DARK HEART OF THE SUN

DARK DESTINIES, BOOK I

S.K. RYDER

Dark Heart of the Sun
Dark Destinies, Book 1

Copyright © 2023 by S.K. Ryder

Published by Hidden Worlds Press
Cover design by 100 Covers

All rights reserved.

No portion of this publication may be reproduced, distributed, or transmitted in any form or by any means, electronic or manual, without the prior written permission of the publisher or author, except for the use of brief quotations in a book review. For permission requests, contact the author.

This is a work of fiction. All characters, organizations, places, and events are a product of the author's imagination, and any resemblance to actual persons (living or deceased), places, or events is coincidental.

1st edition: December 2016
2nd edition: December 2023

Paperback ISBN: 979-8-9893855-1-5
eBook ISBN: 979-8-9893855-0-8

hiddenworldspress.com

I

MISSING TIME

Five in the morning, and Cassidy Chandler stared bleary-eyed into the bathroom mirror, wondering what it was she was seeing. The bruise was garish; there was no other word for it. Purple, green and crescent-shaped, just beneath her left ear, obvious enough not to miss in a casual glance at the mirror during a half-asleep trip to the toilet.

What the hell? She touched it. It ached. "What did I do now?"

"Um. I may have gotten a bit amorous."

She turned to see her fiancée, Jackson Striker, standing in the door like a six-foot-four inch pillar of toned muscle and tanned skin. He scratched the back of his dirty blond head. The expression on his chiseled face approached sheepish—but not quite.

"Amorous?" Two years they had been together, and not once had he been responsible for so much as a scratch on her. If anything, he had prevented quite a few. And now...this?

"Yeah. Don't you remember?" He ambled past and disappeared into the separate toilet. Splashing sounds followed as he relieved his bladder.

"Do I?" she asked her reflection. When had she gotten so pale that her freckles practically glowed? Or was that the light and her tired eyes? Unease curled up her spine as the answer became obvious.

No. She didn't remember.

In fact, she didn't even remember getting into bed last night—much less what may or may not have come after.

She clutched the edge of the vanity as her mind bolted back in time, grasping for something, anything. They had been on a night out together. The date had been Jackson's way of apologizing for being gone so much since they'd moved into his family's home—make that compound—and for not standing up to his vile uncle in her defense. His explanations were somewhat plausible—"every family has a moron"—his regrets apparently heartfelt. After an hour's limo ride and a four-course dinner at Palm Beach's finest restaurant, Cassidy had suggested a romantic moon-lit walk on the beach, just the two of them, like it used to be. Jackson didn't want to. She insisted. The limo pulled into the beach access at ten or eleven, they had taken off their shoes, and...and...

Nothing.

Blank.

The wine she had with dinner had worn off. Nor had there been drugs—not now, not ever. And yet...blank.

Jackson met her eyes in the mirror. How long had he stood there, watching her hatch this panic? His own eyes were bright and fully awake. "You okay?"

She opened her mouth, but something made her hold back the questions flooding her mind. Instead, she pulled her hair across the bruise and forced a smile. "I'm fine."

His answering smile plunged a chill through her. It looked as forced as her own. Still, he dropped a kiss on her forehead on his way out. "Good."

What's happening here? she wondered as she watched him pull on his workout clothes as if nothing were amiss. Who *was* this man? He looked like Jackson, but...

No, you know what's happening. The same thing that always happens. Subconsciously, she'd known it for days, maybe weeks. Inevitable like the rising sun, people she loved always left. Parents, friends, lovers—by choice, by circumstance, by death—she always ended up alone. Even now. Even Jackson. Jackson, the man who had pulled her from the hole she had fallen into after her father's disappearance, her mother's death, her boyfriend's desertion. The man who had lost and suffered as she had. The man who "got her" and claimed he needed her with him for the rest of his life, claimed that he would always "get her" and always be there for her. Yes, even him. Pulling away, separating, moving on. Was it second thoughts about his proposal? She hadn't seen that coming, but he had made his case so eloquently she dared to trust, dared to hope that maybe, just maybe, she had found a partner for life. And now...

Cassidy could barely breathe around the ache swelling in her heart. How could she have been so stupid? She knew better. No one was ever there forever. There was only her. It would always only be her.

"Get some more sleep. I'll see you at breakfast," Jackson called over his shoulder as he shut the double-doors to their suite behind him.

She closed her eyes and allowed the gathering tears to slide free for all of thirty seconds. Then she swiped at them angrily. Nope. This wasn't happening. No way was she going to feel sorry for herself over someone who clearly thought better of hitching his one-percenter life to her barely middle-class self. She was done. Moving on. Next.

Eddie was already wedged into his carrier in the closet where he liked to nap between forays to his kibble dish and litter box. Good. No need to coax the massive Maine Coon from underneath the bed. No need to collect anything but his dishes either. There were still kitty travel supplies in the car. He mewed inquisitively when she zipped him up. "Don't worry. We're not seeing the vet." A plaintive sound as she hauled the carrier out and put it by the door. Eddie, once the wet and starving stray, was now her only friend. "It's going to be alright, buddy. We're going to be alright."

It took all of twenty minutes to gather her meager possessions, stuff them into a carry-on, a duffel, and a backpack, and change out of Jackson's T-shirt—which she didn't remember getting into. Before she put it aside, she held it up to her face and inhaled his familiar scent of soap and sunshine. A well of warm memories opened up, but she squashed them down before they could make her doubt her impulsive decision. Those memories she had made were with a man who didn't exist anymore.

Cassidy moved the bags and now gently vibrating carrier out into the hallway and to the sweeping central staircase. A month she lived here, and she was still overwhelmed. The suite she shared with Jackson was the size of the condo they had shared off-campus back in Boulder. Yet, this suite was just one of six in the Striker mansion, a many-multi-million-dollar maze in which she never failed to feel like a trespasser. Especially now when the lights were low, casting vague shadows over the oriental rugs and across the coffered ceilings.

"God, I don't belong in this place," she grumbled. There had been no warning before she arrived here, straight off a cross-country road trip with Jackson all the way from Colorado. When he spoke of his circumstances, it all sounded so casually normal. His father was in finance, he said, neglecting to mention that "in finance" really meant "head of capital investment powerhouse firm, SICI." And "there will be plenty of room for you and Eddie" translated to "we'll all be living separate lives in the same giant house."

"I didn't want you to love me for my family's money," he had told her with an affable shrug of his brawny shoulders that first day when she stood in the ice rink sized foyer, her jaw hanging open.

Even then she had wondered, *What else haven't you told me, Jackson?*

Apparently plenty, most of which he seemed to have no intention of sharing. Brushing off that hideous bruise as nothing more than a love bite, while her normally reliable memory completely failed her on the details, was merely the latest of these. But it was definitely the last.

She found him in the home gym on her way to the garage. Every morning he was in there, pushing, pulling, and heaving reps to a punishing degree before getting in his six-mile sunrise run. Putting down her bags in the hall, she tucked her hair behind her ears, opened the glass door, and steeled herself. "Jackson?"

He clanked the barbell back into its cradle and sat up. Despite the air conditioning and the fan whirling over his head, he glistened with sweat, his thin shirt soaked through and clinging to his chest and abs. Oh yeah. There was more to love about Jackson Striker than his money. What a pity the inside didn't match the outside.

His bright-gray eyes studied her as he took a swig of water and reached for a towel. It was a vague, shuttered look, not what she'd expect from a man discovering his hollow-eyed, fully dressed fiancé standing in his gym at the crack of dawn. Nor was the tone of voice. "Cassidy? Are you going somewhere?"

"I am." To stop wringing her hands, she buried them in the pockets of her shorts. "I'm leaving, Jack. I'm done. We're...done."

He stared at her, blank-faced and still, except for his right hand. It moved against his thigh, the thumb rubbing over the stumps remaining of his ring and pinkie fingers.

Cassidy held her breath, bracing for the questions, the demands for explanations, the pleas to stay and talk. She would be strong. She had to be. If she wasn't, if she allowed him to seduce her back into this false dream...

"Okay."

Her turn to stare, uncomprehending, but only for a second or two. Then anger flared in her chest. "Okay? Really? *Okay?* That's all you have to say?"

He spread his hands before him with a shrug. "You look like you've made up your mind, Cass. What do you want me to say?"

"Right. I forgot. You don't know how to say anything anymore since you got back here."

"That's not fair."

"But your uncle literally calling me *disagreeable* and *unfit* to be the Striker heir's wife in front of the entire family is?" she snapped back, making air quotes around the terms that had pushed her over the edge. She hoped every ear present still burned.

"We talked about this. He's—"

"Quit making excuses."

"—old-school and hardly ever here. You know I'm okay with you having a career, and it's me you're marrying." It was a statement of fact spoken with hardly a ripple in his calm demeanor.

"You think this is about me *wanting a career*? What the hell is wrong with you?" He dropped his gaze to the towel in his hands. "Your family doesn't want me here. They don't want me with you. Your uncle said what is written all over your father's face. And it's obvious that your mother only tolerates me because she loves you."

Cassidy stopped, thinking of Samantha, Jackson's half-sister, and the only person in this rambling house who had made her at all welcome. No doubt she had seen the last of her, too. That realization, together with the tension she saw hardening Jackson's square jaw, brought her temper down a notch.

Sad is what this was. Sad and expected. The only surprise was how quickly—and why—she found herself on her own again.

"I can't marry you, Jack." She pulled the enormous engagement ring off her finger. "If the best you can do now is sit there and let them insult me and then make excuses for them, how is that going to change once we're married? And living in this house with all of them?" That had been another surprise there: no home of their own. They would live their life as a couple under his family's eyes. The family would own her as much as they already owned him.

The last bit of hope she might have held for them died with Jackson's continued silence. Stepping forward, she took his warm hand in hers and dropped the ring into his palm. "I wish I knew what happened to the man who proposed to me." She hadn't seen him since they got here, when he joined the family business and became consumed by it, tense and cagey, keeping her at arm's length.

Jackson closed a white-knuckled fist around the ring, but his tone remained calm. "This is about last night, isn't it?"

All the anxiety about her missing memories bubbled to the surface. The bruise on her neck pounded in time with her racing heart. She fought to suppress a shiver.

He watched her, waiting for she-knew-not-what. He reeked of sweat. Tension crackled off his skin. He knew what had put that mark on her; she was sure of it. Also, that was no love-nibble. It was a serious injury.

Just a few hours ago, she would have never imagined him capable of hurting her. Now? Seeing him sit there with all that strength, leashed tension and slate gray ice in his eyes? Now she wouldn't put it past him.

"It's about a lot of things," she said, straightening her spine, clutching her bravado. "Goodbye, Jackson."

It took everything in her not to run for the door. The walls seemed to lean in, squeezing her out, away from him, his family, everything. She collected her luggage and continued down the hall.

The entrance to the air-conditioned hangar of a garage was wide, but not wide enough, trapping her between the jamb and her duffel. She put the pet carrier down and tumbled her bags in ahead of her.

Jackson came up behind her. "So, where are you going? Home?" Casual, as if asking about the weather.

"None of your business."

She reached for Eddie. He was quicker, picking up the zippered mesh bag with the colossal cat inside, and headed for her car. Mercedes, Jaguars, and a Rolls Royce. Her little VW Beetle sat near the end of the line, a small, bright yellow accident wedged between Jackson's white Audi sports coupe and his uncle's black Cadillac SUV.

"Colorado is a long way to drive from South Florida," he called over his shoulder. "You should stick close."

Corralling her bags, she huffed after him. "Why? In case I change my mind?"

"You will."

"In that case, Alaska it is," she said. The farther away, the better.

Jackson opened the passenger door and secured the carrier with the seatbelt. A worried meow sounded from within.

Cassidy fumed as she wrestled the clumsy case and bulbous duffel into the car's rear. *I will be back, will I?* True, she had no home to return to. *This* was supposed to be her home. *He* was supposed to be her home. He, the man who was helping her leave. The man who, judging from the consoling murmurs coming from the front seat, was more concerned about losing her cat than her. No, she would definitely *not* be back. From here on out, it was her and Eddie, and no one else.

She slammed the trunk shut and slapped the wall control for the nearest of five double garage doors. It rose, admitting a swirl of sweltering, fecund air into the refrigerated sanctum of fresh wax and new tires.

"Stay close," Jackson suggested again as he opened the driver's side door for her.

"Why would you even care?"

"I do. Believe me, I care." After a brief hesitation, he added, "I love you." Something flickered in his cool, bright gaze. Here and gone in a heartbeat.

She waved at the door he held open. "And you have such a way of showing it, too."

The shadow of a smile curved his mouth. "I know better than to get in your way when you're like this."

Like this? She had never been "like this," whatever he thought that was. Then again, she had never seen him "like this" either. This was just surreal. Right down to her simmering fear over what she'd forgotten and his suspected part in her injury.

She slid behind the wheel. "You should go find yourself a more...suitable girl. Make your uncle happy." *Forget about me.*

Suddenly, his smile was radiant and genuine. "He'll have to learn to deal. You're the only one for me, Cass. Go do what you have to. I'll be here when the dust settles."

Cassidy blinked. Dust? What dust? No, that didn't matter. She yanked the door shut, started the engine, and was out of the garage seconds later.

Down the driveway and well out of view of the massive house, she halted at the wrought-iron gates flanked by life-sized bronze lions. Right would be the most direct route to the interstate, and from there anywhere, including Colorado, which had been home for all of her twenty-two years. Going back there would mean throwing herself at the mercy of her father and his mistress-turned-wife, not to mention their two out-of-control toddlers.

With a groan, she dropped her forehead on her hands atop of the steering wheel. The movement made the bruise on her neck ache. Alaska was almost tempting, far away from Florida with its swamps and alligators and entitled men with more money than soul.

But paradoxically, this muggy hellhole had one thing she'd be hard pressed to find anywhere else. Jackson's influential mother had recommended Cassidy to the editor-in-chief of the local paper for a job. It was very entry level and paid accordingly, but that wasn't the point. The editor, Dave McKinney, was the point. As a respected industry veteran, he had connections at all the major media outlets. Impress him, and she might network her way into a prestigious newsroom and never look back, her career as a champion for truth set and her independence assured.

Conversely, if she disappeared on this man without notice, her professional reputation would be shot before it ever existed.

Plus, she needed the money. Those student loans wouldn't pay themselves off.

With a sigh, Cassidy turned left.

2

Cottage by the Sea

Finding a place for Cassidy and Eddie to stay sounded trivial on the surface. It was anything but in a place like Orchard Beach on a Sunday morning.

The town lay nestled along Florida's Atlantic coast, well out of the way of major urban centers, and featured some of the most expensive real estate in the country. Wealth settled here for quiet anonymity. Affordable housing on short notice didn't exist, and hotels and motels were out of her budget, to say nothing of pet-averse.

Discouraged, Cassidy stopped at a small café by the beach for an early lunch. Though the ninety-plus degree, rotting seaweed scented breeze did nothing for her appetite, she picked at a woefully overpriced burger, fries, and diet soda. Eddie explored the shade beneath the picnic table at the end of a leash, scratching, crunching kibble, and retching up a hairball. She bent down to check on him. His green eyes brimmed with accusation.

"I know, buddy. Being homeless sucks. I'll find us something. I promise."

She scrolled her phone for local listings and picked the brains of the service staff and fellow patrons. There was a roommate opportunity two towns over, but when she called, the room was no longer available.

The universe continued to conspire against her feeble plans at every turn and even laughed at her outright when she settled Eddie back into his bag, where a bright glint caught her eye.

"Jackson, you son of a bitch," she muttered and retrieved the Striker family engagement ring from the wadded up blanket inside the carrier. The rare pink diamond in its antique silver setting was worth the kind of money that could buy a house in this town—the kind of money it would take her a lifetime to scrape together. The thought made her feel queasy with both apprehension and anger. No doubt he expected this to prod her into acknowledging the error of her ways and come rushing back into his fickle arms.

"I should sell this thing and run. Let Jackson figure out how to tell his father it's gone."

Eddie sat in his carrier and watched her, questions in his furry face. The white stripe down his front resembled a tie on a solid black suit and shirt, giving him the distinguished look of his namesake, the pioneering broadcast journalist Edward R. Murrow.

Dubious, the cat cocked his head. Cassidy sighed and slipped the ring onto her right hand. She was no thief. And whatever she might think of the Strikers, losing their priceless heirloom was more than she wanted on her conscience—or risk, from a legal perspective. She'd keep the rock close and return it later. Much later.

Across the street from the public beach was Beachside Havens, which advertised short-term holiday rentals. It sounded pricey, but it was open, and it wasn't like she had other plans lined up. The inventory turned out to be sizeable during the oppressive Florida summer, but still dwindled in light of her requirements. Still, an hour later, she walked out with a key, a month-to-month agreement, directions, and her bank account down to vapors.

It took another half an hour to find the leaning sign at the A1A turnoff to Seagrape Lane. *Mule trail,* she thought as the

Beetle bounced over the narrow, broken pavement winding into the thicket. The beach cottages strung out along the way were all deserted for the summer, their windows shuttered and yards overgrown. By far, the one in worst shape was the most affordable of the lot—her new home.

Number Seven squatted around a small bend at the end of the road, as though trying to hide its shameful condition from the others. A wilderness of subtropical foliage crowded around the ramshackle two-story structure. The paint, which might have been blue at some point, was now a peeling, nondescript shade of fog. Shutters obscured the two upstairs windows while the downstairs porch yawned like a forbidding cavern, giving the impression of a giant head decomposing beneath a blanket of clattering palm fronds. An overgrown bougainvillea, climbing up a support post, splashed a vivid red gash across its face.

In his carrier, Eddie mewed, echoing her misgivings. "Well, it's this or we sleep in the car, buddy."

Outside, the air steamed with brine and shrilled with cicadas. Lizards darted from beneath her sandals. She climbed the creaking front steps, two where there were meant to be three, the middle one long gone. On the porch, two Adirondack chairs battled with a tenacious vine. When Cassidy pushed open the front door, the house exhaled a cloud of thick, moldy heat.

She hurried to the air conditioner controls, only to find them dead. It wasn't for a lack of power, though. The lights worked fine. Their incandescent glow illuminated an interior of polished wood surfaces and gently worn, tropical-print furnishings. A boxy, last-century TV sat in one corner. More modern equipment blinked by its side. She checked her phone. Yes, Wi-Fi, thank God. She hadn't dared to hope for an Internet connection.

The kitchen appliances looked to be as old as the TV, but they all functioned. A dozen bottles of Perrier lined the fridge shelves, sparkling leftovers of the previous tenant, no doubt. She helped herself to one, pouring the cold bubbles down her throat. Opening random drawers and cabinets, she found standard sets of utensils and dishes, a box of crackers two years out of date, and a number of startled roaches. She shuddered and slammed the drawer shut.

A cursory inspection of the rest of the place turned up several empty green bottles, towels wadded up in the downstairs bathroom, and a locked door to the back room. The main bedroom upstairs was dusty, but otherwise adequate.

Beachside Havens apologized when she called, promised maid service first thing in the morning, and would reimburse two weeks' worth of rent for the inconvenience. The air conditioner would have to wait until they could contact the overseas owners.

"Home, sweet roasting dump," she murmured after she hung up. Rivulets of sweat trickled between her shoulder blades. But she smiled when twisting an unmarked nob kicked an energetic ceiling fan into motion. Things were looking up.

With a claw clip from her bag, she bunched her hair on top of her head and got to work opening curtains and windows and locating cleaning supplies. No way would she wait until tomorrow for someone else to make the dump in question livable.

It was, after all, her dump.

Dominique Marchant's first deep breath of the evening brought him the unfamiliar stink of cleaning solutions—and the bone-deep temptation of warm-blooded life.

The small hairs all over his body rose in alarm as he sat up. Expanding his vision, he scanned the darkness in infrared shades of gray. His meager belongings lay scattered among the juvenile furnishings, and the samurai swords hung together in their usual place on the wall beside the locked door. Nothing had been disturbed.

He stretched his preternatural senses outward. No movements, no sounds inside. Outside, the sighing rhythm of the ocean accompanied the lazy chirp of insects. He cocked his head and focused.

There. A heartbeat.

Dominique unlocked the door and cracked it open. Light blazed in the kitchen down the hall. Eyes narrowed, he moved into the living room. There the source of the heartbeat lay curled up on the sofa. It was the largest domesticated cat he had ever seen. When it spotted him, the animal sprang up, arched its back and puffed out its black fur in a hissing display of flat-eared, wild-eyed, bare-fanged aggression. He responded in kind, extending his far more impressive canines and issuing a deep, guttural growl.

The cat wisely reconsidered its folly. Ceding the territory to the superior predator, it bolted for a love seat in the far corner of the room. But instead of sliding under the furniture, the over-sized animal thumped into the low base with a surprised screech. Frantic, it hurtled into another direction—paws skidding on the tiles before finding traction—and galloped up the stairs.

Dominique swayed as it passed, lured by the rush of its agitated blood, but he let it go. The cat wasn't the problem.

Whoever had brought it was.

While he lay in oblivion during the day, someone had scrubbed years of neglect off the floors and furnishings. They weren't here now, but clearly they would be back. Panic rose as he scanned the familiar space and its unwelcome additions—litter box, pet dishes, blaring radio, laptop, chargers, camera, papers...

He shuffled the small pile on the kitchen table. To-do lists, cryptic notes, phone numbers, doodles, a contract...

The tight print hit him like a racing train. In the weeks he'd been here, it never occurred to him that the cottage—legally owned by his mother on St. Barth—might be managed and available for rent. The place was too much of a wreck to be a viable income property. Yet, here it was, written. For very generous terms, one Cassidy Chandler had taken possession on a month-to-month basis.

He dropped the contract on the table and rubbed a hand down his face. *Mon Dieu, non.*

What would he do with a human in his lair? He couldn't even remember his last conversation with one that didn't end with a corpse in his arms. His fangs emerged at the thought. Hunger cramped his belly. This Cassidy Chandler could not—*would* not—survive meeting him. Not here. Not now. Not like this.

Then what?

Then it was all over. Someone would come looking for her, and they would find him instead. He would have to leave. One way or another, either before or after he made a corpse of her, he would have to leave.

"*Non*," he whispered. Leaving was out of the question. This place was all that remained of his stolen life. It was his final tether to humanity, his past, his present, his future. He would exist here—and he would die here.

And he would do it alone.

3

Justice

Hunched low over his bike, Dominique blew across the causeway to the mainland and through the intersection into town at just shy of one hundred miles per hour. An SUV lurched at him from the right. He twisted the throttle, gunning the engine, and screamed past the front bumper so close it brushed his knee. Tires shrieked. Horns blasted. He continued to dart among vehicles. Only a tiny portion of his vampire mind processed the shifting traffic patterns as he traveled toward I-95.

Most of his thoughts belonged to one Cassidy Chandler.

"Merde, merde, merde..."

He was now starving. A meal was about to walk through his door, and every instinct told him to stay and take advantage. He had almost faltered when, on his way out, a yellow car turned onto Seagrape Lane, a woman at the wheel. It had to be her, returning home.

To his home.

His lair.

No. She was not his preferred prey. Not that this mattered to the depraved hunger that ruled him. If it had a pulse, it was prey. What little remained of the human in him still battled the thirst for blood with a bargain—all the blood he wanted, but on very specific terms. *Madame* Chandler did not meet these terms. For now, she was safe—as was what was left of his conscience.

Then again, the night was young.

"Fuck."

The machine between his thighs quivered as he leaned into the curve of the highway on-ramp. The BMW motorcycle's previous owner had tuned the machine to a point where no mere mortal rider could hope to maintain control at maximum speed. Dominique often pushed the engine until it screamed. Within seconds, he moved past two hundred miles per hour, becoming little more than a blur among the snails comprising normal traffic. He was one with the bike. He was one with the night.

He *was* the night.

And day had come to his house.

"*Mon Dieu, aidez-moi.*"

But God could not help him now, if he ever had. Dominique was on his own.

Fort Lauderdale was closer to his lair than he liked, but his hunger was too potent. If he waited much longer, he risked becoming careless. He didn't have to cruise the neighborhoods around Port Everglades for long before an opportunity presented itself—two thugs plying their narcotics trade. As Dominique stashed the bike and let the beast rise, thoughts of the girl disappeared.

From a distance, they mistook him, as they always did, for a potential customer, a rival, or an easy mark. His tall, athletic build beguiled with casual grace, and the tousled dark hair spoke of naïve youth. The silver-studded black leather outfit might have been their only warning of a darker side.

"*Bonsoir,*" he greeted with a dazzling grin. "I have something for you."

They frowned, baffled, but one reached behind him, producing a handgun. "It better be your wallet, punk."

"Much better," Dominique countered with an inhuman growl of anticipation and savored their dawning unease. "Your death."

He dropped the leash that held the beast, and his reason all but vanished, swallowed whole by the primal need to feed.

It was more than the blood. That would have been too crude. No, much as he had prepared a prime cut of beef in his previous life, the beast liked to season its prey with measured doses of horror and hope before marinating it in the terror of certain death. They cursed him and they ran. They struggled and begged. They lost their bowels and cried for God, all to no avail. In the end, he slammed home the powerful fangs and tore with savage abandon.

The hot, coppery blood hit the roof of his mouth in orgasmic pulses. He went faint with ecstasy, pushed deeper, pulled harder.

There was poison in his saliva, in his bite, seeping into the bloodstream. When it reached the brain, the mind of the prey opened to him, showing him in vivid detail precisely what he was destroying. Small lives of ego and greed. One had committed gruesome murders. The other had delivered his own cousin to those he sought to impress and stood by as they raped her to death.

They were the lords of the street. They were above the law.

Until tonight.

Tonight, justice had found them.

By the time Dominique drank the second life whole, his face was wet with emotion. He sat alone between the broken corpses in the dark. The sound of traffic hummed nearby. A siren howled farther away. The beast lay coiled, drowsy with satisfaction. He almost felt human again. He didn't like what he saw.

"When will justice come for me?" Try as he might, it had yet to appear.

He wiped his face and raked his fingers through his hair, pushing the melancholy out of his mind. Then he got up to retrieve the machete he kept strapped to the bike. There was work to be done.

The sky already paled in the east by the time he returned to his lair. His body grew sluggish under the sun's growing weight. Or so it seemed to him. What really plunged him into oblivion every morning, he didn't know. This was only one of many mysteries bestowed on him without benefit of explanation. But there was no mystery about what daylight would do to him. In the horrific months he spent with his mad, inscrutable sire, he had too many opportunities to see the results of blood-drinker bodies left in the sun.

Once off A1A, Dominique silenced the bike and pushed it the rest of the way. Whatever he would find, he was in no mood to deal with it this close to sunrise. His sanctuary lay not quite dark and not quite silent in the predawn hush. The yellow VW Beetle with Colorado plates squatted in the carport, and the windows upstairs stood open to catch the sea breeze. Behind them, sheer curtains glowed with a soft light. She slept up there, his unwelcome houseguest. It took little effort to hear the rhythm of her breath.

He stashed the bike and helmet in the shed, clicked the lock shut, and detoured to the beach. The drowsy shush of the surf greeted him. Wind soughed in the branches of an Australian pine and ruffled his hair in comforting welcome. For a few precious moments, he let the peace settle over him and pretended he would still be there when the sun rose from the ocean. It wasn't long before an anxious shiver rippled up his spine, forcing him to return to the cottage. He would never again feel the sun's warmth.

And perhaps that was all the justice he would ever know for all the lives he had taken.

The houseguest, the intruder, had locked the front door.

"*Merde.*" He never locked the door when he went out. Dominique stepped back far enough to survey his options, and his gaze fell on the open windows of the upstairs bedroom. He hesitated, considering that room...where his father once slept.

Crushing the memories away before they could unhinge him, he hopped onto the porch roof. The window's insect screen was busted. Shadow-silent, he slipped past the curtains, which kept the mosquitos at bay but did nothing against larger blood-sucking creatures.

A rich ambrosia of honeyed fruit and warm vanilla filled the room, and the beast stirred with sluggish interest. Dominique stopped breathing. He was about to speed past his parents' old bed when he saw her. Bathed in the soft glow of a nightlight and clad in only a tank top and a pair of floral-patterned panties, she lay across the rumpled sheets with her arms and legs flung out, offering herself to the breezes swirling from the overhead fan.

He stood transfixed, letting his gaze wander with unexpected pleasure. In his twenty-seven years before this curse found him, he had known his fair share of women, but none quite like this. An active life had shaped that firm body, not starvation dieting and medical procedures. Her heart-shaped face, too, was exquisite, full of stubborn lines and gentle grace, and a mouth with an invitingly plump lower lip. Her head lay in a cloud of russet hair, a lock of which had fallen across her freckled nose and shivered with every breath. On her right hand, an impressive diamond struck an odd contrast with the abused nails and her presence in a place such as this. Alone.

A framed picture stood on the nightstand. It depicted her together with a woman in a bright pink ski-cap, a relative, judging by the similar features. The woman's smile had an air of resignation while the girl's—Cassidy, he recalled—was broad, almost fierce, her eyes slits of blue against intense sunlight. The dark brunette hair streaming from beneath her cap was thick as a lion's mane and shot through with copper.

Dominique cocked his head, considering. She didn't look like she smiled much lately. In fact, she looked exhausted from more than a day spent cleaning his house. The corners of her eyes crinkled with tension even now.

Another pair of eyes caught his across her belly. The cat, coiled like a spring. Unlike its mistress, the animal was wide awake and aware of him. Knowing itself discovered, it scrambled backwards and promptly dropped off the side of the bed with a thump. Growling, it hustled underneath.

Cassidy stirred at the commotion, turning to mumble into the pillow. When her hair fell away from her neck, the slow throb of her vein there caught his attention. In his enhanced vision, it appeared as a flowing ribbon of golden light, a siren call to his basest needs.

He closed his eyes and forced the beast back into its cage. When he opened them again, dread seized him. No longer distracted by his supernatural awareness of her life force, he saw instead the dark, crescent bruise beneath her left ear. Dominique dropped into a crouch, the growing lethargy in his bones forgotten.

Another blood-drinker had fed on her.

But not here. Not now. He would have sensed another immortal presence. The injury wasn't fresh—a day old, maybe two—but it was ugly. The bite had been hard, showing a loss of control or intent to kill. Yet she had survived, the attack aborted. Not only that, she was here, in his lair. Coincidence? The odds were non-existent. She must be compelled, sent here, to him, by another blood-drinker. But to what end? And by who?

He could think of several possibilities, all of them justifying her immediate disposal. Even if it meant he would have to abandon his lair. If one blood-drinker had found him, it was only a matter of time before his mad sire did as well.

If he hadn't already.

The sun was coming, and his thoughts were slippery inside his skull. He had seconds of consciousness left to decide…what? His gaze flew to the girl with the bruise. No blood-drinker could touch him during the day, but she could. If he killed her now, or if he let her live, the result would be the same—someone would get to him today or tonight and would do with him as they pleased.

If she stayed, he could not. He had to find shelter somewhere else. Now.

Dominique got as far as the window. A sky already bright with reflected sunfire scalded his face, forcing him back inside, throwing him to the floor. He lay flat and stared up at the shadows whirling around the ceiling fan. To his eyes, sparks flew from the blades. His ears filled with the roar of the sun barreling across the horizon.

Stairs. His body crawled down the stairs, faltering limbs moving of their own accord, dragging him to safety. As it always did, the beast took over to save itself. Tears streamed down his face as daylight filled the house, singed his eyes, and wrung all the strength from his bones. He bit his tongue until it bled to stifle the agonized howl filling his throat, to conceal his presence from her, the intruder, the spy.

When the door to his sanctuary closed, smothering him in blackness, his body wilted against it and slid to the floor. He reached for the deadbolt, but couldn't feel it, couldn't feel his arm flopping by his side. He didn't know if he had turned the lock, if he was truly safe.

With his last coherent thought, he realized it didn't matter. If she was here to kill him, she would have done it yesterday.

And if she wanted to kill him today...justice had found him at last.

4

PRICELESS LUXURIES

Jackson Striker's life was made of secrets, most of them deadly.

For two years, he had let them fade into the background while he was away from this house, his family, these memories. Let them fade as he found solace and the will to live in Cassidy's arms.

Now he was back, and so were the secrets, the things no human should have to know were real.

Worse. Those secrets now came for Cassidy.

Because he had let his guard down.

The attack had been so fast. Still, he should have been better prepared than the small, full-spectrum light he carried everywhere. A blast of that in the face had surprised the creature enough to chase it away, not kill it. It could have returned. Both their bloodless corpses could have washed up on the beach this morning.

It might yet come back.

Jackson paused at the bottom of the polished oak spiral staircase and gripped the railing hard. Might? No, that blood-sucking demon *would* be back. Cassidy's flight this morning was all the evidence he needed. She was compelled. Compelled to rush into a monster's arms—and certain death.

That is what the serum in a vampire's bite did. Once in the bloodstream, the victim became a puppet, even at a distance.

The vampire could find her or summon her and place into her mind anything it wanted. She obviously remembered nothing about the attack, no longer trusted him, and was hell-bent on leaving him, the man she should trust to keep her safe. Physical restraint would have been the only option to stop her. The resulting damage to their already-shaky relationship would have been irreparable.

To save her—to keep her—he had to let her go.

Bracing for the confrontation to come, Jackson touched the twin St. Christopher medals at the hollow of his throat and started up the stairs to the Striker Foundation's control room. It had all ended in a colossal bungle he would now have to explain. Somehow. His plan was to follow her and put down the bloodsucker well before sunset. It would have been his first kill. It should have been simple.

Only, she didn't B-Line to a vampire's lair. No, she spent hours checking out every hotel and motel in town, apparently at a genuine loss about where to stay. By the time Jackson lost her at a red light on US 1, frustration was eating him from the inside out.

He waited until well after dark to call her. To his relief, there was a touch of familiar temper in her voice. He tried to get a sense of her whereabouts through background sounds. A microwave beeped. Utensils clattered. Drawers slammed.

"Just making sure you're all right, babe," he said, smiling at her clipped retort. There was no hint of the dreamy distraction typical of someone under a vampire's influence. For the moment, at least, she was fine.

That still left a vampire hunting in Orchard Beach, one that could decide to finish what it started. The faster Jackson found and destroyed the creature, the better.

Which is why he now stood before the electronically sealed, steel-core door to the Foundation's inner sanctum, a windowless room on the mansion's third floor. He mashed his thumb against the reader, willing the indicator to turn green with a welcoming warble. Instead, it buzzed red. With a tightly curled fist, he knocked. Hard.

As he hoped—and feared—it was Uncle Garrett who tore open the door, looking like a thundercloud about to hurl lightning. Garrett's scowl eased a bit when he saw his nephew. After giving him an assessing look, he turned away, leaving Jackson to catch the door and follow before it shut in his face.

The scents of ancient paper and oiled leather greeting him. A hint of blood, too, he imagined, the scent of secret history. Forcing a casual air he far from felt, he ventured, "So I'm still not on the Grid?"

"Nothing gets by you, does it?"

Jackson tried not to wince. If his uncle doubted his competence before, he'd deem him useless beyond all hope if he learned what all had gotten by him in the past twenty-four hours. The eyes of the Striker patriarchs followed him from their staid portraits amidst meticulously ordered floor-to-ceiling bookcases lining the round, windowless room. He sensed them judging him, finding him lacking. The way his own father had found him lacking earlier when Warren refused to intercede with his brother on his son's behalf. "You're not ready," he had said.

Maybe. But being ready had ceased to be optional.

"Deep breath," Cassidy would say. "It'll be alright." The memory of her smile settled him as he approached the massive, ornately carved wooden desk in the center of the parquet floor. It was cluttered with yellowed manuscripts. Two curved wide-screen monitors sat off to either side, scrolling data in multiple windows, but Garrett, back in his chair, ignored this as he picked up a pen and continued a note in what Jackson recognized as the Register of Primary Targets.

The silence dragged. Jackson kept his face neutral, his hands clasped behind his back, rubbing at the stumps of his two truncated fingers with his thumb. They were constant and inescapable reminders of the price of impatience. Impatience had lost him his fingertips and gotten his brother killed.

"Shouldn't you be out searching for a new bride?" Garrett said without looking up. His broad shoulders bunched, and light gleamed off his neat but thinning hair that held not a hint of gray. At fifty-eight, Garrett Striker maintained a vigor and fitness level on par with his twenty-four-year-old nephew.

"I have a bride." At his uncle's raised brow, Jackson's hackles rose. "I think you met her when you humiliated her at dinner on Friday. Her name is Cassidy Chandler, soon to be Striker. She—" Whatever else he might have hurled at him died on his lips when Garrett looked up, eyes narrow in warning. "She will be back," he concluded simply.

Taking off his glasses, the older man sat back and tossed them, together with his pen, on the desk. "Attitude. Well, this is new." He considered his nephew. "She's run off, and someday you'll thank me. Trust me."

"She'll be back," Jackson said again. "Trust me."

The alternative was unthinkable. Cassidy had filled much of the hole in his soul left by his twin brother's death. Losing her would be like losing Justin all over again. This time, he wouldn't survive. That stark realization snapped everything into sharp focus and filled him with quiet certainty.

"But I'm not here to talk about my relationship. I came to tell you that I believe there's a target in the area."

"Oh. Do you?" Garrett said in a too mild tone of withering displeasure. "And what would make you think that?"

I saw it with my own eyes. Right. Garrett would nail his hide to the wall and lock his stupid ass out of Foundation assets for the rest of his life. Jackson took a breath and embarked on Plan B. "The so-called gang war killings over the last couple of months. They're—"

"Not vampire victims."

"—unusually violent."

"Exactly. Only a youngling could leave a trail of corpses like that, and no sire would tolerate that much risk of exposure.

They'd put it down before things got this far out of hand. You should really know that."

Jackson did. He, too, had studied the centuries of research. But if he was to keep Cassidy's involvement—and his own botched attempts at hunting—off Garrett's radar, this was the only plausible option for alerting his uncle to a local vampire problem.

"I think this is a new pattern," he offered.

"Now you're reaching."

"Think about it. All these bodies are dismembered, and even if the heads are found, they're too decomposed to prove anything. Doesn't that sound like someone's trying to hide something more than just a murder?"

Garrett sighed and shook his head. "Kid, it's a sad fact that humans can be as brutal as any vampire. But they are humans, and human laws and authorities will deal with them. Not us. We're here for the monsters they don't know about."

"Maybe that's what some bloodsucker wants us to think. Throw the humans off the idea that anything unusual is going on while he kills at will."

"Then at least he's cleaning up the streets while he's at it."

"You can't be serious. What if he expands his menu in the future? What if he already has?"

"Jack, slow down." Garrett gestured for calm with one hand. "These are not vampire victims. There's no precedent for that anywhere in their history or even their legends." He waved at the bookshelves, groaning with those histories and legends.

Jackson shifted his voice into a more reasonable gear. "There could be things we don't know about them yet."

"Not after five hundred years, no. But even if, what do you expect me to do about it? Even if there are vampires involved, we need to know where they spend their days, not where they hunt, which in this case would be random and all over the state. I have genuine leads to follow up on. I can't be wasting my time on wild theories."

Jackson clenched his jaw. Fuck, this was not going the way he needed it to. "Then give me access to the Grid. Let me explore this wild theory and put down whatever I find. I'm ready."

His uncle didn't hesitate. "You were ready three years ago. Not now."

The power of the memories that roared out of the deepest recesses of Jackson's mind took his breath away. He swayed in his shoes and placed his hands amidst the papers on the desk before him. His voice sounded steadier than he felt. "Three years ago, I watched my brother die. The only thing I was ready for was therapy, and obviously I couldn't have that." He had found it, though, with Cassidy.

"When you fall off a horse, you get right back on. Wait this long, and—"

"I didn't fall off a fucking horse," he ground out. "I watched the other half of me get ripped to fucking pieces by something the rest of the world doesn't even know exists." They had survived a nightmare, he and Garrett. How could his uncle sit there spouting clichés while Jackson stood here shaking? "Pieces," he repeated very quietly.

For many seconds, perhaps a full minute, the only sounds in the room were the humming technology and the tick-tick-tick of an antique grandfather clock. Then the leather chair creaked as Garrett sat back and steepled his fingers.

"That right there is why you're not ready to come back," he said, all calm reason. "You've had too much time to think about this. Whatever edge you had is gone."

Jackson wanted to scream. Somehow, he kept it together. "We were twenty-one years old and on our first hunt. We didn't have...an *edge*."

"Just the same. Emotions like this are a serious liability. You're the last of the line. We can't afford to lose you, too."

"I will never be without emotion about—"

Garrett held up a hand. "No one expects that. But you have to learn to channel them, and I don't mean into revenge. That's just another emotion they'll exploit."

The gentle tone—as though he were explaining proper manners to a five-year-old—hauled Jackson over the edge. To hell with controlling his emotions. "Who are you to say that to me? Except for one apparently expendable nephew, you've never lost a thing to these demons."

"Careful."

He leaned in close, got nose-to-nose with the man, lowered his voice to a snarl. "You kill them, but they've never touched you. They can't. You know why? Because you don't give a shit about anyone but yourself and the Foundation. You're like a fucking machine with no more heart or soul than the things you kill."

Garrett shot out of his chair. "That's enough."

Jackson straightened but said nothing more. He held his uncle's furious stare and marveled. So this highly efficient killer was human, after all. Human and feeling more than a little emotional right now. He watched him run a quick hand over his hair and adjust his white SICI company polo shirt before sitting back down.

"I lost Andi to them," he said. At Jackson's baffled look, he clarified. "Antonia Striker."

"My father's first wife?"

"She may have been his wife, but she was the love of my life."

Jackson stared, unsure what to make of this revelation or its implications. "I don't understand. She died in a car accident."

Garrett nodded, his face softening in a way Jackson had never seen on this hard-nosed man, not even when Justin was killed. "She and her four children, yes."

A highway accident. A horrific explosion. Eight dead, Antonia Striker and all her children among them. That's all Jackson knew about how his father, Warren, became a widower at the age of thirty-six. Four months later, he married the destitute socialite Lillian Reynolds, Jackson's mother. Within a year, she gave him the sons he wanted. Sons the Foundation needed.

Jackson's destiny had been sealed at his conception—which would never have happened if not for that accident. A new chill dropped into his belly.

"That's not the real story, though, is it?"

"Not all of it, no." Garrett pushed the pen around on the desk, thoughtful, before he said, "Their driver took their car into the path of a tanker truck. On purpose. We found out about him only much later. Rafael." His mouth twisted with contempt. "He'd been enslaved by a vampire I put down years earlier. He plotted his revenge since the night I took that bitch's head. He infiltrated the house staff, watched us, and figured out how I felt about Andi and her kids. And then...then he made me pay with everything that was dear to me." He looked up. "*Everything.*"

Every hair on Jackson's body rose in silent alarm at the sudden, mad vehemence flaring across his uncle's face. It vanished an instant later.

"But I can't afford to think about any of that, and neither does your father," Garrett continued, all business again. "The Foundation's mission is our purpose. Our only purpose."

His head spinning, Jackson lowered himself into the wingback chair in front of the desk. Because of a back injury sustained long ago, Warren no longer hunted. Instead, he dedicated himself to running the Foundation's legitimate and lucrative business, Striker International Capital Investments, which financed the clandestine operation managed by his brother. Garrett Striker was the most ruthlessly efficient vampire hunter in Foundation history, bar none. Now Jackson knew why.

And it wasn't for lack of emotions. Just a matter of channeling them.

"Until you can say the same, kid, you're not hunting." Garrett waited until Jackson looked up to clarify his point. "Wanting revenge will make you stupid. If you can't set aside your feelings over the night your brother died, you will share his fate." Garrett smiled without humor. "And that would really put a crimp in my retirement plans."

Jackson felt himself calm, felt all that rage...channel. "I was born for the Foundation's mission. Of course it is my life." He clenched his jaw against blurting out how his honed hunter's instincts had hummed during last night's attack. How his mind could focus on logistics and possibilities rather than fear or anger. How he'd driven off the menace and saved Cassidy's life.

With a flashlight.

"I need to start doing my job," he said instead. "I'm ready."

Garrett rubbed his chin, considering. "Isn't your father keeping you busy enough getting you trained to take over the company?"

"Since there's only one of me now, shouldn't I be getting trained on both sides of the business?"

His uncle scowled. Jackson almost smiled.

"Fine. I'll get you set up on the Grid, and you can start doing some research in your spare time. We'll see how that goes."

Jackson allowed himself a small thrill of victory. "Thank you."

Garrett slid his glasses back on his nose and glanced at the monitor. "The other thing you can do is get married and make some heirs before you do get yourself killed. I'll get you a list of some girls who'd be amenable."

"Don't bother. I'm marrying Cassidy," Jackson said and got up to leave.

"The girl who ran off. Right."

"She'll be back." He couldn't resist adding, "She just needs to get past her impulse to hand you your balls on a platter."

Garrett shot him a look that threatened to draw blood. "Please tell me she doesn't still have that ring."

"She'll be back. With the ring." Jackson hoped he sounded more certain than he felt. Cassidy hadn't mentioned the ring when they spoke. No telling where it was. He wouldn't put it past the damn cat to eat the thing.

"For the love of God, kid. What do you think you're doing?" Garrett got up and rounded the desk to close in on his nephew as he might close in on a target. "The last thing you need is a journalist wife digging into this family and asking questions to which she can *never* know the answers. That sort of thing can get us all killed."

This Jackson hadn't even considered. He had always believed that Cassidy would trust him enough to accept that portions of his life needed to remain private. Like every other Striker wife in history.

Or not, he thought with a sudden flash of insight.

"Did Antonia know?"

Garrett went still, his granite gray gaze sharp with warning.

No one not born into the Striker family was ever told about the Foundation's true mission because no one who didn't receive the rigorous early mental training could withstand a vampire's compulsion. Not knowing the truth is how people stayed safe from the truth.

Which didn't mean it hadn't happened.

Garret put his hands on his trim hips. "Do you love this girl?" he said. "Well, don't."

"What the hell business is that of yours? I can control my emotions fine when I need to."

"Not this one, kid. Not love. You can't turn that off and on like anger. Love is bigger than that. It makes you vulnerable. All. The. Time. Vampires—or their slaves—won't hesitate to turn the people you love into weapons that will shred your soul. That's why love is the only luxury a hunter can never afford."

Jackson's mind reeled, scrabbling, trying not to fall into the quicksand pit opening beneath him.

His uncle's smile was thin and sad as he pushed him in. "If you really care for this girl, Jack, get that ring back and let her go. Let her live."

5

What Needs to be Done

Cassidy arrived at work a full fifteen minutes early on this, her second Monday as the *Gazette's* newest rookie reporter-slash-errand-girl. She countered the speculative greeting of the society page maven with a bright "Couldn't sleep. Figured I might as well come in" and hurried past. No point belaboring a super-sized cat crashing through the overheated cottage at the crack of dawn—or that she had moved out of the Striker mansion in the first place. That last bit no doubt had society page headlines written all over it.

She had used the opportunity to take her camera to the beach and watch the sunrise. And get to work early, of course. With rent now looming along with debt payments, the paycheck, though meager, was more critical than ever. The need for a woman to be able to support herself was the most important lesson her mother taught her—by tragic example. Scholarships and student loans had paid for her journalism degree. Time to put that to work—even if the place was the *Orchard Beach Gazette,* a sleepy little paper mired in the twentieth century.

She checked the coffeemaker and office voice mails before returning to her desk and the stack of black folders in her inbox. "Why do so many people die around here?"

A disembodied chuckle drifted across the cubicle wall. "Because South Florida is where people come to die, kiddo."

"Thanks for that cheery insight, Larry. I must be the busiest obit writer in America."

A gray head with a thick walrus mustache poked around the corner and peered at her through horn-rimmed glasses. "It's called learning the ropes. We've all been there."

"I know." She sighed and settled into her chair. "I only wish I could contribute something a bit meatier."

"You did that write-up on the Valieri case for me Friday. Thank you, by the way. I appreciate you jumping in like that."

A warm flush of gratitude infused her. Larry Speicher, a laid-back optimist with an eye to retirement and a reputation for disappearing early on Fridays, reminded her of her long-dead grandfather. She had liked him from the first rumbled welcome and solid handshake. "You know the only reason Dave assigned me that was because court reporting—" She glanced around and lowered her voice. "—is beneath...some people."

"So what? You showed that you're willing to do what needs to be done. Keep that up and you'll go far."

"Some people" showed up right on time. Jim Lawley looked busy just bustling through the front door. Tall and lean, he cut a sharp figure in a tailored shirt and slacks, the consummate professional with places to go and VIPs to see. His phone was a permanent fixture in his hand, and he gestured with it as he barked out his good mornings.

When Jim set a course for her cubicle and the kitchen farther down the hall, Cassidy sucked in her breath and held it, preparing for the migraine-inducing cloud of cologne that wafted around him.

"Good morning, Chandler. How's the coffee?"

Cassidy stifled a groan and schooled her face into good cheer. He wasn't referring to the coffee in her cup. "Fresh and extra strong. Just the way you like it."

"That's my girl." He patted the top of the cubicle wall, his wedding ring clanging on the frame, and disappeared into the kitchen.

"So *not your girl*," she said under her breath and logged into her workstation. The coffee machine was her most sacred responsibility to hear Jim tell it, and one of her duties was to set it up every night for a fresh pot at the push of a button the next morning.

"Good morning, Mr. McKinney," Cassidy greeted cheerfully when the editor-in-chief went past, totting his quart-sized Florida Gators mug. He only nodded in reply, deep creases furrowing his brow.

Before she got too discouraged about the lack of enthusiasm from the man who could make or break her career, she decided the dead could wait a few more minutes. Taking the camera out of her bag, she plugged it into her workstation. The morning's images appeared on the screen. Most were of a spectacular ocean sunrise, an explosion of deep blues and fiery reds that had nudged her grudging respect for the sunshine state up a notch.

"Are you doing something different with your hair, Chandler?" Jim's voice pulled her from her study of one of the other things she had photographed on the beach.

"Felt like wearing it down," she said with a small shrug. Her dark, chestnut hair—twice its usual volume thanks to the scoop-with-a-spoon humidity—was down over her shoulders, covering up all the makeup she slathered over that awful bruise on her neck. Though invisible now, it still ached every time she turned her head.

"Nice look for you. I like it. Very sexy. I hope that Striker kid appreciates you," he added with a wink, and sipped his steaming coffee, which must have been up to his standards.

Cassidy toyed with the impulse to wipe that patronizing leer off his face with the contents of her own cup—or at least a casual mention of the sexual harassment policy. Jim was the golden boy, though. Rumor had it that people got fired if Jim didn't like them. Staying in his good graces was paramount if she hoped to stay around long enough to earn a reference from

Dave McKinney. Not all of what "needed to be done" applied to beating deadlines.

Steeling herself, she took a cautious breath of the cologne cloud.

"Maybe you can help me figure something out, Mr. Lawley, since I hear you're a bit of a fisherman." She swiveled her monitor toward him.

Jim gave a low whistle. "What a mess. Where was this?"

"On the beach. This weekend," she said even though the backdrop was obvious. Before he could ask for a specific location—her new backyard—she added, "What do you think would cause that?"

Interest apparently piqued, Larry shuffled his bulk around the partition. "A dead shark, kiddo? That's not news unless it was murdered by a goldfish."

"Well, something killed it all right," Jim said, leaning closer. Cassidy leaned away as far as she was able without looking like she wanted to crawl out of her skin. "Bull shark, I think. Big mother, too. Definitely an apex predator." He straightened. "In the ocean anyway. That looks like someone caught it and hacked out its throat with a dull knife."

"Why would someone do that?"

Larry snorted. "Get some of these rich kids with their fancy toys high enough, there's no telling what entertainment they'll invent."

"Definitely ballsy. They could have lost a limb or their lives. Just look at those teeth," Jim said.

Cassidy did. "How do you know they didn't? It's a big ocean. There might be a story there."

Larry hid a smile in his coffee.

"Not if we don't know who's missing or injured, and there are no reports of either right now. But...there is a report I need to follow up on ASAP."

"Something gruesome?" Larry prompted. Jim never looked this gleefully grim unless gore was involved.

"Yes. Just got the alert." He waved his phone. "Another body washed up on Marathon this morning. Female in her twenties, on vacation in the Keys. Throat cut. Probably raped, same as the other two. Another one is missing, but no body yet."

Larry scratched his balding head and heaved a disgusted sigh. "Animals."

Cassidy shivered. This wasn't the only killing spree in Florida right now. For several months, an "especially brutal inter-city gang war," as the police put it, left the headless bodies of dealers and pimps stashed in dumpsters and shipping containers around the state. As all of them had rap sheets a mile long, those discoveries rated only a mention on page three by now. But the victims in the Keys, two hundred miles south, were innocents killed in ways that gave Cassidy nightmares. The night two and a half years ago, when three drunk frat brothers "on the prowl" cornered her, could have ended like this—if not for Jackson.

"Do they have *any* new leads?" she said, rubbing the chill off her arms.

Jim shook his head. "I'm going to call some contacts down there to see what I can find out."

"I can call for you," she offered. This horror struck too close to home. In any way she could, she needed to help solve this case and save other women from that fate. That sucking up to Jim Lawley would help save her job and career was almost an afterthought.

"No, thanks. This is too big for a rookie. Besides, I think you've got obits to write." He nodded at the stack of black folders. "Better get busy, Chandler."

"Wait." Cassidy was on her feet before she knew what she was doing. "This is an important story. Two sets of eyes and ears are going to find more than one."

Jim turned away. "I've got it covered."

Do what needs to be done, she thought. "Mr. Lawley, please hear me out." At the pleading note, he swiveled back. "I'd really like the chance to work with you. To, you know, learn the ropes."

Larry flashed a surreptitious thumbs-up beside his cup.

Jim hesitated. "Really. Well, I'm flattered, but I work alone."

"I don't want to share the byline. I want to learn how a real pro works a story like this."

Now Larry closed his eyes and shook his head a little. Okay. That last line was laying it on a bit thick. Jim seemed to think so, too, judging by the exasperated look he gave her.

"Miss Chandler. You have no experience and zero local knowledge. I don't have the time to train you."

"Everybody has to start somewhere. And why am I here if I'm so underqualified?"

"You're here because your future in-laws are this paper's biggest supporters. And that, as they say, is that." He saluted with his mug. "Good coffee, by the way."

Cassidy watched him go with her mouth hanging open. The implications rocked through her. No one here—except maybe Larry—expected her to contribute anything of value. They tolerated her, because they had to. They did what needed to be done to humor the most influential family in town.

She fell back into her chair.

Larry looked apologetic. "Sorry about that, kiddo. Jim's an ass hat. Don't let him get under your skin."

No, Jim Lawley wasn't the problem. The problem was the Striker patriarchs who had just sucker punched the air out of her. How could she not have seen this coming? All the applications she had sent to outlets large and small within two hours' drive. None had openings for rookies. Most didn't even call her back. Not until Lillian Striker got involved.

"Well, if this is really what you want, dear, I can make some inquiries," Jackson's mother had said.

The very next morning, Cassidy scored an interview with the *Gazette's* editor-in-chief, Dave McKinney, legendary newsman, enjoying semi-retirement in South Florida. They had no openings either, but she received an offer anyway, based on, she was told, the strength of her samples.

But did she owe this opportunity to her connection with the Strikers instead? Could her falling out with them take it away? Could one phone call from Warren or—God forbid, Garrett—leave her without a paycheck and without a home soon thereafter?

Without her independence?

How long before that happened? Or had Jackson's father already contacted Dave about her? Was that why her boss looked so distracted this morning?

Turning away, she fisted her right hand into her left, feeling the enormous diamond ring she wore only because she didn't want to risk losing it. Now she realized she stood to lose far more than the ring if she took it off. Deciding on the spot, she moved it back to her left hand. If Jackson insisted she keep it, the clunky thing might as well help her keep this job long enough to establish herself as something more than the biggest investor's future daughter-in-law.

"You okay?" Larry wondered, his sonorous tone gentle.

Cassidy cleared the knot out of her throat and mustered a half-hearted smile over her shoulder. "Oh, sure. I guess that's what I get for overdoing the brown-nosing. Like you said. He's an ass."

While Larry retreated to his cubicle cave, she sat and continued scrolling through her images. Another subject of her early morning photo safari was a giant sea turtle laying her eggs. Choosing the best of this group, she dragged them into the image share folder.

Then she put her camera away, took a fortifying gulp of coffee, and headed for Dave McKinney's office.

To do what needed to be done.

For a long time after waking, Dominique remained motionless, crumpled against the door of his sanctuary, and considered the odd mix of disappointment and relief churning in the pit of his gut.

He still existed.

And he was not alone.

The scent of her living presence permeated the musty air. Country music drifted down the hall, together with the sounds of kitchen activities. Dishes and cutlery clattered. A lid clanged onto a pot. Outside, waves hissed up on the beach and insect song filled the night. It all felt warm and familiar, like faint echoes of long ago nights in busy kitchens, of pristine beaches, laughter, and wine.

Dominique pushed the memories away. He could ill afford to be distracted now with an unknown quantity preparing—he sniffed and his nose wrinkled in distaste—processed cheese food in his kitchen. If she was here to annoy him with her atrocious culinary and musical choices, she had succeeded.

The leathers creaked around him as he unraveled the cramped position his body had held during the day. Maybe he had overreacted this morning. She was not here to end him. No mortal who knew this place as his lair would have to bother moving in to accomplish that. A morning visit to drag his oblivious self into the yard would suffice.

But *did* she know he was here? Did she know what he was? Where was the blood-drinker who marked her?

"What's the matter, buddy? You hear something?" To his heightened senses, the girl's muffled voice sounded as warm as her aroma and as soft as the thump of her heart. Less enchanting was the sharp hiss of the cat, followed by the animal bolting upstairs.

"Oh, c'mon, Eddie, you big chicken. If there's another snake in here, at least show me where it is." Bare feet padded down the hall. Shooing noises ensued from the bathroom beside his room. Drawers opened. Something knocked about. "I know I got them all. *And* the bugs."

Dominique listened, hypnotized by the sound of a human voice in his sanctuary.

"God, I hope I got them all." The laundry closet door opened. Hesitation. A weary sigh. "Fine. Geckos can stay. But you have to eat the bugs." Her warm-blooded scent dissipated as she retreated. A chair scraped across the tiles. Utensils clinked.

He lingered in the darkness. Answers. He needed answers, and the only one who could provide them was this girl, this Cassidy. That made disposing of her out of the question—in theory, anyway. In reality, the odds were stacked against her. Even well-fed, the beast would not want to pass up such a convenient opportunity. If she showed any signs of fear in his presence, what slim control he maintained would evaporate.

That she would be terrorized by a strange man in leathers appearing in her home with his hair caked by blood was a given.

6

THE WAY OF THE FRENCH

There was a naked man in her house.

Cassidy looked up from her dinner and laptop as he emerged from the locked room at the end of the hall. He stretched at leisure, yawned, and pushed a hand through a wild tangle of dark hair. Just when the vision couldn't get any more bizarre, the naked man smiled.

She stopped breathing.

"*Bonsoir*, Cassidy," he said in a velvety French voice. With a little wave, he disappeared into the guest bath. The door clicked shut. The shower came on.

A clump of mac 'n' cheese plopped onto the table from her halted fork. She put the utensil down and sat back. "What. The. Hell." If not for hearing the water run, she might have doubted her own eyes. "What the hell?"

She shut the laptop, silenced Radio Denver, and marched down the hall. A second before she knocked on the bathroom door, she thought better of demanding explanations of a strange man in the shower. Instead, she peered into the gloom of the back bedroom. The light filtering in from the kitchen revealed little more than a twin bed. Bulky black clothes sat piled on top of rumpled cartoon character bedding, and silver-buckled boots lay beside a pair of flip-flops on the floor. Hot, stale air squelched from the interior, heavy with old wood and creeping mildew and something almost out of place. Something...cool?

In the bathroom, the shower cut off. Unwilling to be caught snooping, Cassidy rushed back to the kitchen on bare toes. Had he been in there all day? Was he there yesterday when she all but turned the house upside down, scrubbing it and evicting the wildlife? And today, when the maid service had probably made enough noise to wake the deaf?

Answers. She needed answers. And he better be able to provide them, and fast.

She hovered by the table, food forgotten, wishing she wore something a little less revealing than shorts and a sports bra. She still felt damp from her run on the beach earlier to burn off the mounting anxieties about her job. Her future remained precarious—even after her heart-to-heart with Dave—and now this: a naked man popping up in her house like a mushroom on a lawn. Was there no end to the craziness of this day?

The stranger didn't bother with a towel when he returned to the back room. Cassidy tried—and failed—not to stare. Even in the low light, it was impossible not to notice that fluid grace and confident strength, or those half-moon buttocks. When he reappeared seconds later, he wore a pair of black exercise pants that rode alarmingly low on his slim hips. He moved down the hallway toward her like a long-limbed panther on the prowl.

Cassidy's eyes flitted down and then away from the solid slab of muscle narrowing into his waistband. Given the unenthusiastic state of his male assets, sexual assault probably wasn't on his agenda. The unbidden thought made her mouth go dry. Suddenly, she was far too aware of being alone with him. Only the sound of rolling surf swelled through the open windows, together with the cool, wet smell of the ocean at night. There was no one else around—no one to hear her scream...

A soft crack and hiss snapped her back to the present. The stranger in her house now stood in the kitchen and lifted the bottle of Perrier water he had just opened to his lips. She studied his face for clues. It was as striking as the rest of him, ruggedly beautiful, like something off a GQ cover, complete with a couple of days' worth of beard shadowing his lean cheeks. Jet-black hair clung to his pale neck in damp tendrils, and bold, black brows swept above hooded eyes. When he stopped drinking, a smug smile curved his full mouth, dimpling one cheek. He was watching her as curiously as she him.

"Are you enjoying the view, *madame*?" he said, sounding mildly amused and exceedingly French, his cadence lilting and vowels smooth.

"I wasn't..." she spluttered.

The dimple deepened. "Surely you have seen a nude male before, *non*?"

Cassidy's face flamed. There was "nude male" and then there was *him*, and he damn well knew it. Men like this graced fashion runways and the slick ads for men's cologne. They did not walk out of locked bedrooms in rundown rentals languishing in the middle of nowhere.

His dark eyes danced with obvious delight at her awkwardness, and his smile exploded into a grin that touched an icy finger to her spine. Despite the oppressive heat, she shivered and hugged herself.

"Who the hell are you? What do you want?" she said, shocking herself with how helpless she sounded. A vise clamped around her lungs, squeezing the breath out of her. The surf roared in her ears like an approaching tsunami, scattering her thoughts.

His grin faded, replaced by something much more ominous. *Hunger*, she thought for no reason she could name. Written all over that model-perfect face. And all she could suddenly think about was the dead girls washing up on the beaches of the Keys.

"If...if you're going to rape me, at least be q—quick about it." God help her, but as long as he let her live, it was a bargain she was willing to make.

"*Merde*," he hissed under his breath.

Great going, Cass, she admonished herself as her eyes frantically cast about for potential weapons. If assault hadn't been on his mind before, it was now.

"No," he snapped as her hand went for the discarded fork. He spun away, retreating to the far end of the living room that adjoined the kitchen. There was frantic rustling and a muttered stream of what must have been choice French profanities.

Then something new curled in the air, familiar and sickening: cigarette smoke.

Cassidy sank into her chair and cradled her head in both hands, wheezing, her heart pounding on the back of her tongue. Like evil ghosts summoned by the smoke, countless angry, grief-stricken memories slammed into her, taking her panic attack to a whole new level. Her lungs disappeared.

"*Écoutez!*"

Startled, she looked up and found herself pinned by his gaze. Her breath came in fast, shallow gasps, the panting of an animal caught in a trap.

"Listen to me," he said with an obvious attempt at being soothing, though his accent was now clipped and terse. Leaning onto the back of the chair opposite her, he sucked at the cigarette trembling in his fingers without taking his eyes off her. Twin streams of smoke blew from his knife-blade nose. "I will not rape you. Do you understand this?"

She tried to nod because she did understand the words. But she couldn't get enough air, and her head felt like a helium balloon with its string cut. Her hands convulsed around the table edges to keep her tethered. The room spun. The panic had its teeth into her too deep for her to do anything but fight for breath.

"Breathe," he ordered. "Deep. In with the nose. Out with the mouth. *Lentement.* Slowly. More slowly."

Something about the timbre of his voice reached straight down her throat and into her chest. Her lungs obeyed and expanded with precious air. Slowly. Again. And again. Several more breaths later, she sat back, drained, the drumbeat of her heart ebbing.

He stayed where he was, still pulling at the cigarette, but his hand was steady now. Ashes dropped onto the table, onto the floor. He looked almost as relieved as she felt. "I will not do this thing, Cassidy. I will not force myself on you. Nod if you understand."

This time, she nodded.

"Do you believe me?"

Another nod. He would not rape her. She believed it because if that were the plan, she doubted he'd bother talking her down from a panic attack.

Which didn't rule out a lot of other unsavory ideas he might have up his non-existent sleeve. No matter. As long as it wasn't *that*, she could deal. If she kept her wits about her. Gathering them up, she straightened in her seat.

"How do you know my name?"

"I saw your papers last night." He gestured at the pile in question, which contained her rental agreement. "You were out."

Out grocery shopping. She almost got clipped by a phantom motorcycle rocketing out of the mule trail on her way back. Remembering the black leather clothes and fancy boots in his room, she added "lunatic" to her running list of observations, along with rude, crude, and no respect for privacy. She'd be packing her bags if not for her self-respect and the two free weeks she was due in this dump.

"So who are you and what are you doing in my house?"

He hesitated before shrugging one bare shoulder, which sported a prominent tribal sun tattoo. "I am Dominique Marchant." He reached across and extinguished the cigarette in her bowl of mac 'n' cheese. "And this is, in fact, *my* house."

She stared at her ruined meal, the dish her mother used to make for her from scratch when Cassidy needed cheering up. Like today. "And that was my dinner."

"That is shit," he said, waving at the bowl.

So it was true what they said about the French being rude. His striking good looks paled beside his arrogance and disappeared entirely in light of that filthy cigarette. She looked up, her jaw clenching. That glimmer of amusement was in his eyes again. Deep, warm hazel eyes, alive with unspoken challenge.

She raised a brow. "So what you're saying is you live in this pigsty?"

He turned a chair around and straddled it, folding his arms over the back and propping his chin on his forearms. The intensity of his regard was unnerving. "*Oui*. I do."

"With no AC?"

"I don't need it."

"No food?"

"I eat out, *chèrie*. Every night."

"How nice for you." A wry tilt of his mouth. "At the rental agency, they don't seem to know you're here."

"They don't. I didn't expect anyone to rent this...pigsty, during the summer."

"Pigsty is all I can afford," she said flatly. If he sent her packing, she'd be out of options. Again. Not that she relished having a rude, snooping, lunatic Frenchman for a roommate, but only yesterday she was willing to put up with anyone who would give her a room and tolerate a cat.

Besides, he did promise not to rape her.

She heaved a small sigh. Could the bar get any lower?

Dominique glanced at where her fingers fretted with the Striker engagement ring. "The man who gave you that can afford to keep you much better than this, *non*?"

Cassidy stopped fidgeting. "Well, maybe I don't want to be *kept*. No?"

He searched her face. Flecks of gold glinted in the depths of his eyes where gears tumbled into place. "So he is the reason you are here."

"I don't see how..."

"Is he also the one who bit you?"

Her hand flew to the mysterious bruise on her neck, visible now with her hair up and all the makeup sweated off. *Oh my God, he's right. It does look like a bite,* she thought, aghast. Out loud, she said, "That's none of your business."

"*Au contraire,*" Dominique murmured. "This is my house. The reason you are here disturbing my peace *is* my business."

"Does that mean you're okay with me staying?" Encouraged by his silence, she continued, "It wouldn't be long. Just until I get some funds saved up." Or a raise or better offer, neither of which appeared likely at the moment.

"That depends. Are you here because of that bite?" A long index finger pointed at her neck.

"You don't know when to quit, do you? What's your kinky fascination with a bruise on my neck?"

"What do you remember of how you got it?"

She hesitated, the hole in her memory opening between them, ready to swallow her. What all had she forgotten? Did a total stranger know more about it than she did? Cassidy doused a new shiver of unease with a hearty dose of bluster. "As you said. It's a bite. Want me to draw you a freaking picture?"

"No. Just tell me."

She pushed her chair back and got up. "You're unbelievable. No, I won't tell you or anyone else. It's private."

"Cassidy," he said, his tone softening. "Tell me what happened. Tell me everything."

That voice...it had a tangible presence, a vibration that resonated somewhere deep inside her, caressing her with warmth and understanding. Yes, she did want to tell him. From one moment to the next, the need to talk to someone bordered on desperate. About how lost and confused she felt. How she could no longer trust a man she loved and about so much more bottled up deep inside—grief and disappointment, anger and frustration. Pour it all out in a giant heap to someone who genuinely wanted to know, to him...to...

She blinked. To this haughty bastard who ruined her food, stomped on the memories she nursed in it, showed way too much interest in her personal life, and was bound to throw her and Eddie out anyway?

"I don't think so." She and the cat could sleep in the car.

Dominique sat up as if she had slapped him. Then his face shuttered into a blank nothingness worthy of any pouty runway model. He got up and stalked around her, his presence encroaching on her like a force of nature. She stood, riveted and disbelieving, as he leaned in and sniffed at her shoulder. Tension rolled off him in waves, but he didn't touch her.

Not physically, anyway.

The blow he delivered came as a snarling command. "By this time tomorrow, you will be gone from here."

A moment later, the front door slammed in his wake.

———————

Dominique cursed all the way to the beach.

The situation with this Cassidy Chandler girl was now a full-blown fiasco. It missed being a blood-soaked disaster by only the slimmest of margins.

When she seethed with fear out of nowhere, the beast had torn his guts to bloody ribbons in its frantic need to live up to every one of her worst expectations of him—and more. If not for the cigarette smoke grinding through his lungs, distracting the hunger, he would have lost his last shred of control.

So much for his clumsy attempts at a casual approach. Clearly, even his most dazzling charm could instill terror.

"*C'est un putain de désastre.*" He tore away the flimsy pants and threw himself into the sea. Since his transformation, he no longer floated, making swimming impossible. So he crept along the sandy bottom on all fours to a small reef just offshore. There he spread himself face-down across the coral and algae-encrusted limestone shelves and let the passing waves rock his body into stillness.

His mind raced.

He could not compel her. At least not when she didn't want to be.

She wanted to breathe, so she did his bidding.

She didn't want to tell him about her injury, so she didn't.

It made no sense. If another vampire had compelled her to resist him, she would have done so every time, not only when it suited her. Also, her sudden panic was a lethal tripwire. Any blood-drinker that went through the trouble of sending her into his path would have a better plan for her than immediate self-destruction, such as dragging him out into the sun, for instance. Not only had she not done that, she even seemed oblivious to his true nature.

Unless she was compelled to be oblivious.

Something slithered across the back of his thigh. Dominique didn't move, thrilling to the gentle caresses. Encouraged, the octopus continued to investigate, slipping its tentacles over and beneath him, testing the peculiar, smooth feel of him while he imagined its curious explorations to be the embrace of the sea itself. His heart ached with a powerful, almost forgotten need to be touched like this, with affection and trust.

Closing his eyes, he shivered as the octopus nestled its soft body between his legs, seeking and not quite finding a place to lurk in comfort. This, too, was an intimacy he would never know again. Some blood-drinkers didn't care that their human lovers would not survive a sexual encounter. Dominique wasn't one of them.

His thoughts swerved back to Cassidy, the girl in his lair with the scent of an unknown vampire in her veins. Her blood wasn't all that enticed him, and that interest was mutual. Her involuntary arousal was more than obvious to his heightened senses. But that was insanity. He had taken one life in a fit of passion when he didn't know any better, a tragedy that would haunt him forever along with too many others. Doing it again with a full understanding of the consequences? That would kill what little was left of his humanity.

Deep in his heart, the beast growled its discontent. It would not have her, not tonight and not tomorrow, not any night or in any way.

The octopus emerged across his buttocks and sidled up his back. It probed at the cloud of hair floating around his head. Then it vanished in a hurry, the water jet of its departure washing down his spine. He opened his eyes and shifted his vision. A thousand tiny lives melted from the gloom surrounding him—and a single large one. His body tensed, compacting, readying for the hunt.

The shark nudged him once. Circling around, it returned, aiming for a taste. It underestimated its prey. When the animal would have torn his flesh, Dominique caught it in his arms. Seconds later, its thin, salty blood flowed from its heart and into him, a predator without equal. Soon, the carcass drifted on the reef, attracting the first scavengers.

He settled a distance away, the beast appeased, if not satisfied. Shark blood was the blood-drinker equivalent of junk food—convenient but little else. Sometimes convenience trumped enjoyment, especially tonight when a human slept in his lair. He would stay submerged out here until dawn to avoid that temptation. By tomorrow night, if she had any sense at all, she would be gone and safe from him.

But not safe from the other blood-drinker.

An inexplicable frisson passed through him. Whoever it was, it wasn't his sire. That much he knew from her scent. Was it possible that she was only a casual and already forgotten feed who moved into his lair by sheer coincidence? Possible, yes. Probable? No.

What would the other do with her when she left here? As long as none of it involved him, Dominique had no cause to care. Yet, the thought gave him pause. At best, she would be killed, at worst enslaved—if she wasn't already. He found no pleasure in indiscriminate murder or the cruel games blood-drinkers often played. But if he condemned her to such a fate, was he any better than those who would execute it?

It was a question that still occupied him when the sky grew light and he locked himself behind the door of his refuge.

7

REFUGEES

Dominique Marchant's vehement demands notwithstanding, Cassidy was determined to find a compromise. Finding another place to stay was simply out of the question. She'd lose money she couldn't afford by breaking the rental agreement. Plus, there was her job. She wasn't about to give anyone any cause to dismiss her by spending paid time on personal calls, to say nothing of leaving early to move her belongings yet again.

Instead, she put in a grueling day in the rookie trenches while mentally rehearsing the looming encounter with the ornery Frenchman. They had definitely gotten off to a harrowing start. Somehow, she had to make this work.

All was quiet when she returned to the contested beach digs that evening, and she was relieved to see Eddie and her things had not been evicted to the front yard in her absence. Dumping her bag and blazer on the kitchen table, she kicked off her shoes and released a long breath. The heat wrapped around her like a sauna, soaking into tense muscles and making her relax almost against her will. All day she acted the model employee. She had even refrained from giving Jim Lawley a piece of her mind when he suggested the coffee machine needed detailing with a toothbrush.

On the plus side, one of her turtle pictures ran today under the heading "Local Color" and Dave had been halfway encouraging when she explained about wanting to contribute more. Not that he'd rushed to hand her a choice assignment. "It's only your second week," he told her. "Give it time."

Retrieving a diet soda from the fridge, she popped it open. While she drank, she admired her handiwork. She had poured her time and sweat into making this place livable, even welcoming. The late afternoon sun streamed through the windows, dappling the kitchen and living room with warm yellow patterns. A strange sense of refuge oozed from the wood-paneled walls and hovered around the worn furnishings. Even the faded rugs scattered across the tiles like casual smiles seemed to greet her.

A lot of life had transpired here. Happy life, she liked to think, and for reasons she couldn't quite explain, she felt safe here despite the cranky Frenchman camping in the back room. How long had he or his family owned this place? Was he part of whatever had created the good vibes she imagined? Maybe she felt safe here not despite, but because of him.

Eddie flowed down the stairs and poured himself onto a rug beneath the whirling ceiling fan, where he stretched and twisted with abandon. Cassidy joined him on the floor and rubbed his squirming belly. "Hey there, buddy. Feeling better now?"

Last night she tried to bribe the cat out from under her bed with kitty treats for an hour. He was underneath the bed again—or perhaps still—this morning, brimming with feline misgivings. But now he purred as if he had swallowed a motor.

The back room door was closed. How could anyone sleep in this heat? Was he soaked in alcohol? Knocked out by drugs? How sad. He was such a handsome guy—until he opened his mouth. Cassidy sighed. None of her business. She had enough problems of her own.

She went for a jog on the beach and noodled around with an idea for an article before lounging in one of the creaking Adirondack chairs with a bowl of leftover mac 'n' cheese. Shadows lengthened, and a breeze brushed against her damp skin.

Insects buzzed over the whoosh and mumble of the ocean. A deep sense of peace enveloped her.

It was temporary.

Fresh from a cool, soapy shower, she descended the stairs and spotted him sitting cross-legged in a corner of the sofa, a bottle of Perrier in one hand and a laptop balanced between his thighs. That he wasn't yelling, she thought, was promising.

"You're up," she said by way of tentative greeting, glad for the long, tie-dyed peasant skirt and conservative top she had donned like cloth armor.

Dominique's attire tonight, she was relieved to see, included not only gym pants but also a black, V-necked T-shirt. He ran his fingers through his unruly hair, pushing it off his furrowed brow.

"You are still here."

"Yes. So I am." To buy herself some time and gather her thoughts—and to avoid fidgeting in place—she padded to the kitchen, opened the refrigerator, and stared into it. That's when she noticed an unfamiliar pop beat underlying French lyrics had replaced Radio Denver. He had appropriated her Bluetooth speaker. Well, technically Jackson's, but she was the only one who ever used it.

Right then, a station break identified Radio St. Barth. She inhaled, preparing to tell him exactly how she felt about him touching her things, but then remembered her still precarious situation. So she opted for a diplomatic, "Is that where you're from? St. Barth?"

"*Oui.* St. Barthélémy."

Not in the mood for sweetness, she took one of the Perriers, opened it, and drank straight out of the bottle, trying to recall what she knew of that Caribbean island nation.

"Isn't that where that Italian actress was killed last year? What was her name? Jo-Sebastian-something?" He continued to stare at his screen. "That was quite the media circus, as I recall. Were you there for that?"

Dominique snapped the laptop shut. "Why are *you* still *here*?"

"Sorry. Guess you were." She made a mental note to run some searches for St. Barth. She knew it was small. And, oh yeah, French.

"Look," she said, facing him from behind the kitchen counter. "This wasn't my first choice of places to stay. In fact, it's safe to say that it was my last choice. Though it's growing on me," she added quickly. No point insulting his home more than she already had. "I have nowhere else to go right now." She drank some more of the chilled bubbles before that depressing thought could sink in any deeper. "Besides, there's a contract I can't afford to break. You should have told them you were here."

His expression remained neutral as he watched her.

"I'm quiet. I'm neat. Eddie"—she glanced around, but saw no trace of him—"well, Eddie is obviously the disappearing cat, and I make sure he's always clean. It doesn't look like you're allergic or anything. We should be able to coexist for a bit? Maybe?" she finished with a hopeful grimace.

Dominique took a slow swallow from his own little green bottle. "Your pet is allergic to me."

"He's shy around strangers. At least he doesn't bite. Neither do I, by the way."

As she hoped, that got a smile out of him, one that pressed a rakish dimple into his unshaven left cheek. "Maybe I do." At her confused frown, he waved the bottle in dismissal. "Do you truly have nowhere else to go?"

"Nowhere else I can handle being right now, no."

"Why?"

Cassidy cringed. Here came the questions again. "That's...personal."

He made a small noise that sounded French somehow, set aside the laptop, and unfolded his long legs. "You insist on sharing my home. What could be more personal than that?"

The suggestive purr in his voice sent heat crawling up her neck. She didn't want to go there with him, needed to keep their accidental relationship as business-like as possible. She had no room in her life for more complications, and, God help her, Dominique Marchant had "complicated" written all over him.

"*Détendez-vous*, Cassidy. Relax," he said, getting up. Coming closer, his mood shifted as he leaned one hand on the kitchen counter across from her. "My privacy is very important to me. Yet you are determined to invade it. I want to understand why that is."

She searched his face and found only quiet interest. Okay, so he might have a point. Were their roles reversed, she doubted she would be half so accommodating; that deserved something. She summarized her situation, mentioning a big move, new job, and low pay, but leaving out the personal details—or tried to.

"What about the man who gave you that?" he asked, nodding toward her left hand and the ring.

"Well, he's not here, obviously."

"Is he still in Colorado?"

She shook her head and studied the ring, remembering how Jackson had presented it to her on one knee two days before they both graduated—she with her journalism bachelor's, he with his MBA—both of them full of excitement and hope.

"So he is dead?" Dominique prompted.

"No. We..." *broke up, but I'm still wearing this because I might be out of a job if I don't and will be financially sunk for eternity if I lose it? Nope. Keep it simple.* "We're taking a break." A long one.

"Because of the bite?"

She gasped. "What the...what is it with you and that bruise?"

"It makes sense, *non?*"

"No. It doesn't." Agitation rippled through her. Before he could push the issue further, she went on the attack. "And to be perfectly honest, neither do you."

His eyes widened a little. "Oh?"

"An obvious hunk like you hanging out here all by yourself? Sleeping all day and disappearing all night? What gives?"

"Ah. I knew you were enjoying the view."

"Don't change the subject."

"Like you?"

"What are *you* doing here, Nick? I can call you Nick, right? Who are you really?"

That seemed to bring him up short. His mouth opened, but whatever was about to fly out didn't. Instead, the expression on his too perfect face softened, and Cassidy was pleased to think she had made her point. Then the corner of his mouth lifted, and he practically purred when he said, "Perhaps I am a depraved, French serial killer hiding from justice?"

She stared at him, trying to read this new mood. Really? They'd only just met, and he was going for dark humor? Well, if that's how he rolled, she'd bite. "Oh, a *French* serial killer, is it? Good to know. I'd hate to be here with a criminal who might actually have some manners."

Now it was his turn to look befuddled. She lifted a brow in challenge. With a small shake of his head, he upended the Perrier to his lips.

Male model, she reasoned, watching his throat bob. Probably lost his contract because he couldn't check his attitude at the door and camped out here to nurse his wounded ego. Well, she wasn't about to coddle it. She had too many things to worry about to be dazzled by those looks.

When the bottle settled back down on the worn yellow laminate countertop between them, it was empty. His agile fingers idly spun it in place. "I have an allergy. To the sun."

"Don't tell me. You sparkle," she countered. He looked up and tilted his head, mouth pursed to hold in a retort or a smile, hard to tell which. She looked more carefully; his skin did seem fair enough to blister if exposed to anything stronger than a forty-watt bulb. "Um, sorry. I do know that's a real condition."

His eyes rounded, incredulous. "What? Sparkling?"

"No. Sun allergy. But it's kinda strange that you're avoiding the sun on a tropical beach, of all places."

He watched the bottle in his fingers again, a small frown drawing his black brows together like the wings of a bird. "This house belongs to my family. They don't know I'm here. I would like to keep it that way."

"Fine. But the rental agency is trying to reach the owners about the busted AC."

His head snapped up. "Tell them to stop."

"Are you going to fix it, then? Assuming you're not throwing me bodily out of here, which is about what it'll take to get rid of me, by the way."

Another one of those long, searching looks as if he were trying to read her every thought. Then he abandoned the bottle, and returned to the living room where he sprawled on the sofa, facing her, his arms outstretched across the back. After a moment's though, he inclined his head. "You may decide to leave on your own."

"I doubt that."

"There are house rules."

"House rules?" Okay, that sounded promising. Armed with all the best intentions to take every single one to heart, Cassidy settled in the nearest wicker armchair and folded her legs underneath her. "Shoot."

"If you are drinking my water, you will keep us both supplied. I don't enjoy going to the store."

She opened her mouth to protest, then saw the half empty green bottle clutched in her hand. "Expensive habits."

"My least expensive habit, actually. Consider it part of your rent."

Cassidy smothered a spike of irritation with forced good cheer. "Fine. Perrier it is. And anything else in the fridge, while you're in there. Be my guest. Help yourself to snacks."

"Help myself?" Somehow, he managed to appear aghast and eager at the same time.

"Really. I don't mind."

"Oh, I think perhaps you would." He shook his head. "No matter. Your groceries are safe from me. Except for the apples and eggs, there is not one piece of actual food in this house. It is all processed shit."

"Wow. Do you feel better getting that off your chest?"

"I will give you the money for the Perrier, if you like."

"That...would be good," she agreed, taken aback by the unexpected offer. "What other rules?"

"Your speaker. When I'm here at night, it will stream Radio St. Barth." He held up a hand to forestall a protest. "Consider it rent for using my Internet connection, *non?*"

Cassidy sucked in a breath. Her hands clenched around the bottle. "Radio Denver is all I have left of home."

"Listen to it when I'm not here."

Which might be most of the time, she thought, calming herself. And it was just a radio station, easily changed.

Dominique leaned forward, elbows propped on his thighs. "Your speaker—and how you use it—is a blessing, *chérie*. I had not considered this until I heard your Radio Denver. I have not felt so close to home in over a year."

The soft tone and the casual endearment touched her in a way she didn't expect. "Sounds like we have something in common."

"*Oui.* We are both...refugees?"

Tears stung her eyes without warning. "Yes. That about sums it up." She cleared her throat and swallowed. "Okay. We share the speaker. What else?"

He produced a crushed pack of cigarettes and a lighter from his pockets. Tapping one out, he lit it and pulled hard. Cassidy slumped back in her seat, heart dropping. "How often do you do that?"

"When I need to."

"When the cravings hit, you mean."

His smile didn't quite make it into his eyes. "*Oui.* Cravings."

"It doesn't bother you that those things are going to kill you?"

"This?" He studied the smoldering tip. "I should be so lucky."

"It's not a joke, Nick. I watched my mother die of lung cancer, and she wasn't even the one smoking. It's a horrible way to go. I wouldn't wish it on my worst enemy. Not even you."

A haunted look fled across his face. "My condolences on your loss, but I promise you, you would not like me much if I did not smoke."

She wrinkled her nose. "That assumes I like you at all."

"I know you do."

"Like hell."

He inhaled again, his face tense with concentration, and exhaled on a heartfelt sigh. *"Oui, chérie. Exactement.* Like hell."

Cassidy waved off the pollution drifting her way. "Are we done?"

"Do you agree with all the rules?"

"Yes," she said, trying not to breathe too deeply. Smoking would have been a deal breaker had she known about it beforehand. But there had been no evidence when she arrived. Chances were he rarely smoked, and at the moment, it was likely only to annoy her. At which he succeeded in spectacular fashion.

"Then you can stay."

"Thanks."

She got to her feet, preparing to retreat upstairs, when he stopped her with, "I don't sparkle in the sun."

"Really. Imagine my surprise."

He gestured with the cigarette. "I smoke. Maybe...with your help...I can show you sometime."

"Right." She snorted and headed for the stairs. "Just what I need. A comedian for a roommate."

8

TRAIL OF BLOOD

Every night and every morning, Jackson called Cassidy to keep tabs on her state of mind. The serum in her blood might yet lure his target into the open.

Or so he told himself.

Uncle Garrett's warnings barely registered before Jackson brushed them off. He could not give up Cassidy any more than he could stop breathing. Without her, there was no ground beneath his feet. The last few days made this abundantly clear. He had to convince her to come back to him, letting him keep her safe—even if she would never know why or from what. She was his rock and his moral touchstone. Without her...without her, he would turn into Garrett's cold, brutal clone.

By reaching out so often, he hoped to remind her of the friendship on which their relationship was based, the trust they once shared. He had been forced to break that trust, and now had no easy way to repair it without putting her in even more danger.

He didn't push. He respected her desire to keep conversations to brief courtesy check-ins. But tonight, Friday, she was worked up enough to share more about "a guy at work" who stressed her to the point of ranting. Jackson's immediate—and not so brilliant—advice was "come home, babe, and forget the job. You don't need to put up with that shit."

The long silence told him he'd stepped in it. He scrunched his face, mentally kicking himself. "Cass—"

"Apparently I do need to put up with that shit," she told him with an icy calm and disconnected.

"Fuck." Jackson slammed his phone on the desk, grabbed a pen and flung it clear across the Foundation library. It bounced off the canvas of great-grandfather Grayson Striker and clattered to the polished wood floor.

Why did she have to make things so difficult for herself? How much of this stubbornness was because of that vampire's attack on the beach? Did she remember any of that yet? Didn't sound like it. And what about the ring? He would sooner cut off another finger than ask about it, but she hadn't said a word all week. Not one. It could be anywhere by now. Though he liked to think she kept it with her, allowing it to remind her of him and their past. It might even be the reason she still answered his calls.

Jackson raked his nails over his scalp and tried to rein in his mounting frustration. Time enough to worry about that later. He had a vampire to find and kill before it found and killed Cassidy. Which was easier said than done. Uncle Garrett kept him chained to a desk, verifying targets tossed up by the Grid—everywhere but Florida—while Garrett jetted off to destroy them on his own. Two vampires put down this week, and he was hot on the trail of a third. Garrett claimed he'd rarely been so productive. Jackson had rarely felt so useless.

All of this would change in an instant if he could convince his uncle that there was a target right here in Orchard Beach. The gang war casualties still looked like his best bet. Better by the hour, actually. Through the network of Striker contacts, he had secured police and coroner reports that left no doubt in his mind that someone or something was trying to hide the true cause of death. Every victim found to date was exsanguinated, a fact not released to the media and attributed to the beheadings and possible "other unknown events" by medical examiners.

Jackson stared at one of the enormous monitors on the library desk. It still made no sense. Leaving bloodless corpses was too obvious. No vampire would risk discovery like that. Most vampire activity was masterfully disguised and invisible to the human world. The older the vampire, the greater the control, the fewer the clues. But when a youngling vampire was first made, there was usually a pattern of people falling mysteriously ill and then disappearing. Violent deaths often followed. At that point, a limited window of opportunity opened for the Foundation to locate and destroy the youngling and, with a little luck, the sire as well. With even greater luck, a whole nest. Such events popped up at random and in no particular order.

And they hadn't happened in Florida in years.

"Nothing ever happens in Florida," Jackson muttered.

Potential leads appeared and disappeared on the monitors as the Grid examined the never-ending stream of news data in real-time. Only the most promising leads would trigger closer examinations.

"Nothing happens in Florida...now." He ran a thumb down the side of the keyboard, thinking. The supposed "gang wars" had been raging for weeks, but where and how did this violence start? Authorities had offered no concrete explanations.

Jackson spent half an hour building a new algorithm and two hours pouring over the historical data it retrieved. Bit by bit, a new trail of clues emerged from the shadows of time. These were unusually violent deaths, immediately preceded by disappearances of deliriously ill individuals who were often related to, or at least knew, the victims. Normally such things would trigger the Grid, but these all happened in out of the way places from where reporting was often delayed enough to render the information useless. Taken together, however, a trail became obvious. A trail that had been winding its way around the globe for years—right to his doorstep.

9

Blood-Child

Six nights and still Dominique lived. Every sunset found him awake again in his bed, untouched, his veiled invitation to drag him into the sun and watch him "smoke" ignored. He kept the entrance to his sanctuary unlocked, even tried to leave it ajar, but there the beast drew the line and forced him to shut it. His sense of smell told him that Cassidy had not touched the door, much less opened it.

It wasn't for a lack of encouragement.

When he encountered her in the evenings, he made a point of being as obnoxious as possible, even as he drowned in the Caribbean-blue depths of her eyes. He provoked her at every opportunity, forcing her to think about him and learn to despise him. He offered no promises about repairing the AC and let her resulting complaints go unacknowledged. Her appalling culinary skills were easy to condemn, and beyond that, her clothes, her habits, her work, even the hair she couldn't seem to tame...everything was fair game.

He needed her to think of him and puzzle him out on her own during the day when she could come find him and end him, whether on purpose or by accident, it mattered not. Revealing his true self and asking outright was not an option. Her terror would cost him his control and get her killed on the spot. The chosen tool of his imminent demise was fragile indeed.

Once Cassidy's fury was sufficiently stoked, Dominique spent the rest of his nights hunting to the point of gluttony. The more blood and terror he consumed, the less the beast was interested in her increasingly familiar presence. It was peace of a sort, the first he knew since being transformed. He hadn't even checked on his automated searches in days. Months of scouring the Internet had turned up nothing useful about actual vampires and no trace of the cure he once hoped to find.

He was resigned by now that the only way to escape this existence was death. The certain knowledge that the next dawn could be his last edged every instant with a transcendent clarity that he relished as thoroughly as the hunt. Every night was a treasured gift, every dawn a quiet farewell. And every morning, as the sun approached the horizon, he lingered by her bed and studied her sleeping face, filling his last conscious thoughts with the woman who held his life in her hands.

Returning from the hunt on this early morning, however, Dominique's sense of peace evaporated when the cottage came into view. His skin prickled with an instinct he knew to trust.

Another vampire was near.

He let the alarm run through him and melt away, maintaining a relaxed attitude as he let the motorcycle roll across the untended yard. Instead of taking the bike to the shed, he propped it beside the porch to give him easy access to the machete sheathed along its side.

He swung down and removed the helmet and gloves as quickly as he could while still presenting a picture of casual carelessness. His nostrils flared in the night air, sifting through the dense brine for any hint of scent that would betray the intruder. There was only the vaguest trace of something that shouldn't be there.

Slowly, Dominique turned and scanned the shadows, all his senses keyed to the limit. Tiny life forces of nocturnal scavengers went about their business in the shrubbery. None of them had either the size or the white-cold brilliance of a vampiric aura. His anxiety mounted as he stood there in the open, but retreating inside would blind him to the threat. Seconds crept past. He stood perfectly still.

And then he knew.

He didn't even look to confirm the flash of insight before bolting straight up a cabbage palm and plowing into the blood-drinker hiding in the tree's crown. The intruder had hovered right above him and could have dropped on him at any time. Incensed, Dominique seized the other vampire and hurled them both into space.

At close range, he recognized the scent. This was the fiend who had left the mark on Cassidy. Rage drove out his fangs and tightened his grip, digging claw-like fingers into the thick neck. He would not suffer this miscreant to live.

They crashed to the ground in a tangle, but instead of pinning his foe, he tore at nothing but dirt and air.

"Such spirit, young one," mocked a voice behind him. At last Dominique registered something else that the fog-shrouded forest smell betrayed. His unwelcome visitor was older and stronger than Dominique by many decades, if not centuries. His own wintery scent betrayed him as a youngling and would for years to come. This unwelcome visitor would have no reason to take him seriously, much less fear him.

Or let him live.

Dominique jumped to his feet, anticipating a lethal attack. The intruder sat on the ground, legs wide before him, his head tilting as he looked at Dominique with soft, unfocused, brown eyes. A ragged, blood-caked caramel beard covered most of the rest of his face.

"I do not hunt your territory." Dominique snarled to cover his mounting unease. "But this is my lair and mine alone."

"You have her." A gap-toothed grin of childish delight appeared in the grimy beard. "The sweet riddle."

"She is not your concern."

"But she is. She is. I have searched for her, you see. So much more there is to find in her blood."

Not a casual onetime feed then. Nor had this vagrant sent her here or it wouldn't have taken him this long to find her. No, this one had tasted Cassidy, spared her, and now claimed her as his. An unexpected sense of possessiveness surged through Dominique. All his instincts settled and focused, preparing for battle. He wouldn't be caught off-guard again.

Nor would it be the first time an older blood-drinker tragically underestimated him.

"You will not have her, *vieillard*. She is under my protection."

"But I must. I must know the answer to her riddle. She is the light that casts the shadows of all our fates. She is the beginning and the end, the life and the death. She is...*everything*."

The stranger was on his feet and had Dominique's head in his grasp in an instant. He jerked back with a guttural growl of warning. His body compacted around his bones as the beast rose.

A manic light glinted in the wide eyes. No trace of fang showed in the beard. "Don't you see that?" he said with hands outstretched, beseeching, lost in his madness. "Don't you sense that, young one?"

The fervent declaration rattled Dominique in ways he didn't understand. "All I see is a lunatic blood-drinker."

The old vampire giggled.

Dominique's flesh crawled. He could not allow this madman to exist another night, knowing of his lair and lusting after Cassidy's blood. Wishing he had carried his swords tonight, he was about to dart for the crude weapon lashed to his bike when the intruder spoke again, this time sounding almost reasonable.

"Then you see only the shadows, blood-child." Scowling, he shoved back his matted hair, but made no effort to straighten the stained flannel shirt or ripped trousers. He wore no shoes. "Like all of them. You can't see the light. The possibility. Magic has come among us and all you want to do is drop me with your blades."

Blades, Dominique thought, stunned. Not a reference to the single machete, but the two samurai swords. What else did this stranger know about him? More importantly, how did he know it?

A hundred other questions vied for space on his tongue, but the one he voiced was, "Who are you?"

His visitor brightened and bowed with a dramatic flourish. "I am Serge. I am he who sees." When he straightened, his good cheer vanished. The stare with which he skewered Dominique made his insides squirm.

Merde. Of all the blood-drinkers he had encountered since being forced to join their ranks, the only one who didn't try to kill him on sight was also certifiably insane—or playing an elaborate game. Serge might only be entertaining himself before he killed the presumably helpless youngling and turned to the truly helpless human he craved.

"Tell me, blood-child," he said, his tone serious now. "What is your best skill? To kill others like us...isn't it?"

"Are you asking for a demonstration?"

"Before you became one of us, you didn't kill anyone, did you?" When Dominique couldn't stop the ironic twitch of his mouth, Serge placed a grubby hand on his chest. "Oh, my mistake." He looked at Dominique with renewed interest, his head bobbling a little from side to side. "Your skill with your swords—your ability to survive—is your gift. It was so when you were mortal. Now it is perfected in you."

Dominique's fists tightened at his sides. How did this scatter-brain know about his martial arts training, much less how he used it? How long had he been stalking Dominique? And how had he not noticed before? "*Fils de pute.* I killed no one with my swords before coming to this cursed existence."

Serge ignored the outburst. "When I was mortal, my gift was seeing things that would be. It is this that my sire made perfect in me." He pinned Dominique with that piercing, mad look again, his hands wringing before him, expectant. "Do you see?"

Dominique scoffed. "You see the future?"

Exuberant nodding.

"Then do you see how I will remove your head with my swords if you do not leave my property and never return?"

The hands dropped to his sides, disappointed. "Ah, blood-child. You won't kill me. You need me too much."

"I need no one."

Serge bobbled his head again, squinting. "You will. The redemption you seek cannot be earned on your own."

Dominique almost sneered. If this lunatic were truly clairvoyant, he would know that Dominique would soon be ash, rendering the question of redemption irrelevant.

"She is the key," Serge said, his voice dropping in a way that made the back of Dominique's neck prickle. Then he took a step back, his gentle eyes opening so wide they seemed to swallow his shaggy face in unadulterated awe. "And you...*you* are the lock." Slow shake of the head. "The world of night will never be the same." Suddenly, he cackled and clapped his hands together. "You need me, blood-child. Yes, you *need* me!"

The last word still hung in the air when Serge disappeared in a blur. As the tension drained from Dominique's body, anger took its place. He'd actually been tempted to believe the madman, though he wasn't sure why or even which part. Serge was a derelict, lost to humanity and blood-drinkers alike, a fringe element of existence, little better than a ghost or a nightmare.

Worst of all, he had dared to feed from Cassidy.

"If I see you again, I *will* kill you," Dominique promised under his breath.

He pushed the bike around the cottage and into the shed. As he snapped the lock into place on the door, he decided to stay close to home for a while. He had fed well enough this week. He could afford to spend a few nights hunting down and eliminating this threat before it got any closer to Cassidy.

On the porch, he dug the house key out of his pocket. Since she insisted on locking the front door and every downstairs window, he carried this now to avoid a repeat of his awkward trip through her bedroom. As he slid it into the lock, he hesitated.

She is the key. You are the lock.

A pulse ran through him, deep and powerful, a sense of recognition.

Don't you sense that, young one?

Something unseen shifted around him. Dominique shivered.

He turned the key and stepped inside. The door swung shut in his wake, muffling the sounds of the night and wrapping him in a cocoon of her quiet breathing and drowsing heart. He extended his senses toward her, his fellow refugee, his chosen executioner, and felt...something. Like a tug at the base of his heart.

Dominique bedded down in his sanctuary and waited for the day to claim him, perhaps for the last time. "*Cassidy est la clé,*" he whispered. Yes. She was the key. To end his suffering. If—no, *when*—she could...unlock his mystery, his lock.

She is the light that casts the shadows of all our fates. She is the beginning and the end, the life and the death. She is everything.

"*Absurde.*" He would kill that irritating old bastard and be done with him—if Dominique survived the day. If he didn't...Serge would be free to indulge his insanity with Cassidy.

He dragged his leaden limbs back to the door. There, the sun almost had him again, but he made it back to his bed before collapsing. This time, he was certain his door was locked.

10

A Conversation in the Dark

Cassidy was desperate. Night couldn't get here soon enough. Yet the swelter of the summer day lingered far into the evening. The drawn drapes and the fan spinning at maximum above her prone form didn't even make a dent in the agony. An invisible ax lay lodged in her forehead while her stomach roiled.

It was without a doubt the worst migraine of her life.

Not surprising, really, the way the last few weeks had gone. Nothing changed for her at the *Gazette*, but rumors swirled among the staff about newsroom legend Dave McKinney actually retiring by the end of the summer. If true, that left her with three months to impress a man who hardly knew she existed to give her the sort of reference that could launch a career.

Rumor also had it that none other than Jim Lawley would take over the editorial reins. God help her.

Frustration and anxiety were taking over, and there was no one left in her life she could vent to. Certainly no family close enough to care. No close friends either; overwhelming personal responsibilities had left little time for a social life in high school. Her mother had passed just before she started college, so for those first two years she barely functioned enough to make it to classes, much less build friendships.

Then, the last two years, there had been Jackson.

Jackson, whose regular calls puzzled her as much as they reassured her. At least someone was thinking of her. In desperation, she had tried to talk to him, but his glib solution to her problems—drop everything and let him take care of her—made her bristle. Amazing how he still knew her so little. Staying in touch or not, he was as good as gone. Like everyone else who had ever mattered.

Samantha, Jackson's half-sister, was more sympathetic. Proud not to be born a Striker, she expressed great pleasure at Cassidy's willingness to confront the Striker patriarchs—which, she confessed, was more than she could say about "baby brother." Still, she was his loving sister. Cassidy wasn't going to tell this woman things she wouldn't have told Jackson. She couldn't risk him or his uncle sabotaging her chances with Dave—if they hadn't already.

Then there was a roommate who enjoyed tormenting her. Even though their paths only crossed after Dominique woke and before he left the house, those brief moments were fraught with tension. Whenever she tried to keep the peace, he would irritate and criticize her, always with a side of attitude. Any night now, he would tell her how to breathe.

No, wait. He had already done that when they first met.

"Air conditioning, you bastard," Cassidy groaned and gasped as pain radiated through her brain. "How can you live in the tropics and not have air conditioning?"

Unbelievable that this was still an issue. He continued to dismiss her complaints with an offhand remark about looking into it sometime soon. Enough was enough. As he requested, she had told the agency that the AC worked fine once she figured out the controls. Tomorrow she would call back, report it broken for good and demand immediate repair. To hell with his privacy issues.

On the upside, she only had to deal with him an hour a day, if that. Otherwise, she had the place to herself. Plus, with that chip on his shoulder, there was no risk she might start to "like" him, God forbid. One flippant comment, one arrogant glance, one whiff of cigarette smoke—*especially* the damn cigarette smoke—and that was the end of any accidental daydreams those striking good looks might have inspired.

Civil conversation was beyond the Frenchman, and Cassidy had almost reached the point of ignoring all the sniping—with one exception. She'd left a copy of the paper containing her Valieri case write-up lying around. He read it, found it lacking, and told her so.

"I'm doing my job the best I can, the way I'm asked to do it," she fumed.

"Congratulations," he said, sounding bored. "You are living up to their low expectations of you."

The words rankled every time she recalled them, which was often. He knew nothing about the challenges and biases she faced, and yet, a small part of her wondered if there was a grain of truth there. Writing obits, answering phones, and making coffee was as exciting as everyone, including Dave McKinney, believed she ought to get. And so it was.

"No, it's not," she croaked now into the oppressive gloom. All she needed was half a chance, an opening, a *crack*, and she would surprise them all. She had to wait for it—like she waited for everything else—and she would be ready. *And I don't care what you think about it. You're a total stranger and a colossal pain in the ass.*

A total stranger who even now crawled out of his bed.

She heard him down the hall, unlocking the door; a soft sound, it still slashed through her head. She regretted not having gone up to her room. It had been so hot up there, impossible conditions in her fragile state. So she collapsed in the living room, the coolest, darkest spot in the house. By now, she was certain she wanted to die. The agony in her head had hold of her entire body, turning her limbs to rubber and churning her guts.

"What's the matter with you?"

She cringed at the harsh words rattling her skull. "Shhh. Migraine." She felt, rather than saw, him stand over her. The fan whirred, bathing her in a muggy breeze and sounding a bit like a wobbly jet engine to her ears. "I can't deal with you tonight," she whispered. "Go away and let me die in peace."

But he didn't go away. "Do you have medicine?"

"Shhh. Yes, I do, but it's not working this time." Not one iota. She wanted to sob with helpless fury. No doctor had yet told her with certainty what caused these migraines, though extremes in temperature and humidity were prominent suspects. Surprise, surprise.

The act of speaking heaved her stomach. "Oh God." She moaned, curled over the side of the sofa, and let it happen. The late lunch reappeared. Suddenly cold, she shivered, heard her own pitiful retching, felt tears wet on her face. An arm wrapped around her shoulder and a gentle hand held back her hair. She opened her eyes. Was that a bucket? Where had that come from? She heaved again.

Cassidy became aware of Dominique beside her, his hands on her, supporting. She dropped her head against his firm thigh and was vaguely thankful that her cheek met material and not bare skin. "Just kill me now."

"Not tonight, *chérie*," he whispered and pressed his palm against her clammy forehead. His touch was deliciously cool. She must be running a fever, too. The mother of all headaches.

"Feels nice."

"I know."

Of course. If it wouldn't hurt so much, she might have rolled her eyes.

"Are you done?"

Cassidy queried her stomach, then hazarded a small nod.

He pushed her back into the sofa cushions as though she were a rag doll being placed in a drawer. "Stay still."

He carried away the bucket, and she heard him flush the contents down the toilet. The fridge opened. Plastic rustled and glass bottles clinked. He opened one and poured. Then he crouched by her side, pressing a cold glass into her hand. "Drink."

The commanding tone left much to be desired as bedside manners went, but she was too weary to argue. The chilled, sparkling water washed the sour taste of vomit from her mouth. "I'm sorry."

"For what?" he wondered, sounding surprised.

"Being sick."

He said nothing, and she was sure that come morning she would be mortified. But now, here in the dark with her head threatening to split open like a ripe melon, that didn't matter. Nothing did.

Something cold and squishy settled on her forehead. "A bag of frozen peas," he explained. "I wrapped it in a towel for you."

"Nice." She sighed. "Thank you."

"Does this happen much?" His voice was so soft, she could barely make out the words.

"Never this bad. I think it's the heat. And humidity." The silence stretched. "Too bad we don't have air."

"Too bad you eat shit, too."

Her indignation rose through the haze of pain. "I had salad for lunch."

"And something deep fried."

Just remembering made her feel green, even more so when she realized how he knew this. "Yeah, that's it. Blame the victim. I'll keep a bucket nearby next time. You won't have to put yourself out on my account again. I promise."

His deep breath brushed against her cheek. Damn, he was close. Though she was too sick to care. A peculiar clean scent wafted over her. Pure somehow, like snow.

"I have a sister who suffers like this," he said after a while. "I used to watch over her. Before..."

Sorrow skirted the edges of his indifference. In the stifling quiet, she became weightless, adrift in timeless nothingness. With him.

"What happened?"

A blanket of silence folded around them. Only the fan whirled. "She married and moved away."

"You don't sound happy about that."

"On the contrary, I am very happy for her."

"But not for yourself."

"Is it that obvious?"

"Written all over your face. When I can see your face. When you're not skulking around in the shadows." She adjusted the makeshift ice pack on her temple. The cold numbed the pain, but only temporarily. It would be a long night.

"Then we have that in common as well, *chère*."

Her sluggish brain turned this over. "Is it that obvious?"

"*Oui*." The word caressed her ear. "I have to go. Will you be all right?"

Her body was a quagmire of sensations—agony and relief, fire and ice, longing and dread. No, she was nowhere near all right, but she would manage on her own. She always did. "I guess I'll live."

"You will," he confirmed with a flip in his voice that made her relax. The cockiness she could deal with. But whatever had just passed between them...that she couldn't even comprehend in her present state.

"A kingdom for some air conditioning."

It took her a full minute to realize that she was alone in the dark.

II

Being Human

Dominique leaned on the splintered porch railing and waited for his world to stop tilting. She had taken him by surprise. Every other evening, she met him with either verbal assaults or cool indifference, but never like this, never weak and vulnerable. Her plight carried him back in time in a whirlwind of emotion he didn't know how to contain. A half-forgotten human impulse led him to comfort her.

That and he needed to save the rug that carried so many precious memories.

How easily the past resurfaced. How powerfully.

Geneviève.

Dominique's proud elder sister was a frequent sufferer of migraines and hated anyone seeing her in that condition. Anyone but him. Nursing her was a natural reflection of his love for her, and he had done it gladly until she married. Her husband was a good man, but in Dominique's opinion, far from good enough for one of his sisters. The protective streak he felt for both his sisters ran deep. For Anastasie, he had even killed...

He gasped as the memories swerved into far darker territory with horrific clarity. Shedding his clothes, he bolted for the beach and the ocean, letting the waves swallow him.

He hurried along the sandy bottom, battling the water's drag on his limbs. His frustrations mounted. Without thought, he moved toward a skiff anchored on the shallow reef hugging the shore. The sole occupant, engrossed in meditative contemplation of the night sky and mirror-calm sea, startled violently when Dominique flowed over the side like some mythical merman.

"What the fuck—"

A deep, inhuman growl rumbled in Dominique's chest, and the long canines extended with sweet anticipation. The prey's eyes bugged to a comical size. Then fear exploded out of the human's every pore, filling the air with acrid spice that roused the beast fully. The intended meal bolted over the side. Dominique had him by the scruff before he hit the water.

"The sharks will have you soon enough," he rasped, hauling back his flailing catch. "I promise to be quick."

"What do you want with me?" the man wailed, voice high with hysteria. "What the fuck are you?"

The beast replied by tearing into the bulging neck. The poison saturating his saliva surged into the human's brain, claiming the mind along with the body, nourishing the vampire.

His name was Matt, he was no derelict, and beyond smoking the occasional joint, he never broke the law. He had spent the afternoon fishing, seeking the meaning of life with a hero sandwich and a six-pack of beer, and decided that when the new job came through, he would finally ask Christine to marry him. She was mellow like him and her warm smile always soothed him. And she put up with his fishing addiction. She understood him and accepted him. He was content just now, just before that naked freak got into his boat—

Dominique slumped on the cooler. Blood and seawater sluiced down his torso, the beast quiet in his heart. He stared at the deep slash in the dead man's neck and stupidly thought of Christine and how she would never know how important she had been to Matt. Christine, the woman who accepted this man despite his need for solitary communion with his boat and fishing tackle.

Dominique chuckled and pushed the hair out of his eyes. On his face, seawater erased his tears. Trivial human nonsense. What he wouldn't give to have his life be so simple again.

He pulled up the anchor, started the engine, and headed into deep water. After leaving the body to the sea, he went north, moving with the prevailing current. By dawn, the skiff would be miles away, its owner presumed lost to a rogue wave or clumsy accident.

Morbid curiosity drove Dominique to wonder if Matt had caught anything at all. In the ice chest, five silver bodies stared back at him with blank, glassy eyes. What a waste to let them rot in there, their small fish lives given in vain.

Then an even stranger thought occurred to him. His forehead pinched into a frown. An insane thought.

Before he could consider the reasons too closely, he bundled the catch into a plastic sack. Then he slipped over the edge and down to the sandy sea floor, leaving the skiff to motor on by itself. Package in hand, he plodded back to shore, his mood growing buoyant. It was a ludicrous idea that risked much and was bound to complicate everything. But it felt deeply, undeniably right. A warm, familiar echo from his human past.

So be it. If he was to lose his reason in her presence, it might as well be this.

When he reached the beach behind the cottage, his disposition turned ugly.

"You are most entertaining, young one," Serge greeted. He sat cross-legged in the sand.

He realized that the old blood-drinker must have witnessed him feeding, a profound violation of privacy.

"Did I not tell you to never come near me again?"

"Will you club me with your catch?" Serge wondered with a glance at the bag of fish clutched in Dominique's hand. The silly grin faded into uncertainty. "Poor feeding, those. Not much blood, you see."

"What? Does your vision fail you? Don't you know their purpose?"

Serge looked Dominique's nude body up and down, his head cocked. He nodded, gently at first, then with vigor. "I see the ember of her light in you, blood-child."

"Make sense," Dominique snapped, crushing the unease quivering up his spine. Whatever else this lunatic may be, he was perceptive. Or were the nerves his ramblings struck mere coincidence? "I have no patience for your riddles."

"I told you. She is the key, the light that casts the shadows," Serge said as though explaining a simple lesson to a small child. "She is everything. But you need my help, or—"

"None of our kind ever helps anyone but themselves."

Serge's shoulders twitched in the ragged flannel shirt. "Sadly true, that. Mostly."

"Why are you hounding me? Because you tasted her once, and you want more?"

Serge unfolded his legs beneath him, rising to his feet in the same motion. "Well...no. Yes. But..."

Dominique had heard enough. This filthy beast had enjoyed what he denied himself so ruthlessly—Cassidy's blood, her life, her spirit, her mind. Serge knew them as Dominique never would. In a flash of fury, he lashed out and gripped Serge's forearm, eliciting a surprised yelp as he swung the vampire nuisance up in an arc and slammed him back to the ground so hard clouds of dust puffed up around him. Then he stomped down his bare foot, aiming for the beard-encrusted throat, only to strike empty sand with a jarring thud. Serge had already slithered off. Wary, the pest crouched a short distance away, sand dusting his face and tangled hair. The huge brown eyes beseeched him like those of an old stray dog, watching for the next savage kick to come his way.

"Go anywhere near her again, and I will end you," Dominique growled, trying to cover his unease at this display of helplessness from one so much faster and stronger. He would have to make good on this threat, and soon. If she was to remain safe, this vagrant blood-drinker would have to die before Dominique did.

"You believe *I* threaten her?" Serge chortled, straightening again, but maintaining his distance. "What do you imagine *you* will do to her?"

The words were a hard slap to Dominique's raw nerves. He knew very well what he, a youngling with tenuous control over the beast, would do to the girl if he gave in to any of his lurid lusts for her.

"She will live," he declared for his own benefit almost more than Serge's. "She has to."

Serge rolled his eyes. "Silly child. You see it. I know you do. You need me to stop you from destroying her. Accept what must be."

"You intend to keep *me*...from harming Cassidy?"

"See? You understand."

"I understand you take me for a fool. She is nothing to you but a pawn in your games. She doesn't need your protection. She has mine. And I need *nothing* from you."

The disappointment in Serge's drooping expression was unexpected and profound, and elicited an unwelcome pang of sympathy in Dominique. Was this old lost one really only looking for a connection with another blood-drinker?

Dominique groaned inwardly, already regretting what he was about to do, but realizing that it would happen with or without his consent. This way, at least, he could monitor the threat more closely. "Stay if you like and watch. From a distance," he added quickly when Serge's face lit with eagerness. "She must never see you. And one foot inside my house..."

Serge mimed a blade cutting his throat and nodded. "And if you bring one sharp tooth anywhere near her, none of that will matter. You understand, yes?" he said with giddy good cheer.

Dominique understood. The idea of an outside force keeping the beast in check was not unwelcome, but why Serge would do this mystified him. Older and therefore stronger, he didn't need an excuse to destroy a youngling without a sire's protection. If Serge surprised him while unarmed, odds would not be in Dominique's favor. He could have done so half a dozen times tonight alone. As for his so-called gifts of premonition and visions of a meaningful future involving a mortal woman...giving this any credit at all was the way of madness.

Inside, Cassidy still lingered on the sofa, the makeshift ice pack limp on her forehead, and her breathing unsteady, nostrils flaring. One small light cast the room in soft shadows. An open bottle of Perrier sat on the floor next to her.

"Back already?" she mumbled.

"Passing through."

"Great. Have fun."

He crouched down beside her, removed the bag of soggy peas, and put his hand on her forehead. "Not much better, is it."

"A little." She didn't open her eyes, but her head pressed against his fingers in a gesture of unconscious trust that lodged a lump in his throat.

"You should be in bed."

"I should have air conditioning, too."

His jaw tightened. He had no need for climate control and was leery of strangers in the house during the day. Then again, what was more foolish than letting an unsuspecting human live with him? Not much.

He touched her chin with one finger. "Look at me, *chérie*."

She turned her head, exhausted from her battle with the headache, too exhausted to maintain her defenses or her temper. She blinked, trying to focus on him, her eyes dilated and glassy like those of the fish in his bag. "Out skinny dipping?"

"*Oui.*"

Her nose rumpled. "You stink."

"I caught dinner," he explained, unable to keep the amusement out of his voice. In her presence, he seemed almost absurd to himself.

"How nice for you. Hope it was good."

"You will have to be the judge of that."

"Me?"

"*Oui*. Dinner tomorrow is on me."

"You're kidding."

"I intend to prove my culinary skills to you."

"You...cook?"

"Surprised?"

She studied him for a long moment. "I just don't know what to make of you, Nick."

"Sometimes neither do I," he admitted. "You should get some sleep now."

"I can't. Everything hurts."

"Nothing hurts," he told her, pitching his voice into compulsion, driving past what remained of her resistance. She didn't resist. She welcomed the relief. "Sleep now." As her eyes drifted shut and her breathing deepened, he couldn't resist one last whisper. "Dream of me."

12

A MATTER OF TRUST

When Dominique emerged from the cottage, fully dressed in his leathers and boots, he stopped and cocked a brow at the figure hovering in the shadows. "Not a foot."

Serge glanced at his bare feet, then around the porch. He backed down the stairs, slow with reluctance. Tripped up by the missing step, he tumbled off into a sprawling heap.

Dominique bit back a groan. "I do not trust you."

"Mutual, blood-child." Serge sat up, making no attempt to brush off the sand and dry weeds clinging to his rags. "Dream of you? Devious."

Without comment, Dominique walked to the shed and prepared to go out. Serge followed. "You can't...must not influence her. You'll ruin everything."

"Truly? What am I ruining?" He had rolled out the motorcycle and put on his gloves.

"I told you. Everything."

Dominique straddled the machine and pulled the helmet over his head. "Do you even hear yourself?"

The old one paused his erratic gesturing to take careful notice of him. "Are you leaving?" The bike hummed to life. "But you already fed. And you shouldn't leave her."

Dominique couldn't agree more. "I'm not leaving," he said, clapping down the visor. "*We* are." He moved with lightning speed, twisting around, grabbing Serge by an elbow and hauling him across the seat behind him. Then he sped out of the lane, and, once on smooth asphalt, gunned the engine.

His hijacked passenger's shrieks overpowered the bike's high-pitched whine. Frenzied, Serge clamped onto Dominique with bone-crunching force and wailed like a siren for a mile before Dominique freed one of his arms enough to slam an elbow into the body barnacled to his back. He felt several ribs snap outright, and the crushing hold loosened. By the time he turned into the Publix parking lot ten minutes later, Serge was reduced to quiet trembling.

"How many centuries have you seen, old fool?"

Serge held up three fingers.

"Things have changed, *non?*"

With a vigorous nod, Serge staggered off the motorcycle and looked the machine over with a wary eye. Built for high-speed stealth, it was completely black and aerodynamic. "Faster than a frigate," he said, thoughtful. "Drier, too."

Dominique popped off his helmet and tried for patience. He knew there were blood-drinkers like this, creatures whose minds were as locked in the era of their making as their bodies. He never thought he'd spend time with one, and he wasn't sure why he bothered with Serge.

"Can we do that again?" Serge wondered, an odd excitement sparkling in his eyes.

"*Malheureusement,*" Dominique muttered. Unfortunately. They would do this again and again for as long as Serge lived and Dominique needed to leave Cassidy and the cottage to hunt.

Or shop.

He eyed the brightly lit store with some trepidation. It was his habit to compel someone to supply him with Perrier water while he waited outside, but tonight's list was rather more complicated. He would have to enter and blend in. Given his black leathers and pale skin amidst the tanned tourists in shorts, tank tops, and sundresses, that would be a challenge. He almost reconsidered his ludicrous offer to the girl.

"Easy pickings," Serge mused, eyeing the mortal shoppers.

"*Merde.* No pickings. Stay out of sight. And I need cash," Dominique called over his shoulder. "Find some." That should keep the nuisance entertained scouring the lot for dropped change.

He swiped a pair of dark sunglasses from the rack by the door, snapped off the tag and put them on to stop his eyes from watering in the artificial glare. Then he maneuvered a cart through the store with as much haste as might be humanly reasonable. He deflected curious glances with dazzling smiles and compelled the cashier—after two attempts and removing the sunglasses—into accepting the pack of gum he handed her as payment in full.

When he arrived back at the bike in the far corner of the lot, there was no sign of a derelict blood-drinker. He put down the bags, shoved the sunglasses up into his hair, and surveyed the area. Nothing. He inhaled. No blood. No blood-drinker. "*Merde.*"

He listened. Over the hum of the lot's lights, he heard the *booping* of the ATM where a line had formed. The woman just finishing rounded the side of the store. He took several steps to his left to watch her. "Here you go, you poor thing," she told a huddled figure with a bright, cold aura. "Get yourself a warm meal and a clean bed."

"God bless you," replied a familiar voice, teetering on the verge of giggles. "You never saw me."

Dominique stood beside him an instant later. "What are you doing?"

"This is an amazing time, blood-child. So much treasure, so quickly." He pulled a thick stack of bills from his pocket. "Much money, yes?"

Several thousand dollars, and here came the next good Samaritan.

"God bless you," said Serge, the decrepit panhandler. His head bobbled and eyes sharpened. "You never saw me," added

Serge, the blood-drinker, and the donor turned on a heel and left, oblivious.

Serge sighed with contentment. "So much drier than a frigate."

He let Serge finish collecting his loot, took it without comment when the old pirate presented it to him—apparently uninterested in anything but gold and blood himself—then shoveled him back onto the bike and hung the grocery bags off his arms.

At the cottage, he let Serge wait outside while he stashed the perishables in the refrigerator and ghosted up the stairs to check on Cassidy. She was still in her bed where he had deposited her earlier, but the bunched sheets bore mute testimony to restless sleep. Even the cat seemed to want nothing to do with her thrashing limbs. It perched on top of the dresser, watching him with wide, worried eyes.

He arranged the money for her to find in the morning, complete with a brief note of explanation. When he looked up, Serge's bearded face stared from the other side of the curtains draping over the open window. He growled a warning. Serge pointed to his feet, which, being on top of the porch roof, were technically outside the house.

"Nick? What's wrong?" Cassidy still sprawled across the sheets, her eyes closed. Dreaming. Of him. Brows creased in consternation. "Oh, right," she mumbled. "Everything."

No doubt of that. And there was nothing he could do about most of those wrongs. Most but not all, he decided as Serge poked his head past the window frame to see the girl, his feet still outside as ordered. Dominique almost went for his swords, but the look of awe on Serge's unkempt face stopped him. Unhinged he may be, but Serge was as enchanted by Cassidy as Dominique, and he wouldn't hold against the old one what he couldn't conquer within himself.

Pushing Serge back, he slipped out the window with him and dropped them both off the edge of the roof. "Another ride?"

Serge's eyes lit up like a child's on Christmas morning.

Dominique did not disappoint. As they streaked up I-95, weaving around traffic and construction, his passenger's initial shocked shrieks soon gave way to delighted yelps. By the time they reached Jacksonville, Serge had taken to riding surfboard style by standing on the tiny shotgun seat, swaying with the movement, his laughter uproarious.

When he tried to climb over Dominique to stand on the handlebars, Dominique deemed the moment right. He swerved hard toward a semi, throwing Serge off balance. But instead of spilling under the churning wheels, Serge leapt, jabbed his fingers into the aluminum side of the trailer, and clung like a demented bat. Dominique would have preferred him incapacitated, but this would do as well. The imbecile was off his bike and two hundred miles away from his lair.

Mission accomplished.

Riding low, he shot past the truck and aimed for the next exit ramp when the bike lurched beneath him.

"Blood-child, this is glorious," Serge shouted as he dropped on top of him from the semi's cab. The truck's brakes squealed, the driver panicked by the acrobatics unfolding in his headlights. "Again!"

Dominique nearly took them off the road with the frustration roaring through him. Remoras suckered onto the underside of sharks were easier to dislodge than this *putain d'idiot*. He veered toward another truck. Serge sailed off on his own, blurring across the trailer's roof and launching himself into space off the cab at the perfect instant to slam back on top of Dominique. He howled with glee. The bike would go no faster, could not outrun the lunatic as he surfed three more trucks, whooping and laughing all the way.

He aimed for the rear of the next semi and lost his passenger the second he came within range. This time, instead of trying to pass the truck quicker than Serge could move, he slowed and dropped out of sight behind a van heading onto an exit ramp.

Two minutes later, the highway blurred beneath his tires again, going south now, going home. He allowed himself a relieved sigh. The fool could go get lost in the city now. He might even forget all about Dominique and Cassidy. With any luck at all, he had seen the last of Serge, he who sees nonsense.

He tried not to recall that as of late, luck was rarely on his side.

———

Cassidy knew she was dreaming, and yet she couldn't wake up. In her dream, the heat of the sun rising beyond her bedroom windows morphed into bone-gripping cold, and the sheets became drifts of snow shifting beneath her hands and feet. The babbling radio alarm was drowned out by the howl of wind sweeping down from craggy peaks.

She had to find him.

The air was thin and brittle up in the mountains, and the sky such a dark blue it bordered on black. Nothing survived here but the wind. Snow slithered as she staggered.

"Cass? What are you doing here?"

Jackson's voice was the only thing recognizable about the man-shaped bundle of winter gear, its features obscured by a hood, goggles, and mask. She shook her head, her hair whipping about her face. Her lips moved, but no sound came out.

He couldn't help; she had to find him on her own.

"You're going the wrong way, Cass," Jackson called as she trudged towards the barren cliffs. "There's nothing up there." His voice faded, shredded by the landscape, eaten by the sky.

Damn it, I don't have time for this. Where are you? What do you want from me?

Her bare foot slipped on something buried in the snow. She bent to dig down. A body. She brushed snow off the prominent cheeks and forehead and out of the hollows around the eyes. She sat back. Stared.

What are you doing here?

Dominique opened his eyes. The pupils constricted to invisible pin-points in the glaring sunlight. The hazel irises glittered with gold flecks. A smile spread wide. Then he laughed into the sky. The sound echoed off the mountains before fading away, vanishing the way his body vanished, melting into the whiteness without a trace.

She reached for him. *No!*

With a shuddering gasp, Cassidy came awake. Her heart raced, and her limbs felt sluggish and sore, as though she had climbed the mountain for real. Sweat trickled down her sides. Morning sunlight stabbed to the back of her eyeballs. Clasping both hands over her face, she groaned and rolled to her side.

She had spent an entire night in the same bizarre lucid dream. Every time had been a little different, but every time, she found him. And every time, he vanished. Dominique. Why the hell wasn't she dreaming of looking for Jackson? Or hiding from Jackson?

Eddie mewed where he sat at her feet, his thick tail wrapped around neatly placed paws, green eyes huge with inquiry. She stole a glance at the clock. Seven-thirty-four. She should be half way to work by now. "Shit."

A thick stack of bills beside the radio caught her eye. Hundreds, fifties, and twenties half obscured a note of exquisite handwriting. *For AC repair. D.*

"About freaking time." Though she'd have to talk to him about coming into her room...

The air rushed out of her. Misery-soaked memories rushed in. She pressed a hand to her forehead, mercifully free of pain after a long night dreaming in a bed she didn't recall getting into. But it took no imagination at all to fill in the blanks.

She flopped back into her pillows. "Holy shit."

13

In Vino Veritas

That evening, she knew the cook was up when the music changed. The soulful country tunes drifting up the stairs like cool mountain air disappeared, replaced by a sophisticated cosmopolitan beat that sounded more European than Caribbean.

"Good bye Radio Denver, hello Radio St. Barth," she muttered and gathered her damp hair in a tight coil before it dried too much and explode back into its usual cloud of frizz. This crazy hair, never meant for a tropical climate, was a gift from her mother's Irish ancestry...

Grief surged up out of nowhere. After two and a half years, these spells were rarer, but they had lost little of their power. She picked up the picture of her mother and herself from the nightstand. Her mother's gorgeous auburn hair was long gone at that point, and she would only live one more week after that last outing into the mountains. She had rallied with almost manic energy, defying death for as long as she could, living every moment until the last. "Because I know how few I have left," she had said. "That's an incredible gift. It makes life so much sweeter."

No, it doesn't. There had been nothing sweet about those last desperate days. Cassidy would have done anything for more time with her mother, her only family. She put the picture down and wiped at her eyes. "Seize those moments, honey," her mother had also said. "Don't let a one of them get past you." God, she was trying. Sometimes she even managed not to fumble them.

Her stomach growled, reminding her of another potential fumble. Deciding to take Dominique at his word when she found the fridge stocked to capacity, she hadn't eaten since the blueberry muffin Larry had shared with her this morning. By now, she wished she had at least had a snack. Why could Dominique not get up on time? Talk about wasting a lifetime's worth of moments.

Not that she was in any great hurry to see him. Not after he held her hair while she spilled her lunch and then carried her passed out self to bed. Her face flamed with chagrin every time she imagined it.

Eddie hustled into the room, his ears back, shaggy body low to the floor, and disappeared under the bed without so much as a glance in her direction. "I know the feeling, buddy."

Shorts and tank top seemed too casual for a presumably French-themed meal. But alternatives were limited. Really, unless she wanted to wear work clothes, there was only one, a blue and green knit dress she had bought because she hoped Jackson would appreciate its clingy profile. Not that he had noticed the first and last time she wore it at that disastrous family dinner.

With a sigh, Cassidy pulled on the dress and tucked the plunging neckline into respectability. She didn't bother with shoes, and applied a bare minimum of makeup, mostly powder over the bruise on her neck. In the mirror, every ounce of awkwardness she felt about the dress—and last night—radiated from her face in spades. Resigned, she summoned a smile, squared her shoulders and descended the stairs.

In the kitchen, the rattling of pots and pans competed with the French pop music. The chef was his usual somber self in the black workout pants and V-neck T-shirt, the former comfortably loose, the latter tight across the lean muscles of his arms and torso. A pair of flip-flops and a red-and-white checkered apron completed the incongruous ensemble. The unruly hair was confined by a thin leather strap, emphasizing the striking planes and angles of his face.

She stood and watched him lay into a pile of vegetables with a serious knife, which he wielded with the casual ease of long practice. After more than a week of bickering, this was as unlikely a scene as the one last night. The man was a walking, talking contradiction.

"*Bonsoir*, Cassidy," he said without looking up. "Are you feeling better tonight?"

"Much. Thank you," she said, swallowing a fresh wave of embarrassment.

He glanced at her. His cheek dimpled with a heart-stopping smile. "I'm glad."

The plate of French bread suddenly looked very interesting. She perched on one of the bar chairs at the counter, retrieved a slice, and spread it with a thick green paste that smelled enticingly of olives and spices. She chewed slowly, enjoying the flavor while he retrieved a bottle of wine and a glass.

"Dressed, dry, *and* civil," she said. "I'm not sure I know who you are anymore."

He sent her a sideways look of pure mischief. "*Madame*, you know nothing of who I am."

And there he was, the Dominique she knew, sharpening his tongue for an attack. Much better. "Oh, I know you're a pain in the ass, insufferably full of yourself, and have zero respect for privacy."

He paused in the application of corkscrew to bottle, baffled.

"I could have found the money on the kitchen table. There was no need to leave it in my room."

"Ah." A final twist and pull uncorked the wine. "I was there anyway, *chère*, to make sure you were all right."

"Well, it makes me uncomfortable. Don't do it again."

A tiny frown furrowed his forehead as he splashed some wine into the glass. "As you wish, Cassidy. *Paix.*"

She stared at him, disoriented by the argument that wasn't, and his expression brightened. "Peace?"

"Peace," she repeated. No, she didn't know him. Not at all.

He pushed the glass toward her. "Tell me what you think."

Grateful for the change of subject, she sipped. Flavors of fruit and earth washed over her tongue in a pleasant swirl. She licked her lips. "Mmm. What is it?"

Unrestrained pleasure lit his face. "French."

"Of course." She scoffed, but couldn't help smiling. "Silly me."

He filled one glass and pushed it toward her.

"And you? Where's yours?"

"None for me," he said with a rueful little noise. "I'm driving the skillet." With that, he turned back to the stove where things sputtered and bubbled.

Cassidy drank more of the wine. Mellowness settled in her bloodstream. Considering his words, she added "recovering alcoholic" to her mental list of observations. Well, at least he had the willpower to stay on the wagon. Her opinion of him ticked up a smidgeon.

She watched him cook. Every movement was sure and precise. Lean muscles flexed in his bare forearms. Strong, capable arms. Arms that had carried her to bed... Damn. Time for another slice of bread.

"About last night...thank you. But...you didn't have to do that. I could have managed."

"An old habit," he said, sounding a little distracted as he uncovered the marinade pan and moved several filets around in the sauce with a pair of kitchen tongs.

"Really? You carry unconscious women to bed often?"

"I did a little more than that, *non*?" One filet landed in the skillet and sizzled forcefully.

"Yes. You did. None of which you had to do." And none of which required discussion while preparing dinner.

"An old habit," he said again, working the fish in the pan, his expression unfocused. "You make me remember so many."

"And...is that a good thing?"

"*Peut-être.* We will see." He nodded toward a sheet of paper lying on the kitchen table. "I see you got a quote for the air conditioner."

"Yes," she said, eager to change the subject again. "It's outrageous, isn't it? The entire system needs to be replaced. I got a verbal quote from another company that was actually four hundred dollars more. Tomorrow I'll call—"

"I already signed this one. I will give you the rest of the money."

"You did? Just like that?"

"This is basic maintenance of my property, *non*? It should be done. What did you expect?"

"Oh, I don't know. I guess I expected an argument. Can't imagine why."

He flashed a quick smile that threatened to melt her insides. "I can see reason—when I want to."

"Then I'll get it scheduled. Thanks." She shook her head, as relieved as she was exasperated. "You drive me insane, Nick." No, he wasn't a Nick. He was mysterious and raw, as surreal as he was charming, both obscure and blinding in the same breath. That beautiful mouthful of a name fit him as snugly as his shirt. "Dominique," she amended.

He crossed the kitchen to top off her glass, his expression not quite smug, but also not quite innocent. "I know," he murmured. She could have sworn he purred.

While she nursed the wine and nibbled the bread, he worked the stove, adding ingredients, checking consistencies, adjusting temperatures. Her mouth watered with the aromas of savory spices and sizzling meat swirling in the air. "You look like you know what you're doing."

"My parents trained my sisters and me," he said slowly, as though digging for every word. "We were raised in the kitchen of our restaurant. When we were old enough to hold a pot, we were put to work."

"Restaurant? Your family owns a restaurant on St. Barth?"

"*Oui. Maison de la Mer.* On the beach. You can watch the sunset over the sea from the patio."

On the speaker, right on cue, a woman made an announcement in rapid French, followed by the Radio St. Barth tag line and more music. She imagined a tiny dot of land in the sea, bathed in sunshine, surrounded by warm oceans, and frequented by visitors from the most glittering capitals of Europe. An island awash in comfort and peace. Paradise. "And you left that for...here? Why?"

He didn't respond right away. "Islands are sometimes too small."

"Ah. I see." Relationship issues. Of course. "Think you'll ever go back?"

"I doubt it." He picked up the bottle and added a measure to one of his pots. Then he filled her glass yet again.

"Hey. If you keep this up, you may end up having to carry me to bed again."

"You are obviously enjoying it. I'm glad someone is."

"Or you're trying to get me drunk so you can take advantage of me." Of course, just saying that out loud was proof that she was already there. Her inner censor—never the keenest to begin with—was packing it in for the night.

Mischief drowned the shadows in his expressive eyes. "If I was going to do that, *ma chèrie,* I would not need you drunk on anything but me."

"Oh, you think I'm that easy, do you?"

"No. I am that good. Seduction is my gift."

"Good God. Does that hurt? Being that full of yourself?"

That dimple again. "You like that about me, *non?*"

Her mouth dropped open. The attitude apparently had no limit. Before she could decide whether to be offended or charmed, he extended a steaming cooking spoon in her direction. "Here. Try this for me."

She gave the sauce a grudging sniff. The creamy herb smell was a flavor punch to her sinuses that made her inhale deeply. Irresistible wickedness followed in short order. Two could play this game.

Very deliberately, she put her lips around the tip of his utensil and closed her eyes, savoring the flavor. The taste was exquisite, delicately bold and deeply warm. Though her senses swam in culinary ecstasy, she pulled her face into a frown and made an elaborate show of licking her lips and tasting the spoon again as though undecided. When she stole a peek at the chef, she was pleased to see the dark scowl and slack jaw. He looked like he had forgotten how to breathe.

"Mmmm. I guess it's all right."

"Liar." He leaned across the counter, and she froze, breathless with anticipation of she-knew-not-what. He hovered closer, his sudden nearness overwhelming her senses.

"It is a sweet, sighing orgasm on a spoon," he whispered against her ear, his accent as rich and smooth as the sauce. The words curled down her spine, a tingling ripple that engulfed her in liquid heat. When she shivered, he drew back. His face left no doubt that he knew precisely what effect he had on her.

Maybe two could play, but clearly, only one could win.

Cassidy cleared her throat with an awkward cough. "Okay. That, too." His strangely bottomless eyes drew her in with relentless power. Everything in her wanted to look away, back away, but she couldn't move an inch, not until he turned. Then she had to hold on to her seat to keep from sliding out of it, all the bones in her body gone to jelly.

"You're not subtle, are you?" she said, borderline senseless between the alcohol and a hunger for more than food.

"I don't know what you mean."

Like hell you don't. She drank more wine out of sheer frustration and confusion. Add "sensual force of nature" to that list. Was there a woman alive who wouldn't fall into his arms?

His mouth continued to twitch with quiet amusement as he arranged the fish, vegetables, rice, sauce, and garnish on a plate in a display worthy of a foodie magazine cover. He placed the serving before her with a flourish. "*Et voilà. Bon appétit.*"

What's for dessert? she thought and immediately chastised herself. Maybe it would be better if they kept arguing.

But it took only one forkful to clear her mind of everything but the food. Tempting as it was to wolf it all down, the symphony of flavors made her linger over every morsel.

"You like it?"

She nodded, honestly humbled and done pretending otherwise. "It's the best thing I've ever eaten."

"I thought it might be."

"Aren't you having any?"

He shook his head. "It is too early for me to eat. This is for you."

"All this? Just for me? I don't know what to say."

"'Thank you' will suffice."

She savored another mouthful of the perfectly done, delicately flaky fish and searched her limited French vocabulary; this food deserved nothing less. "*Merci beaucoup.*"

"*De rien,*" he countered, looking pleased. "Do you think you will want more?"

"Definitely." These dainty gourmet portions wouldn't cut it.

A second filet hit the skillet.

Drunk with flavor and wine, she gestured with her fork. "This is better than sex. Hands down."

Dominique chuckled. "I'm flattered. But if that is how you feel, you obviously have not had the right lover."

"Uh-huh. And let me guess. You're volunteering to remedy that?" *What the hell am I saying?*

He sobered a little. "You should not try so hard to seduce me, Cassidy. You would not like what you find."

"Me? *Me* trying to seduce *you*? I thought seduction was *your* gift."

"Then you underestimate yourself."

Cassidy tried to smother a grin as she mopped up the sauce with a chunk of flaky, perfectly done fish. The stunning Dominique found her "seductive?" The idea made her giddy. Then again, she could blame the wine for that as well.

"So?" she ventured when he refilled her plate a little later. "*Are* you trying to seduce me?" Yes, the censor had definitely checked out. It lay in a drunken, snoring stupor in the corner of her mind.

"No. I'm not." He sounded more serious than he had all evening.

"That's not what it looks like from here."

"Then I owe you an apology." He set the plate back down in front of her and refilled her glass. Again. "Please don't take this personally, but my...needs...are different."

He returned her questioning look with an air of detached expectation.

"Oh," she said, realization dawning. "Really."

"I apologize if I led you to think otherwise."

"Well, no, that's good, actually." She sipped the wine. "I mean, seriously. My life is upside-down right now." Her gaze strayed to the ring on her finger, safe from accidental loss and probably helping her keep her job—and, whether or not she wanted to admit it, a constant reminder of Jackson and what they once shared. Jackson who kept calling, kept listening, kept making a show of caring—while he kept himself at an emotional distance.

And Dominique? Beautiful, mysterious, charming, and physically present—but emotionally orbiting a star even farther out than Jackson.

Also, gay.

She stared into her glass and shook her head in sad wonder. *How did I not see that one coming?* How desperate was she for meaningful connection to be done in by a delicious meal and meaningless banter? Or was the wine to blame for that, too? Well, at least this time she hadn't invested years into a relationship before it fell apart. There was that.

When she met his eyes again, Dominique watched her with a stillness that bordered on the uncanny. "I'm here just for a little while. No telling where I'll end up." Or when he would disappear without warning. With a rueful smile, she added, "Thanks for stopping me from getting carried away."

"*De rien,*" he said, and for a moment she thought he looked as disappointed as she felt.

14

ALLIANCES

Dominique busied himself cleaning utensils in the sink while her rampant desire swirled in the air like a rogue wave, threatening to suck him under, cave in his skull, and crush his reason.

Without warning.

While she made love to his cooking spoon, his imagination served up vivid scenes of pushing her across the kitchen counter and claiming her body, her blood, her mind. Her life. His canines and cock both ached in readiness. Nothing but the pulse in her neck and the sweet scent of her arousal filled his awareness.

She had surprised him in the worst possible way.

His fault, all of it. What was he thinking, plying her with this much wine, whispering of sweet orgasms, and speaking of exquisite lovers? Just watching her enjoy the meal he prepared for her made him delirious with pleasure. By also encouraging these flirts, he couldn't have pushed his own limits any harder if he tried.

And he had shattered hers.

Cassidy bolted for her phone when it rang on the living room table, a desperate grab at distraction if ever there was one. Her gait was a bit unsteady, as was her greeting to the caller. He had no trouble picking up the male voice on the other end, demanding to know if she was all right.

She sagged into the sofa cushions and buried her face in one hand. "Really, I'm fine. Just in the middle of dinner. I wasn't watching my phone for texts."

"You're not eating right, are you," the caller challenged, and Dominique's nerves rippled with mild irritation.

"Jackson, please don't lecture me. I get enough of that from Nick—" Her expression twisted into a hideous "oh shit" grimace as she half curled into a fetal ball. The caller, Jackson, requested an explanation. "Nick-*e*," she croaked, hand over her eyes. "Nicky. My roommate."

Dominique froze, ambushed by a gut-punch of memories of the last time anyone called him by that name. He forced himself to focus past the agony and listen to Cassidy's awkward explanation of her living arrangements.

"You don't need to worry about my diet. Nicky...is a chef, so...she cooks for us. Gourmet food. It's delicious." She glanced in his direction, her wide, blue eyes beseeching him to understand.

He did, but he didn't like it, and the hairs on the back of his neck rose in agitation when Jackson asked to see her before leaving on a business trip. Dominique leaned across the kitchen counter, straining to hear every nuance of their conversation. Tight impatience in Jackson's tone, uncertainty in hers as she stared at the ring on her finger. As the exchange continued, she turned over her hand, hiding the diamond.

"I'm sorry, Jackson. My schedule is pretty full. Maybe when you get back." She cut the connection without waiting for a response and flopped into the cushions, head thrown back.

He admired her invitingly bared throat before recalling himself. "Do you love this man?"

"I really don't know anymore," she said, sitting up. "Right now I...can't be near him."

"Why?" he asked with studied casualness and made careful note of her teeth catching on her bottom lip.

She broke into a sudden fit of giggles. "The mansion got too small."

As Cassidy finished eating—now with a tall glass of Perrier water—her story poured out. At the center of it all was Jackson Striker, the man whose ring she wore with such uncertainty. Their connection ran deep, forged in a shared understanding of grief and recovery Dominique couldn't help but envy. For all his passionate but ultimately superficial relationships, he had known nothing even close.

Everything changed once she arrived at Jackson's home and encountered his wealth and family. They frowned upon her common aspirations and the life she imagined for herself and Jackson. Cassidy spoke in vivid detail about how it all came to a head the Friday before her arrival at the cottage when the Striker patriarchs took their heir's future wife to task soon after the main course was served.

"It was like the Spanish Inquisition, and nothing I said was right. They made it obvious that the last person they want Jackson to marry is a middle-class career girl who is in no hurry to procreate."

"But...Jackson asked you to marry him, *non*?"

"He seemed to have forgotten that bit." She hesitated, hurt edging her face. "He just sat there, right beside me, and didn't say a thing. I needed him to be there for me, and...he didn't even look at me."

"*Trou du cul*," Dominique murmured. "Asshole," he clarified at her questioning look.

"That's what I said." She laughed and wiped at a moist eye. "Although I probably shouldn't have shouted it at all three of them before storming out of the dining room. I think Jackson's mother was on the verge of fainting."

Dominique smiled, admiring her spirit and wishing he had been there to see it, wishing even more he could have defended her. He had known scores of women—and more than a few men—who would have conveniently forgotten their principles in favor of a life of plenty.

"He apologized later, and I couldn't stay mad at him. He said his father and uncle are traditionalists, but as long as we didn't upset them too much...or call them names,"—she groaned—"there was no reason we couldn't live the life we wanted. Everything was...good. Almost."

He finished turning off the stove and setting the dishes to soak in the sink. Leaning back across the counter, he emptied the Perrier bottle into her glass. "Then why are you here?"

Her hand surreptitiously reached for her neck. Dominique waited.

"Something happened," she began. "I woke up with this and...I have no idea how it got there." A small shrug and a dismissive wave. "I can't even think about it. It's like my mind bounces off something when I try. Like it was so traumatic I'm blocking it out."

He said nothing, silently encouraging her to go on while renewed anger at Serge scraped at his nerves. The old fool was stronger than this. There was no excuse for leaving that mark on her neck and such turmoil in her mind.

"Jackson knows what happened. I can see it in his eyes. His whole attitude toward me changed overnight. He got so distant. I..." She shook her head.

"What did he tell you? About that night?" He maintained a tone of almost disinterested calm, but inside he seethed. What else had that blood-drinker imbécile done?

"He didn't tell me. I didn't ask." After a moment, she added, "For all I know, he did this to me."

He did not! Dominique swallowed the words he could never explain. She radiated pain and confusion, and he ached with the need to ease her anguish.

"Maybe he doesn't truly know what happened," he offered. "Otherwise, why wouldn't he tell you? If he loves you?"

She looked unconvinced.

"Love knows no secrets, *non*?" he said, wishing he would have no secrets from her.

Cassidy held his gaze as though she sensed his deeper sentiment. "No. It doesn't."

For a while she fell into thoughtful silence while he finished tidying the kitchen, lost to his own speculations and drifting on the lyrical rhythms from the speaker.

"Tell me about yourself, Dominique. You've listened to my tale of woe. Let me return the favor."

He hung up the towel and apron and retrieved two more bottles of Perrier before replying. "No one should have to hear my...tale of woe. It is not fit for"—*humans*, he thought and set one bottle before her—"a friend."

The smile curving her beautiful mouth soaked into his skin like the warmth of the sun. "Then tell me what you would tell a friend." She took his offering and broke the seal. "I'm a good listener."

———————

Reluctant to break the spell by stepping onto the front porch and finding what he knew lurked there, Dominique lingered in his corner of the sofa, long after Cassidy found her bed—under her own power—and listened to her breathing deepen.

"Foolish child. You cannot outrun your destiny."

He closed his eyes, blocking out the commentary from outside, grasping at the fleeting sense of contentment. He had told her about his life before, in sketchy terms at first, then in increasing detail as he allowed himself to remember what he would never know again—the smiles of his family, the voices of his friends, the electric-blue of the Caribbean Sea under a mid-day sun. Strange how speaking of these things made them almost real once more and less the echoes of insufferable loss.

Folded into the sofa's opposite corner, Cassidy took it all in with interest, respecting his wish and never asking the one thing she surely most wanted to know—why did he no longer live that life? By the end, Dominique thought he might have told her if she had asked. He almost believed she would nod and understand.

But only almost.

For a few more moments, he held onto that dream. Then it evaporated together with the elusive humanity he cultivated for her. A soft growl vibrated in his throat.

From outside, there was a chuckle. "Your fate will always find you."

"As will you, it seems," Dominique said, feeling weary. Why hadn't he put this one down yet? On the porch, he found Serge blending into the shadows in an Adirondack chair.

"You need me."

Dominique leaned against the rail and crossed his arms. "What I need is for you to tell me what happened the night you fed from her," he said so low only another blood-drinker would hear him—not a human sleeping by the open window above them.

"I saw the light in her soul." Serge beamed as if proclaiming a miracle.

"And you did what? Exactly?"

"I drank, of course. I had to know her mind, see her light. It was..."

"What compulsion did you put on her?"

Serge looked mildly offended at having his proclamation cut short. "To not see me. Nobody ever sees me." This with a wistful sigh.

"Did you compel the man she was with, too?"

"The man?"

"Her man." Blank stare. "He was there that night. You compelled him also?"

"Oh, no. No, he is not her man."

Dominique fought for patience. "Regardless, he was there. Did you drink from him?"

Serge gasped, then shook his head, muttering, but stopped when Dominique growled a warning. "So impatient, blood-child." He straightened a little and looked away. "He was...repulsive."

"Repulsive," Dominique repeated. If an accurate description—and he couldn't think how—that could explain Cassidy's sudden reluctance for her fiancé's company. If Serge reached this conclusion while deep in her mind, he might well have accidentally compelled her to feel likewise. "Repulsive how?"

The old blood-drinker had that far-away look again, his voice soft. "He has a light, too. But he is not her man."

"You are useless," Dominique snarled in sheer frustration. It was all he could do not to slam the door behind him. The beast slithered behind his ribs. Only one thing would appease it. Pulling on his leathers and boots wasn't even a conscious decision.

He steeled himself for an argument on the way out, but Serge didn't even hesitate before leaping onto the back of his bike. "You need me with you," he declared, chuckling. "Yes, you do."

———

That night in her dreams, she knew where to look for him—or thought she did. He wasn't there. The hole she dug held only rock and ice.

"Are you hungry?" he asked from where he sat, cross-legged, on a boulder. His bare skin merged with the snow's glare, making his body blend into the background. His hair flew in the wind, shiny and dark. She had mistaken it for a raven in flight. His eyes were untouched by the smile on his lips.

Cassidy huffed and staggered out of the snow grave, her yellow nightshirt fluttering around her. "How long have you been sitting there watching me dig this freaking hole?"

"I have been here all along. You haven't looked in the right place."

Exhausted, she sat down next to him. Her bare toes curled into the snow as though it were sand. "This is too warm."

"It is a dream."

"I know. But it's too warm. Have you ever even seen snow?"

"Once. I didn't like it."

A new shape appeared before them, heavily bundled. "Roommate, is it? Nice, Cass. Real nice."

"Why are you here, Jackson?"

"Shouldn't you be asking *him* that? Doesn't he own any clothes?" A mitten-covered hand gestured wildly.

"It's a dream."

Dominique inclined his head to whisper in her ear. "He doesn't know that."

"But you and I do. Why are we here? What am I looking for?"

"Me."

"Well, I found you. Now what?"

He stretched his face toward the sun, his pale features all but invisible in the light, as though drawn on the wind itself. "That is up to you, *ma petite.*"

"I need to get some sleep. I'm leaving now."

With a soft *whump*, she fell back into the snow. He looked back down at her, his face now obscured in shadow. Then she could see through him. Seconds later, he was gone.

"You drive me insane, Dominique."

The wind laughed. In French.

15

Lost in Translation

"Damn you, Dominique. You and your ludicrous ideas." Cassidy pinched the bridge of her nose and gave her burning eyeballs a minute to rest. This was going to take all night. Though it had sounded like a brilliant idea yesterday, now she was tempted to blame that on the wine as well, right along with her mortifying attempts at seducing a gay man.

They had talked until one in the morning. It was a charmed life he had lived on the island paradise of St. Barth. She listened, fascinated by his words and the warmth and beauty animating him as he spoke. After a while, she sensed an undercurrent of sorrow in his words, but she didn't ask, loath to disturb his happy recollections with questions about an obviously much less carefree present.

When the conversation shifted to her own life and work, he had some definite opinions and ideas about how to seize initiative. Which was why she still sat at her desk, long after everyone else cleared out, wanting only to bang her head against her cubicle wall.

On Dominique's suggestion, she had taken Jim Lawley's most recent piece and rewrote it in her own voice and with her own spin on the details. Even Dave McKinney could see how much better it was. Not that he said so. No, instead he tried to reason with her.

"Why are you so desperate to pick a fight with Jim? You're young. You've got bigger things waiting for you than the *Gazette*, Chandler."

For a moment, she was confused. How could he be making predictions like this when he'd hardly seen enough of her work to form an opinion? Because he wasn't, she realized. It was her supposed imminent marriage into the Striker clan he referred to, not any future career in journalism.

Cassidy bristled with barely contained indignation. "Mr. McKinney, this is my first job in a career I have wanted since I was eight. Regardless of how I ended up here, the fact remains that I *am* here. I want to stay here, and I want to contribute to the best of my abilities."

When he still looked dubious, she leaned in with another angle, seizing more initiative. "Wouldn't that be in the *Gazette's* best interest? Unless, of course, you actually feel that my work isn't up to your standards, in which case I'd appreciate any help you as my editor can give me to improve."

He gave her the long-suffering look of a man who really didn't want to deal with such decisions—a man thinking of retirement sooner rather than later. Her shoulders slumped. It must be true, then. Dave was leaving, and Jim would keep her in obits and coffee machines from here on forward. This might not be the only chance she ever got, but it was the chance she had right now. And she would not let it go this easily.

"Mr. McKinney. Please. I—"

"Okay, Chandler. Okay. You've made your point." Dave swiveled his chair around and fed the evidence of her crime to a shredder. Then he handed her a business card for Garcilla Health Systems, a Miami-based company about to announce a massive expansion, including a center in Orchard Beach. He wanted a full write-up on them as well as expected economic and community impacts on the area. By tomorrow.

"I'm on it," she promised, intending to work all night if necessary. Which she did, though not for the reasons she expected. The name on the card, Rosa Garcia Lopez, PR rep for Garcilla, didn't speak English other than to say that she didn't, and Cassidy spoke even less Spanish. Apparently Miami really was American in name only.

After tracking down all the English-speaking sources she could, she groped her way through various Spanish sites and tried to read between the lines of the auto-translated results. Slow progress, but she kept at it. Failing was not an option.

She ignored her phone's chirping, knowing it was only Jackson with more pester-texts after she had let his earlier call go to voice mail. But when it rang again, her concentration shattered. She had half a mind to ignore the unfamiliar number, but as tired and cranky as she was, the possibility of getting to hang up on a telemarketer was too tempting to resist.

"Yes?"

"Where are you?"

She blinked, stunned. "Dominique? Where did you get this number?"

"From your phone."

"Great. Remember that discussion we had about privacy?"

"You left it on the kitchen counter last night."

"Okay," she said, letting that sink in. Privacy meant nothing to him—sort of like clothes. "So you're calling to see where I am? Don't tell me you miss me."

"Would you like me to make dinner again tonight?"

She glanced at the wall clock. "Crap. I had no idea how late it is."

"Where are you?" he asked again, making her hesitate. Did he seriously feel entitled to keep tabs on her now?

"Well, not that it's any of your business, but I'm in the office working on my new assignment. Which is due tomorrow, and which I got because of your crazy idea. How's that for an explanation?"

There was a pause, as he must have considered the grinding quality of her tone—and ignored it. "Congratulations. I knew you could do it."

"I'm not so sure." She sighed. "Would you believe the people I have to talk to don't speak English? And most of what's been written about them is in Spanish."

"And...you don't speak Spanish?"

"About as well as I speak French."

He made a pitiful little noise. "Oh, you are in trouble." The way he pronounced "trouble" with a sonorous, nasal quality and a round, rolling R, made her insides quiver.

"I don't need you to tell me that."

"Come home and eat. I have an idea."

She had serious doubts about his ideas at this point. Still, she was hungry and nothing more could be accomplished here tonight. She dropped the research and article in progress into her personal cloud drive and headed out.

Fish was on the menu again. Dominique showed her a freezer full of them. Brain food, he said. Afterward, with her stomach pleasantly full, but her head still clear of wine, they sat together on the sofa, bare feet propped on cushions on the glass table-top, laptops balanced on their thighs. She typed while he read through her sources and gave her the highlights. He was fluent in Spanish.

"Be careful, Dominique. If you keep this up, I may forget about not being your cup of tea and all."

"You should never forget that, *chère.*"

"Fine, fine. But I owe you a hug. Is that okay?"

"I don't know. You might bite."

"Hilarious."

"I know," he said, his smile all mystery. "I amuse myself."

She squelched a pinch of disappointment. After the trials of the day, his calm, confident strength was a soothing balm, a promise of safe harbor. But a promise was all it was. Companionable lounging on the same piece of furniture and reminiscing about happy times was as much as this gay man was willing to give his new female friend. Which was, of course, for the best. At least she knew where things stood with one guy.

The phone in her bag chirped, and Cassidy was about to dig it out when the last document disappeared from his display, replaced by a dragon of animated blue flame against a black backdrop. The creature held a login box in its claws, and Dominique entered the longest password she had ever seen. Cryptic techno-babble poured across the screen, some of it in ominous red lettering.

"What are you doing?"

"Looking for an unlisted phone number."

She leaned closer, hovering by his shoulder to watch, even though nothing much on the display made any sort of sense. "Aren't they unlisted for a reason?"

"Like network passwords?" The corner of his mouth lifted in irony. She had defaulted the Internet connection four times before he agreed to share the Wi-Fi password.

"Uh-huh. So what are you gonna do? Reset the phone company?"

"I'm checking personnel records."

Startled, she looked closer. The screen still made little sense, but "Garcilla" figured prominently in the text scrolling past. "Wait. You *hacked* Garcilla's network?"

Right on cue, a new window appeared, inviting him to search by employee name or social security number. Señora Lopez's private information popped up seconds later.

"If it is on the Internet, it is mine."

"You're...you're a hacker? *That's* what you do?"

"Not *a* hacker, *chérie*. *The* hacker."

"So I'm living with a criminal after all," she murmured.

"I'm also very good at writing malware."

Cassidy sank back into the sofa cushions. "I don't believe this. What other laws do you break? No, don't answer that," she added quickly when he looked like he actually might. "I don't want to know. Honest. I need plausible deniability all the way."

His eyes flashed with silent laughter. "Suit yourself." Grabbing his phone from the side table, he dialed a number from the personnel file.

Before Cassidy could comprehend all the ramifications and tell him to hang up, Rosa Garcia Lopez's tiny, surprised voice pitched from the speaker. She had answered none of the numbers on her card earlier and sounded in no mood to conduct business at this time of night on this number either.

He spoke in brisk Spanish. When Cassidy's name came up, she froze in shock, the specter of guilt by association looming large. He made a calming gesture, placed the phone on the table, and pulled her laptop across. He began adding to her notes in English. The conversation continued for a while, Rosa's disembodied voice becoming relaxed, babbling more. He sounded all charm, making encouraging noises as he worked.

She leaned in against his shoulder, reading. From time to time, she got distracted by his scent. Perhaps she shouldn't be surprised that she was dreaming of snow. His cologne, or shower gel, or whatever it was really did smell like that—like ice on a winter day so cold it glittered.

"*Et voilà*," he said when the call concluded and he handed back her laptop. "You can now write an article so boring it will put to sleep the paper it is printed on."

"Who did you tell her you were?"

"Your research assistant."

She choked a little. "Did she ask how you got that number?"

"I'm an excellent researcher?" he offered with a wink.

"You're a good liar." The words were out of her mouth before she could bite them back. He had stolen Rosa's private number and lied to her about who he was. While Cassidy had heard of reporters who thought nothing of doing much worse to get a story, this felt different. This wasn't her spinning facts to a faceless stranger. This was someone she knew doing so on her behalf with a casual ease that took her breath away.

Dominique studied her face, his smile fading. "When I need to be."

"Have you lied to me?" She wasn't sure why that should matter. They were only strangers passing in a cottage, after all. Yet somehow, it did.

"No," he said after a hesitation that was just this side of too long.

"Right." She took a deep breath. "Sorry. You helped me out big time here, and I'm being an ungrateful twit. Thank you, Dominique. I mean it."

"*De nada.*" He shut down the hacker software. "My pleasure."

The velvet sound of that last word moved through her like a soul caress. It felt so natural to lean against him, sighing, drawing strength and comfort. "What can I do to pay you for this?"

He put his laptop aside and fidgeted in the pockets of his gym pants, forcing her to back away. "One morning you will think of something." He stuck a cigarette between his lips, but paused when he caught sight of her scowl.

"Is that necessary?"

"*Oui,*" he said, and flicked the lighter. His face narrowed as he drew the smoke.

She held her breath, shut her laptop, and got up. "And here I thought I might start liking you. My mistake."

Smoke streamed from his nose and mouth, though he did at least turn his head away before exhaling. He smiled a little. "No mistake. You do."

"You conceited French pain in the ass."

"Please don't take this so personally. This is my problem, not yours."

"But it *is* my problem," she fumed. "Do you know what that filthy stench reminds me of? My father."

Unlike her, Dominique had no trouble hiding his true thoughts behind a blank expression, which was annoying enough. Added to the smoke, every friendly thought she might have entertained evaporated.

"My father has smoked all his life, but he's still healthy as a bull and busy screwing a woman half his age while my mother died of the cancer she developed from his second-hand smoke. And oh, yeah, when my mom got sick, he ran off to his mistress because he couldn't deal with what was coming."

The more the chemo tore down his wife, the more time Cassidy's father spent away from home. And the night an ambulance had to take her mother to the ER because she had a fever so high she was incoherent, he didn't answer his phone and didn't show up until three hours later. "Traffic," he had hedged. "Lousy signal." As he drove them to the hospital, she had begged him to try harder, to step up, told him that his family needed him. He'd hugged her and promised he'd do better...

Hot tears welled in her eyes, and Cassidy blinked, fighting to keep her composure. She didn't see her coward of a father again until the funeral—two years later. He'd left her to deal with all of it: her mother's decline, the house, the bills, plus school. At sixteen. Alone.

With a shaky breath, she squared her shoulders. "So no. Not something I can just ignore."

Dominique watched her, completely transformed from easygoing computer hacker and "research assistant" to the poster boy for aloof reserve. After a brief hesitation, he pulled another drag from his cigarette.

"Jerk." Gathering her laptop, she marched up the stairs, but stopped when he called her name.

"If it bothers you so much, I won't do it in the house anymore." He dropped the cigarette into the Perrier bottle.

"Thanks, I guess." Not much of an apology, but more than she had expected.

He got up and collected his things with impatient move-ments. What other laws would he break tonight? The speed limit was an obvious one. What or who was he running from? Or to? She couldn't help feeling like she was part of the problem, a thought that came with a stab of resentment. There was no one left in her life she could trust to give her a straight story.

His face empty as a china doll's, Dominique disappeared down the hall.

"Good night," she said, but received no reply.

Five minutes later, curled in her bed with Eddie, she listened to the sound of the shed behind the house being unlocked and the motorcycle starting up. It was only a revving engine, but it sounded angry to her, furious even. It raced away into the night.

Screaming.

16

Nothing to See Here

Serge lay in wait for him by the shed. "You play a dangerous game, blood-child."

Dominique ignored him. He didn't need the derelict to chastise him over how close he'd come to ending her life tonight. She had startled him with her touch, brief as it was. The heat of her body searing into his skin all but shredded what was left of his reason, especially after her insistence on honesty. He had almost shown her the truth. Almost.

He swung onto the bike, pulled the helmet over his head, and started the motor. Then he waited. When Serge hesitated, he revved the engine, and the pest leapt aboard. Dominique sped out of the yard, down the lane and onto A1A as though launched from a slingshot, hurtling away from the ever more irresistible temptation of Cassidy.

She shouldn't be there. He should have tried harder to get her to leave that first night. Now it was too late. Much too late. Her innocent acceptance of him, allowing him to forget for a time what he had become, was a drug he could not refuse.

It was now more than just allowing her to live for an ulterior purpose. Now, he wanted her to live because he enjoyed her company, because her laughter chipped at the black ice in his chest. Because she trusted him, even needed him. Because he could help her, and she wanted to help him in return.

Because in her eyes, he was human.

He jammed the brakes. The bike skidded sideways toward the shoulder, tires shrieking. Serge sailed off in a long, flailing arc and disappeared into the brush.

Dominique sat stunned by the realization; he needed Cassidy as he had needed no one before—and so did the beast. Even now, his hunger for her crawled in the marrow of his bones. Inescapable. It would happen. He would find himself at her bloodless throat with no idea how he got there. It was only a matter of time.

Serge emerged from the shrubbery, a bewildered expression on his scruffy face. Several cars that had slowed to gawk continued on, satisfied—or perhaps disappointed—that no one lay dying on the side of the road. He stopped, opened his mouth, closed it again, speechless at last. A shirt sleeve was gone and both pant legs hung in tatters.

Dominique pushed up his visor. "Did you not see that coming, old fool?"

Serge shook his head emphatically.

"But you know what I will ask next?"

He nodded, a grin splitting the beard. "You need me," he purred. His eyes glinted with a sudden, mad light as he straddled the front tire, gripped the handlebars, and leaned close. His cool forest breath washed over Dominique's face. "Say it, blood-child. *Tell me.*"

Dominique thought he might choke on the words, but speaking them was as inevitable as what would happen if he didn't. "I need you...to teach me...how to keep her safe—from me."

Visibly puffing up with satisfaction, Serge hopped on behind him. "Finally. I was beginning to think she would be half-dead before you understood."

"You might have explained it better."

The idea hadn't even crossed his mind until last night when he watched Serge hunt. The bloodthirsty pirate left no corpses. While he helped himself to a measure of his prey's blood, he played with its mind, twisting it to turn away from whatever evil it contemplated and instead pursue the opposite course. There were at least two former drug dealers and one corporate lawyer in Miami who now felt called to a life of service in the church. The implied amount of control over the beast was staggering.

"You weren't ready." Serge slapped a jaunty rhythm on Dominique's shoulders. "You are now. We proceed. Go."

He fought the temptation to fling the nuisance off his bike again, but as he had relegated himself to the position of student, he would have to endure the teacher.

Though only to a point. While the lesson belonged to Serge, the rest of the night would remain in Dominique's hands. Which is why, five minutes later, he pulled into the parking lot of Orange Blossom Manor, Orchard Beach's poshest resort.

"No, no, no, no, no." Serge moaned, thumping Dominique's back. "You're not ready. Not ready. No."

"Make up your mind," Dominique grumbled. "Wait here."

He left Serge to orbit the parked motorcycle, whining his distress, and strolled into the lobby, just another tourist needing a room. Determination focused his compulsions to a fine point, and it took only one try for the desk clerk to hand over a key card with a welcoming smile. After a quick stop in the sundries shop, he located the suite, got the water running in the Jacuzzi tub, and returned to the bike via a back stairway.

"Come with me."

"No." Even Serge's voice trembled. "This is bad. This is very, very bad."

Dominique smiled, displaying his fangs. Regarding his own future, the fool was correct. Serge's world was about to tilt on its filthy axis.

Grabbing a bare, grimy elbow, Dominique propelled him to the back stairway. Serge whimpered every step of the way, but fell silent once they were in the plush, fourth floor hallway. Eyes rolling, head bobbling, he cleaved to Dominique, clearly not trusting the unfamiliar space to let him pass unscathed.

Two teenage boys stopped in their tracks at the spectacle, and Dominique let the compulsion fly. "There is nothing to see here." Their faces neutralized, and they walked away.

Moments later, he opened the door to the suite, pushed Serge inside, and maneuvered him across the room.

"What are...what are you doing?"

"Making you invisible."

When Serge spotted the steaming tub, his arms and legs shot out to catch the bathroom doorway like steel grappling hooks. "NO!"

Dominique shoved. "*Si!*"

Serge shrieked in protest, and Dominique clamped his hand over the gaping, hairy mouth. "Listen to me, *imbécile*. We are not hunting the streets tonight. More than human eyes will see us, and cameras cannot be compelled into ignorance." He sniffed at the matted hair. Dirt. Garbage. Rancid blood. "And *nobody* can be compelled to forget your foul stench."

Serge shook violently, his eyes locked on the tub swirling with suds. He made a sad, humming noise and Dominique removed his hand. "But...does it have to be water?"

"*Oui*. Water. It cannot hurt you. You know this, *n'est-ce pas?*"

Serge gave him a mournful look. "You have never been keel-hauled, young one."

Dominique stared at him.

"It's horrible. You either get cut up by the barnacles or you dro—" He let out a high-pitched yelp as Dominique, taking advantage of his momentary distraction, shouldered him across the bathroom and into the Jacuzzi. Serge flailed, sloshing water and foam over the edge and across the floor. Finally, he anxiously settled onto the built-in seat and eyed the suds as though they might be conspiring to smother him. Already the ragged clothes and hair leeched grime into the hot water.

Dominique stood over the scene, hands on hips, drenched. "Did you find any barnacles in there?"

Serge looked up, a dog trapped in a downpour. "You are cruel, blood-child."

"We are only getting started." Dominique pulled off his jacket, tossed it out into the room, and retrieved a large bottle from the shopping bag. "Wait until you see what shampoo can do."

It took well over an hour, but by the time Dominique was done scrubbing, rinsing, trimming, and shaving him, the vampire who stood before him, swathed in a towel, was unrecognizable. Even Serge seemed transfixed by his own reflection. His face, excavated from decades' worth of beard and filth, had the typical lean blood-drinker lines but also a softness natural to the age at which he was made. And the hair, once a dull tangle, turned out to be a riot of caramel curls. Only the eyes were the same—owlish, brown, and not entirely focused.

Serge touched his bare chin. "I haven't seen this since...before." Then, on a low growl, his eyes pooled into black caves and the canines extended between his lips. In a flash, his flesh tightened around his bones until he had the gruesome, skeletal appearance of the beast.

Dominique tensed, his own primal instincts rising to answer the challenge. Amidst all the bungling idiocy, he had forgotten how much older—and stronger—Serge was, a potentially fatal mistake. But the moment passed, and Serge reverted to a benign human form that could no longer be mistaken for a vagabond.

"Effective."

Dominique forced a casualness he far from felt. "There are some new clothes on the bed. Go find something that agrees with you."

Alone in the bathroom, he studied his own reflection. The two day's growth of beard shadowing his cheeks had taken a year of rampant feeding to appear. He picked up the razor and scraped it over his jaw. Glistening black stubble rained onto the wooly mop of Serge's beard already in the basin. When he was done, the mirror reflected a clean-shaven face of innocent male beauty.

"Effective," he agreed.

Serge looked a paradox; in the navy board shorts and teal shirt and with his bouncing curls half obscuring his face, he presented the image of a seasoned surfer—who had never seen the sun. Dominique sighed. "If anyone asks, you are from Canada." He glanced at his own pale arms. "We both are."

Nobody asked. They received little more than curious glances as they made their way to the resort's beach-side pavilion. A live band strummed off to one side and a cheerful crowd buzzed around the tiki bar. There were young couples, retirees, families, and children. Their warm, living essences drenched the air.

"You are not ready for this, blood-child."

Dominique glanced at the surveillance cameras mounted in the area. His canines ached with the eagerness to feed. "That is why you are here. Teach me."

The old one continued to look uncertain.

"You have made another, *hein*? Taught another?"

The fluffy curls shook. "Never."

Dominique didn't know whether to be furious or dismayed. He settled on somewhere in between. "Then you and I shall both learn tonight—for Cassidy."

He found a seat at the bar and ordered a bottle of Corona he didn't touch. All his senses keyed on the maelstrom of life flowing around him. Not reaching out and taking it at will required tremendous effort, and he threatened to come undone when a pair of chattering women settled beside him. Before they could attempt conversation with him, he dug for cigarettes. He had yet to light one when a soap-scented Serge sidled up to his other side, fidgeting, and pressed his face against Dominique's shoulder. "As you wish, blood-child," he whispered. "For the sweet one."

Serge spoke in tones so low only Dominique would hear them over the thumping music and raucous laughter. He told of intention and action, of pacts with the beast and focus of the mind, of battles with the self and a truce bargained in blood.

Some concepts were not unlike those he had long practiced for martial arts. Control was all. Control over the self. Lose it and lose the battle.

But the beast—the hunger—often had a will of its own. It claimed control when it pleased, and even now chaffed with impatience. The thought of keeping it leashed much longer seemed as hopeless as confining fire in a cage made of straw.

He studied the lighter and cigarette in his hands. "Have you ever heard of a cure? For us? An end to this torment?"

"The sun." Serge shrugged. "Why would you want that?"

"Why would anyone want to sit here on a beautiful evening wanting only to tear open every vein he sees?"

He clasped Dominique's shoulder. "Understand this. You are...*young*," he said with grave emphasis. "Remember yourself as a mortal youngster with his first bottle of drink." He leaned closer, leering. "Your first kiss with a promise of more? It is like that, you see. A fever. That powerful."

Not wanting to get any closer to the woman sitting on his other side, Dominique fought the urge to lean away from Serge. "And?"

"And then you grow up and learn to pace the drink and savor the women. But in our case—" He sat back and lifted both hands. "Well, growing up is lengthy business, yes?"

"How lengthy?"

Serge watched him light up and waved at the resulting smoke. "You poor child. Your sire was of no help to you at all, was he?" He sighed. "Too old, that one, to remember anything of before."

Dominique almost dropped the cigarette. "What do you know of him?" If Serge was another spawn of that creature, possibly a loyal one...

"Easy, blood-child. I know only what I see in your future." Before Dominique could bristle with contempt, Serge added, "I can smell his strength in you. Use it to do this. You can. I have seen it."

Dominique pulled on the cigarette, fighting for calm. "In my future?"

"Yes."

He muttered a choice French curse. Did he really believe this nonsense now? No, of course not. But regardless of how Serge phrased it, this was more to go on than he had in a year of nights. "How?"

"Simple. You always remember what matters more than the blood."

Which, thanks to the biting smoke, he could taste in the back of his throat and felt oozing in his lungs. "Survival," he said, glancing at the all-seeing surveillance cameras. "The beast cherishes survival most."

"Good. What else?"

The woman, who had almost faded from his awareness, laughed, recapturing his full attention. The pulse beneath her ear thumped with life, and her hair was almost the same color as...

"Cassidy," he whispered.

Serge nodded, beaming with satisfaction. "You care about something more than yourself, and you can override the hunger." More solemnly he added, "You more than care for her; she is everything to you."

Dominique swallowed the blood in his mouth and crushed the cigarette in an ashtray. "*Oui.* She is."

The woman radiated heat like a boiling pot. He imagined he could feel her heart pulsing against his bare arm where Cassidy had touched him earlier. "What do you see...*exactement?*"

"You should try to drink before you wear yourself out."

"What do you see?" he insisted. "For her?"

Serge leaned on the bar and turned Dominique's untouched beer with his fingers. His head moved from side to side as if debating with himself. "I see light."

"Sunlight?"

"No. Light. Soul light. It streams from everyone, but much of it is weak and of no consequence. But sometimes...yes, sometimes it's like watching a sunrise. Like the sweet one."

Dominique could imagine it. He felt it every time he looked at Cassidy—and not only in terms of his secret hope that she would expose him to the actual sun.

"What does that have to do with seeing the future?"

"Because a light like that casts shadows. Long, strong shadows. It is these I see falling through time."

"So what happens?"

Serge dropped his gaze and shook his head. "Shifting, always shifting. Hard to focus."

"You don't know, do you?" Dominique scoffed, angry that he had believed, even for an instant.

"I know one thing that is for certain. The shadows cast by her light will consume you. Me too. Maybe more, or even all. So hard to explain." He tried, groping for words, then leaned his head to the side, exposing his neck. Inviting. "Drink. See for yourself."

Dominique's mind went blank. Not because of the offer of blood, but because of the offer of *vampire* blood. Nothing was more sacred to their kind, or more private. To drink from another was to know their thoughts for a while, their true selves. The old one offered him what usually, but not always, only sires granted their younglings—complete trust and raw honesty.

Also, every unhinged thought in that inscrutable mind.

"No. I cannot." Not if it were the last blood on earth.

Serge bobbed a careless shoulder, but his gaze remained troubled. "As you wish. But then take this." He reached past Dominique and touched the elbow of the woman with Cassidy's hair. When she turned, Serge flashed her a beguiling gap-toothed smile. "My son is eager to meet you."

Dominique murmured a greeting along with his compulsion and paused long enough to kiss her cheek before homing in on her pulse—thinking only of Cassidy with every beat of her heart.

17

STORM FRONTS

A storm was brewing. Jackson called and woke her up early on a Sunday morning to tell her so. A tropical depression, he said, forming over the Bahamas. High winds and flooding were expected at the beach by midnight. She should spend the night elsewhere.

Cassidy was still halfway tangled in the latest bizarre dreamscape featuring snowy mountains and Dominique's riddles, but she did, eventually, register a threat far more serious than the weather. "Wait. How do you know I'm by the beach?"

"Did I say that?"

Her jaw set hard. So much for keeping her new address concealed from him. "Yes. You did."

"I...um...saw you drive in that direction after work the other day."

"You're *spying* on me?"

Alarmed by her sharp tone, Eddie popped from the wadded sheets beside her, his green eyes round with questions.

"No, I was...oh, hell. Yes. I followed you home last week. I had to make sure you're somewhere safe."

"Oh? And does my place pass muster?" Outrage had her as wide awake as three cups of espresso. "Not exactly Striker standards, I bet."

"Babe, listen..."

"I'll have you know it's got a top-of-the-line AC system." Brand new, in fact, as of two days ago.

Jackson laughed. "Well, sounds like a winner, then. It's supposed to hit ninety-four today."

"I don't think you spying on me is funny."

"I wasn't...oh, for fuck's sake, Cass. Would you rather I'd put a GPS tracker on your car? I know where you work, you know."

Cassidy hung up. He knew where she lived. This meant he could stop by any time here, where she was alone—or might as well be. She rubbed the goosebumps off her arms. The thought disturbed her more than she could say.

All day long, she watched for Jackson, but all remained still on Seagrape Lane. Almost eerily so. There wasn't even a hint of a breeze, and the sky lay like a humid, hazy blanket over the landscape, trapping the oppressive heat.

She braved the sauna-like conditions for a gas and grocery run that included bottled water, canned goods, and a flashlight—just in case. She also collected an assortment of newspapers and a tub of on-sale butter pecan ice cream to celebrate the weekend and her career finally lurching forward. After pulling that Garcilla Health article out of her hat by the deadline—with more insightful detail than expected—Dave had been impressed enough to send another, much more straight-forward assignment her way. Life was looking up.

While the outside boiled, a pleasant stream of cold air washed over her as she read the papers and spooned sweet, frozen goodness into her mouth. She also monitored the TV for weather updates. Energetic debate surrounded whether the storm had slowed or stalled or was on the verge of changing direction. There were live shots up and down the coast—mostly at tranquil beaches—but The Weather Channel's top hurricane pro had set up shop in Titusville. "...high likelihood of landfall here some time in the early morning hours, possibly strengthening to..."

Titusville was nowhere near Orchard Beach. Cassidy put the excited back-and-forth on mute. Far more interesting were the local headlines of violence and mayhem playing out around the state.

Head Found in Restaurant Dumpster
Employee who made discovery treated for shock

Florida Man Trapped in Port-A-Potty
Uses gun to shoot lock, hits passing patrol car

West Palm Beach Steps Up Surveillance
Additional police patrols to discourage gang activity

Wisconsin Woman Missing in Keys, Search Launched
Disappearance fits recent pattern, authorities say

As she read, she wished she had another non-Floridian—or anyone, actually—to discuss all this with. She picked up her phone and considered the depressingly short list of contacts when Eddie placed a paw on her elbow. He was lying on his back beside her, the picture of feline bliss, the white stripe on his chest and belly ruffling in the cool air current.

"Just chill, you say?" she asked him, scratching his vibrating throat. He closed his eyes, content. She sighed. Life would be so much easier as a cat.

For dinner, Cassidy cooked a pot of mac-n-cheese with peas and a boiled egg. It was comfort food that would forever remind her of her mother. Often, it also made her think of all the people she had lost.

By the time her bowl was empty, she added another loss to the tally. Eddie, her faithful companion all day, roused from his snooze, dropped to the floor, and stretched with a toothy yawn. Then he shook out his shaggy coat and padded away. "Hey, where're you going?" The cat didn't hesitate in his climb up the stairs. "Oh, suddenly my company isn't good enough for you either?"

"I told you he is allergic to me," Dominique said as he emerged from the hall and headed for the kitchen where he helped himself to a Perrier. Once again, his attire was limited to the well-worn gym pants, his hair tucked behind his ears. He still maintained the clean-shaven look he had adopted last week.

"And a cheery good evening to you."

He drained the bottle before eying the pot on the stove. "You are eating shit again."

"Oh, we're back to that, are we?"

"If you waited for me, I could have made you something superior."

"A body could starve waiting for you to get up. Or do you want me to haul you out of bed when I'm hungry?"

A smile ghosted across his face. "You could try."

"Right." The installers had clanged and banged around the house for the better part of Friday, impossible to miss, yet he emerged that evening looking surprised to find the house twenty-plus degrees cooler. "I know better."

"Pity."

"Besides, why would you care what I eat?" she said as her attention caught on an updated weather bulletin. The wad of green radar signature over the Bahamas was "wobbling." Great. "I take it you're staying in tonight?"

When there was no response, she turned to find him watching her with an odd expression she couldn't even begin to place. "What?"

Dominique looked away and shook his head. "Nothing." He pitched the empty bottle in the recycle bin and headed for the door. "*Bonne nuit*, Cassidy."

"What the hell," she muttered when the door closed behind him.

So he preferred spending the night in a tropical downpour rather than talk to her. Or even not talk. If only he'd stick around and make at least an attempt at tolerating her presence.

With both hands, she massaged her forehead, willing away the niggling threat of a migraine. God, this was getting old, this business of people disappearing on her—even the irritating gay roommate. It shouldn't matter. He was almost a stranger, after all. And yet...it did. Tonight of all nights, with a storm threatening, she would be alone...again.

Fifteen minutes passed before Cassidy realized she hadn't heard the motorcycle start up. Not that he was dressed for riding. Maybe he was on the beach. Whatever. He was a big boy and could take care of himself.

An hour and another weather bulletin later, Cassidy still sat and stared at the screen where the weather reporter in Titusville was practically bug-eyed with excitement. "...now definitely showing signs of strengthening," he reported, and, "Effects could be felt as far south as Palm Beach and..."

"Wonderful," she grumbled and turned down the volume. The rumble of high surf was obvious now, even through the closed windows and over the drone of the AC. Dominique wouldn't be crazy enough to go swimming in that, would he? Or had a rip current caught him and carried him out to sea?

Guilt set in. He might lie washed up on the beach in need of medical attention while she sat here nursing old grudges. "You're a freaking pain in the ass, Dominique, I swear." She toed into her flip-flops, grabbed her phone and flashlight, and stepped into the restless night.

18

SNEAK ATTACK

Cassidy shivered as she descended the porch steps, her feet automatically navigating the missing one. In all the time she'd been here, she'd never gone out after dark. Cassidy looked around at a landscape full of rustling shadows. Warm wind, heavy with weather, brushed against her skin and tugged at her ponytail. Above, scattered clouds hustled like sails through the sky in the vague light of a quarter moon.

She was alone.

"Uh-huh. What else is new?" With a shaky breath, she pushed aside her apprehensions, switched on the flashlight, and made for the beach.

She spotted him when she crested the dune. Not a lifeless form in the sand, but a figure advancing along the water's edge in precise movements, bare torso edged in moonlight. Back and forth he went, pausing between bursts of activity, wielding a stick of some sort with such force it hummed in the wind. Every motion radiated power and purpose. Fascinated, she stood and watched.

A minute later, he stopped and looked at her.

"I just came to see if you're okay," she called, giving a half-hearted wave. "I didn't mean to interrupt." She wasn't sure he heard her over the thundering waves, so she walked closer. "The storm is moving again. They say it'll get nasty here in the next couple of hours."

"Do they?"

With her light politely averted, she could make out little of his face beyond the occasional glint of his eyes and the silvered edges of his straight nose and high cheekbones. But the smile in his voice warmed her. "You should not be out here, then."

"Well, that makes two of us." She glanced at the stick, a piece of driftwood. "What are you doing, anyway?"

"Practicing control."

"Oh?"

"It is a Kata, a martial arts practice. It helps to focus the mind." Tossing aside the stick, he lowered himself and draped sleek, muscular arms over drawn-up knees.

Cassidy sat in the sand beside him and switched off the flashlight. A sense of déjà vu swept over her. In one of her recent dreams—high in the mountains, in the snow, in the too-warm sun—they had sat like this, together in companionable conversation, and all was right with the world. She sighed but refrained from leaning against him as she did in the dream.

"So you practice Kung Fu, too?" A useful skill for a covert government operative, which was her latest theory about him. Though which government he might work for was debatable.

He glanced at her. "Aikido."

"What's the difference?"

"Different origins and purpose. Aikido is a Japanese martial art that focuses on avoiding conflict. Control is everything."

"And going after them with a stick is the backup plan?"

"Sword."

"Of course. Off with their heads."

"*Oui.* If required." He sounded dead serious.

"Interesting hobby."

"It is a discipline. I hold the rank of Shodan, first degree black belt."

Despite herself, she was impressed. "Chef, hacker, motorcycle stuntman, and now a black belt? Is there anything you're *not* good at?"

Dominique laughed without humor and turned back to the foaming waves. "Many things, but mostly... I seem unable to avoid trouble."

The sudden bitter edge took her aback. Genuine anger vibrated behind those words. Her gaze dropped to the faded tribal sun tattoo on his left shoulder. It had a solid black core.

"What kind of trouble?" she asked, feeling like she was stepping over a cliff.

He snorted. "Why would you care?"

"Why wouldn't I? I like to think we're—" She stopped, recalling their earlier exchange. His sidelong glance told her he thought of it, too. "Friends," she said softly.

He considered. "*Mon amie.* My troubles are dangerous."

"I figured as much." When he remained silent, she added, "It might help to talk about it."

"Perhaps." He paused as if gathering unpleasant memories. "The life I knew before...the life I told you about...that all ended one night when my sister, Anastasie, was attacked." Another pause. "There were three of them, rich, drunk tourists. It was a complete coincidence that I found them when I did." His voice all but disappeared, and Cassidy strained to hear him. "Two of them held her down and covered her mouth while the third..."

She closed her eyes. Cold nausea punched her gut.

"Aikido is a defensive art," he continued. "But at a certain level, if there is a loss of control, defensive techniques can become...lethal."

Cassidy tasted tears in the back of her throat. "Did you? Lose control?"

He gave her a long, searching look. "I did."

Nodding, she wiped at her face with the heels of both hands. "Good." His silence told her all she needed to know. No details necessary. Taking a life was no small thing, even when in self-defense. "Was your sister okay?"

"In a manner of speaking."

That, too, spoke volumes. While her own harrowing experience had been over two years ago, her flesh still crawled with the memories of rough hands grabbing her, ripping her clothes, shoving her into the dirt.

On impulse she said, "Teach me. Right now."

"Teach you what?"

"How to defend myself. Like you defended Anastasie."

"Oh, *chérie*. That takes many years of dedicated practice."

"There must be something that would give me a fighting chance?"

"Perhaps. But why?"

"Because—" Her eyes stung with tears. Like gritty stones, she pushed the words from her mouth. "Because I was her once, not that long ago. On campus. Some jocks thought I'd be...fun." She swiped at her eyes. "Jackson saved me from the worst of it, but he just used his fists. It's how we met, actually. Our first three dates were on a shooting range where he taught me how to use a gun. But I don't like them. I refuse to carry one with me."

Dominique was silent for a long time. "Nothing I can teach you will save you against someone with a gun. The bullet always wins."

"I know."

"*Très bien,*" he said softly and rose to his feet in a single fluid motion.

Cassidy scrambled upright and faced him, hyper-aware of the subtle power of his presence, the lean muscle in his torso and arms—and the gym pants that rode too low on those slender hips. Above all, though, she was aware of him as a weapon, capable of defending those he loved—to the death if need be.

In the beam of her flashlight, he spent half an hour showing her basic maneuvers, simple ways to get out of holds and inflict great pain, and touched on using an attacker's own momentum against them. Most importantly, he taught her to gain control of a wrist.

"Once you have control of the wrist, you have control of him. With control, you have power." He illustrated this point with a gentle twist of her arm. She dropped to her knees with a yelp.

Cassidy was more than impressed. These techniques were potent and potentially more effective than a firearm, since the target would never see it coming. Intent on absorbing all she could, she paid close attention. Dominique was an accomplished instructor, and all business as he demonstrated. Again and again, she found herself right up next to him—or flat in the sand. He used only enough force to make his point, yet he expected no such consideration from her.

"I don't want to hurt you."

"Not possible. And if you don't practice properly, this will do you no good."

Cassidy tried harder and soon realized he meant it. She really couldn't hurt him. She stopped *trying* to defend herself. In her mind, his shadowy form morphed into the shapes of her nightmares. He touched her and it was other hands she felt, other arms she grasped and other bodies she sent slamming to the ground.

As though sensing her need to vent years of helpless anger, he ceased giving her direction, letting her do as she wished—until her foot came flying out in an all-out assault on his groin in a most undisciplined move. He twitched his hips out of reach, leaving her foot to connect with nothing. Off balance, she landed hard in the sand. The jarring impact rattled her out of the frenzy she had worked herself into. She lay, catching her breath, appalled by what she had almost done.

"Oh my God, Dominique. I'm so sorry." She propped herself up on one arm. "That would have hurt."

He stood nearby, just beyond the flashlight's reach, quiet, not even breathing hard. At the horizon behind him, lightning snapped and flickered.

"Maybe a little," he conceded, and she was relieved to hear the wry humor in his voice. "I think you have had enough for your first lesson. We can practice again tomorrow, if you like."

She got up and brushed the sand off her. It flew away in a cool gust, and thunder rumbled over the crashing waves. High time to get indoors.

"Thanks. I would like that. Assuming I can still move tomorrow." Every muscle in her body felt bruised.

"Ah, *ma petite,* have I worn you out?" he cooed.

She snorted. "In your dreams."

He laughed, a rich, warm sound of palpable joy, and something deep inside her resonated with the power of a struck gong.

Cassidy moved before she was fully aware of what she intended to do. It was as if something pushed—or pulled—her toward him, urging her to shatter whatever boundaries still remained after the intense physical contact of their practice. She stepped in close, slid her hands up his bare chest and kissed him, feather-light, on the corner of his mouth. A tremor ran through him before he froze completely. She smiled against his cheek and whispered, "Sneak attack."

What an excellent fit they were. Dominique had only a few inches over her five-six frame, unlike Jackson who, at six-four, towered well out of reach. This felt like a puzzle piece snugging up with its neighbor, clicking into place.

The idea hit her with disorienting power. She hardly knew him. How could this feel so right? The wind brushed his hair against her face, and her senses swam with him and the night. And snow.

Unable to step away as she intended, she closed her eyes and lingered, drifting in the dark, savoring this surprising sense of connection, knowing without a doubt he felt it too when he leaned into her. His hands slid up her arms in a slow caress, but he didn't embrace her.

"Cassidy, *ma petite*...no..."

"You would defend me if I was attacked," she whispered into his ear. "Wouldn't you?"

"I would tear them to pieces," he whispered back.

The vehemence in his husky voice almost made her believe it. She turned her face to look at him, only to find his mouth on hers, tentatively tasting her lips. A razor-sharp blade of desire sliced through her.

Oh my God, what's happening? This couldn't be right. She tried to push away, but only broke the tender kiss. He didn't hold her, but his proximity alone seemed to tether her in place.

"Dominique, what are you doing? I thought I—" She gasped when he kissed the sensitive skin beneath her left ear. His hands settled at her waist. "I thought I wasn't your cup of tea."

"I never said that, *chérie.*"

She trembled with indecision—and anticipation. So easy to step away from him and put a stop to this. But he had been right when he claimed seduction as his gift. Just another moment then, one more minute of all her nerves zinging, of being high on him.

Leaning her head to the side, she bared her neck, inviting more.

His arms came around her, drew her close. His body, hard against hers, vibrated with tension. A tiny alarm clanged in the back of her brain. There was something she should remember or know, but didn't. It was quickly silenced by the warm craving sliding down her spine and pooling at its base. Damn, but the French pain in the ass knew how to nuzzle a neck.

With a moan and a vague hope that he wouldn't leave a hickey, Cassidy surrendered.

The stormy night vanished.

She stood in the middle of a deep-green meadow at the edge of a burbling creek. Fir, water, earth, and snow rode a cool breeze that soughed through the impenetrable forest all around. In the cobalt blue sky above, an immense, brilliant helix slowly turned. The more she watched, the more it pulled at her.

Cassidy became weightless, as though she were coming apart, disappearing into the spiral.

Suddenly, Dominique knelt at her feet, staring up at her, his face awash in emotion. She marveled at the deep, obsidian beauty of his unblinking eyes. Even on the mountain, she had never seen him like this. She had never seen his tears.

She joined him in the grass. "What's wrong, Dominique?" Wind tousled his hair, blowing it across his eyes. She brushed it aside and placed her hand against his cheek. "Dominique? What are you doing?"

19

I Am Here

Rapture!

Her blood slid down his gullet as rich and intoxicating as the finest wine. All but senseless with lust, Dominique drank her glorious essence and plunged at last into her mind.

He groaned, ecstatic at the cool, green oasis of light that welcomed him. Her bright emotion was the clear spring water quenching his thirst, her soul the gentle wind that blew the filth from his own. He fell to his knees, sobbing as though witness to a miracle.

In a way, it was. The oasis reached out for him...touched him.

Dominique? What are you doing?

The shock of it brought him up sharply, reminded him of where he really was, what he was really doing. The beast all but tore him apart in its eagerness to have her. *Know me!*

She did. She truly did.

His control in tatters, he fell into her, every fiber of his being yearning to merge with her, to drown in this ferocious ecstasy. The image of her in the sunlight dimmed as the shadows in the forest pushed in.

No, wait, she called. *I found you. Don't go.*

Dominique blinked into a night heavy with storm and foreboding. He lay flat on his back, pinned down by a furious blood-drinker. Laughter bubbled in his throat, though whether from relief or hysteria, he couldn't say.

Serge took a tight hold of the back of his neck and pulled him close. "Tear me to pieces, will you? Tell me, blood-child, what should I do with you then? Do you remember nothing of what I've taught you?"

Dominique sobered. Cassidy's blood...he could still taste its sweetness, smell it in the ozone-laden air. "*Mon Dieu*. What have I done?"

Serge shoved him over and got up, but before he could touch her inert body, Dominique was by her side. With gentle hands, he rolled her onto her back. She was breathing, her heart strong. He went light-headed with relief. In the physical contact, he sensed shadows welling in her mind, unconscious and confused, but very much alive.

Her hair had come undone from its tie and the wind cloaked her face in the silky mass. Brushing it aside, he tensed at the sight of her. The scent of blood rose from her like steam off a pot, and he pressed his mouth flat against a fresh surge of hunger. The puncture wounds on her neck were already healing, but still oozed.

Serge, crouching across from him, sighed. "You are not ready to feed from one you want so desperately. Why did you?"

Canines firmly sheathed, Dominique bent down and applied his tongue to clean and heal the wounds until only two tiny pink marks remained, obscured in the remnants of the bruise. When he lingered an instant too long, relishing her warmth, her nearness, Serge gripped his shoulder in unmistakable warning.

He slapped the hold away and sat up. "At least I didn't leave ugly damage."

Serge ignored the barb. "What did you see, blood-child? In her blood?"

"Light," Dominique said, not sure where else to begin. Also, somehow the experience felt far too private to share with the lunatic—even if said lunatic had proved useful these past few nights by teaching him to feed without killing. Or trying to. While he had learned to exert a measure of control over the beast, Dominique still lost himself more often than not, and Serge ended up pulling him off his meal.

"Of course you saw light. What else?" Eager now, Serge scooted closer.

Dominique growled a warning. He wouldn't put it past the old pirate to take advantage of his lingering confusion to make another attempt on Cassidy's blood.

Serge retreated half the distance he had advanced.

"It doesn't matter what I saw. What does it mean that she was *aware* of me? She saw me in her mind." His voice dropped even lower. "She saw the beast in me."

Serge became still, a statue with curling hair drifting about his pale, stony face. The unblinking eyes cut straight through Dominique and into another reality.

A chill seeped across his shoulders. "What do you know?"

"You cannot compel her, can you? Not without her permission?" Serge read the answer in Dominique's exasperated look. "No, no, of course you can't." Wringing his hands, he turned aside. "But of course. Of course. So clear now."

"The only thing clear is that you see nothing," Dominique sneered. "Again."

He looked down at Cassidy. So vulnerable and yet so brave. Her spirit was as gentle as it was hardened by experience. Would his sister, Ana, have found such strength within herself if he could have stopped her attackers in time?

Could she have found it had she lived?

The thought of her death didn't overwhelm him with quite the power it usually did. That was past and done. This magical young woman whose very presence blunted so many horrors of his existence, who was aware of him in her blood...she was the present.

He still perceived impressions of her thoughts. Curious, he touched Cassidy's forehead to amplify the effect. A scene playing in her mind flickered to life with startling clarity: snow under an indigo sky, wind whistling through jagged mountain peaks. Cassidy drudged through the drifts, anxious...calling his name.

Ici, chèrie, he thought at her on impulse. *Je suis ici. I am here.*

To his amazement, she calmed. *Finally,* she thought. *I'm glad you're safe.*

Dominique was too stunned to move. This was impossible. This was not how the poison worked, not with humans. Two-way telepathic links happened between blood-drinkers who fed from each other, but never between a blood-drinker and a human. In a human mind, the poison was a means of exerting control, nothing more.

Never this.

Cassidy frowned. Her consciousness separated from the dream and wobbled toward the surface like a disoriented bubble.

"I see it on your face, blood-child. She hears your thoughts," Serge said in an awed whisper. "Rare that. Very rare."

"Stop speaking nonsense." Dominique's frustrated hiss was obliterated by a rumble of thunder. "What does any of this mean?"

Cassidy stirred. As her eyes fluttered open, Serge disappeared into the shadows blanketing the dune, but Dominique heard his delighted cackling—and the words that dropped a lump of ice into his gut.

"It means what I told you from the beginning. She is your key. She unlocks you. She *knows* you."

Dominique tried to look casual as he gazed down at her, though his soul trembled at the notion that she would know what he had truly done.

Cassidy blinked. "What...what happened?"

What indeed. Keeping his face averted from the flashlight's beam, he assumed a cocky attitude. "I kissed you senseless, and you liked it."

The hoped-for retort didn't materialize. She said nothing as she sat up. Confusion hovered around her like a shroud. "No. Not that." Her eyes cast about, searching, and she whispered, "It felt so real."

"Ah, *chérie.* This is not the reaction I was trying for."

Cassidy gave a small, self-conscious laugh and gathered her hair back into a ponytail, refastening the tie with a twist of her wrist. "All right, all right, Casanova. I admit it. For a guy who doesn't like girls, that was—" She cleared her throat. Heat plumed in her cheeks. "Yeah, that wasn't half bad."

"Only half?"

Her reluctant smile was full of appreciation, melting the apprehension from his heart. His relief was short-lived.

"This is going to sound weird, but...I think I...was dreaming." She paused, chewing her plump lower lip in thought. "Was that just me? It felt like maybe...I don't know."

The wise thing would have been to shrug and brush her questions aside. But the experience affected her deeply enough to risk mentioning it, even though it was so improbable. If he dismissed her now, she might well withdraw what little trust she granted him. And that, he knew, he could not endure.

"What was this dream?"

"That...I wasn't alone."

Dominique sensed the web of memory mesh behind her eyes. He watched and waited, already tasting ashes in his mouth.

Encouraged by his silence, she added, "It was like being inside a cocoon of some sort. Very peaceful."

Relief surged through him. No, she wasn't telling him everything, but neither was she afraid. She knew him as no mortal ever had and lived to tell him so.

What would she recall later? How much of his true self had she sensed? When would she know the first whispers of genuine terror? *Not tonight. Please, not tonight.*

Though he was going to tell her tonight—or at least some of where his journey into darkness began—but she had surprised him with her reaction, her own past, her request. She had surprised him with her kiss. She even surprised him when he fed.

"You are a strange woman," he murmured. "I kiss you like you have never been kissed, and all you have to say is that it was...peaceful? I may be eternally wounded."

A shy smile curved her full, soft mouth, and he ached to kiss her again. Just a kiss, just a touch, just a moment of that indescribable harmony. He didn't dare act on the impulse, though. One near disaster was enough for tonight.

"Um, yeah. About that." She scrunched up her face. "Hate to tell you...friend...that didn't feel all that platonic."

"It wasn't," he purred, throwing himself into this far safer topic with abandon.

"So...you changed your mind about trying to seduce me, then? But I thought...well, this would be so much easier if you were gay," she finished, visibly deflating and radiating a confused mixture of disappointment and desire.

"I appreciate beauty in all its forms," he said, choosing his words carefully. "I take my pleasure where I find it." This had been true of his life before, and it was true still. Only now his pleasures cost lives.

"You're a strange man, Dominique," she mused.

"The strangest, truly."

Lightning split the roiling darkness, washing the beach in a series of blinding flashes. Cassidy leapt to her feet. "The storm. We need to get inside. C'mon."

Dominique's eyes watered with pain from the flashes of brilliance. By the time he regained his vision, she stood over him with the flashlight. "Any day now, Casanova."

Still preoccupied, Dominique let her lead the way back to the cottage. Serge trailed behind them, humming sea shanties. Fierce gusts of wind barreled off the heaving water, carrying clouds of salty spray. They whistled through the Australian pines and thrashed the sea grape shrubs. The storm promised to be powerful, a fair match to the turmoil in his heart.

But nothing compared to what waited for them back at the cottage.

A small, white sports car sat in the crumbling driveway. A man in khaki shorts and a yellow polo shirt paced beside it, a cell phone pressed to his ear.

Cassidy stopped in her tracks. "Oh my God. Jackson."

20

THINGS NOT SAID

The temptation to walk up to Jackson with an obscenely good-looking, scantily attired Frenchman in tow was almost more than Cassidy could resist. Much less tempting was having to deal with Jackson's inevitable reaction. The less they had to discuss, the faster he would leave.

She hoped.

"Ah *chère*, you wound me again," Dominique said when she asked him to stay out of sight.

"I couldn't explain you if I talked all night." Not to Jackson. Hell, right now, she wasn't sure she could explain him to herself.

"Cassidy? Is that you?" Jackson shouted over the rising wind.

"Do me this favor, Dominique. As a friend. I'll send him away as quickly as I can."

Without waiting for a response, she jogged toward the cottage and into the light shining from its front windows.

"Cass. Thank God." Jackson scooped her up, smothering the breath out of her with a massive hug. She went stick stiff in his arms. "I was about to call 911."

"What are you doing here?" she squeaked, pushing at his chest until he let her go.

"They upgraded this thing to a tropical storm an hour ago. You didn't answer your phone or my texts. I had to make sure you're all right."

His worry struck a small, guilty chord in her. Still furious with him for spying on her, she had not only ignored his attempts to reach her all day, she had turned off her ringer altogether.

Plus, she had been busy learning self-defense skills from a half-naked, maybe-not-gay man...who then kissed her senseless.

"Right. Sorry," she muttered, pulling the mobile out of her pocket long enough to see notifications scrolling off the bottom. "I guess I didn't hear my phone over all the noise on the beach."

Jackson glanced around. "What the hell are you doing out here?"

She shrugged. "Watching the storm come in over the ocean?"

"What? Alone? At night?" He looked incredulous.

"Yes. What of it?"

"This is serious weather, Cass," he said tersely. "You don't go for a stroll in it. Especially not by yourself in the middle of the night, twenty fucking miles from nowhere."

"And surprise, surprise, I'm perfectly fine anyway." *I think.* "I'm going inside now to avoid getting hit by lightning. And you should leave."

When she tried to pass him, he grabbed her arm. "No, you're obviously not fine. I know you, babe. This isn't you. You're not this stupid."

"Are you seriously calling me stupid now?"

"What? No." He let go of her and made a calming gesture with one hand that even in this low light looked forced. "Honestly, I'm only here because I was worried sick about you."

Thunder rumbled, rising over the roar of the surf like a mountain on the move. The ominous sound vibrated through her.

"Well, as you can see, I survived my very dangerous nighttime expedition to the beach. Now you better go before the weather really hits."

Jackson didn't. He looked pained. "Actually, I think it's time for you to come home with me. This storm is coming this way now and building faster than they predicted. There's no telling how strong it'll be when it gets here. And this—" He waved at the cottage. "This may not..."

Cassidy followed his gaze...and gaped. There on the porch, silhouetted against the lit living room window, a familiar figure leaned on the railing. *Freaking bastard.*

"This house has survived worse," the figure said, sounding just this side of bored. "Are you not going to invite your guest in, *chèrie?* This is no night to be outdoors."

Jackson propped his hands on his hips. "Who the hell are you?"

"I am Dominique. I live here."

Jackson glanced back at Cassidy as though expecting her to deny those words.

She didn't. She couldn't. She huffed an exasperated breath. "My landlord."

"And roommate," Dominique clarified, his voice dripping with smug satisfaction.

Jackson headed for the cottage with a determined stride. Cassidy trailed after him. He came to a halt on the top step to stare at Dominique who turned enough for the light to edge part of his angular face.

Though she couldn't imagine how he'd moved this fast, he now wore a pair of snug black jeans and a dress shirt, also black, unbuttoned to mid-chest, long sleeves rolled up his muscular forearms. The wind fluttered the silky fabric around his torso and tousled his black hair. He could not have looked more devastatingly attractive.

"I see," Jackson said, sounding dazed.

Cassidy leapt at the chance to take control of the situation. "Dominique, this is Jackson Striker. He was just leaving." She fiddled with the ring on her finger. If ever there was a time to give it back, this was it.

Dominique's eyes flickered to her. "Your fiancé, *non?* Or perhaps not?" he added with a knowing, suggestive tone that made her face burn.

Jackson bristled beside her. "So. This is *Nicky*, is it? Nice."

Dominique looked the other man over and arched a critical brow. "So this is the brave Jackson Striker. *Charmant.*"

"You're a...guy."

One corner of Dominique's mouth tugged upward. "You noticed."

"Delightful company you keep these days, Cassidy. Do you think you might have mentioned this?"

"It's not what you think. He's letting me rent a room cheap. That's all." She stopped toying with the ring. This situation had reached critical mass. Insisting he take it back now could turn it nuclear.

Jackson didn't look away from Dominique for even a second. "Really? And why would you do a silly thing like that? What's your interest in my fiancée that you would let her disturb your peace all the way out here?"

With arms crossed, Dominique leaned his shoulder against a porch post and slanted her a quizzical look. "You must know how stubborn she can be. She wanted to stay with me. Who am I to argue with such determination to get away from you?"

Damn it, what do you think you're doing? Cassidy placed a calming hand on Jackson's arm. The frantic ticking of his pulse beneath her fingers made her speak with care. "Don't let him get to you, Jack. He's obnoxious by nature."

"I'm French," Dominique clarified without missing a beat.

"And gay," she snapped.

He leveled one of those heart-stopping smiles at her. "But you like that about me, *non?*"

"Oh, gay!" Jackson burst out. "Is that it? Well, that makes everything all right then, doesn't it?"

"Jack, will you listen to yourself? What's gotten into you?" Cassidy said, bewildered by his escalating reaction. Of course, he wouldn't shrug off the woman he was ostensibly still engaged to living with a strange man out in the middle of nowhere, but going postal on the guy after a reasonable explanation? She'd seen Jackson lose it once before when he hammered her attackers with his meaty fists. She knew he skated awfully close to that edge now.

And this time, she also knew, he kept a handgun in his car.

Definitely *not* the moment to give him back that damn ring.

Dominique produced a cigarette from somewhere and lit it with an impatient flick of his lighter. Sheltered in his cupped hand, the orange flare cast his features in eerie shadows.

"Please don't make a big deal out of this, Jackson," she tried again. "It's not worth it."

"Are you out of your mind? What am I supposed to think of—?" He trailed off to watch Dominique exhale a long stream of smoke as though he had never seen anyone do such a thing.

"Such delicious fighting," Dominique murmured. "If you and Cassidy are going to have make-up sex, may I join?"

Cassidy gasped. "What the hell is wrong with you?"

He gestured at Jackson with the cigarette. "He may have no balls, but he might be fun. You tell me?"

Jackson's muscles bunched under Cassidy's hand. Veins protruded from his neck and forehead. At this point, she had half a mind to punch Dominique herself—if not for her recent first-hand knowledge of what an Aikido black belt was capable of. Armed with nothing but his temper, Jackson was hopelessly outmatched.

Unless he went for his gun.

"Cassidy, do you have any idea—?" Jackson began, hoarse and red-faced with fury. He finally met her eyes. "Do you have *any* idea what this is doing to me?"

"Prude." Dominique sniffed.

"Stop it, both of you," Cassidy ordered, slapping her hand on Dominique's chest and inserting herself between them. "I'm sorry, Jack. I didn't mean to upset you. But for now, I'm living with a first-class jerk. Deal with it. God knows, I've had to."

Jackson grabbed both her arms. "Come home with me, babe. Right now. We'll work everything out. I promise."

For the space of several heartbeats, she considered agreeing. Never had she seen him so desperate, so unreasonable.

Lightning cracked through the sky, washing the scene in a harsh flicker that revealed the truth. Despite his impassioned words, there was no love in that desperation, only anger. He was practically snarling with it.

Thunder rattled the glass in the windows and vibrated in her bones. "I'm not going anywhere with you."

His grip tightened. A moment later, spiraling her arms up and out, Cassidy shook him off with one of the simpler Aikido moves Dominique had drilled into her. Surprised, Jackson stepped back and staggered over the missing porch step, nearly taking a tumble. After he regained his footing, he stood in the yard and looked up with an expression of bewildered fury. "Don't do this. You don't want to stay here. It's dangerous here." As if to underscore the point, more lightning split the sky, followed by the first fine spattering of rain.

She backed into Dominique and fought to keep her voice from trembling. "Then you should leave. Now."

"I won't leave you here," he insisted, starting toward her.

"She does not want to go with you." The soft but unmistakable menace in Dominique's tone startled her and stopped Jackson mid-step.

Cassidy rubbed the goosebumps on her arms. "I'll be fine, Jack. Just go."

Jackson looked like a bottled explosion in want of a corkscrew. Again she thought of the gun he kept in his car and remembered Dominique's words about there being no defense against a bullet.

"Please?" she cajoled.

"What the fuck, Cassidy." He shook his head as if trying to dislodge something from his brain. "You seriously want to stay here? In this dump? With this...this asshole?"

"For now, yes. Yes, I do."

Dominique shifted his weight behind her. "I wonder what that says about you, Jackson Striker."

"Or you," Jackson countered.

"Okay, that's it," she declared. Whatever was going on, the high-voltage tension humming between the two men crawled all over her skin. "I've had about enough of this pissing contest. Jackson, you need to go. We can talk about this when you've cooled off."

He seemed in a mood to try dragging her away again, but he raised his hands in a gesture of reluctant surrender. "Okay. If you're sure. Fine." He took several steps backward. "I'll call you tomorrow."

Hard rain swept in on a cool gust, and Jackson hurried to fold himself into the sports car. Then he sat, staring at them through the windshield. He did not, to Cassidy's immense relief, reach for his gun.

"He is not for you," Dominique murmured. "He does not know you."

"Oh, and you do? If you did, you wouldn't be here right now." She reached over, snatched the cigarette out of his fingers and flung it into the rain. "Would it have killed you to stay out of sight? To say nothing and not push every button I didn't even know he had? What the hell were you thinking? Right now, I swear, I don't like you. At all."

Dominique remained silent and unmoving as they watched the Audi rumble to life. The glaring LED headlights swept over them before cutting into the darkness of the narrow road. Within seconds, all traces of Jackson vanished into the night and an onslaught of rain.

Bone-deep weariness sucked at her limbs. Cassidy paused at the door on her way inside. "Just stay out of my way."

She didn't expect a reply. And she didn't wait for one.

21

This Dream

Cassidy's words echoed in Dominique's heart like a curse. He deserved her contempt, but he could have done nothing other than what he did. More than anything, he needed Cassidy to stay. Never could he allow Jackson Striker to persuade her away, or even threaten to take her by force. That man was a spoiled brute, entirely unworthy of her.

He stood in the dark, listening to her steps retreat up the stairs, letting the wind-driven rain swirl around him. Another presence climbed over the far rail of the porch and shook itself, flinging water in every direction.

"Wet," Serge declared with heartfelt disgust.

"Your powers of observation are staggering."

"Yes, yes, they are," he agreed as he settled himself. He had lost the new shoes, Dominique noted, as well as several buttons from his shirt.

"I am in no mood to deal with your insanity tonight. Either be still or find a hole to crawl into."

Serge chuckled. "Ah, young one. Your patience is gone, but no one lies dead. You're learning."

Dominique gave a derisive snort. "You would have stopped me."

Curtains of rain whipped around the cottage. Wind rushed in tormented trees.

"Maybe."

He narrowed his eyes at the wretch dripping in an Adirondack chair. "*Maybe?*"

"Some things, blood-child, have to play out as they will. Like you and he."

"This hot-head and I? You see a future for us?" he mocked, then added on a darker note, "It will be very brief. That I can promise."

"Your shadows overlap."

Dominique clenched his teeth against demanding specifics and impatiently swiped at the wet hair hanging in his face. "You are useless. *Complètement.*"

Serge chuckled. "But you made no bodies tonight. Whose fault is that?"

"*Oui.* It is your fault that I am hungry."

Serge growled with satisfaction, but said no more. That Cassidy lived tonight because of Serge was understood—as was Dominique's gratitude.

After a while, Dominique found himself in the other chair, his companion all but forgotten as the storm moaned around the cottage.

With part of his awareness, he listened to the house creaking under the assault, ready to leap into action should serious damage occur. The rest of him puzzled over the riddle of Jackson. For all the time he had spent with Cassidy, for all the supposed depth of their relationship, he seemed not to understand her driving need to be her own person. No supernatural insights were required to see how Jackson trying to exert his will over her only pushed her away faster. And yet, the man seemed anything but stupid.

The storm still rumbled across the sodden land an hour before dawn, but the torrential rains finally eased to a determined drizzle. During the night, an already leaning trunk of a towering cabbage palm gave up the fight against the winds and crashed to the ground across the mouth of the driveway, cutting off the cottage from the rest of the world. Dominique roused himself and went to heave it aside.

For a while, he stood and let the darkness embrace him. But the peace he longed for would not come. He was a raw nerve standing there with rain dripping from his face, and his clothes soaked through.

When he returned, Serge still sat in his chair and stared into space, expression blank, lost in his private madness. Dominique passed him without comment and entered the house.

Power had gone out, killing all the annoying electronic hums. Only the sounds of a sleeping woman's soft breathing filled the uneasy gloom. He stepped into the tub in the downstairs bathroom and let scalding water pound over him. The heat warmed him, making him feel almost human.

He lathered and washed. When he found his cock swelling in his grip, he lingered there and recalled with perfect clarity the soft weight of her in his arms, her willing mouth on his, her sighs against his face. The beast did not begrudge him this meager comfort. Without the presence of a human's mind and blood, it cared nothing for what he did or experienced.

When he finished, Dominique pressed his forehead against the cold tiles. Despair dragged at his heart. An eternity of nights spent battling the hunger and jacking off in the shower is all he could look forward to. Though perhaps now that she had declared her unqualified dislike of him, eternity would not be all that long.

He toweled off as his thoughts raced on. He never wanted to know her fear, but was her disgust—not of the beast, but of him, the man—any easier to bear? It shouldn't matter. She would never meet the human version of Dominique Marchant. That man was dead. And yet...

Seconds later, he slipped through her door. The cat's head popped up. It retreated beneath the bed with its usual haste.

Cassidy lay among mounds of rumpled sheets, evidence of restless sleep and troubled dreams. The windows stood propped open to random gusts of damp sea air, which cooled the room, now that the air conditioning was out. The only thing covering her was a faded yellow shirt emblazoned with a sleeping kitten. "I don't do mornings," the lettering declared, making him smile.

With no particular intent, Dominique crept into the bed beside her. He moved closer and inhaled her natural perfume. With his expanding vision, he basked in the web of swirling golden life surrounding her.

Her eyes opened, blind in the darkness, then closed again. She reached out one hand, let it brush against his face, and mumbled, "You promised not to come in here."

"Please don't hate me," he whispered. His heart pinched with regret and fear. He had rarely felt so helpless.

She didn't reply, drifting near sleep and then rousing again when he nuzzled into her hair, inhaling deeply.

This time, when she touched him, her fingers lingered on his face. Imagery flowed from the physical contact and swamped his awareness, and he saw himself as she had seen him in the oasis—on his knees, staring up at her in shock, the beast in his eyes.

"I don't hate you." Her whispered words echoed in their incredible link, and his heart unclenched ever so slightly.

"Do you want me to leave?"

Again that long, long pause. "No."

She believed she was dreaming. It did feel like a dream, even to him. The beast slept, and in its place, the man rose.

She caressed his face, her desire filling his mind, her breath brushing his shoulder. He wept when she kissed his cheek.

It means nothing, he chided himself. *She does not know the real you. Or that you are truly here.*

But oh, to be part of this dream...

Taking his face in both hands, she kissed his mouth in a slow, bold, soul-deep way that left him weak with need. For one sweet moment, he let her. For one sweet moment, he allowed himself to believe this was real.

For one sweet moment...he was human.

Then she pressed her soft warmth against him. His recently satisfied cock stirred—and with it the hunger. His humanity slipped. Pulsing rivers of blood now glowed beneath her skin.

Somewhere nearby, Serge growled a warning. Dominique ignored it.

What he couldn't ignore was the searing pain against his cheek.

With a gasp, Dominique broke the kiss and pulled her hands off his face. The engagement ring glinted. *Silver.* In casual contact, silver caused little more than a tingle. Pressed against his skin like this, the metal caused stinging blisters to erupt.

He set his jaw hard. Jackson's ring had saved her—from him.

"I'm sorry, Dominique." Cassidy sank into her pillows with a weary sigh. "I'm sorry I'm a girl."

"*Non...*" He stopped himself. What could he say that wouldn't break this spell? Or promise what he could never deliver? Her breathing deepened as she drifted back to sleep, back to dreams he could sense as being colored by longing and edged with regret.

He kissed her forehead before reluctantly sliding out of bed.

Serge hovered in the doorway, ready to yank him from the brink of disaster. Dominique shoved past him. The patter of bare feet followed him downstairs.

"You did well, blood-child."

"*Connerie,*" he hissed. "She is no longer safe with me. I want her too much."

"But you need her. She..."

"What I need is for you to go away. I will not go near her again tonight." Only because mere minutes of night remained.

Leaving Serge by the front door, Dominique turned down the hall—and stopped. When he was here to change his clothes earlier, he had moved too fast to notice, but something was off.

Something about the angle of the door. Something about...he lifted his chin and scented the air, half hopeful, half terrified. But it wasn't Cassidy's scent that lingered in his sanctuary.

It was Jackson's.

Quickly, every nerve in his body buzzing with alarm, Dominique moved through the room, smelling for traces of the man. There were few—the door, the light switch, handles on several dresser drawers, a hint on the hilt of the *katana*—but they were strong and deeply offensive. Of course, he would have searched the house for Cassidy earlier, but this small, shuttered space held enough interest to distract him from her possible troubles. Why?

Suddenly Dominique regretted having so little control that it never even occurred to him to "speak" with Jackson in private, to have his blood and know his mind. The beast only wanted to rip open his throat and be done with him. It still did. Now more than ever.

"It's getting late, blood-child."

Dominique whirled around with a warning snarl. Serge stood just inside the door, looking as inoffensive as it was possible for a soggy derelict blood-drinker to look.

"Who do you smell in here?"

Serge didn't meet his eyes.

"Did you know about this? Did you know he would invade my lair?"

A slow shrug.

"Of course you didn't." Serge had been on the beach, watching over Cassidy the entire time. He wouldn't have been aware of Jackson at the cottage any more than Dominique was. "You want this to 'play out as it will,' do you? Then let it. Tonight, I will find Jackson Striker, have his blood, and know his mind. Consequences be damned."

"But you already know his mind."

Dominique opened his mouth to fling another retort, but then he froze, his world tilting. He had seen, heard, and smelled everything about the man, and only one explanation made any kind of sense at all. "He...knows."

Serge bobbed his head. "He does."

Stunned, Dominique sat on the edge of his bed. "But how is that possible?" His sire hadn't been big on giving instructions, but about one thing he had been very clear—no human could ever know of them and be allowed to live.

Serge snorted. "So much more is possible than you can comprehend, young one. But for now—" He held out his hand. "Come spend the day with me in the ground. You are no longer safe here."

The sun was close. Too close. Already he could feel his body growing sluggish, and the thought of leaving his sanctuary filled him with dread. Serge, with his greater age and strength, could function for a few more minutes and could help him find new cover in the ground—like a corpse.

Dominique didn't move.

It was a good day to die, and a good way, too. Perhaps Jackson would spare Cassidy the truth about his fate. Perhaps he would let her remember her obnoxious French roommate only at his best. Remember the kiss that would be the last glimmer of joy he would ever know.

An otherworldly calm settled over him. "I will stay here."

Serge made a panicked little sound.

"This will play out as it will, *mon ami*." Dominique stretched out on the mattress, his energy draining away as fast as water from a sieve. "Watch over her for me," he whispered.

Then the memory of her kiss enveloped him and carried him into oblivion.

22

Island Tales

Jackson needed the bastard alive.

That was the only reason he wasn't back at Cassidy's place right now, taking the initiative, putting down that bloodsucker holed up with her. Instead, he paced the Foundation's library, nursing impatience, waiting for Uncle Garrett.

Controlling a live vampire required the Foundation's more specialized facilities—to which only Garrett had access. Garrett, unfortunately, was also the man of the hour in his official capacity as SICI's Director of Security.

Jackson balled his fists with impotent frustration. Last night's harrowing encounter still twanged in his nerves. The shuttered bedroom should have been a clue. Yet the idea of a vampire sharing its lair with Cassidy was so outlandish, he couldn't entertain it until he stood face-to-face with the creature and got a good look at that too-flawless skin and those too-penetrating eyes. And the attitude.

Obviously, Cassidy was compelled to stay there. Yet even Jackson, who knew her so well, hadn't recognized the effect. She didn't come across as distracted or confused or like someone coerced to act against their interests. The compulsion was deep, evidence of unusual skill. And the fact Jackson had walked away from the confrontation, even though completely unprepared, proved his own self-control under pressure.

Both his father and uncle were wrong about him. Jackson Striker was ready to hunt. He was more than ready. He only needed to nail down his uncle long enough to make that clear.

The opportunity presented itself moments later when the electronic lock unlatched, and Garrett strode into the room like a remnant of the storm itself. "Is this where you've been hiding all day?"

"Waiting for you, yes. You said two hours five hours ago."

"That damn tree took out a corner of the roof and four windows. Niagara Falls ran through the building half the night. Freaking controlled chaos this morning, because there's too damn much money on the line to be closed on a Monday. Everybody was there."

Garrett dropped into the leather executive chair behind the main desk, every line of his trim physique radiating impatience. "Everybody was there *except*, of course, the future president of the company. Don't think that wasn't noticed, kid. Your father's going to tear a chunk out of you the size of Texas when he gets his hands on you. I can promise you that."

"There's work to be done for the Foundation. There are lives at stake."

"Sorry to tell you this, but sometimes the hunt has to take a backseat. When our resources are threatened here at home, a vampire halfway around the world gets a break."

"How about one in fucking driving distance?"

This gave Garrett pause. His sharp gaze narrowed. "Did I miss an alert from the Grid?"

"This is way off the Grid, trust me. If the Grid knew about this, it would stroke out."

"Skip the drama. If you're sitting on something critical, why didn't you say so?"

"Oh, I don't know, Uncle. Maybe because you cut me off in mid-sentence when I called? And could it be you haven't checked your voice mail because you saw I called, and what could I possibly have to say that's in any way important?"

Garrett let out a long breath. "Very well then. Let's hear what you've got, and make it good."

Jackson sat on the edge of the desk, turned the keyboard around, and typed the codes that brought up his research. He had put the last pieces together early this morning to complete a picture that would take the Foundation to maximum alert.

"We don't have much time, but you're going to have to hear this to fully appreciate it."

He explained his new search method, the algorithms that scanned historical data for markers of vampire activity and connected them by proximity and similarities. As the trail of red dots plotted out on the screen, Garrett retrieved a pair of reading glasses from a drawer and leaned forward as he put them on.

"About two decades is as far back as we can go before the data becomes too fragmented, but there's no reason to think this activity pattern didn't start much earlier. Centuries for all we know." While Jackson called up various supporting documents and images in one window, the dots kept popping up like drops of blood on the other, annotated with dates and numbers dead and missing, all along the world's coastlines. Eventually, they crept up the eastern shores of South America, into the Caribbean, and stopped at Grand Cayman, south of Cuba.

"While some of these were blips on the Grid, the delay in getting data from these remote places always kept the probability low. But over time, the pattern becomes obvious. Everything points to one or more vampires traveling, siring younglings as they go. Given the locations and time frames, I'd say by boat."

Garrett dropped his readers on the desk and rubbed the bridge of his nose. "All right. Nice detective work. But the last bit of information you have here is six months old. What does any of this have to do with...driving distance?"

"Possibly a great deal."

"Possibly? Jack, I've been up all night and all day. I don't have the patience to play games."

"And I've never been more serious. About anything. There's more. Lots more. Do I have your attention, or am I doing this on my own?"

Garrett heaved another sigh, then slid his glasses back on his nose. "Continue."

Jackson forced himself to calm down. This was too important. "Going north, Cuba would have been the next logical place for them to strike, but that's a digital blind spot for us. And here in Florida..." He trailed off meaningfully.

His uncle gave him an exasperated look. "There's no way you can spin the gang war killings to fit this."

"Maybe. Maybe not. A moot point, in any case." Jackson still believed those fatalities to be vampire victims, but he had no concrete evidence to pin them on his primary suspect. Which didn't matter since said suspect was practically in custody already.

He pressed a key, and the blood-spattered map zoomed in on one particular dot marking a tiny Caribbean island. "St. Barts is where things get interesting. What happened there and when it happened, nail it down as a place where our traveling ghouls dropped anchor."

"Over a year ago."

Jackson ignored the dismissive snort and spoke with all the conviction of certain knowledge. This was so much more than a youngling vampire playing at being human, and he would make damn sure Garrett understood the full magnitude of what he had uncovered. To that end, he laid out his evidence as though in a court of law.

Exhibit A was Jean-Paul Marchant—handsome, olive-skinned and middle-aged—successful restaurateur and father of three, found by his wife one evening without his head. Three weeks later, Jean-Paul's youngest daughter, Anastasie, met the same fate.

Garrett's face went hard with disgust as he studied the gruesome crime scene photos. He would recognize them, as Jackson had, as classic vampire victims. "What a waste."

"It gets better." Jackson called up Exhibit B: an image of a woman whose voluptuous beauty and seductive smile were instantly recognizable even to a pop culture Luddite like Garrett Striker.

"That's that actress who got killed there, isn't it?"

"Yes. Jeovana Sebastini, Italy's rising star." Her naked body washing up on a posh Caribbean beach and the investigation that followed had been international front page news for weeks. Several people were arrested. No one was ever charged.

"Don't tell me she—"

"Was found dead only a day before Anastasie Marchant. Not a drop of blood left in her. She got to keep her head, though, even if her neck was a mess."

He schooled his face into neutrality before paging to Exhibit C. The Dominique he had met was nothing like the tanned and grinning man on the screen now, an equally delighted Jeovana hanging off his arm.

"This is Dominique Marchant, age twenty-seven, Jean-Paul's only son. He was reported missing, presumably kidnapped, the same night his father died." Jackson cycled through a few more images of the couple, mostly long-lens paparazzi shots, each racier than the last. His teeth set hard at the thought of Cassidy in the same house as this cocky Caribbean gigolo. Even if the guy weren't a bloodsucker, Jackson wouldn't want him anywhere near her.

Garrett rubbed his jaw, considering. "So she had a connection to that family when they became victims and became one herself. But why would anyone think her boy toy was kidnapped?"

"Retribution. The week before Dominique disappeared, he came to his sister's defense and ended up killing a guy with ties to the Columbian cartels. With his bare hands." Jackson paused, relishing the rare flash of astonishment on his uncle's face. "Officially, Dominique died about six months after that while trying to escape his captors. Supposedly, there was a gunfight at sea. His body was never recovered, of course."

Garrett looked dubious. "What are you implying? That he was turned? You realize that makes no sense, right, kid?"

"Compared to a Columbian cartel keeping a prisoner on a yacht for six months before blowing his brains out?" To say nothing of a vampire cooking up such an elaborate ruse in the first place.

"That family lost two people to vampires, and the actress clearly got caught in the middle. That can't be a youngling's doing. The sire would never allow it."

"I'm thinking the sire didn't have a choice." He flipped to yet another image of the human Dominique, this time looking fierce in a wide stance and draped in the full black-and-white garb of the Aikido martial arts discipline. His opponent hung suspended in mid-air before him, tumbling on his way to a hard impact with the mat. "Our suspect here's an Aikido black belt, highly disciplined. Though I'm guessing he lost it when he killed one of the guys he caught raping his sister, Anastasie."

Jackson said it without emotion, but somewhere in the pit of his stomach bloomed the reluctant recognition that he could well do the same for his sister, Samantha. He nearly had for Cassidy. He shoved the wellspring of sympathetic rage back down beneath the icy calm of the hunt. "If you add that skill set to the strength and speed of a vampire, what you get is—"

"A youngling on steroids."

"Operating independently of a sire, yes. Or at least trying to, and capable enough to avoid getting put down by either the sire or anyone else who might object." Like that piece of work that had attacked Cassidy on the beach. That one seemed too unhinged to be the mastermind of such a sophisticated pattern, much less sire someone like Dominique. But chances were good that his presence was no accident. He had to be part of whatever game was afoot between the youngling and his sire. He had to be part of their nest.

"Interesting theory."

"No, not theory. Fact. And not even the most interesting one." Jackson leaned forward, moving in on his virtual kill. "I've seen evidence that he's a master of compulsions and can already feed without taking lives." He would have to if he operated with no sire to control him. And that he fed from Cassidy was indisputable; no bloodsucker would waste such an opportunity. Plus, she had looked a tad pale last night.

Then there was the whole cigarette smoke thing. No vampire could stand being near the stuff, yet this one sucked it down on purpose. What the fuck was that about?

"It takes years for them to master those skills," Garrett said, searching his nephew's face with increasing interest. "Unless—"

"Unless the sire is stronger than anything we've seen in a hundred years."

Garrett became still.

The young ones, hungry and undisciplined, were easy to track, trap, and destroy. But the old ones were the Foundation's ultimate targets. They could vanish for centuries, killing at leisure and spawning armies of new monsters to prey on the living. They often passed great strength to their younglings, making them equally difficult to locate and destroy within a very short time. Old vampires were like an undetected cancer in the body of humanity. The mere suspicion of one in their sights was monumental.

It took under half a minute on the grandfather clock before Garrett added it all up. "You're saying an ancient vampire is traveling the world by boat, and...is here? How can you be so sure?"

Jackson smiled with satisfaction as he glanced at Dominique on the monitor, then back to the man who looked at him as though he had never seen his nephew before.

"You and Dominique should meet. Today."

23

Unresolved Mysteries

Dominique woke, still drifting in the peace of his conviction that he would never wake again, and decided Jackson Striker was useless. Either the man didn't understand half of what Dominique gave him credit for, or his intentions were not as hostile as they appeared. As the latter seemed unlikely, Jackson must be as clueless as he was useless. He allowed himself a groan of sheer misery, but stopped when he detected the aromas of a kitchen in high gear accompanied by the familiar clattering of pots and utensils. Beneath it all, Cassidy's heartbeat thumped, relaxed as she worked against a backdrop of American country music.

With a brief touch of his lips, he recalled the passionate kiss in her bed this morning and smiled. She may well remember it as a dream, but remember it she would. So did he. He also remembered how close he had come yet again to doing her irreparable harm.

His good spirits fading, he sat up and looked around. No trace of Serge. He had half-feared the lunatic would carry him away and bury him in the dune, but there hadn't been time. Dominique was still here, another night alive and faced with a quandary he could no longer escape. He wanted her—*needed* her—like living things require air. That these feelings were mutual to some degree was obvious from her dreams, her touch...her kiss.

But what if she acted on those impulses while wide awake? He could not risk responding to her. He could not be a true mate to her, and it was unforgivably selfish to seduce her away from a man who could, even if that man was an idiot. What to do about this, though? He didn't know.

He shrugged into his sweats and a fresh T-shirt, finger-combed his hair and confirmed the cigarettes and lighter in his pocket before heading for the kitchen.

He got as far as the hall.

The enormous black-and-white cat lay flat on its belly, pawing with intent savagery beneath the door to the laundry closet and oblivious to the blood-drinker standing over it. Dominique watched it work and felt a pang of sympathy for the little hunter. Prey was so close, yet out of reach.

He helpfully pushed open the door, and the cat pounced. Then hissed. And growled. A long black ribbon of muscle shot out and serpentined down the hall. The little hunter bounded after the snake, swatting and snapping at the slithering tail.

"Eddie? What're you doing?"

Before Cassidy could step into the hall, Dominique moved with lightning speed and grabbed the intruder's head. The serpent coiled around his arm, frantic. The cat looked up, astonished.

"You're welcome," he told it.

Cassidy skidded to a halt. "Oh my God. How did that get in here?"

Realizing what had happened, the feline predator relinquished the prize. It trotted away, moving upstairs with an unhappy grumble. Dominique watched it go with a rush of unexpected pleasure at the little brother's irritation instead of terror. Something had changed, and he was fairly certain it wasn't the cat.

"I don't even want to know how you can touch that thing," Cassidy said with a shudder. "Well, don't just stand there. Get it out of here." She made shooing motions toward the door as she retreated.

When Dominique stepped onto the porch, he spotted Serge moving in the shadows. His face popped over the rail, all smiles.

"Blood-child, you survived the day."

Dominique tossed the snake into the bushes behind Serge. "You were wrong, old fool," he said under his breath. "Jackson is even more useless than you."

He didn't wait for a reply before returning indoors.

"Thanks for taking care of that," Cassidy called over her shoulder as she worked at the stove.

"Thank your cat. He found it."

He moved closer. Two pots boiled vigorously, one steaming vegetables, the other agitating a sack of boil-in-bag rice. The oven, too, was in use. Inside, he spied four servings of salmon and crabmeat rolls, ready-made by the local supermarket, judging by the discarded packaging on the counter. An enormous leap forward from macaroni and cheese. He was inclined to be impressed.

"I know. Sometimes I wish he wouldn't be so good at tracking those critters down. If I don't see it, I'd be happy not knowing about half the stuff that gets in here."

Dominique's smile tasted bitter in his mouth. "I'm sure that some things he finds...you do not see."

She gave him a searching look, but said nothing.

He opened the refrigerator and retrieved a bottle of Perrier. Of all the things he had enjoyed before, this was the only one left to him. More or less. He would have preferred the softer San Benedetto sparkling water from his restaurant days, but this worked well enough. The bubbles soothed him, and he found that water lessened the need for blood. His Perrier habit saved lives.

For a while, he watched her poke at the rice bag and the vegetables as though the constant attention would speed up their cooking. Muscles flexed in her sun-darkened arms, and her half-gathered, copper-shot lion's mane brushed bare shoulders. A navy-blue tank top hugged her torso, delineating the lines of her back. A skirt of tie-died turquoise reached to her ankles. Sand clung to her heels.

He took a tentative breath, seeking her scent. The baking fish smothered the air, but he caught the distinctive fragrance of her blood—and immediately wished he hadn't. *Merde*, he was hungry.

It would be better to leave. Now. Let her assume he was still put out about the events of last night. Let her believe he was moody, temperamental, and reprehensible. All that was true enough and would only be fair to her. But he remained rooted to the spot. He needed to hear her speak her mind tonight, understand what conclusions she had reached during the day.

Preoccupied with her cooking, she held her silence.

"No microwave?" he prompted. "No macaroni and cheese?"

"I know you don't like either." She hesitated. "I doubt this is up to your standards, but I'm hoping you'll cut me some slack."

"It is a commendable effort. Are you expecting company?"

"Why? So you can pick a fight with them, too?" she wondered without turning from the stove.

He leaned against the kitchen counter, half-crossing his arms, swirling the bottle as he struggled to formulate the apology she deserved and which he was unable to voice. He wasn't at all sorry for antagonizing the man who claimed her, and he would not stand here and say otherwise.

"You're still upset."

Her shoulders drooped a bit. "No, I'm not. I should be, but I'm not." She shot him a brief glance, taking in his surprised expression. "Jackson was as big an ass as you were. I have never seen him like that, but I have some idea where he's coming from. What I can't figure out, though...is you."

"*Moi*?"

"*Oui*. You." She turned to face him now, clutching the wooden spoon in one hand. "What were you thinking? After I asked you to stay out of sight, why were you there anyway? And why did you provoke Jackson like that?"

"Is that truly such a mystery?"

She shook her head. "I know what it looked like, but...no, I don't know. I thought we were friends. Friends don't go out of their way to wreck each other's relationships."

"Is that what I have done?"

"Is that what you wanted to do?"

To this, he had no answer.

"So what was that?" she asked again, her voice soft with confusion.

He emptied the bottle while wondering what he could tell her that was both true and comprehensible. He needed her and felt as protective of her as he ever had of anyone—even if what he had to protect her from was himself.

That last was no small feat. Only two weeks ago, this scene here with her so close and emotionally raw and him not having hunted in days would have been unthinkable. His ability to deny the beast right now was as remarkable, in its own way, as her attempt at an actual meal.

And somehow, miraculously, they had done this for each other.

He chose his words with care. "I wanted to make sure that this man is worthy...of my friend. She deserves to be cherished."

Her lips flattened, keeping the thoughts whirling behind her eyes from spilling out of her mouth. What finally emerged was, "You don't think he is worthy of me, do you?"

"I think he means well for you." The only positive thing he could get himself to say about Jackson Striker.

Cassidy considered. Then she nodded, a shadow of regret passing over the unsettled oceans of her eyes. "Friends. All right then." She turned back to her pots and away from what was really on her mind and his. "Well, you were a jerk, my friend. But so was Jack, and he's come to his senses, I think. He came by here earlier to apologize in person."

"Did he?"

"He even brought that creep of an uncle with him and made him apologize, too, for how he treated me that night at the house, if you can believe that."

Suddenly, Dominique wasn't sure what to believe about Jackson Striker. "Would it not have been easier to call?"

"Ya think? That was my question, too." She fished the plump-to-bursting bag of rice out of the bubbling pot. "He said they were near my office, and when they didn't find me there, they came here. God, that was awkward." She sliced open the bag and emptied the rice back into the pot. "I managed to get off a little early today so I could get this organized. I hope you're hungry."

"Starving," he said, envisioning Jackson's plump veins.

"Oh, good. The salmon is almost ready."

He blinked. "What? What are you doing?"

"Isn't that obvious?" He stared at her, dumbfounded, and she continued as though speaking to a two-year-old child. "I'm cooking dinner? Jerk or not, I owe you after all you've done for me. So tonight, my friend, I'm going to feed *you* for a change."

He choked down the impulse to laugh. Or cry. He wasn't sure which. He settled on a strangled "I cannot."

"You just said you're starving."

"I have to be somewhere."

She sighed. "Yeah. I wanted to talk to you about that, too."

"About...that?"

"Remember how I said I wanted to help you?"

"You cannot. No one can."

"Well, what if I can?"

His lips twitched. She looked so grim and sure of herself, as though made invincible by the might of her cooking spoon. Though the determined set of her mouth and flashing eyes made him wary. Suddenly she had the air of a lioness stalking prey for more reasons than her unruly hair. "You do *not* know what you are talking about, *mon amie*."

She turned off the stove and oven and came close enough for him to feel her living heat push at him. "What if I do?"

"Then you are a fool for still being here." All his nerves stood on end. *Did* she know? No, she couldn't. She wouldn't offer him regular food if she did. In fact, he wouldn't be standing here; he'd be a pile of ash by the front door.

"No argument there," she said, further confounding him. She put down the spoon, pushed her hair behind her ears, and pressed her hands together before her. The lioness gathered herself to pounce. "Hear me out, please. I think I can help you. But I'll need your help to do it, and I'm guessing that won't be easy for you."

Her heartbeat reverberated in his skull. Hunger sharpened to a fine point in his gut. His voice emerged as a hoarse rasp. "Outside."

From the porch, he scanned the shadows for Serge, Cassidy's guardian angel, but the pest was nowhere to be seen. *Merde.*

He lit a cigarette, feeling her watch him, praying there wasn't enough light for human eyes to see his shaking hands. As she couldn't abide smoke, she kept her distance and her arms firmly crossed with displeasure.

"What is it you think you know?" he said when he felt somewhat sure of himself again.

"I...did some research today. For a story. I found some things from St. Barth."

Alarm zinged through him. "What story?"

"The local gang war." She fell into an expectant silence.

His mind reeled with the implications, refusing to consider the much more unsettling fact of her mentioning his island home. "Why are you writing about that?"

"I suspect that it's not a gang war at all. I think there's something else going on." She hesitated, glancing at the cigarette. "Will you...can we talk about this?"

He flicked a blob of ash to the ground. She knew nothing. He was hungry. He should be gone. "What would this have to do with me?"

"Because of what happened to your family."

His fingers gripped the porch railing so tight the wood creaked in protest. Venomous mists of memory engulfed him. The beast churned. Deliberately keeping his movements to a minimum, he drew hard at the cigarette.

He should have told her to be still, to forget whatever she thought she understood or wanted to do. He should have bent her to his will on this. His sanity depended on it. Instead, it was her voice weaving a spell around him.

"I found the articles about your father and sister in *Le Journal*. Had to use the online translator again, but I got most of it. I can't tell you how sorry I am."

Still, he said nothing.

"I have a theory, Dominique, that what happened there and other islands and what's happening here are related. The...well, there are similarities."

He should leave, but his morbid fascination belonged only to her earnest, innocent voice.

Organized crime, she reasoned, a violent cartel making a play for dominance in international markets. His father must have stumbled on a smuggling operation run by one of his suppliers and paid with his life. Since he, Dominique, had been reported abducted, she reasoned they wanted to use him for their own ends—as a hacker perhaps, or for his martial arts skills. Likely they used his sister Anastasie to coerce him, possibly Jeovana, too, for Cassidy had found the paparazzi pictures of them together. She speculated these women were killed to force his hand, but he got free and now hid from these mysterious perpetrators, probably to keep what remained of his family safe.

He listened, entranced, and as charmed as he was stunned by her absolute conviction of his innocence in all of it.

"So," she concluded. "How close am I to the truth?"

He couldn't keep a facetious smile from forming as he finished the last of the cigarette and stubbed out the butt against the porch rail. She had found the bloody trail to his past, yet the truth escaped her. "What do you propose to do with this theory of yours?"

"I want to propose writing an article about it, throw some light on these connections. The gang wars are already national news, so what I write should get broad attention, too, and stir up some more investigations. These bastards need to be stopped, or at least slowed down. But...I need you to tell me what you know."

He shot her an incredulous look. "You believe I'm being coerced by a criminal organization which thinks nothing of cold-blooded murder, yet you expect me to simply tell you what I know?"

"I wouldn't use your name."

"Ah. I would be an 'anonymous source?'" He gestured vaguely with one hand. "That will not help your credibility, *ma chère*, or keep me safe if what you suspect is true. If such an organization exists, they will notice your reports, consider your *inside* information, and start watching your every move. They will find you, and then they will find me."

"Oh." Her brows drew together at this wrinkle in her logic.

It was a genuine wrinkle. Though not a formal enterprise, "they" existed, and if they had an agenda, it had nothing to do with dominating the world of organized crime. But one of them could well notice her evidence—her so-called anonymous sources—and draw the correct conclusions.

"In any event, I cannot help you," he continued. "There is nothing I can tell you about any of this. Now I have to go." He left her standing there on the porch and went to dress for a night in South Florida's urban jungles.

On his way out, she met him in the living room with a sheaf of papers in her hand. "You're lying to me."

He gave her his most intimidating look, but the foolish girl would have none of it. She had been around him too long, had seen too much of his former self, the self he had resurrected for her and now maintained by the slimmest of margins.

"Dominique, please let me help you. This is eating you alive. No one should have to live like this."

"Write what you will, but leave my family out of it. They have nothing to do with what is happening here, and there is nothing I can tell you."

"If that's true, then why are you here? Why are you here when you should be with your mother and sister who need you more than ever right now?"

"Stop," he snarled. The lioness was going for his proverbial jugular, and it wouldn't take much more before he returned the favor in a literal sense.

She was adamant. "No. I won't. Not until you explain why—if I'm so wrong about everything—you let your family believe *this*." With a snap of her wrist she held up one of her papers, a printout that included his picture. His obituary.

He recoiled even as he admonished himself. He should have seen this coming the moment she mentioned St. Barth.

Her voice lost its strident edge. "If you aren't hiding from something terrible, why does everyone you care about believe you're dead?"

Because I am. Because I should be. He had intended to be dead, truly dead, by now and had made great efforts to create the trail culminating in the obituary she brandished, the closure his mother and sister so desperately needed.

Dominique took a single step forward and leaned his face into hers, capturing and holding her huge blue gaze. He held nothing back, driving the command into her obstinate mind with a virtual sledgehammer of will, her supposed resistance to him be damned. "You will *never* speak of my family again. You will write *nothing* about them or me. Never!"

She flinched, and a slight tremor raced through her body.

Fear.

He spun away. The beast slithered, reared up. What had he done?

"I'm only trying to help." Her voice wobbled near tears.

Dominique savored the memory of her blood, felt the razor edges of his teeth against his lips, and his vision colored in the psychedelic hues of the hunt. All that was human in him drained away and in seconds would be gone completely.

As the hunger surged, he opened the door and flung himself into the night, clinging to one overriding truth. *You will help me,* mon cœur. *When you know what to do.*

24

MISSING INGREDIENTS

Jackson's latex-covered fingers itched to touch—and claim—the samurai *daisho* set hanging on the wall. Like their current owner, these weapons were a deceptively delicate, lethal work of art. He couldn't help but admire the tiny golden dragons tucked in the neat wrapping against the ray skin grips. Or the dragons curling around the brass hand guards. More dragons, rendered in gold, spiraled along the polished ebony scabbards themselves.

Yes, these long, curved blades would be spectacular over the fireplace in the mansion's living room. A worthy trophy of his first kill.

"Don't. Touch. Anything."

Jackson shot an irritated look over his shoulder. "What kind of idiot do you take me for?" Though he had touched the blades, the first time he saw them. Before he knew who owned them. Not something he was about to admit to his uncle.

"Sorry, kid," Garrett said and continued slowly sweeping the HD camera around the room, recording every detail of the vampire's cluttered lair for analysis. "Just making sure. We can't afford to have him catch our scent here. They're like rats. If they smell humans on a trap, they won't go near it."

Jackson turned to the disheveled twin bed. That the vampire spent his days here was obvious—just not today when Cassidy was safely out of the way. Had he been here yesterday when they came to collect his unconscious body and found her all but guarding the place? Or had he, like Garrett warned, already caught Jackson's scent in here and would never return? Did the vampire even suspect what Jackson knew and plotted? That last dire possibility was the only thing that had kept them from pushing in here past Cassidy yesterday. Such an act would not have guaranteed a capture, but would have raised or confirmed plenty of suspicions.

"Fuck," he muttered.

"Patience is mandatory in this business," Garrett said and powered off the camera. "Okay, we're done. Let's go."

Jackson took one last, longing look at the swords and retrieved the rolled body bag sitting by his blue-covered feet. They wouldn't be carrying away any vampires in it today. "Better luck tomorrow."

"Longer than that." Garrett closed the front door behind them, securing the lock he had picked earlier with impressive skill. "Every time we come here and don't find him, we're reinforcing our scent in the air of this place. We don't want to risk driving him away."

Jackson worked his jaw in frustration. "So what? We just wait? How long?"

"At least until I get back from Chile." A jet already waited on standby. The Chile lead had popped up last night, strong and without warning, too good to ignore. And apparently, too good to allow Jackson along for the kill. Though Garrett's official excuse was that with Warren tied up in critical business negotiations all week, someone had to be available to coordinate things in case the Grid popped another hit. Never mind that the Grid reported all the facts to them through their phones.

Jackson tossed the body bag into the back of his uncle's black Cadillac SUV and slammed the hatch. He got in, peeled off the latex gloves and polyethylene shoe-covers and stuffed them into the center console compartment together with Garrett's.

Garrett cursed under his breath as he navigated the behemoth vehicle down the bumpy, narrow lane winding back out to A1A. The encroaching vegetation screeched along the SUV's polished sides like nails down a chalkboard, and Jackson couldn't suppress a smile. There was a reason he suggested taking his little Audi for this mission, and next time they certainly would if for no other reason than that Garrett's living room on wheels would be in the shop getting a fresh coat of paint.

Once they were back on the paved road, Garrett picked up on his nephew's sullen silence. "Promise me you won't do anything stupid while I'm gone."

"How can I?" Jackson snorted. "I'll be too busy being useless."

Garrett regarded him thoughtfully and seemed to make a decision. "Well, maybe not. If you're up for it, there is a bit of field research we need to do."

———————

Cassidy had expected to work hard to prove herself to Dave McKinney. However, that this would require seeing her life flash before her eyes—repeatedly—in the space of one afternoon was a revelation.

After her drive down I-95 and back—through a string of torrential downpours, no less—she returned to the office borderline shell-shocked. But she had her in-person interviews, her pictures, and her seen-it-done-it tale of Garcilla Health Systems in action. To her great relief, most of Garcilla's employees spoke English fine—when they wanted to.

Dave's reaction when she reported in was a grudging half-smile—and two more assignments on stupid-short deadlines.

Do what has to be done, she told herself and marched to her desk.

As she worked, she could feel Jim Lawley seething from across the room. The day she had delivered the original assignment on time and against serious odds, he had thrown a massive, highly unprofessional fit. Not until Dave took him aside and spoke with him in private did he calm down.

If only Jim would stay silent, too. The sniping just kept on coming. The coffee wasn't up to par, there was a typo in an ad she proofed, and dead people weren't getting enough respect around here. Today was no different. Late afternoon found him and his obnoxious cloud of cologne lounging at her cubicle's half wall and revving up the malice. She was looking hassled, he suggested. No surprise. The business could be rough. How long was she planning to struggle on before calling it quits?

Cassidy did her best to ignore him, which only got him more riled up. By the time he told her outright that she was all but taking food off his family's table by "stealing" his assignments, he had worked himself into a red-faced lather. She pretended to keep working, grateful he wasn't able to see her screen where she was by then furiously typing nonsense. No way in hell would she give him the satisfaction of a response.

Jim was comical, she told herself, compared to that high-strung roommate she had to deal with. A whining mosquito, nothing more. It didn't help. *Breathe, Chandler. In with the nose. Out with the mouth.* She winced. Damn that Frenchman for being the one whose voice she would hear right now.

The rest of the cubicle farm was silent. Twenty coworkers had gone all ears and no mouths, and Jim, whose carefully coiffed hair was looking a bit ragged, launched into the grand finale. He was not, he announced in strident tones, going to let himself get sidelined by an "ass-kissing, wannabe rookie with a rich boyfriend."

Cassidy spoke before she knew she was doing it. "Jeez, Jim. If it's that important to you, shouldn't you be at your desk writing something?"

Jim turned purple.

"Just saying," she amended, wondering if he was about to drop of a stroke.

"Hear, hear," a disembodied baritone chimed in.

He glanced around as though only now noticing that they weren't alone. Some brave souls had raised their heads far enough to level disapproving looks at the Gazette's out-of-control golden boy.

In an astonishingly calm tone, he said, "I'm going to bury you, Chandler. That's a promise." With that, he stalked away, smoothing his hair with one hand as he went.

Cassidy sat back in her chair, clasped her hands in her lap to stop them shaking, and concentrated on breathing.

"He's a chihuahua, kiddo. All yip and no bite," Larry's rumbling voice advised from the next cubicle. "You just gotta let him yip till he's hoarse. You did great."

"Right." she had another word for it, but her attempts to file a harassment complaint with the office-ad-min-slash-hr-department had yielded only a pro forma response. Basically, a "welcome to working life in small town Florida" shrug. God help her, she couldn't get out of there fast enough.

Taking her own advice, she returned to her work in progress. But Jim's words haunted her. Of course, he wanted her to quit—since she wasn't kissing his ass anymore—but why would he think she'd even consider it? Dave was giving her opportunities. Sure, it was challenging, but no way would she throw away a chance for a good reference.

What else could she do anyway? Tuck tail and give Jackson a chance to redeem himself? Right. The Striker patriarchs would make her life miserable until she finally packed up and...

Her fingers stilled on the keyboard. Is that what was happening here? Is that what Dave told Jim? Would he save himself the trouble of firing an important supporter's presumed future daughter-in-law by loading her down with work until she failed and...quit?

The realization squashed her into her chair. It was so obvious. Jim Lawley's threats were the least of her worries. She was being quiet fired. How long could she keep up this relentless pace?

For a full minute she sat, staring at nothing, stunned. Then she steeled her spine and filled her chest with new resolve. She had cared for her mother, managed their house, juggled medical appointments and dwindling finances, *and* finished school. This clown show? This was nothing.

And she could keep it up for as long as she had to.

Cassidy didn't realize just how much she needed Dominique to be home until she saw the open shed in her car's headlight beams. More than that, she needed him to listen as she talked through her troubles and picked his freakishly brilliant brain for perspective. Assuming, of course, he accepted her apology for digging into his life. She'd mentally practiced it all the way down and up I-95.

But as they had been this morning, the motorcycle was gone, the downstairs bedroom empty, and the house silent.

So it was happening again. He had left. Refused not only her sincere offer of help but also her friendship. Refused her. No explanation, no nothing. Done and gone. In record time.

"Wow. Just...wow." It didn't matter that she expected this. The disappointment was sharp as shattered glass.

Eddie came to greet her, circling her legs, herding her non-too-gently toward the cabinet with the cat food. She filled his dish on autopilot, shoved leftovers into the microwave, and tried hard to bury her hurt with anger. She couldn't. The dreams were too vivid, haunting her even when she was awake. Especially that last one while the storm raged outside. The easy intimacy had felt so very right, a respite from reality. Except, even in her dreams, Dominique Marchant had no actual interest in her.

But that embrace on the beach before Jackson arrived and everything had gone sideways? That felt like...interest. She sucked at her bottom lip, thinking. No kiss had ever transported her as this one did, clear into an alternate reality. Definitely not a dream. And Dominique had been there with her...with enormous ink well eyes. Exactly as they were last night when he told her to never again talk about his family. That had certainly been real, not to mention surreal.

She hugged herself against a shiver. Either the boundaries between reality and imagination were blurring, or her sanity was on shaky ground.

The microwave and her cell phone went off in tandem, rattling through her head. She struggled to sort out the pinging and chirping before reaching for her phone. "Dominique."

It wasn't. But at least it wasn't Jackson either; it was his sister.

Unlike her half-brother, Samantha Reynolds was the most sensitive and compassionate person Cassidy had ever met. She heard the weariness in Cassidy's voice and radiated warmth in her own. Before long, Cassidy was sharing the highlights of her work-life frustrations, and Samantha, with her front-row seat to her mother's marriage to a Striker heir, deduced the rest. In her informed opinion, as long as Cassidy stuck to her guns, all would be well. Baby brother needed her in his life just the way she was, willful and strong, and Samantha hoped fervently that they would work things out.

"You are his rock, sweetie. I see it in his face every time you're in the same room together."

"Unless his father or uncle are in there with us," Cassidy said, snuffing out a twinge of guilt. There were sides of Jackson she was sure even his ever-loving sister wasn't aware of.

A morose sigh floated across the line. "I know. He gets all moody and tense. I used to think it was grief and depression, but now that I've seen him light up around you, I know he only does it with them. It's weird. I can't figure it out."

Strangely, that made Cassidy feel better. "So it's not just me then."

"No, it's not." She braced for another subtle plea to give Jackson another chance, but sensing her mood, Samantha's tone lightened. "Maybe they've cast a spell over him. I used to think they were sorcerers, you know."

"Seriously? Why?"

"Oh, it's what my imagination came up with when I was nine and got to peek through a door I wasn't supposed to. Warren's library up on the third floor? The one with the electronic lock? Well, it's a vault for the rare books he collects. The walls are covered in shelves full of these big old volumes that look like they'd contain spells for world domination. So I decided he and Garrett were wizards." On a mysterious note, she added, "Come to think of it, I've never found a shred of evidence to the contrary."

Despite herself, Cassidy laughed. And she kept laughing as they together imagined the Striker patriarchs in sorcerer outfits, complete with flowing robes and pointed hats, casting spells over smoking cauldrons. Tension washed off her in a torrent. Magic indeed. "Thank you, Sam. I really needed that."

Samantha still giggled. "I think you could also use a mini vacation. Are you up for a road trip this weekend?"

"Where to?"

"A yoga conference. A friend of mine had a family emergency and won't be able to go. It would be a shame for the fee to go to waste."

"I don't know," she hedged. Samantha's circle of friends were all dedicated yoga practitioners. Cassidy enjoyed the occasional class, but an entire weekend of tying herself into knots and minding her breath seemed daunting.

"Oh, c'mon, it'll be fun. And besides, it's Key West. You can't live in Florida and not go there."

"Wait. Key West?" She straightened, her reporter instincts kicking into high gear. Jim had exhausted all his leads on the epidemic of murders happening in the Keys, but he had yet to get in his car and drive his butt down there. His loss.

"What time do we leave?"

Dominique hunted for five nights, traveling throughout several southern states, leaving a trail of dismembered bodies, drowning his misery in blood. And finding only more self-loathing. No, there was no help for a thing like him.

Which is where Cassidy came in.

Since she had yet to figure out the truth about him and put him out of his misery, she would have to be told and given instructions, but in a way that wouldn't terrify her and provoke the beast. Straight forward and non-threatening—if such a thing were possible—with an escape route in place would be best. He would no doubt have to face her revulsion, which was as it should be. He deserved her judgment in the name of all he had done, and he was ready to receive it in this, his last night on earth. Except...she wasn't there to dispense it.

Well past midnight, he approached the cottage and found it devoid of both human and vampire life. His imagination offered a raft of explanations, all of them alarming: accidents, illness, attacks...Serge changing his mind about keeping Cassidy safe.

Dominique rushed inside, tasting the air for any trace of blood and finding none. Only the little brother lay rolled in a living room chair, reassured of his territorial rights during Dominique's extended absence. On seeing him, the cat roused and trotted upstairs. Additional makeshift food and water dishes, along with several litter boxes, were tucked away in the kitchen and living room. Enough provisions to last for days.

A paper lay on the kitchen table, a note, the handwriting hurried and sure.

D,

As you are clearly unaware, it's a common courtesy to let the people you live with know when you plan to be gone for more than a day. In case you get back this weekend, know that I'm attending a conference in Key West with Samantha and will be back Sunday night.

C.

PS: While I'm there, I'll also do some digging for the story we discussed. Looks like I won't need your help after all.

Panic crawled over him like a swarm of hungry ants. Young women had been abducted, raped, and killed on those islands for months. Before Cassidy distracted him, he had intended to go there himself to hunt down the perpetrator and enjoy the sweet terror of a truly guilty soul. Now she, the most important—and most vulnerable—person in his life, was putting herself right in the path of the lethal danger waiting there.

For half a minute, Dominique felt like a truck had run him down. Then he turned toward the door and the waiting bike, ready to follow her south as fast as the machine could carry him. But a dark suspicion made him stop and look back down the hall to his room. A second later, he was there.

The antique swords still hung on the wall, now free of Jackson's scent, but always full of memories, some of them good. The swords had been a gift from his once closest friend, in honor of attaining the rank of shodan. Dominique let his fingers trace the golden dragons winding around a smooth scabbard and brass hand guard. Another dragon lay embedded in the hilt's cord wrapping. More than mere strength and skill, these creatures represented wisdom and cunning, traits every martial artist aspired to. He was certain that, unlike the Samurai warriors who had used these blades to end human lives in centuries past, his own use of them to end non-human lives involved neither wisdom nor cunning. Only raw skill and desperation to survive. Only defense, never offense. And he never used them to hunt...

Before he could think about the reasons and circumstances too closely, he took the scabbards off the wall and slung them across his back.

25

AURELIUS

Based on what little he knew of Jackson's sister, Dominique tracked her and Cassidy to the venue of the only yoga conference currently underway in Key West. The Casa Marina Resort was at the island's southern end, and by the time he walked into the lobby, dawn was close enough to make his shoulders hunch with dread. The night clerk, at the end of her shift, didn't need much of a compulsion to share their room number and hand over a key to the closest available suite. There, Dominique hung out a "do not disturb" sign and took refuge cocooned in a bedspread behind a locked bathroom door.

When he emerged at sunset, he was both surprised and relieved to find the two women already asleep again. As getting into the room unnoticed was not an option, he loitered by their door, listening for Cassidy's breathing and heartbeat. Assured of her wellbeing, he was about to leave and see to his own business when he heard her sigh and rustle out of bed. Next came running water, pulled zippers, and rattling clothes hangers. A few minutes later, he retreated when the door unlatched, then watched Cassidy step into the hallway from the far end of the hall. She wore the same blue and green dress he had found so enticing the night he first made dinner for her, the one that hugged her torso and fluttered above her knees. Her chin rose with determination as she adjusted her neckline and looked around, orienting herself. The moment her gaze swerved in his direction, he ducked into an ice machine alcove.

She walked past his hiding place, her sandals smacking the soles of her feet in a purposeful rhythm, when he caught her familiar scent. His knees turned to butter in a hot skillet. It was her natural, sensual perfume but magnified tenfold by hormones and enveloped in the earthy richness of menstrual blood.

Dominique bit his lower lip bloody to keep from moaning. He'd be able to track her blindfolded in a windstorm—as would every other vampire on the island.

With mounting apprehension, he watched her ask for directions at the front desk before marching out the door, map in hand. He considered intercepting her, but could think of no plausible reason to explain his presence. Once she crossed the street, he resigned himself to providing a discreet security escort and went to retrieve his swords.

The neighborhood surrounding the resort was semi-residential. Scattered tourists walked the narrow streets, which were lined with homes and motels tucked into rampant tropical foliage. Even through the muggy stench of overripe fruit and dank mildew, Cassidy's scent was obvious. He found her again just as her steps slowed along a white picket fence, something in the shrubbery drawing her attention. Pausing in the darkness by a gumbo limbo tree, he dared to hope she might have changed her mind about going out. Then the shrub clucked drowsily, and her shoulders slumped with relief. Shaking her head, she left the feral chickens to roost in peace and continued on her way.

"*Femme têtue,*" he muttered under his breath, and merged into the shadows in her wake.

Pedestrian traffic swelled after the next turn, and on Duval Street, the sidewalks swarmed with Saturday night revelers. The road itself ran thick with creeping traffic, ranging from sports cars to bicycle rickshaws. Art galleries and souvenir shops jostled for space with tattoo parlors and raucous bars. Music blared from every second open window. The balmy night was heavy with possibility, and Cassidy, camera now in hand, looked determined to witness it all.

Dominique grew bolder, fluidly weaving through the crowds behind her. Few glanced his way, finding the sidewalk performers and a drag queen parade more interesting than his leather-clad ninja vibe. His own attention was captivated by her riotous ponytail. That and her beguiling scent; it twined like a silk thread through the stench of sweating, energized humanity, and dragged him along like a toy on a string.

She studied the posted menus of several restaurants but entered none of them. Checking the offerings himself, he thought he knew why. Compared to the meals he had prepared for her, the fare seemed uninspired.

When she paused in front of a gay strip club, her cheeks blooming with color, he smiled. Later, at an elegant little piano wine bar, there was a wistful look in her eye, and he agreed. He would have joined her, explanations be damned, had she chosen to linger here. She didn't.

She didn't settle on an establishment to patronize until she reached the far end of Duval. Stunned, he watched her disappear into the milling interior of the least likely place to capture her interest.

Once again, she caught him off-guard.

Limits, like time, were fluid here one hundred miles from the mainland.

As Cassidy walked, marveling at the teeming, carefree vibe, she couldn't help thinking of her mother's decree to "seize the moment." She had certainly seized the one that had brought her here, and everywhere she looked, others were doing the same. A fantastical variety of decadent, sensual life streamed around her. Restaurants and bars bustled amidst colorful shops and beautifully restored mansions. Street performers dazzled with acrobatics and stunts, and vendors hawked trinkets and vices. And all of it was drenched in cloying perfumes, tangy spices, and pungent sea.

Flushed and breathless, she forced herself to refocus on her original reason for accepting Samantha's invitation. While she did attempt to keep up in the human knot-tying workshops for her friend's sake, ultimately, she was here to help another friend and possibly launch her career.

That this "friend" didn't want her help was beside the point.

Since arriving yesterday, conference activities and a threatening migraine had monopolized her time, and tomorrow they would head back home. If she was going to do this, it had to be tonight, which is why, an hour before midnight, she walked into Sloppy Joe's.

Though it was widely known that two of the murder victims were last seen alive here, business didn't appear to be suffering. Cassidy stepped through the wide-open doors and into the throng of inebriated patrons.

Paraphernalia of Keys lore, including several giant stuffed fish, covered every inch of wall space, and a sea of flags and banners fluttered along the ceiling in the icy blast from an industrial-strength AC system. The entertainment rattling the rafters was only a little more sober than the audience. Cassidy wished she were drunk as well when she paid attention to the lyrics, which extolled the male performer's abiding hatred of vaginas. No one else appeared to notice, much less mind.

"Yep. No limits," she murmured and snapped a few more pictures before putting the camera away and sliding up to the large bar dominating the center of the cavernous space. By the time she secured a cup of light draft, she also located a free barstool and did her best to blend in with the party atmosphere.

Sipping at the froth, she considered how best to bring up the subject of the murders and with whom. The bartenders were way too busy, and the security guards flanking the bar would know better than to dish dirt to a visitor, much less a reporter. One of the locals then. She scanned the small low-key groups clustered at tables along the walls when a hand grabbed her knee and slid up her thigh.

"Hey, babe," said a gust of stale beer breath.

Before she could turn away, a mouth crushed hers, pushing her hard against the edge of the bar. She shoved at the stranger. A foul tongue squirmed between her lips. Her legs were in no position to do any damage as he had come at her from the side, but his hand definitely went where she didn't want it.

"Control the wrist, control the body," Dominique had said. Yeah, right. No chance of that at this point. She grabbed his bottom lip between her teeth and bit down hard.

He jerked away. "Bitch!"

As though in slow motion, she saw his arm move back, hand forming a fist. Her mind blanked with shock.

The blow never came. Instead, her assailant—little more than a scrawny, drunken boy—jolted around.

"Last warning, junior," a new voice said with quiet authority. "Stop harassing the ladies and go sleep it off. I won't tell you again."

The boy squirmed against the man who held him with a massive arm across his thin chest. His lip bled bright crimson.

"Fine. Lemme go, you motherfucker."

"Go home," her savior said. He released the boy who stumbled into several other bodies on his way out the nearest door.

"I'm so sorry about this, miss. Are you all right?"

She looked up into the concerned face of a man of early middle-age with calm, blue eyes. She nodded and wiped at her mouth with a napkin. "I am now. Thank you."

He brightened and leaned closer to make himself heard over a new crescendo from the band. "I'm so glad. Please accept my apologies for my nephew." He placed a sincere hand over the front of his yellow Hawaiian shirt, which was tucked into pressed and belted khaki pants. "Zack is really a decent kid.

Just young. I'll make sure his father hears about this. And the language," he added emphatically. There was a tinge of an accent she couldn't place in the genial voice.

"Your nephew? Is he even old enough to drink?"

"As of last week, yes. Still trying to figure out his limits, though." He stuck out a hand. "I'm Aurelius. Friends call me Arie."

She accepted his firm grip and gave her name with a smile. His tanned skin complimented a neat head of thick brown hair. A pair of stylish rectangular glasses rode his aquiline nose.

"Can I buy you a drink to help make up for his behavior?"

She gestured at her full cup. "I'm all set. Thanks. But...there is something you might help me with."

"Name it. If it's within my power, it's yours."

"Do you live here?"

"For a couple of years now, yes."

Well, well, well. Ask and ye shall receive. "So maybe you know some things about the recent murder spree around here? I would love to hear a local perspective."

"You're joking."

She shook her head.

Arie rubbed his prominent cleft chin, considering. A heavy gold watch flashed on his beefy wrist. "Tourists don't usually want to hear about things like that."

"I'm not a tourist. I'm a reporter."

"Ah, media. I see. We've certainly had a few of those lately."

"Would you mind talking to one more?" She added a flirtatious lilt to her words. A jovial grin was her reward.

"Not at all. If that's all it takes to make up for Zack's lousy manners, it'll be my pleasure. Come and sit with me over there, away from this." He waved his hand, dismissing the ongoing saga of the gender wars.

"Not your thing either, huh?" she wondered as they settled at a table near an exit.

"Zack's thing. I promised I'd take him out to a place of his choice tonight." He spread his arms wide and made a "there you go" face. "Kids."

Warming to her new acquaintance, Cassidy pulled a notebook and pen from her bag and flipped to a blank page, pen poised. "So, what can you tell me?"

"Anything you want to know," he promised. "And then some."

Dominique slipped down a side street and, under cover of deep shadow, grappled up the wall. No sooner had his feet touched the roof than his hackles rose. "You."

Serge sat, hugging his knees and rocking gently in the same corner Dominique intended to leave his swords to minimize the attention he would draw in the bar.

"Blood-child," he greeted, sounding despondent.

Dominique charged up to him. "Where were you when she ambushed me with my past and pushed me to the brink of violence?"

"I was there, but you didn't need me. You are strong enough."

He grabbed Serge by the shirt collar. "That was the *one* time *she* truly needed you."

"It's all happening as it must."

Dominique dropped him, disgusted. "And now why are you here? Following me?"

"Her. I follow her. Always."

"Oh? She told you where she would be? Or did you divine this with your second sight?"

Serge frowned. "I, too, can read, young one."

"You were inside my house?" Dominique demanded. Clearly, he'd been gone too long.

"For her, yes. At sunset, she was gone. I had to know she was safe. Since you were busy pillaging," he added with a sniff.

"I am here now. I will keep her safe."

Serge's eyes slid away. "You will try."

Apprehension slithered through Dominique before he could squelch it. He pulled the scabbards over his head and set them on the ground. "Make yourself useful and watch these."

"You will need those."

"Against a throng of drunken mortals?" he scoffed. "That is not what—"

Suddenly, the bumbling blood-drinker had him by the arm and spun him around to face him at close range. His eyes radiated naked terror. "Your fate and hers will be sealed this night."

Dominique shoved free and backed away, his youngling heart spooked and pounding like a war drum. "Stop toying with me. Your insanity is not my priority tonight. *She* is."

"I know." Serge's curls shivered around his face as he trembled. "The future is now. Tonight. I see it clearly. You will sacrifice for her. You will sacrifice...everything."

For a moment, the grim tone made Dominique's flesh crawl. Then he raised both hands, warding off he-knew-not-what, and shook his head. "I do not have time for this. Watch the blades."

Serge stared at the swords on the asphalt roof. The dragons on the scabbards almost seemed to move in the low light. "It has been an honor knowing you, Dominique Marchant."

At street level, Dominique took a moment to collect his nerves and convince himself yet again that he placed no stock in Serge's premonitions. This was easier when they promised light and joy, things that could never again be a part of his existence. Believing in his own death, however...that was easy. But tonight?

"Impossible," he muttered and headed for the bar. Tonight, he had no time to die.

He spotted Cassidy before he even entered. A filthy drunk cretin had attached himself to her like a barnacle right there in the middle of the sea of bodies. She struggled, but could not chip him off, her rising panic whispering in what remained of the link forged by his poison in her blood.

Dominique maintained just enough control not to send people sprawling to the floor in his rush to get to her—and he had just enough sense to stop in his tracks when another came to her aid.

Melting into the shadows by the restrooms, he became still, all his senses locked on the scene of Cassidy and her rescuer, watching every nuance of their movements, listening to their words. His eyes narrowed and vision shifted. The milling auras of the human crush emerged. Dread whispered through him. Cassidy's golden life energy rippled with agitation, and the amiable stranger charming her...he glowed a cold white.

Vampire!

Dominique flattened himself to the wall, tense from his toes all the way up to his scalp. He had expected this, of course. Tonight, she was like a bowl of peaches and cream amidst a banquet of stale bread and water, impossible to resist. But what he hadn't expected—would never even have considered—was a creature such as this.

The harder he strained to hear the other vampire's heart, the greater his fear became. Then he heard it—a single beat.

This was no ordinary blood-drinker. This was a monster with a heartbeat slower than anything he had encountered before, except for one—his own sire. This incarnation of the beast, calling itself Arie, was immensely old and powerful—and knew how to apply bronzing lotion with skill.

Instinct told him to retreat and cede the territory. Let this ancient beast have the bar, the town, the island. He'd be fortunate if he escaped unnoticed.

But Aurelius's chosen prey was the one human here Dominique could never let him have.

"You will sacrifice for her. You will sacrifice...everything."

A snarl of fury vibrated in his throat. She lived in his lair and he had fed from her. The beast claimed her as his. And she wouldn't even be here in this insane pursuit, if not for him. In every way, it was his responsibility to keep her safe. No matter what.

"You will try."

If not for the wall holding him up, he might have slid to the grimy checker-tiled floor. He closed his eyes, free-falling into helpless rage. Serge was right. Even with his swords, Dominique had little hope of surviving the night.

And for Cassidy...there was no hope at all.

A scuffling commotion in the hallway brought him back to the present. He glanced over his shoulder—and stilled. Of all the people he might have expected to see appeasing a foul-mouthed drunk careening out of the men's room, Jackson Striker was the very last.

26

VERTIGO

Jackson walked out of the men's room and came to a hard stop. The figure standing at the end of the narrow hall had its back turned to him, but he would have known that unkempt mop of black hair and the arrogant bearing anywhere. And if there was any doubt, the leather jacket, pants, and boots in the eighty-degree night sealed the deal.

Fuck. How does this shit keep happening to me?

Go to Key West, his uncle had told him. Investigate homicides that barely register on the Grid. While he was relegated to this playpen—and presumably out of immediate trouble—Garrett was off to South America, going after the sure thing. But once Jackson learned his sister and Cassidy would be there too, he agreed. If Cassidy was enslaved to the vampire "roommate," she would go nowhere without his permission—or without him. Away from a familiar environment, even a supernatural being might trip up and become an easy mark for someone who knew what to watch for.

Clearly, Jackson had been right on both counts. Though he would have rather not found out by practically falling over his target outside the bathrooms in the rowdiest tourist trap south of Miami.

He gave himself a mental shake and assessed the situation. The vampire appeared agitated, loitering there, watching the crowds. One pale, long-fingered hand pressed flat against the wall, the other fretted and fisting by his side. Jackson felt his own hands balling. So the bastard was hungry and looking for dinner. Nice.

Taking a moment to collect himself, he touched the St. Christopher medals hanging around his neck. One had been Justin's. Feeling it together with his own never failed to infuse him with his brother's calm certainty. It also never failed to remind him of what could go wrong if he lost his focus.

This was it; the hunt was on.

There was a strip of sticky trackers in his pocket. Fingering them, he calculated his chances of not only escaping the hallway unnoticed but also planting a device in passing. Tag him or not, if the target noticed him, Jackson would lose the element of surprise. But the thought of biding his time in the men's room galled him.

An intoxicated man bursting out of the door and slamming into his back decided the matter for him. As they staggered together, the stranger spewed a stream of vomit-flavored obscenities that drew glances from everyone in earshot.

The guy could have thrown up all over him. Jackson wouldn't have cared. The real problem was the vampire swiveling his head around and going extraordinarily still. Much as Jackson would have liked to pretend not to be aware of him, at such close quarters he would have looked ludicrous to try.

He sent the unstable patron on his way with an apology and faced the most dangerous youngling vampire on Foundation record. Dominique Marchant regarded him with a veiled stare that made his flesh crawl. How anyone could look at that face—even half obscured behind a sweep of disheveled hair—and not see a viper lying in wait was beyond him.

Jackson smirked without humor. "Nicky. We have to stop meeting like this."

"Are you here for her?" the vampire asked. Jackson had to strain to hear him over the clashing music and revelry.

"What if I am? You're here on a girl's night out, I take it?"

"You useless piece of shit."

He only half-pretended to restrain himself from violence while in his pocket his fingers peeled one of the three trackers off its strip. At about the size of a small Band-Aid, the units were the smallest the Foundation's labs could manage. The tiny battery activated when it separated from the backing and died some twelve hours later.

"Sorry to disappoint you, but I have better things to do than stand here and be insulted by you. If you'll excuse me?" Tracker at the ready, he made to shove past his target and leave.

A vise grip closed around his wrist, shaking the tracker off. "You don't even realize she's here, do you?"

A moment of true terror seized Jackson before he could drown it in an emotional smokescreen of outrage. "Let go of me," he ground out between clenched teeth.

In the next instant, he was yanked up close to the inhuman body. Then his back slammed against the wall. The vampire leaned into him so intimately Jackson wanted to crawl out of his skin for a whole new set of reasons.

"Look," the bloodsucker whispered by his ear, the word barely filtering past the blood pounding in Jackson's head. The cold, clear smell of winter wafted over him, disorienting in the sweat-soaked tropical night. "Out there, at the far side of the bar. Do you see?"

Jackson turned his head enough to scan the crowds. Hyper-aware of his exposed neck mere inches away from a set of fangs that could savage him in seconds, he almost didn't register Cassidy. But there she was, beer in hand, looking alluring in that figure-hugging dress she had purchased especially for him. She wasn't wearing it for him now, though, and the stocky man she was talking to so animatedly clearly enjoyed the view of her cleavage. Judging by the way her beautiful heart-shaped face glowed and the ponytail bobbed as she nodded, he was laying it on thick, too.

"Looks like she's having a great time," Jackson said, doing his best to sound as if he wasn't reaching the limits of his capacity for shocking revelations. *What the fuck is she doing here alone?* Last he heard, she was sleeping off a migraine.

As though reading his mind, the vampire provided an explanation. "She is researching the local serial murders for a story. She does not realize she has already found the killer."

"Right. I can see what he wants from her, all right." Not that he'd let that happen, of course, but first he had to get some business taken care of. His right hand was back in his pocket and fishing for another tracker. "What's it to you anyway? Does she know you're stalking her now?"

The vampire stepped away and moved deeper into the hallway. "Stop being an ignorant prick and get her out of here before he does. I understand what he wants from her. You have little time," he added, looking past him.

Cassidy and the stranger had slipped off their chairs and headed for one of the many exits. Panicked indecision turned Jackson's brain to oatmeal. Tag the first vampire he had a genuine shot at or save Cassidy from...? No, he could catch up with her. Or...maybe he wouldn't have to. The stranger pulled out a chair for her and she sat, producing a notebook and pen from her bag.

Jackson released a long, relieved breath, but now his fingers were sweaty in his pocket, making a mess of the tracker's sticky surface. He needed more time. His nerves hummed with tension. His target seemed to vibrate in tandem beside him.

"If you feel that strongly, then what are you doing skulking in the shadows? Some *friend* you're turning out to be, Nicky." He was stalling, but it was a genuine question. If the vampire considered Cassidy his property—and why else would he be here?—keeping to the sidelines while someone else put moves on her made no sense.

"That man is dangerous to me."

Jackson sneered. "Don't make me laugh."

Two seconds later, he realized what his nervous outburst implied. He glanced at the vampire—and confirmed the unthinkable. Those cut-right-through-you eyes read the truth on his blanching face.

There was a reason the Striker Foundation had been around for so long—absolute secrecy. No vampires knew that there were free, uncompelled humans who knew they existed, to say nothing of hunting them with such dedication. With this single revelation, he had undermined centuries of work.

If vampires didn't kill him, Garrett surely would.

"Don't look so surprised. It's not like you're not obvious or anything," he said, looking the vampire up and down. There was a sticky tracker ready to go on his finger at last. Time to plant it and get out while the bloodsucker was still off balance.

His target arched a neat black brow. "As are you."

Oh, fuck no, Jackson thought, fighting for the appearance of calm. *You don't know a fucking thing about me.*

The vampire leaned in close again, his voice dropping even lower, the French accent honey thick. "Allow me to enlighten you further. That *man* with her, he has several *thousand* years over me. If I had *any* illusion about surviving a confrontation with him, I would not ask a useless asshole like you to intervene."

Jackson jerked his head around, attention swerving to Cassidy's companion. An ancient! Right there in front of him! The coloring had thrown him off. Built like a small truck, the guy wasn't especially handsome, but without obvious flaws. And how he carried himself spoke of a man half his apparent age, strong and confident—and completely oblivious to the fact that a hunter had him in his sights.

Cassidy wasn't just in danger; she wouldn't survive to see tomorrow, unless he extricated her. But that would draw attention to himself and risk exposing the entire Foundation and its mission, something to be avoided at all costs.

Then again, he already had the full attention of one vampire here. Caution clearly had left the building.

Dominique obscured himself and his telltale aura in shadows as he watched Striker set out on his mission. On the surface, Jackson blended into the scene well with his two-day beard, tan shorts, leather flip-flops, and a beer bottle emblazoned tank top which displayed his impressive chest and biceps. But the human's racing heart and muscle-bunching tension were unmistakable to vampire senses. His only hope lay in them being interpreted as the natural reactions of a jealous man.

The chances of a human suitor dissuading Aurelius from his chosen prey were slim but still better than those of a youngling challenger, even amidst a thousand humans. A blood-drinker that powerful could whisk Dominique away and finish him before anyone knew he had been there.

Jackson walked up behind Aurelius and clapped him companionably on the shoulder. "Hey, buddy. Thanks for looking after my girl, but I'll take it from here."

Fascinated horror welled inside Dominique. The human was either insane or had, all evidence to the contrary, no true understanding of what he was dealing with. Or maybe he did; he tuned out Aurelius now in favor of Cassidy who looked up from her notepad.

"Jackson? What are you doing here?"

Aurelius watched with quiet interest as the human man explained how he saw her leave the hotel and was hoping to find her for a late dinner to talk. The ease with which he spun his tale gave Dominique pause. There was more to Jackson Striker than met the eye.

Cassidy wouldn't budge. "I'm sorry, Jack, but I've got a great lead here. I'm going to finish this interview. Go have a beer, and I'll come find you as soon as I'm done. Okay?"

"No, you won't," Aurelius said, drawing Cassidy's attention. "He's leaving. Aren't you, young man?"

Jackson still refused to face the ancient vampire, refused to meet his eyes, refused to make a compulsion easy.

Cassidy blinked up at him. "Oh, you're leaving?"

"With you, yes. You and I are going to go have dinner. Now." He reached for her notebook, but she grabbed it with both hands and clutched it to her breasts.

"I'm working. This is important to me. Why can't you see that? Why is it always about you?"

"Please, babe. Don't make a scene," he implored, taking hold of her arm. "This is all about *you*. Trust me."

"Buddy, can't you take a hint? She's busy," Aurelius snapped under his breath.

Jackson held Cassidy's angry, bewildered look. "And I love her."

Her mouth opened, but no words emerged. Then she looked back to Aurelius who spoke with venomous tenderness.

"He will tell you anything to ruin your story, sweetheart. He is rude and selfish and cares only that you do what he wants."

Dominique felt ill with impotent rage when he heard the compulsive undertone in the voice deepening the hook of trust he had already slid into her mind. *No, no, no,* he chanted silently. *Do not listen. Leave with Jackson,* ma belle, *leave now!* Je t'en supplie! It was a desperate attempt to reach her. But whatever remained of the telepathic link between them, it was too weak to break through Aurelius's spell.

"I know," she said and twisted out of Jackson's grip. "Please...just go."

Hearing the disappointment in her voice, Dominique wanted to charge into a bare-handed attack, a move guaranteed to get him killed and leave her even more helpless.

Jackson, however, had no such reservations.

"You son of a bitch," he snarled and spun around to level a right hook at Aurelius's jaw.

The ancient one easily caught the human's fist in his hand, and when he captured his eyes as well, the air rippled with the power of the compulsion he hissed at Jackson. "Go find your bed and forget you ever saw me. Now!"

Dominique could feel the effect clear across the room, able to resist only because he had expected it. *Merde.*

But Jackson's defenses were shattered. All anger and determination drained out of him as he straightened and pivoted away. For him, Aurelius had ceased to exist. "See you in the morning, babe," he said without looking at Cassidy.

Then he stepped out into the night and vanished into a stream of pedestrians.

27

Silent Heart

Maybe following a random stranger wasn't one of her brighter ideas. Still, they were in a crowd, and everything about this stranger was warm and casual. The timbre of his voice reassured Cassidy, as did his amiable smile.

The frozen key lime pie on a stick he insisted she try didn't hurt either, though she probably should have refused the second helping, and definitely the third. "I love these," he told her. She couldn't disagree. Tangy lime and dark chocolate. What was there not to love?

They turned onto a side street, and the hubbub fell behind. Arie was a talker, relating fascinating tales of his youth in Rome—the games, the intrigues, the wars. Fascinated, she tuned out everything else, and by the time they stopped at the end of a narrow lane, she was decidedly lost.

Murky darkness everywhere, alive with rustling trees. The only light in the immediate vicinity seeped through a crack between boards nailed across a downstairs window of a modest, two-story structure. She could just make out a decrepit porch and weed-chocked stairs. Moldy decay hung in the muggy breeze like the scent of homeless ghosts.

"Where are we?"

Arie turned to her with an amiable smile. "We're here, sweetheart."

"Where the last victim died?" She looked around. A short, dead-end pathway, lined with other homes or possibly sheds—she couldn't be sure in the darkness. There were no signs of life. "No one heard her scream?"

"They don't scream. They moan."

"Really? That's...odd." Odd, too, how disoriented she felt with every nerve suddenly prickling for no reason she could name; though she thought she ought to.

"Come, let me show you."

She hesitated but accepted his offered hand. With chivalrous flair, he guided her up the two creaking steps. The front door opened, and a rangy figure appeared, silhouetted against the weak interior light.

"Took you long enough. Not only the sorriest tits in the whole place tonight, but you make me wait for it on top of it. My junk's like a rock, man."

Cassidy's jaw dropped. Arie, however, didn't seem at all unsettled to find his nephew at a crime scene and spouting attitude. He tucked her hand into his elbow as though preparing to shepherd her down a scenic path.

"And you are disobeying my orders by keeping that light on."

"Just 'cause you can see in the fucking dark, don't mean I can."

A hard edge slid into Arie's voice. "Don't make me regret you."

Zack's mouth snapped shut on whatever other grievances he might have had. He stepped aside, glowering, as Arie escorted Cassidy through the door, tugging her a little when her feet became reluctant. The young man's eyes, burning fever bright, bored into her. He reeked of sweat and greasy hair, and the bite she had left on his lip still oozed a little. Blood was smeared on the threadbare gray T-shirt hanging limp on his sparse frame.

Unease and confusion bubbled in the back of Cassidy's mind. She didn't know where she was, and wasn't sure why she was there. Impressions jumbled around her head with no meanings attached, like figments of a dream...

Of course. Another dream. She was still at the hotel, and nothing here was real, not even the stink of rot and stale urine. She closed her eyes and tried to transport herself to the cool, clean mountainside. But when she looked again, squalor still surrounded her. Great. *Jackson's already been by. Wonder when Dominique's gonna show up.*

A single battery-powered camping lantern teetered on a wobbly little side table and illuminated the cramped interior. The remnants of countless takeout meals lay scattered together with dog-eared magazines featuring large-breasted women in provocative poses on the covers. The thin, soiled mattress in the middle of the floor gave her pause.

Zack slammed the door behind them. "Small tits, brunette, *and* she bites. You *know* that's not what I like."

Arie inclined his head as he looked her up and down, assessing. Something was different about him. "She is what I want tonight," he said, as though speaking to himself. "Her spirit is strong, and her scent is...extraordinary."

"Oh, fuck you, man. *Scent.* Who gives a shit if there ain't no tits?"

The words didn't register with her so much as the angry frustration behind them. A shiver ran through her. Something was wrong. She ought to pay more attention. Her thoughts slogged through mental mud.

Arie leaned in to slide his nose along her jaw, inhaling. She flinched, but otherwise remained rooted to the spot. Not because he restrained her. No, her legs simply wouldn't obey her commands. Apprehension wormed through her belly. *Only a dream,* she told herself. *Creepy but harmless.*

"She is ambrosia," he murmured. "Warm and ripe and spiced with lime and chocolate sweetness, and...ah, yes. I thought so." He stepped back to regard her, lips puckered with disapproval.

He didn't wear his glasses anymore, and his eyes… Her head swam. She'd seen that hyper-dilated stare before…somewhere.

"Interesting." He poked a finger under her chin, lifting it, pushing her backward right up against a wall. She winced when he rubbed a hard thumb over the remnants of the bruise she kept so carefully covered with makeup.

Zack came up behind him. "Motherfucker. Is that what I think it is? How is that even fucking possible?"

"It's old news, and not local. She's a reporter from Orchard Beach, didn't you say? Colorado before that?"

She muffled an affirmative, and he released her to sag against the wall. Impossible to look away from those bottomless eyes. It was like being pulled into an abyss.

Arie's mouth curved into a thin, hard smirk. Some of his teeth looked a little too long. And sharp. "Are you ready, sweetheart?" He held out his hand to her, and she took it without deciding to. Her bag slid off her shoulder and thumped to the floor.

"F-for what?"

"To learn how they died, of course. What they felt. For your story."

Yes. Yes, of course she wanted to know. She had to. For the story.

She also wanted to vomit as he led her to the stained mattress.

Zack cackled like a manic clown.

Then the room spun around her, and she lay crushed against Arie's barrel chest. Something wasn't right. She should get away. But her limbs were limp and useless dead things against those arms, thick and solid as tree branches. He even smelled of trees. She closed her eyes to float in a forest of evergreens on a hot, dry day.

"Don't be so stubborn, sweetheart. Relax," Arie purred. "Enjoy."

Sensual promises whispered through her body. Ice spread in her gut.

"I'll be with you to the end." He nuzzled against her neck.

Silly to resist. He was her friend, after all. She sighed.

Then a breath of stale beer brushed her face and withered the evergreens. Hard hands groped beneath her dress. Brutal fingers dug into her flesh.

Memories crashed over her. Memories of a deserted path on campus. Three men, reeking of beer, holding her, pawing at her, tearing at her clothes...

"She is mine," said a new voice. A familiar voice.

The mental fog thinned a bit, and a wave of nausea surged up her throat. No, this wasn't just wrong; she would die here.

"What the *fuck*—"

"Shut up," Arie snapped.

Her assailants stood over her where she lay sprawled across the foul mattress. The boy had his hand on the fly of his jeans. Arie had a restraining hand on the boy's arm. Neither one looked at her.

Cassidy scrambled to uncooperative legs. Out. She had to get out. Plenty of windows, but all boarded up. Another door. She lunged for it, found it locked. She threw herself against it, bounced off, stumbled in a pile of garbage, panting. Panic swelled in the back of her mind. If she didn't escape, she'd be the next dead body washed up on the beach.

Drugs. The asshole drugged me. How could I've been so stupid?

She spun toward the front entrance.

And stopped. A column of black leather stood inside the door.

"Holy...shit," Zack murmured.

Cassidy almost laughed. A dream. It was only a dream. A crazy, freaking nightmare of a dream.

Arie pushed Zack in her direction. She hardly noticed when the boy took a hold of her arm.

"Dominique Marchant. What a rude surprise. You might have knocked." When there was no immediate response, Arie chuckled. "Yes, I know you, pup. Your reputation precedes you."

"You have something of mine," Dominique said. He sounded almost bored.

Arie glanced at Cassidy. "Yes, I thought I detected someone's punk in that. Impressive, for a pup. It seems everything your esteemed sire says of you is true."

"Do you believe everything said by madmen?"

Malevolence split Arie's face in a brilliant sneer. "That madman is the only reason I haven't finished you yet."

"Truly." Something between a sneer and a yawn. "*Magnifique.*"

With that, Dominique stalked into the room like a great cat claiming territory. Boot heels thumped a dispassionate rhythm against the floorboards, leather clothing creaked, and the ornate hilts of the dragon swords protruded over his shoulders.

He stopped to look at her, his eyes pools of black ink in the snow of his blank, beautiful face. She could feel him thrum with leashed energy.

"Dominique?" It was him. And it also wasn't. She had never dreamt of him like this before. He always made an impression in life as well as in dreams, but now...now he took her breath away.

Zack dropped her wrist and backed away, uncertain. "What the fuck, Arie? This guy a friend of yours or what?"

"Well, now. That all depends on how far he wants to push his luck tonight. Won't it Dominique? Or should I say...Nico?"

Dominique gently grasped Cassidy's chin. A tingle raced along her jaw and down the back of her neck. She shuddered.

Hear me, Cassidy. Do not be afraid. No matter what happens.

He hadn't moved his lips, yet she heard him. Heard the words and what lay beneath them, beneath the mask of his face: nameless terror.

"Get me out of this nightmare," she whispered through welling tears.

"Yeah, I don't think so," Zack mocked. "So you guys sharing?"

"I don't share," Arie said with no small contempt.

Trust me, Dominique's silent voice said again. Then he released her and faced the older man. "Nor do I. She is mine."

Not what Arie wanted to hear; his mood darkened considerably. "You can't seriously imagine I would let you walk away with this morsel, do you? Out of the generosity of my *silent* heart?"

"Oh, fuck no," Zack declared with such vehemence Cassidy flinched.

Dominique held out his hand, and she grabbed it as though diving for a lifeline. His fingers closed hard around hers.

"You will let me walk away with her because you do *not* want to explain to *him* what happened to me if you don't."

"Oh, I won't have to. You're leaving, alone. I suggest you take that offer; I won't make it again." The tone brooked no argument.

"Hell, yeah," the boy confirmed, and Cassidy clenched a fist with the urge to punch him just to shut him up already.

In her other hand, a tremor raced through Dominique's fingers. *No fear.* Her nerves bristled, knowing that he tried to convince himself as well as her. But when he spoke, he sounded in complete control, his voice a dark, fluid vibration in the air. "You will not stop me. You will forget about her. You will forget you ever saw me."

Arie's eyes narrowed into black slits. "You...arrogant...little...*mongrel.* Do you even know who you are insulting?" He paused a beat before finishing with a thunderous roar. "I don't give a shit who your sire is. I've put pups like you down in every age since the reign of Nero, and *you* will be no exception."

Fear. It stabbed through Cassidy like a jagged knife. She flinched toward Dominique, cleaved to his side. But instead of gathering her close and protecting her, he sent her sprawling to the filthy floor.

"Son of a bitch," she cried, not sure what hurt more—the jarring impact or the betrayal by a supposed friend when she needed him most—again!

Dominique leaned forward, his arms wide in invitation. "Then come—"

Arie morphed into a flash of yellow that streaked at Dominique and...past him, then through the back wall in a deafening crash. Dominique appeared a short distance away, untouched.

Cassidy stared at him, then glanced at the crash site. Pieces of wood and chunks of plaster clattered in a quaffing cloud of dust. "What—?"

"Oh, you're so dead, man," Zack said, shaking stringy hair out of his eyes. "Shoulda run when you had the chance."

Dominique kept his gaze trained on the hole in the wall as he slung the swords off his back in a surreal blur of movement. Empty scabbards rattled to the floor, kicked aside. The long, gleaming blades whirled, hummed, and moved into position, crossed low before him.

Very calmly, he said, "Come and get me, old man."

Wind rushed through the room, kicking up the debris in a swirl of motion. On the room's far end, though, there was nothing but the ragged hole. A thump, the swish of swords, a grunt, a sharp cry of pain. Cassidy spun on a heel and stared, slack-jawed and uncomprehending, at the fantastical scene of Dominique stuck halfway up the wall. His face twisted in a hideous grimace.

It took her several seconds to understand that what kept him pinned up there were his own swords. Both their hilts protruded from his chest.

The boy, who reeked of lust and refuse, laughed. "Told ya, ya shoulda run."

Rage and pain tore through Dominique. He'd let his own terror render him blind to the true extent of the threat posed by the ancient Roman, all because of Serge and his fearful babbling. The price for that mistake would be his life—and Cassidy's.

Arie sneered at him. "Stupid child."

Dominique slammed his hands and heels into the wall and arched his back against the hand guards of his swords. Every movement sliced more lung, flesh, and bone, even as the wounds tried to heal around the cold steel planted on either side of his frantic heart. Piercing the heart would have been a mercy. It wouldn't have killed him, but the blood loss would have rendered him unconscious—and of little entertainment value. A cry of agonized frustration ripped out of him.

"No, stop this, please." Cassidy's voice, so soft and human, wrapped around him, calmed him. She rushed closer, stared up at him, wide-eyed with confusion and shock. "How the hell... Oh my God, Dominique..."

No, this wasn't how he wanted her to learn the truth about him. At least there was no scent of fear from her, only outrage. He tasted blood in his mouth, felt it flow from his nose. He tried to smile for her and failed. She didn't believe this was real. Like the sweet kiss in her bed, this, too, was just a dream.

And in her dream, her fingers wrapped around the sword hilts—and stopped. "I don't know what to do."

"Pull, Cassidy. Pull them out." Not that he truly believed she could—or that Arie would let her—but right now he'd take any chance to save her life, no matter how remote.

She dropped her hands. "I can't. I might kill you. Stay still. I'll have to call 911."

Arie tossed back his head and boomed with laughter. "Sweetheart, you really don't know what we are, do you?" He appeared all too eager to explain.

Dominique growled a warning.

"Jeez, you don't know when to quit, do you?" the boy chided.

Cassidy stepped back, increasingly bewildered.

"I'm sorry, Cassie, *mon amour*," Dominique said quickly. "So sorry I brought you into this." He swallowed a gob of blood, coughed. "So sorry...that I cannot save you. Forgive me. I beg you."

She shook her head. "I don't understand."

"I hope you never will."

The boy snorted. "Someone hand me a fucking box of tissue."

Aurelius cast his minion a disapproving look before crossing his arms and leaning against a wall. He looked thoughtfully composed despite his disheveled appearance. His bright shirt was un-tucked, one sleeve hanging by a shred. A hole gaped at the knee of his slacks and both shoes were gone. Thick hair stood on end around his brutish face.

"This human means that much to you? You would give your life for hers?"

"*Oui.*" No hesitation.

"What?" she squeaked, looking between them. "No. No, this is crazy. What are you talking about?"

The ancient one ignored her. "Well, I won't ask for your life, pup. But I will demand your loyalty and obedience until I can deliver you back to your sire, who, I suspect, will be most grateful."

Dominique couldn't suppress a violent tremor. Death. He wanted death, not hell at the hands of the creature that had made him. But even this would not be too high a price for her life. "And she walks free."

"With no memory of this night." The Roman's voice was low and mocking. "Or you."

"*Oui,*" he whispered, wretched, and watched tears glint in Cassidy's eyes. She may not understand the literal deal he had just struck, but she understood the meaning. "Send her away. Now."

Aurelius reached out and pulled her close in front of him, draping one arm possessively across her shoulders. "Then again, I may not be as strong as you where she is concerned. She is so very"—he made a show of savoring her scent while his free hand traveled suggestively over her belly, tugging at her dress, and squeezed one breast—"tempting."

Cassidy squirmed like a landed fish. The stink of her mounting horror overpowered the pong of blood and damp filth.

Dominique snarled. "You have me. You do not need her."

"You forget yourself. What I don't need is to make bargains. What I want, I take."

The wretched boy giggled. "Got that right."

Cassidy whimpered, and Arie's eyes flared with the darkness of bloodlust.

"Wait."

Every head turned as one to the door. A familiar, bug-eyed face peered around the edge. "These two," Serge began and cleared his throat. "They are under my protection."

28

Awakening

Arie released her.

Cassidy managed half a step before her legs buckled, and she sagged to the floor, trembling and gorge rising. Nothing made sense. Worse, everything was getting horrifically weirder by the moment.

A compact little man in torn, stained clothing scurried, mouse-like, into the room. She had never seen him before, yet he seemed familiar—in a not good way. Not that this mattered right now, so long as he wasn't a friend of the evil duo.

Arie gave the new arrival a narrow look. "Under your protection?"

The little man nodded, eyes huge, the springy curls around his head bouncing. He glanced at Dominique, who had gone so still he looked like a grotesquely posed mannequin. The stranger rubbed his neck thoughtfully. "Headstrong, that young one. You know how they are." With a casual gesture at Cassidy, he added, "This is all that keeps him reined in, you see."

She tried not to move, not to breathe, and wished she could disappear into the floor. She couldn't begin to guess at what was going on here, except that the consequences of failure would be fatal.

Again, the little man cleared his throat. Drumming his fingertips together, he sheepishly looked up at Arie. "They are my responsibility, they are, both of them. Apologies if they overstepped their bounds; it will not happen again."

"So...you guys got a convention going on here this weekend, or what?" Zach scoffed.

Arie tilted his head to the side as he regarded the new arrival. "You are not his sire."

"I taught him everything he knows. That makes him mine."

"I would like to see you tell his real sire that."

One shoulder hunched up, dropped. "What that one cannot appreciate, I gladly take into my care." He took two steps backwards, bowed at the waist, and placed a hand on his chest. "Again, apologies." Turning on a bare heel, he bustled for Dominique. "We will be going now and leaving you to your business."

"*They* are my business," Arie countered.

The stranger grabbed both sword hilts and pulled. Dominique's eyes rolled into the back of his head as the blades slid free. Boneless, he tumbled to the floor, but stirred within seconds, struggling to his hands and knees in a pool of his own blood.

Cassidy's belly squelched, and she screwed her eyes shut. *Not real, not real, not real. None of this is real.*

The little man squealed with alarm. He had trouble keeping the swords under control. A razor-sharp tip whizzed past Dominique's ear, and he dropped flat to the ground. "*Merde!*"

"Sorry. Sorry, blood-child. Ungainly things. I don't know how you...oh!" The blades swung behind him and one sliced neatly through a small, rickety table. He side-stepped to escape the collapsing furniture and cascade of dog-eared magazines, pulled the offending sword to the front again, and leapt straight up, halfway to the ceiling, to prevent amputating one of his own feet. Finally, he landed in an awkward crouched tangle of limbs and metal.

Cassidy felt faint as she realized the longer of those blood-soaked swords had stopped mere inches from her face.

The little man peered down the blade at her, chagrined. "Apologies."

Arie boomed a hearty laugh. "Incompetent fool. You wouldn't have lasted a day in the Roman army."

"Maybe so," the stranger agreed, straightening. He glanced furtively over his shoulder at Dominique, who had regained his feet and leaned against the wall, face blank of all emotion. Then he jammed the longer blade into the floorboards beside Cassidy where it stuck and swayed. She stared at it, stupidly wondering if he meant for her to use it somehow...and what her odds of accidentally dismembering herself might be if she did. Frozen in place, she looked up to see him study the other blade with a strange, glassy look in his eyes. The gap-toothed grin stretching his mouth made her insides shiver. This was a madman—with a lethal weapon.

"But you know," he said, sounding wistful. "Blackbeard liked me just fine."

She didn't see him move, only heard the steel whistle as he vanished. A blood-curdling scream rent the stillness, and something heavy thumped to the floor. Cool wetness spattered her, and a sharp, pine-forest smell exploded in the air.

Suddenly, Dominique stood beside her. No, not Dominique. She stared up, mesmerized and horrified at...at the *thing* wearing his clothes and hair. The face was still blood-smeared but had somehow...compacted into a skeletal apparition with glittering obsidian spheres for eyes. Powerful teeth—fangs!—glinted in his gaping mouth. The neck was nothing but tendon and bone, and his fingers, claw-like, curled around both dragon sword hilts. A guttural growl vibrated in the surrounding air, a low sound that thrummed with primal savagery.

The grim reaper incarnate.

Oh. My. God.

"You fools!" Arie roared. "You will pay for this with your wretched lives."

Then he was gone, and so was Dominique. Wind gusted through the room. The front door banged open and then slammed shut.

"Holy fuck. Holyfuckfuckfuck...," Zack jabbered. He pressed against the wall, inching toward the hole in the back of the room, but his eyes bugged at something next to Cassidy.

An arm. An *arm* lay beside her, thick-muscled and mottled tan below the elbow, pure white above. Blood flowed from the cleanly sliced shoulder. The wrist wore Arie's clunky gold watch.

Horrified, she shot to her feet and stumbled away. The wetness she had felt...blood. Raising her hands, she found them covered in red. Her stomach heaved and emptied in an acrid stream of pie and chocolate that splattered on the ancient floorboards.

Thunder reverberated through the house. Something massive crashed into the door, making it jerk on its hinges. A rapid-fire *twok-twok-twok* hammered the outside wall—steel hitting wood—swords missing their mark.

"Motherfucker!" Zack cursed.

Cassidy turned to see the boy pull a long, vicious-looking knife from a sheath she hadn't even noticed before, and head for the shattered remains of the back wall. Something moved amidst the pile of broken boards, a figure clutching at his belly. It took her a moment to recognize it for the little man who had morphed from clumsy curiosity to arm-amputating demon. The moment after that, she recognized Zack's intention, too.

"No!" she shrieked, galvanized out of her nauseous daze. Nightmare or not, this stranger saved her life and gave Dominique a fighting chance. No way would she allow anyone to harm him now. She scrambled to her feet and rushed across the room. Loose garbage scattered under her feet as she bounded over the awful mattress and dove for her bag. Hoisting it into position, she charged at Zack like a mother bear in a rage. He spun around, brandishing his knife, only to have it knocked out of his hand by a mighty swing of the bag. When he lunged for her, bare-handed, she swung the other way. The bag met the side of his head with a crack she hoped was his skull breaking and not her camera.

He staggered back. "You crazy fucking bitch."

"I've had about enough of your filthy mouth." Fueled by a mixture of fear and fury, she went after him, swinging her improvised weapon and forcing him into a tumbling retreat through the hole in the wall.

Shaking, Cassidy turned to the stranger—and went faint. He wasn't clutching his belly. His bloody fingers gripped the splintered end of a two-by-four protruding from his gut. "How are you still alive?"

"I should not be, sweet one," he said, grimacing. "But I'm glad I lived to see you fight for me. All will be as it must."

She dropped to her knees beside him, hands hovering over the unthinkable damage, helpless. "We need to get you some help." She reached for the phone in her bag when a blood-slimed hand closed over her wrist so fast and hard she yelped. He loosened his hold. She met his eyes.

All the air rushed out of her. Those eyes...they were too big for his face, and too black. Like Dominique's were black. Like Arie's were black. Bottomless and cold.

"You're the same," she whispered. "All three of you. What—"

At the other end of the room, the boarded-up window exploded in a cloud of shattered glass and wood. The leather-clad grim reaper crashed through it, back first, as though shot from a cannon. With swords flying out to his sides, he back-flipped the moment he hit the ground and sprang upright just in time to deflect the snarling, one-armed monstrosity flying after him.

An instant later, the Arie creature blurred towards Cassidy.

Something struck the back of her neck and shoved her down, slamming her face against the impaled man's chest. Wind rushed around them, full of dust and bestial growls.

Dear God! What is this?

The grip on her nape eased. She sat up and pushed her hair out of her eyes with trembling fingers.

"We are not the same," the man who shouldn't be alive said, voice labored.

His hand slipped off her shoulder, and Cassidy realized he had pulled her out of Arie's way, saving her.

"The Roman, you see, he will kill us all. But Dominique, he will die for you. As will I." Those black gemstone eyes ensnared her, held her immobile. When he continued, it was in a voice so warm and resonant it felt like her own thoughts. "Do not fear me. I am your devoted servant. And never, *never* fear Dominique. He needs you, and he will destroy himself before he brings you any harm. Do you understand, sweet one?"

The calm falling over her was otherworldly. Nothing existed but this man and his words and the absolute certainty they conveyed. Her voice wouldn't work, so she nodded.

"Good. Then run now. Run as fast as your feet will carry you."

"But you—"

"Run!"

Cassidy sprang back as if jumping from a coiled snake. She snatched her bag, her sole weapon, and bolted for the door. Outside, after the lantern light, the night rendered her almost blind. She groped along, past the gate and onto the street where she could see the distant streetlamp.

Driven on by the surreal chaos flitting through the darkness all around, she ran, sandaled feet pounding the cracked sidewalk. Explosive crashes and inhuman roars moved from building to building. Mini tornadoes stirred trees and bushes at random and swept past her several times. Always, they were followed by the rapid-fire sound of steel meeting wood, metal, or anything else that got in the way.

Cassidy was almost at the intersection when someone slammed into her from behind and hooked an arm around her shoulders. "Bitch, you're not going nowhere," the beer breath hissed into her ear. "This is all your fault, and you're gonna pay. Big time."

She filled her lungs to scream but stopped when a cold, hard edge pressed up under her jaw. "Don't even think about it. I know how to use this on pretty necks."

Among the moves Dominique had taught her was one that might shake him off and break some fingers in the process, though that wouldn't stop a knife from doing some serious damage.

Then again, if none of this was real, that shouldn't matter, right?

But she wasn't sure about that anymore, not entirely.

Zack shoved her through a gate and into a small yard where two tiny solar-powered landscape lights glowed among the weeds. Another dark house. God only knew what horrors waited in there—or what he would do to her once he got her inside.

She tried for distraction. "What do you want with me, anyway? I thought I'm not your type."

"My junk don't give a shit right now, and you still owe me for biting me."

Cassidy shuddered. *No. Oh, no...*

She made herself heavy in his arms, feet dragging, sandals peeling off.

"Stand up, bitch." His grip on her tightened, crushing her neck until she wheezed for air.

His hold loosened when a clucking commotion erupted beneath them. A chicken blustered hysterically, beating frantic wings against their legs. Zack wobbled. Metallic debris rattled underfoot. "Shit."

Without thinking, Cassidy pushed off the ground and backed into him hard.

Together, they tumbled into a bush that was apparently home to the chicken's many friends. A flurry of clawed and feathered outrage rose. Birds squawked and flapped everywhere. Talons and wings scratched and pummeled her arms, breasts, and face. Ignoring it all, she jabbed a thumbnail into the crook of his arm to force the blade off her throat. With her other hand, she grabbed at his fingers on her shoulder and yanked back until the joints wilted.

Zack screamed. The knife flashed and slashed—straight into her arm. Red-hot pain followed and seared the truth into her brain...

This is no dream.

29

Know Me

The old Roman's missing arm gave Dominique no advantage. It only leveled the odds—somewhat.

Arie might have let him live under their bargain. More likely, regardless of the deference he claimed for Dominique's sire, he would have ended Dominique when the novelty of toying with him wore off. It was the unwritten law of their kind: An unsupervised youngling had no right to exist.

By claiming him as his, Serge had sealed his own fate.

He had also bought Dominique one last opportunity to save Cassidy's life—if he survived long enough for her to escape. When he saw her running through the street, his determination redoubled, while Arie's rage exploded beyond all measure. The Roman would not let her go, not on account of a mere youngling's challenge. Two thousand years of ego forbade it.

Dominique understood how to use an opponent's anger against them, but Arie had discarded his human instincts centuries ago. Even in the haze of fury, he attacked with devastating cunning, countered every offense with crushing power, and never repeated a miscalculation.

Between massive blood loss and young age, Dominique's reactions were sluggish, his strikes desperate, his escapes narrow. All his strength now derived from the one hope that the longer he held on, the better Cassidy's odds of survival were. He wanted to die believing that she lived, that a last tiny piece of his human soul would survive in her memories of him.

It was not to be.

Her fear surged through her link to him even before he heard her terrorized screams. The power of it dropped him to his knees on the side of a pitched roof, rendering him near senseless. One-armed Arie flew at him from a banyan tree, ready to deliver the fatal blow.

And so it ends, he thought. But the relief he had imagined at his imminent release from this hell was crushed by the knowledge of her certain death.

The death of an innocent.

The death he had brought her.

The death that outweighed all others.

The Roman was airborne, dropping against the star-spattered sky, claw hand outstretched, reaching for his throat, fangs bared. The beast in all its primordial glory.

Something—blind instinct or maybe providence—made Dominique wait to twist aside in the last possible instant. As he did, he swung the short *wakizashi* sword up from beneath. Even if Arie saw it, he had no time or means of avoiding his fate. The impact shuddered through Dominique's forearm as cold steel slid through muscle, then bone, then free again, out into space.

The body crashed into him, the claw scraping along his jaw, but the head kept going, gushing blood over his face. Together, they slithered down the metal slope and hurtled over the edge.

Dominique shoved the dead weight away in mid-flight and landed in a gathering of toppled garden gnomes. He closed his eyes and marveled at the all-too-human trembling in his limbs, the nameless thrill of having survived the impossible.

"Get up, you cunt!"

He sucked at the air, his attention snapping back into focus. Blood drenched the night, both vampire and human, laced with rage and fear. Blind, out-of-control hunger roared in his ears.

On the other side of the house, Cassidy flailed against Arie's sadistic little slave. The scent of her free-flowing terror sent the beast into a frenzy. It wanted them both. It wanted them now.

Then the boy caught sight of him, and everything changed. The human dissolved into a pool of pungent mortal fear.

And for Dominique, all else ceased to exist.

"You fucking killed him?"

The beast snarled, hungry for blood, for life, for terror. *Know me!*

The boy tightened his hold on Cassidy, who had gone still. Her round stare was riveted on Dominique...on the beast. "You touch me, she dies."

Dominique dropped the bloody swords; he wouldn't need them for this. His voice throbbed with the power of his need. "Leave her. You are mine."

"N-no." But the knife quivered and slid out of limp fingers. He knew Dominique for what he was. He could see death coming for him.

The beast grew delirious with anticipation. *Know me!*

The boy—the prey—staggered to his feet, turned, and stumbled through the thicket toward the weed-choked picket fence and the street beyond. Dominique had him by the neck long before he got there and slammed him against the ragged trunk of a palm tree.

Too easy. He shook with the effort to not rip out the bobbing throat with his teeth, to open wide that sweet, hot fount of blood. This meal had to be prepared with care, the experience savored.

"Did you enjoy seasoning his meals with your cock? Did they all die moaning for you?" The words were sand grinding in his parched gullet.

The boy shook violently and lost control of his bowels, further fouling the moldering air. He stared into the beast's bottomless gaze as though into the maw of hell itself.

Dominique leaned closer, letting the prey feel his breath on his face. "Tell. Me."

"Y-yes," he sobbed. Spit drooled from his lips, and a rich fog of guilt and fear flowed from him, soaking into Dominique's senses like the vapors of overproof rum. "I h-helped him catch 'em. M-made 'em feel what he w-wanted to t-t-t-taste...I'll help you, too...I'll b'yours. Anything you want, anything. I'll do it."

"Truly." The beast's voice rustled low and dry, the raspy whisper of death itself. "But I do not want just anything from you. I want...everything."

The prey bawled and convulsed when the fangs sliced open the jugular. Dominique silenced the frantic, gurgling screams by crushing a hand across its mouth. Fists and fingers hammered at his face and shoulders as he slithered into the prey's mind, plundering memories and shattering illusions.

Zack wasn't compelled, not really. His thrill at raping the women as they died in his master's arms was genuine. Afterward, he considered it a special challenge to dispose of them, often using the bodies again at his leisure. He was drunk on the imagined power of it all, never aware of his insignificance in the eyes of the ancient one. Dominique made sure he knew it now—just as he knew of his mind being raped and his blood leaving his body. Zack understood why he was dying and how. There was no mystery, no confusion. Only the clearest, most unmitigated experience of terror imaginable. Terror pulsed into the vampire, together with the blood, in warm, shuddering, orgasmic explosions of ecstasy.

Know me...

The feed surpassed Dominique's wildest expectation, and he tried to draw out the death as long as possible. Still, eventually, a final tremor juddered the limbs, and the heart stuttered to a halt. Only then did the beast release him.

He stepped back and swayed as the body collapsed to the ground. He closed his eyes and ran his tongue around his lips to catch the last of the blood. He moaned.

He smelled her.

She still bled, still reeked of temptation, wreathed in anxiety bordering on panic. For the first time, it didn't matter. He was so completely satisfied, nothing could have persuaded him to ruin this exquisite aftertaste by feeding again.

Cassidy sat on the ground amidst the weeds, disheveled and blood-spattered, drawing shallow, open-mouthed breaths as she surveyed the scene. Uncertain, he remained still, resisting the urge to disappear into the darkness. There was nothing more he could hide from her, no truths to spin, no secrets to keep. His soul lay before her, bare and defenseless as a newborn.

"*Je suis désolé,*" he said, his voice not quite steady. "I am truly sorry you had to see this. I had hoped that you would find out...differently."

Was she lost to him now? Was the dream over? Despair pulled at his limbs, and everything in him wanted to flee from this moment—and the darker ones yet to come. But he remained, waiting.

For her.

For his fate.

Time as Cassidy knew it ceased to exist. There was nothing but this one singular moment. This dream-not-dream haze of impossibility, her brain simply could not grasp. It was like wrestling eels. She had *not* just seen what she had seen. This wasn't real. Couldn't be. Just no.

But the stench of gore was certainly real. The ferocious sting of a deep gash in her arm was indisputably real. And the blood—she touched it with a fingertip—looked very real. There was a lot of it.

She turned back to the crumpled body—a body! Filthy hair, filthier clothes, limbs akimbo, frozen with a terrorized expression. He had touched her, said things, wanted to... And the other one, Arie...

Revulsion rolled up her gorge. She bent to the side and retched up a stream of sickly sweet lime and chocolate.

That flavor, too, was real. Oh, so real. "I love these," he had said, but she'd eaten them alone, because...

Her lungs disappeared. Only a thin filament of air wheezed through her windpipe. She curled in on herself, hugging her knees, squeezing shut her eyes. In her ears, a jet engine was prepping for takeoff.

"Cassidy."

Oh God, Dominique. What had he done? What had she seen? It couldn't be. But... She sucked at the air now in noisy, choking gulps. No air. There was no air. Where had all the air gone? She dug her fingers into the ground, tried to writhe, a fish flopping on land.

"Cassidy...Cassie *mon amour*, listen to me." A comforting murmur. The familiar French lilt. She tried to focus. She was safe now, he told her. It was safe to breathe now. Slowly. More slowly. Very slowly. She shuddered with the effort. "*Bon.* In with the nose. Out with the mouth."

Still so hard to get air, but as she uncurled, it started coming, bit by bit. Along with the metallic reek of blood.

"Slowly." A hand entered her field of vision, offered palm up, asking a question. It was smudged with dirt—and blood—but somehow seemed to glow. So pale. Skin that didn't see the sun. Sun allergy. *Sun allergy!* Her head felt light again.

"You are safe," he repeated. She'd never heard a more soothing tone from him. So unlike the other noises she wasn't sure she had heard him make. "Neither of them will ever touch you again. I promise."

For another moment, she stared at his hand, a still point in a world gone quicksand, then she reached for it, grabbed hold. A lifeline. Thus securely anchored to a point in time and space, she closed her eyes and concentrated on breathing. Impossible to say how long they were like this, silent and alone, before she found her voice again. "I know," she whispered, opening her eyes. "Thank you."

Dominique was crouched before her, his gaze quietly riveted to their filth-caked, clasped hands. He still looked like what she thought she'd seen, and she wondered how she hadn't noticed it before. The flawless pale skin. The stark beauty of his face. Those changeable liquid dark eyes and apparently equally changeable strong white teeth. The silent grace. The effortless strength. Oh God, *the sun allergy.*

Even the outfit—black leathers and silver-studded boots—underscored the truth like an industrial sharpie. Most convincing of all, though, was the blood that smeared his face and caked his hair.

"Will you let me help you?" he said so quietly she almost didn't catch the words in the chorus of crickets that had started up again.

A bubble of hysteria broke free before she could pop it. "Oh, now he asks. What happened to just charging in?"

He looked up from their hands. No, not their hands, her arm—the one that was dripping blood. "This is different. You might misunderstand."

Cassidy wasn't sure anymore what it was she understood or not. Only one thing seemed gospel at this point—if Dominique Marchant, whoever—*whatever*—he was, meant to hurt her, he would have done it long ago. With a tight bob of her head, she agreed.

Gently, he turned her arm and brought it to his mouth. His hold was light. Had she wanted to yank it away from him, she could have. As it was, she only felt her eyes saucer as he licked at the wound the way she might have enjoyed an ice cream cone. The wound's sting faded, replaced by a soft tingling prickle. Her mouth went slack when she realized what was happening—he was healing her injury by...licking it.

"You sure you're not just looking for dessert?" she whispered, all but breathless with wonder.

The corner of his sensuous mouth quirked up in that charming dimpled smile she knew so well. "It is deeper than I thought. I will need something a little stronger."

With that, he retrieved the discarded knife, wiped it on his thigh, and pulled the edge hard through his palm. A gleaming ribbon of blood flowed from his relaxed fist and across her wound, soaking it liberally before he closed his hand over it. He held tight as an army of ants erupted under her skin, making her squirm and gasp. The crawling died down within seconds, and he released his hold, only to dip his dark head back to her arm, this time to clean up the remnants of their mingled life essence.

What did that taste like to him, she wondered, and in the same instant knew that by doing so she stepped over a line into another world—a world in which the supernatural was real. Mesmerized, she curled her fingers to brush against his cheek. In response, Dominique pressed her palm against his face and closed his eyes as though savoring the contact.

"None of this is a dream, is it?" she said, full of awe. "You...really are...a vampire?"

He stilled so completely, he might have been a statue. He seemed to wait for something. When it didn't materialize, he relaxed, but didn't meet her gaze. "*Oui*. I am. A monster."

"You saved my life; I'm not about to question your methods."

He pressed a kiss into her palm before releasing it, then turned to the slumped corpse three paces away. The dead eyes stared at nothing. "That I did not need to do. That I wanted to do."

An impulse which, if she was being honest with herself, she had shared, and now second-guessed if for no other reason than that death might have been too easy a punishment. "What else could you have done?"

"Make him believe anything I want. Things that would turn the rest of his life into a living hell."

Her mouth formed a small, silent O.

A wry twist curled his lips, and he lifted one insouciant shoulder. "That would have required more control than I had."

"I see." She nodded to herself, eels slithering again. "So...what are you going to do with...him?"

"Nothing," Dominique said after a moment's thought. "The DNA evidence will link him to the dead women. Which may be what his master intended all along when he was ready to move on."

"And Arie has? Moved on?"

"The sunrise will take what is left of him."

Sun allergies, she thought again and busied her hands with stuffing her over-humidified hair back into its tie. "He was a lot stronger than you."

"He was about two thousand years stronger."

She startled. More eels.

"I should not have survived."

"I'm really glad you did." And not just because if he hadn't, her fate would have been unthinkable.

Dominique said nothing.

Suddenly, she remembered something else. "What happened to that guy who helped us? Did he make it?"

He glanced around as though he expected said guy to pop from a bush. "I don't know."

"He was a mess. We should go check on him." Help someone, yes. That she understood. That she could do. Her world may have just come off its axis, but there was yet a shred of meaning and control to hang onto.

Thus galvanized, she accepted Dominique's shoulder to steady herself as she got to her feet. Then she collected her sandals and bag while he picked up his swords. When he held out his hand to her, she took it without hesitation and let him guide her back into the darkness, back to the house where the nightmare had begun.

Never had Dominique confessed his true nature to a mortal and not ended up killing them—even those he loved. Never had a mortal known him and not known fear. Yet, here she was, Cassidy Chandler, holding his hand, not a hint of apprehension in her heart, her trust in him complete.

He mulled over this miracle as they walked, but could find no obvious explanation. All he knew was that his heart swelled with gratitude. All that was certain was that he would do everything in his power to not betray her misplaced faith in him.

The camp lamp still glowed, lying on its side against a wall inside the house. Through the shattered window, Dominique could see tiny movements in the rubble at the back of the room. He could also smell the enormous quantities of blood.

"You should stay out here." Better yet, she should run again. Serge would be in no condition to make wise feeding decisions.

"He's alive?"

"Barely." He squeezed her hand before letting go. "You are safe out here. If you so much as hold your breath, I will know."

She nodded and hugged herself.

He found the old buccaneer where he last saw him and in no better shape. Serge stopped his futile writhing. A look of pure awe crossed his face. "Blood-child. You are victorious."

Dominique gripped Serge's slick wrists and pulled. The body came off the thick wooden stake with an ugly sucking noise. Pieces of broken ribs and spine were visible in the mangled gut. As Serge settled groaning to the floor, the injury began to right itself, vertebrae realigning with small pops, new intestine bulging and fingers of muscle and tendons stretching to contain them. Other areas of the supernatural body provided what was needed to rebuild the damage; Serge paled and withered by the second.

His senses, however, remained keen. "I told her to run."

Dominique sat beside him. "She wasn't fast enough. She also witnessed far too much."

"Yet, she is here," he proclaimed, as though it were a miracle.

"She worries about you."

Serge's eyes rounded. "She does?"

"The morning sun will restore her common sense," Dominique muttered and retrieved a discarded shirt from the debris field, then got to work cleaning his weapons.

Serge chuckled before breaking into a coughing fit.

"You wrote me off," Dominique said when Serge fell quiet again. "You all but declared me dead, and because of that, I almost was. Grateful as I am for your meddling, I can't help but wonder why you came back."

Serge's smile was hesitant. "I saw it." Emotion glittered in his hollowing eyes and choked his hushed voice. "Blood-child, for the first time, I saw my own light. I cast a shadow through time now. I cast a *shadow*."

Dominique placed a hand on the bony shoulder and thought he understood. By coming to his aid, Serge had stepped from obscurity into the stream of life. Whether only in his delusions or as a true oracle, it didn't matter. He was no longer only an observer. He mattered—perhaps for the first time in three hundred years.

"*Merci beaucoup, mon ami,*" he murmured.

A deep sigh lifted the emaciated chest. "No. Thank *you*."

His belly had regenerated, but the skin covering the broad dent was thin and raw. He wouldn't be able to heal much more without feeding, which at this point meant he would make a corpse—or three.

Dominique finished wiping the blood off the *katana*, and studied the tiny dragon tucked into the hilt's wrapping. The moment he had struck the killing blow tonight, he had almost felt guided by something. The way he felt guided now. "Do you truly think of me as yours?"

A rare, lucid smile lit his haggard face. "Ah, blood-child. You belong to no one but yourself. I'm honored that you tolerate me, that you'll let me play a part of your future."

Raising a brow, Dominique returned the blade to its scabbard, but he didn't argue. Not anymore. Serge truly was the sire he never had, and the father he would never have again. By the time he cleaned and sheathed the *wakizashi* as well, he had come to a decision. Removing his jacket, he set it aside with the swords.

Serge gazed longingly out the broken front window. They could both hear Cassidy's steady heartbeat outside. He turned away. "Would you...find me someone? And maybe...stop me making a mess?"

"Maybe I have something better for you," Dominique said. When the old one looked up, confused and black-eyed with hunger, he extended his arm, blue-veined wrist up. "Know me."

30

Angel of Death

The fog finally cleared when Cassidy caught her reflection in a restroom mirror. A battle field survivor stared back: ripped and tattered clothes, bloody smears across her face, debris-studded hair. She looked down. Nasty scratches marked her arms. Dirt caked under her nails. Every inch of her evidenced the fight of her life. How had she walked past the café patrons outside without someone calling an ambulance or the police?

Oh, right. The vampire told them not to see her.

The eels slithered again. Cassidy leaned on the little porcelain sink and tried to steady her wobbly nerves. Real, all of it was real. Dominique, her obnoxious French roommate, wasn't part of the world as she knew it, and thanks to a graphic front-row seat to his reality, her own had all but collapsed. Nothing but quicksand lay at her feet. The only stable point anywhere was...Dominique.

The Angel of Death himself.

"My guardian angel," she whispered. An immortal who had killed another immortal to save her mortal self. That, after all was said and done, was the most startling revelation of all. She mattered to him. She mattered to him more than his own life did. That knowledge alone infused her with calm strength.

Internal balance somewhat restored, Cassidy cleaned herself up, combed out her hair, and buried the ruined dress she once so carefully selected for Jackson's benefit in the wastepaper bin. The plastic bag Dominique handed her earlier contained a new T-shirt dress, sapphire-blue with laughing yellow suns. The irony made her weep before it made her laugh.

They walked along Duval Street together, the girl with the cheerful new dress carrying an oversize shoulder bag, and the pale, graceful young man in black leather carrying samurai swords across his back. He had cleaned up, too. His damp, ebony curls framed a clean, flawless face. His black clothing didn't show the stains, but a faint scent of blood wafted off him along with the ever-present smell of...

"Snow," she murmured. "Is that your natural scent? Winter?"

"It is the mark of the very young."

Arie had smelled like a pine forest, also pleasant and natural. And an odor of wet moss hovered around the other vampire, who went his own way once he recovered from being run through with a two-by-four.

She pushed that memory aside. "I saw pictures of you in the sun. Obviously you were...not like this until recently."

"Fourteen months, seven nights, three hours and counting."

"Oh. Not keeping track or anything, I see."

"Except for the last twenty-one nights, every moment has been an absolute nightmare."

"Why—" She stopped in her tracks when she realized his meaning. Twenty-one nights ago, she had moved into his cottage. "Oh."

The dimple in his cheek deepened with a soft smile that made her breath catch. He really was seduction on two legs. Also immortal and...haunted.

"How did this happen to you?"

"Unthinkably bad fortune. Come. You should eat." He ushered her onto the paved courtyard of the wine bar she had admired earlier, where piano music tried to create a reprieve from the rambunctious atmosphere of the street. A hostess seated them at a table beneath the canopy of an immense banyan tree.

After the server departed with Cassidy's order, she sipped ice water and waited.

Her vampire companion sat with one booted ankle propped on his thigh. Absorbed in thought, he traced the cast iron patterns of the tabletop with long fingers. "I have told no one this story," he began. "Though I tried to tell you once...the night of the storm."

"You ended up giving me self-defense lessons." And God only knew how he had managed not to kill her.

Dominique nodded, his mouth twisting in a bitter line. "I told you about that night when I...rescued my sister, what I did...the man I killed." He seemed to reconsider telling her anything more, then clasped his hands over his belt buckle and continued, the words coming quiet and slow, as though being extracted one by one out of his memories. "A blood-drinker was there, watching from the. Maybe it was the violence that caught his interest, but he chose me as his next youngling. At that moment, my fate was sealed. I never even saw him, but he fed on me every night for a week. It's how a human is weakened so that when they are given vampire blood, they will transform."

He paused to drink half his water. "I was so sick, I could barely walk, but I answered his silent summons that night and came to him and his companion. I think I knew even then that they were not human." He drank more of his water, slowly, while Cassidy waited, riveted, watching him wrestle with memories he clearly wanted to keep buried.

Eventually, he continued, "I didn't remember how I was given the blood until much later. There is a madness that takes a newborn youngling when their humanity is burned away, when they are nothing but hunger. There is no memory, no reason, no...conscience."

He gazed into the street. The barest hint of emotion flickered across his beautiful face before he turned back to her, inclined his head, and concluded with an air of forced nonchalance.

"And so, the price for saving my sister is that I live in eternal night."

For a while, Cassidy said nothing, even though her mind bubbled with questions. He had far from told her everything, that much was obvious in his tight smile and narrowed eyes. But the undercurrent of rage she heard in his voice warned her not to go there. Not now or yet, or possibly ever. Instead, she asked about the effects of the sun.

"I feel it like an enormous weight that crushes me into unconsciousness. If I were to be caught in it long enough, I would burn to death. My...sun allergy," he added on a wry note, relaxing. She stared at him. "Given a choice, I would prefer to die by decapitation."

He explained other things that could hurt him—fire and silver—and debunked an extensive list of folklore—garlic, mirrors, running water, wooden stakes, and coffins. Cassidy's cheese basket and wine arrived, and she dove in, discovering she was famished despite the morbid topic. Halfway through the first cheese-stuffed roll, she noticed Dominique's amused scrutiny. "What?"

"I enjoy watching you eat, especially when I cook," he added, warm delight flooding his eyes.

Feeling her cheeks warm, she finished the roll. "So, how did you end up here? In the 'sunshine state?'"

His expression shuttered. "I'm hiding."

"From what?"

"From other blood-drinkers. But mostly from my sire." He looked like he was going to say more, but then flattened his mouth against the words. His eyes flickered across the milling masses in the street. Were there other vampires out there, listening in?

"What about the other one I saw tonight?" she ventured over the rim of her wineglass. "Who is he?"

"Serge," he said with a sigh and leaned back to look into the tree's dense lattice of branches. "Serge is a friend. The only one I have."

She followed his gaze. Nothing up there but deep, green shadows. Yet, she had the uncanny sense that something was looking back. It was the vampire next to her that looked at her, though. Or rather, at her exposed neck. "Sorry. Didn't mean to"—she tucked in her chin—"tempt you, I guess."

Dominique laughed. "Ah, Cassidy, *chérie*, you tempt me whenever I'm near you and often when I'm not. In every way," he added, sobering. "As I know I tempt you."

Her face burned with the sensual insinuations. Being tempted but believing there was no reciprocating interest was one thing. This was quite another. Literally another, she was sure, but she opted for the safer option. "So you do like women, then."

"*Oui*, very much." The look he gave her all but undressed her on the spot, and more than her face heated with it. The dream of lying in his arms and tasting his kiss suddenly blazed in her mind.

She reached for the wine, trying to distract herself, but put the glass back down before tasting the contents, recalling the last time she indulged in alcohol in Dominique's presence. Maybe this hadn't been the safer topic after all. "And...you want my blood, of course." She cleared the frog out of her throat. "But you never—"

The way he tilted his head and the mischief sparking in those gold-flecked eyes told her everything and more.

Cassidy touched the faded, mottled bruise on her neck. "You did? But...but this bruise...I had that before I met..." She looked at him sharply, her mental gears tripping into place. "This is a vampire bite, isn't it? That's why I don't remember how it happened?"

Dominique nodded, his expression souring.

"Was this you?"

"No," he said, looking scandalized.

"Okay then."

Several leaves fluttered from the tree above. Dominique gave them grim regard as they landed on the table.

"But do you know who it was?"

"Someone who will not touch you again while you are under my protection." The ragged edge in his voice wasn't quite human and didn't encourage follow-up questions. Not that she needed any; she'd witnessed, in blood-curdling detail, what it meant to be under Dominique Marchant's protection in the supernatural world.

He finished his water and softened his tone when he spoke again. "I did not leave a mark. And you remember more than you should."

Her brows gathered. "I do?"

"The night of the storm," he offered with obvious reluctance.

"The storm...oh, the...hug?" *And oh my God, that kiss!*

His expression told her he knew what she was really thinking. "The bite is painless when I want it to be, and it heals quickly. The way your arm did."

"I had a dream...a vision." She hesitated. "Was that part of it?"

He gave her a long, unhappy look. "That doesn't usually happen. It surprised me. I almost killed you because of it."

She reached for a fortifying sip of wine. "No, you didn't."

"*Sotte,*" Dominique said, and shoved his disheveled hair back with an angry stab of his hand. "Little fool. Why didn't you run the night you met me? Why are you even still speaking to me now, after all you've seen?"

She had no answer to his first question, at least not one she could put into words, but the second was surprisingly easy. "You're my friend, aren't you? Or was all that as fake as you pretending to be—"

"Human," he finished, shaking his head. "*Non,* Cassidy. What I feel for you is real. I concealed the truth about what I am from you because I knew you were not ready to hear it. For reasons I don't understand, I cannot make you do or believe anything against your will. The way Aurelius did."

The memory sent a shiver racing across her shoulders. How easily that ancient vampire had blinded her to every sign of danger.

Dominique sighed. "Because you can choose to ignore my compulsions, I had no way to tell you this without risking you...reacting badly. I feed on terror as much as on blood. I would have been powerless against my need to drink your fear. You would not have survived."

Her mouth went dry. "I see. Is...is that why you disappeared after...after the last time we spoke?" They had argued about his family, but those words now refused to form on her tongue. God, he really had compelled her. And yes, she had let him. She had been too frightened not to.

And he had run.

The vampire leaned closer, his warm voice becoming as liquid dark as it had then. "Hear me now, Cassidy. At sunrise, you must forget this night and all you know of me. Leave my lair and never think of me again. You will never be truly safe in my presence. No mortal is."

A sensible suggestion, given the night's harrowing events. Considering the last few weeks, however, also pointless. If telling her would have gotten her killed, then not telling her had saved her life right from the beginning—and every night since. Even the nights he was gone. The nights he didn't trust himself around her.

He meant her no harm. He never had.

"Sorry, but I can't do that, Dominique. I'm not afraid of you. And you need more than one friend."

He hissed something in French under his breath and sat back. But his lips twitched with bemused resignation. He would understand if she changed her mind, his expression said. Perhaps he even expected her to.

Instead of arguing, Cassidy reached into her purse and re-trieved a pink plastic bag which featured the logo of a Key Largo gift shop. "This is for you."

"Ah, *chérie*, you shouldn't have," he drawled, but his coun-tenance registered reluctant interest as he opened the bag, then fell into shocked surprise when he unfolded the black T-shirt inside. A pirate skull grinned back. "Bad to the Bone" read the caption.

"I had one like this."

"I know. I threw it out the first day when I cleaned. It had something sticky—" She shook the inevitable conclusion out of her head. "It was pretty filthy. I thought I ought to replace it. And to apologize for all the grief I've caused you, which was clearly more than I imagined."

The corners of his mouth lifted. "*Merci.*"

"You're welcome." She watched him study the print. "Is that how you see yourself?"

"It is what I am."

"Well, I think you're wrong about that, my friend. You're not 'bad to the bone.'"

He arched a quizzical brow. "Did you forget so soon?"

"No. I will never forget what you showed me tonight. But as I see it, your bones are the only things bad about you. The rest of you is just plain old pain in the ass."

"Mmm, *non, chérie*" he purred, his smile growing mysterious. "The rest of me is French."

31

GRAY AREAS

The sunrise following Cassidy's night of supernatural discoveries was both more magnificent and more terrifying than any she had ever experienced before. She watched the sun emerge from the Atlantic as she knew Dominique ached to see it—and never would again—in all its liquid fire beauty and promises of new beginnings. Tears tracked down her cheeks. For him, the only thing such splendor now promised was a horrific death.

For her, as the night drained away, all traces of eternal magic seemed to go with it. Reality re-asserted itself, if perhaps a bit off kilter. How could any of what she had witnessed be real? Even leaving aside for a moment the whole beings-out-of-horror-myth aspect, a cold-blooded killer had saved her from another cold-blooded killer. She had come *this* close to never seeing another sunrise herself. This wasn't the sort of thing you just shrugged off. This was where sensible people called the police, packed their bags, ran for cover, and/or generally lost their shit.

Yet there she sat, doing none of these things. Instead, she swiped at tears and pulled the borrowed meditation shawl closer around her against an uneasy shiver. Maybe she was too confused, she thought, or stunned to really react. Or maybe just exhausted. She had returned to the room only two hours ago. Lying on the bed, staring at shadows, she listened to Samantha sleep, and tried to decide if she'd rather still be as blissfully oblivious as her friend. Eventually, she climbed into the shower and let the hot water beat away what grime and filth remained of her night.

The commotion in the bathroom roused Samantha, who had the annoying habit of waking up fully caffeinated. "Sunrise meditation," she beamed and shook out her thick braid into a wavy wheat blond cascade. "What an excellent idea."

Well, an idea anyway, Cassidy supposed as she followed the yogini to a secluded spot on the resort property. They settled cross-legged onto the plush lawn and faced into the soft sea breeze. But while Samantha sat, eyes shut, communing with the universe at large, Cassidy watched the sunrise and contemplated an alternative universe entirely.

Her hand found the thin scar on her arm, caressing it, remembering what all had come after the cold-blooded killing. The scrapes on her face were gone as well, and the memory of Dominique's soft tongue healing them made her sigh all over again. "Poison," he called it, the substance in his saliva that caused it. "Miracle" was more like it. Had she known beings such as him existed when her mother lay dying of cancer, she would have searched the world to find one—and promptly gotten herself killed. These were vampires, and how they dealt with mortals had become abundantly clear only hours ago. Not Dominique, though. He was the exception.

Or was that only what she told herself?

She cared for him. He made her laugh, helped her out of jams, even risked his immortal life for her. He seemed drawn to her the way she was drawn to him. There was no denying it. Cassidy's heart was at serious risk of being stolen by this vexing and seductive Frenchman.

But that was just the surface. She'd be every kind of fool if she let herself forget the horrific apparition killing that terrified boy. This too was Dominique Marchant. In her mind, these two sides of him had yet to merge into the same being.

And what if she really fell for him? How long before an immortal vampire would tire of tip-toeing around a fragile human and simply left? *Well, at least it won't be because he died.*

A lone figure bounding along the beach interrupted her morbid musings. His tall, tanned, and muscular body was instantly familiar.

"Jackson," she called with a guilty jolt. She'd forgotten all about him.

"Shhhhhh," Samantha admonished on a long, dreamy breath.

"Sorry." Cassidy got up and hurried after him. "Jackson. Wait."

He slowed, but not because he heard her over his ear buds. Done with his morning run, he now moved on to his cool-down stretches. He looked startled when he spotted her jogging his way, the borrowed teal shawl fluttering around her.

"Are you all right?" Cassidy asked.

The brow over his nose pinched tight. He leaned forward into a hamstring stretch. "Why wouldn't I be?"

She hesitated. According to Dominique, a chunk of Jackson's memories had been twisted and obscured. There was no telling what he remembered—or how.

"You seemed upset last night," she offered, wrapping the shawl tighter around herself.

"And you're surprised?"

"Well, I—"

"Turned down a romantic dinner because you were too busy touring strip clubs with your gay roommate. What the fuck did you expect?" He switched legs and glanced at her astonished face. "Yeah, I saw you. Nice, Cassidy. Real classy."

She stared at him, speechless. So he had filled in the hole in his memory with random bits of imaginings, concocting a hybrid reality all his own. One in which she was the bad guy.

"I'm sorry," she managed, regretting she didn't have that damn ring handy to throw at him. It was still zipped into a pocket of her purse back in the room.

He gave her a long, hard look, his jaw muscles bunching, before walking away.

Cassidy watched him go, nerves jangling. It was Jackson, but it also wasn't, and she was the only one who knew it. The only one who knew why.

For the first thirty miles of their drive home, Samantha talked non-stop over a chipper Calypso beat thumping through her Prius. The music grated on Cassidy's exhaustion and the topic—yogic wisdom gleaned at the conference—felt inane considering her own new reality. Vampires existed. People had died. Jackson was broken. Nothing about this day was in any way normal, and pretending that it was made her want to crawl out of her skin.

Instead, she sucked at her lower lip and stared out the window. But the swirling blues and greens of the passing scenery only brought to mind Dominique. He would never see such sun-drenched tropical splendor again. Her heart broke a little more for him.

Eventually, Samantha picked up on the silence from the passenger seat and began asking gentle but prying questions. Was Jack being a jerk? Did Cassidy want to talk about it? She'd understand. The woman was the effervescently beautiful, warm and empathetic older female version of Jackson. It would be so easy to talk to her. But where to begin without sounding unstable, high, or worse?

No, best to stick with the safely mundane topic of Jackson. "I don't know how many ways I can tell him we're over. He's not hearing me." She had confessed that much to Samantha on the way down and had been met with understanding along with disappointment. "And then following us down here?" Not to mention following her out into town and flying into a jealous rage when he found her chatting with a promising source. Who, as it had turned out, wanted to drink all her blood, but it wasn't like Jackson would have known that. "To be honest, it's getting creepy."

"He doesn't take no for an answer. No Striker ever does," Samantha said with a troubled little shake of her head. "I still hope you two can work things out, but I confess, he's not making that easy. He's more like his father and uncle every day."

Cassidy's tired brain turned this over and spotted an opening. "The would-be sorcerers?"

Samantha brightened. "Ha! Right. I did say that, didn't I? Warren and Garrett are secretive enough, that's for sure. And Jackson, too, come to think of it."

"What if..." Cassidy searched for the right words while tightening her ponytail against the wind blasting through the open windows.

"What if? What if what?"

"What if they are?"

"What if the Strikers are a clan of wizards?" Samantha's soprano voice rose another octave.

"Right. What would you do if you found out? If you discovered some one-hundred-and-ten percent irrefutable proof?"

She glanced over and saw Cassidy's intent expression. Her delicate brows rose over the rim of her Ray Bans. "You're serious."

Cassidy was grateful for her own cheap, oversize sunglasses hiding her bleary, no doubt somewhat manic eyes. She forced herself to relax and not look like a candidate for the nearest mental health clinic. "The conference...something someone said got me thinking about the supernatural. And I didn't get much sleep last night," she tossed in for good measure and scrunched her shoulders.

"Really." Samantha looked dubious, but turned down the radio and brushed at the bright strands of hair blowing across her face. "Well then, I guess my reaction would depend on what kind of wizards they are."

"How do you mean?"

"There are good wizards and bad wizards, right? Which one do you think Jack would be?"

"I—I have no idea."

"That's important," she counseled, getting into the theory that wasn't a theory. "If he's a sorcerer who uses his power for evil, well, that wouldn't work for me. But if he does good, now *that* would be cool," she finished, adding, "Maybe I should ask him."

Which one was Dominique? Which version of him was dominant? "What if he's both? Like...a gray area?" Understatement of the century.

"True. Nothing is ever black and white." Samantha bunched her mouth to the side in thought. "I guess that would depend on what I could accept. Where I'd draw the line. But I'll tell you this. If I find out Jack is secretly an evil sorcerer, I'm moving in with you. Do you think your roommate would mind?"

Cassidy had told Samantha only what her brother already knew about Dominique—French, cooks, gay, infuriating. Trying to imagine the vampire's reaction to another clueless human showing up at his door, she didn't know whether to burst out laughing or faint. She did neither. Just stared at her friend.

"Oh, relax, sweetie. I was kidding," Samantha cajoled with a reassuring grab of Cassidy's arm. "I'm sure he's no sorcerer. The French cook is all yours. But I won't say no to a dinner invite."

Cassidy smiled at the other woman's carefree laughter. It was all so clear to her. Black and white and a bunch of gray in between. Just draw a line and pick a side.

Not so easy when it came to Dominique. It wasn't even a question of life or death. He had saved her life, but he had done it by killing with ruthless delight. By doing so, he perhaps saved many others who Zack might have preyed on even without Aurelius.

Also, he killed to feed—to survive—following a law of nature that ruled every predator on the planet. Except that no other predator came camouflaged as an intelligent and seductive human being. Dominique did. That made him extraordinarily dangerous.

But did it make him evil?

Cassidy looked out over the simmering, tropical day. The vampire was right; she should run from him as fast and as far as her Beetle could take her. He gave her that option by allowing her to walk away despite what she knew of him.

Which was precisely why she would do no such thing.

———

This was the day Jackson would bag his first target. According to his phone, the micro-tracker he planted on that presumptuous bastard of a bloodsucker last night hid at the end of a tiny lane too narrow to park in. He left the Audi at a curb around the corner and resigned himself to going for a walk in the already broiling mid-morning sun. He'd deal with the logistics of hauling out a comatose vampire once he had found the creature.

It wasn't the first wrinkle in his morning and probably wouldn't be the last, but he could deal. Just like he dealt with Cassidy. Though he wanted nothing more than to grab her and haul her away, he knew there was no escape for either of them at this point. She was under that baby vamp's control and would do whatever he commanded. Jackson couldn't trust her not to kill him in his sleep. The youngling had it out for him, no question, and in Cassidy he had found his perfect weapon.

They won't hesitate to turn the people you love into weapons... Garrett's words still mocked him.

"Fucking bastard," Jackson spat under his breath, not sure which one he was more pissed at, his uncle for being right or Nicky for proving the point. He should put the bloodsucker out of his misery on the spot.

His bloodlust cooled when he thought of presenting a live capture for his uncle's inspection—and then trapping the powerful sire as well. Maybe even a whole nest, including the fiend that had first attacked Cassidy. The sire couldn't be far. Anything that old and powerful wouldn't tolerate a youngling getting away and leaving a trail of bodies for long.

Already brimming with his expected victories, Jackson homed in on one of the decrepit little houses in various stages of renovation. Just the sort of place vampires liked to hole up in.

"Now let's see who's useless," he muttered.

As he let himself into the tiny yard, the gate's squeak barely rose above the high-pitched buzzing of cicadas. Several large flies hummed past his face. Many more gathered over foul smears on the ground and...

Jackson stopped. "What the—"

The body lying in the weeds was that of a young man, more a boy, really. The paper-white features were frozen in a silent, skyward scream, and the throat gaped with a ragged, fly-encrusted tear.

Jackson's gorge rose. Ferocious memories of his brother's death crashed over him. His feet refused to cooperate as he scrambled back, getting tangled in the clanging carcass of a bicycle. He grabbed at the post holding up a sagging porch roof. Compared to Justin's slaughter, this was surgically tidy, but the cause was unmistakably the same.

He stood, eyes closed, breathing past the stench until the panic subsided. Sweat dripped down his face and neck. He wiped at it. "Okay, buddy. You're done." When he found the bastard, there'd be no need for a body bag.

But the tracker wasn't inside the house. His phone reported it lying behind it. Jackson squashed a spike of anger. If the tracker had come off, he was screwed.

Mosquitos whined hungrily around his head, and he swatted at them as he picked his way through tangled, tropical vegetation into the backyard. There was a fire nearby. The acrid stench of it was getting stronger.

Baffled, he came to a stop before several small mounds of pristine white sand. Some shreds of fabric poked out of them. The tiny device perched on top, blending in with the yellow and black floral pattern of what remained of a Hawaiian shirt.

A cool quagmire opened at the bottom of his mind. Something wasn't right. Reluctantly, he bent to tug at the shirt remnants, retrieving the tracker. As he did, the sand shifted, spreading like a liquid. Feather-light particles drifted into the air. No, not sand...

Ash.

And not just any ash.

The piles had a shape to them, unmistakable now that he allowed himself to see it. Jackson swallowed hard, tasting ash, smelling fire—wood fire, old fire—and the complete disintegration of an ancient vampire.

An ancient vampire tagged with his tracker.

A tracker he didn't remember placing.

A tremor raced up his back. He scanned the yard, desperate for any clues that could shake lose his obviously altered memories. His eyes fell on another, smaller pile of ash a few paces away. Hidden in deeper shadows, it retained its original skull outline. Something had separated the head from the body. Something like a sword.

A sword like the ones in the youngling's lair.

Jackson's heart pounded in his ears. Traces of ash glittered everywhere, glinting even in the vegetation swaying overhead and on the roof itself. Vampire blood in the light of day. Deep gouges pockmarked the weathered wall. He could almost see the tips of swords hitting there, powered by an inhuman strength...locked in a battle to the death...between two utterly mismatched opponents.

And in the middle of it all...Cassidy.

The fog in his brain cleared explosively, and a storm of memories engulfed him: his encounter—no, *alliance*—with the youngling; his struggle to wrest Cassidy from an ancient monster; and his complete failure to do so. Yet, she had survived the night.

Because of Dominique—who had not failed.

Jackson's legs buckled, dropping him to the ground. He stared at the ash around his knees. It slithered and flowed, fluid as the truth.

32

Alone in the Dark

"You found me," Dominique said as she slogged up to him in the knee-high snowdrifts. He sat on a rock, wearing his gym pants, arms propped on one drawn-up knee. He looked pleased. Then she saw his pitch-black eyes.

"Doesn't the sun hurt you?"

"It's not real."

"Oh. Right." She sat next to him, catching her breath. "Why are we still here?"

"Because, *ma chérie*, we are not yet done."

Cassidy woke with a start. Silver moonlight replaced the snow glare. The icy wind became the blast from the AC vent. Eddie made a loaf beside her, paws and tail tucked in, his round eyes and swiveling ears keyed toward the door and the sound of the downstairs shower running.

So I'm alone in a house with a vampire...at night.

She had spent so much time imagining this scenario during the day it almost didn't register as extraordinary. By the old radio clock on her nightstand, it was four-thirty-two, Monday morning. Three hours of sleep, if that. Exhaustion still fogged her brain. She wanted to see him. She wanted to talk to him.

She wanted to sleep.

Cassidy put her hand on Eddie's back and closed her eyes.

Moments later, the massive cat scrambled across her in a mad rush to get off the bed, heedless of the sharp claws digging into her belly.

"Ow!" she cried, curled up, and rolled over...only to find a vampire.

Dominique lay on his side, head propped on one hand, wet hair slicked away from his luminous face. She glanced down the lean, muscled length of him, poured there so gracefully. He wore the usual black gym pants, the new "bad to the bone" shirt, and an amused expression.

"Very sneaky," she said. "Didn't you promise to stay out of here?"

"Do you want me to leave?"

Déjà vu swept over her with the remote timber of his voice. "That depends. Have you eaten?"

Small smile. "*Oui.*"

"I see. Did you kill anyone tonight?" Might as well get that out of the way.

He sobered, stared at her. "Why are you still here?"

"Why wouldn't I be?"

"After all you have seen? It did not occur to you today to pack your bags and go?"

"I didn't say that." She propped herself up on one elbow, facing him. "But I decided not to."

"You are insane, *madame*," he declared with a quiet vehemence that rippled down her back.

"I'm going by precedent. You haven't hurt me yet. I don't believe you will. What I know or don't know doesn't matter."

"You know *nothing.*"

That not-quite-human hiss in his voice should have made her flesh crawl. Yet, she felt remarkably unperturbed, and not just because her life depended on remaining calm. Her faith in him was absolute. She wasn't sure why, but understood that this was not the time to question it. "Maybe not, but...I know enough to have my theories."

His brows shot up. "More theories? *Vraiment?*"

"Yeah, that last one was way off base. But given what I've learned since...well, now I think you hunt—and probably kill—most...every night." She paused to gauge his reaction. Rapt interest. She forged ahead. "I also think you kill those with the most guilt because they are the most terrified of what they must believe is the devil himself coming for them. And...I think that deep down, when you feed the beast, you...enjoy it."

After an interminable silence, he said, "This does not frighten you?"

"Would I be here telling you this if it did?"

"Your cat is smarter than you."

"Eddie knows what you are?"

"He recognizes me as the superior predator."

"Huh. And you haven't hurt him either. Interesting."

"He has wisely avoided me. As should you," he added, a new edge in his voice.

Cassidy chewed her lip, considering. "You're being more of a pain in the ass than usual. This isn't you."

"And you are being more foolish than usual. You only *think* you know me."

"Then why don't you tell me how close I am with my theory?"

"Your theory is not nearly grim enough."

"Enlighten me?"

He didn't hesitate. "The first body I drained was my father. And my beloved little sister, Anastasie, for whom I committed murder"—he waved a dismissive hand—"her I killed, too."

Cassidy swallowed hard. She'd asked for it. "That's...grim."

"And Jeovana, my beautiful Italian love," he crooned. "I buried my cock between her thighs and my fangs in her neck until she lay dead in my arms."

Goosebumps swarmed down her arms. How had Dominique gotten so close? He tilted his head as if he might kiss her. The tip of his nose brushed hers. Her senses swam with him, his beguiling scent and leashed power, the sensual promises in his every graceful move.

She wanted more.

She wanted to flee.

She froze.

"You see, *ma petite folle*, I am deadly to everyone near me," he whispered at her ear. "Everyone...is...prey."

"Did—" She swallowed again to wet a mouth gone dusty dry. "Did you have a choice?" The way he had a choice now? He smelled her in a move identical to how Arie had assessed her, nose sliding along her jaw. Still, she could not make herself back away. "Prey instinct" had kicked in. She dared not show weakness.

The vampire in her bed became motionless.

"Answer me." She gulped. "And don't start lying to me now."

He retreated just far enough to read her expression. "I am a greedy bastard. I always have been. I take my pleasure where I find it. I leave the bodies where they drop."

She shook her head. "No. No, I don't believe that."

"Yet it is the truth." His chin lifted and eyes narrowed, nostrils flaring, a predator incarnate. "Tell me, *ma petite,* do you still want to feed me?"

A thin shard of apprehension slid through her. "Didn't you say you already...ate tonight?"

"I'm in the mood for dessert."

She became aware of how her heart pounded behind her ribs. Judging by his sharpening regard of her, he heard it, too.

"I'm guessing you're not really giving me a choice. Are you?" Maybe that wasn't a bad thing. If he drank her blood, that might rekindle their strange mental connection, and she could figure out this bizarre mood. She turned her head, exposing her neck.

But instead of taking the anticipated bite, the vampire tossed aside the sheet covering her and slid a hand up her thigh.

"What are you doing?"

He pushed her back into the pillow and rucked up her sleep shirt, exposing her stomach. Several of the scratches Eddie had left there were deep enough to bleed. Dominique lapped at them in quick, tiny flicks of his tongue, getting as much of the blood as he could before the wounds sealed.

Lightning forked along her every nerve, but she bit back a moan and bunched her hands in the sheets. What was happening? Why was he like this? So different from.... Her breath hitched. So different from the last time he was in her bed. When she had touched him, and kissed him, and, yes, craved him.

Not a dream. Real, all of it. *Oh my God.*

Done "healing" her belly, he looked up, eyes huge and dark, mouth hard and smug. "You remember."

Cassidy glared at him.

"Do you remember what you wanted of me?" His hands moved to her hips, where his fingers hooked into the utilitarian underwear that secured a pad for this month's edition of female misery.

She sucked at the air when his intention dawned on her. "Don't you dare."

The vampire lowered his face to her crotch and inhaled. A small anticipatory growl followed.

Cassidy made to scramble away, but his hold on her hips became crushing even as his weight shifted to pin down her kicking legs. He looked up at her, and suddenly, for an instant, she was back on campus that night, saw other glittering eyes, felt other powerful hands. For an instant, time vanished, past and future were one, realities overlapped. For an instant, her mind emptied as completely as her lungs.

Then she caught herself, could almost hear him—or another version of him—telling her to breathe, to be aware, to use an opponent's strength against them. Tall order in this case, but it was all she had to go on.

"Dominique, no," she said as calmly as she could manage when he started sliding off her underwear. "Not like this."

He replied with a cold smirk. "Blood is blood."

"I'm hurting. This is not fun for me."

"But it is entertaining for a greedy, bloodthirsty bastard such as myself. Also, you will feel better once you relax," he added on a bland note and made to settle down to business.

Her hand cracked against his cheek almost before she knew it. "I. Said. No."

Time stopped.

The vampire became preternaturally still. Darkness flooded his eyes, gleaming in the moonlight like expanding pools of ink in his narrowing face. The other side of him, the side she hadn't reconciled with him yet, surfaced. The "beast," as he called it, taking shape right in front of her.

Cassidy drew a shaky breath. "You are no better than the monster you killed in Key West."

The metamorphosis completed in a matter of seconds and should have been terrifying to behold. Sad, disappointed tears welled in her eyes instead. So much for Dominique, her eccentric new friend. So much for daring to hope they might have something more—or at least something that might last.

The skull leaned toward her. Ice brushed her face when it spoke in resonant, inhuman tones. "Do you hate me yet, Cassidy?"

She said nothing. Neither did she blink as the tears welled from her eyes.

"Good." His voice took on that persuasive pitch that vibrated right through her. "Go to sleep."

Exhausted in every way, she accepted the compulsion without reservation. She wanted to wake up in the morning and believe none of this had been real.

With the last flicker of her conscious mind, she felt him move and opened her eyes one more time. He had turned away toward the moon floating over the sea. Not a trace of the beast remained on his exquisite face.

What was there instead strangled her heart.

33

UNREASONABLE REQUESTS

The pounding came and went, a giant, hollow drum rising and falling. A voice babbled, too. Something nudged her shoulder. Soft bristles brushed across her face. A whiff of kitty breath.

Cassidy rolled over, sputtering. "Goway…"

The radio cheerfully announced another hour of uninterrupted music for her workday enjoyment. She blinked gritty eyes at the digital clock. Nine a.m. Monday.

Shit!

"Cassidy? Where are you? Answer me."

"What the—" De-tangling from the sheets, she staggered out of bed, Eddie underfoot, almost tripping her.

She stopped as Jackson charged up the stairs. They spoke at the same time.

"What the hell are you doing in my house?"

"Why the fuck aren't you answering your—" He raised a placating hand. "I was worried sick about you when you didn't answer your phone. I've been trying to call you for hours."

"So you broke in?"

He glanced over his shoulder at the wide-open door. "The door was unlocked."

She blinked, unsure. Leaving front doors unlocked at night wasn't her habit. But then she didn't live here by herself.

"Cass, are you all right?"

Sleep and shock clouded her brain. "I need coffee," she muttered and thumped down the stairs.

He eyed her critically as he stepped aside. "Were you still sleeping?"

"Mmm. What was your first clue?" She shoved the rat's nest of her hair out of her face and made a half-hearted effort to straighten her sleep shirt, the one announcing she didn't do mornings.

"That's not like you. Why aren't you at work?"

Cassidy cringed, remembering. Jim was bound to pee himself with glee. Not only did she not have a story, she couldn't even manage to show up to say so. Then again, Jim and his issues seemed oh-so-trivial after this weekend.

With an impatient flick of a hand, she slammed the front door shut and turned around. "I felt like sleeping in, okay? Obviously, I had way too much fun touring strip clubs in Key West."

Jackson met her glower for a long moment before dropping his gaze as though consulting notes stenciled on his sneakers. "I'm sorry, Cass. That was a shitty thing to say."

"Oh, you think?"

He looked up. "Can we talk?"

Mystified by this conversational turn, her temper stalled. "Let me make some coffee first."

"I could use some myself," he agreed, smiling, and bent down to acknowledge Eddie's greeting with a scratch behind the tufted ears. Once she got the coffeemaker perking, she opened a tin of Friskies and filled the cat's dish. Abandoning their visitor, Eddie trotted over and dove into the serving as if he hadn't eaten in days.

"Greedy little bastard," she muttered—and froze as the words triggered vivid memories of another self-proclaimed greedy bastard. Or rather, a greedy "beast." She swallowed hard, her chest tightening. No, not a dream, but a living nightmare.

Closing her eyes, she saw Dominique as she remembered him—the chef who so expertly practiced his skills in this kitchen, never so much as sampling a single thing he prepared. Not to mention an accomplished martial artist, a swordsman, a Frenchman...a broken heart.

She put out a hand against the cabinet to steady herself.

"Babe? Something wrong?"

"Um. Dizzy." She straightened and forced a reassuring grimace. "I really need coffee."

That surreal instant before she fell asleep...*that* was the Dominique she knew, not the ruthless predator who had come to her bed. He had looked wretched beyond words.

"You sure that's all it is? You're looking...pale."

"Am I? Well, I've got my period, too. Just to add to the weekend drama."

"Oh. I'm sorry," he murmured, instantly awkward. "Still bad?"

"No. Much better." She dismissed the subject with a wave of her hand, wishing she could forget Dominique's unorthodox suggestion as easily. What the hell had he been thinking? He must have known how she'd react. Well, maybe. That slap had shocked him as much as it had her.

What the hell was I thinking, picking a fight with a vampire? Just how close to death had she come by pushing him like that? Why had that thought never even crossed her mind?

The coffeemaker still gurgled, but there was enough in the pot for two half cups. She left Jackson's strong and black, the way he liked it, and added sugar and a splash of milk to hers. As he sipped, she took several gulps from her mug. The caffeine went to work, clearing her head and returning her to the problem at hand: Jackson Striker in her kitchen. He wore shorts and sneakers and a polo shirt, not the suit and tie SICI head office demanded of its future president. He glowed with health and calm confidence.

"So," she ventured. "What did you want to talk about?"

He studied the mug in his hands. It was emblazoned with a French flag and a silhouette of the Eiffel Tower. Her own boldly proclaimed "I (heart) St. Barthélémy."

With a stifled sigh, he put the cup on the kitchen counter. "Did you hear about the body they found in Key West yesterday morning?"

"I did," she replied and decided there was enough fresh coffee in the carafe to top off her serving.

"The official story is 'animal attack.' Feral dogs."

"Official?" Cassidy clutched the pot handle as though it could anchor her to solid ground that no longer existed. The back of her neck prickled with dread.

Jackson walked to the mouth of the hallway leading to Dominique's sanctuary and, hands on hips, stared into its dim depths. "I know better; I'm the one who found the body."

She clutched her coffee close. The news report had mentioned no names, just a "real estate investor wishing to remain anonymous" who discovered the gruesome scene.

He pivoted back to her now, speculative. "You know what happened, don't you? I can see you do. I'm guessing you had a front-row seat."

The mug slipped a little in her grip. She put it down. "What are you saying—"

Jackson hurried to her side and closed his large hand over her icy fingers where they splayed on the counter. "Babe, I know. I know everything. And I remember what happened at Sloppy Joe's. I saw the mortal danger you were in." A muscle in his jaw ticked. "I tried to save you, but I never had a chance. Because I'm...I'm only human." The last bit was so low, she barely caught it, yet the words thundered in the room.

"You...you *know*?"

He gave a tight nod. "I do."

"Since when?"

"I...well, since I met him."

"Oh." Extracting her hand from beneath Jackson's, she picked up her mug and drained it. He watched her, hawk-like, as she tried to gather her darting thoughts. "Why didn't you tell me?"

"I had no idea how you'd react. Or how he—"

"No. No, that's not what I meant. You didn't just realize that...there's this whole other reality out there when you met Dominique. You must have known about it. And judging by your reaction, you knew plenty and probably for a while. Don't you think that's something you should have mentioned before you asked me to marry you?"

Jackson looked as astonished as she'd ever seen him. "Where the fuck would you expect me to start?"

That gave her pause. "Right." She pushed the hair out of her face again and blew out a long breath.

"You didn't tell anyone else, did you? Like Sam?"

Cassidy guffawed. "You're joking."

"Good. They're very protective of their privacy," he added with authority.

"Are they?" With an askance glance, she zeroed in on the follow-up. "Just what all do you know about them, Jackson? About...vampires? And since they're so secretive, how would you know it?"

She knew she'd hit a nerve when he reared back, his face darkening. He opened his mouth, closed it, then shook his head, tried again. "The Striker family has known about vampires since the sixteenth century. It's strictly on a need-to-know basis because, as you may have noticed, interacting with them is risky."

Cassidy nodded. "So why do you?"

Another hesitation. "Business."

"So all that money..."

"Look. I didn't come here to discuss Foundation business with you. Now that you understand what's going on—"

"The Striker Foundation? So that's like a vampire financial management company?"

"You need to get out of here."

"What? Why?"

"You can't stay here. You realize that, right?"

"Why not?"

Jackson paced a small, frustrated circle and shoved the fingers of both hands through his spiky hair. "Do I have to spell this out for you? You're living with a killer." He waved at the hallway. "He killed his own father and sister, for fuck's sake. *And* his girlfriend."

Cassidy's knees went wobbly, and she locked them tight. "I know," she whispered.

His eyes rounded and brows shot up. "You *know*?"

"He told me."

Jackson stared at her. "I see. And—what?—that's okay with you?"

Again she remembered the unspeakable misery that was Dominique's face this morning. "There's more to it than that."

"No, there isn't. He's a youngling. That means self-control is not in his skill set."

Cassidy bristled. Jackson may know about vampires in general, but even though he had obviously done some digging, he knew nothing about this one in particular.

"He can't be that bad at it. I've lived here for weeks, and I'm fine."

"And you're going to stay that way." He spun 'round and headed up the stairs, long legs taking them three at a time.

"What? Jackson, what are you doing?"

"That bastard's done a number on your head, babe," he called from her bedroom. "Obviously you're not listening to reason right now, and later it'll be too late." Drawers opened and slammed, punctuated by the sound of zippers being torn open.

"Wait. No. Stop." By the time Cassidy put down her mug and reached the bottom of the stairs, Jackson appeared at the top carrying her duffel with a pile of clothes erupting from the gaping opening.

"Let's go," he ordered, coming down.

She backed away. "I'm not going anywhere with you."

"How often do I need to say this? You're not safe here, so you're coming with me. I'll take care of everything. I promise."

He held out a hand to her. That tense grimace masquerading as a smile made her feel like she was looking at a younger version of Garrett Striker. Cassidy crossed her arms and let her voice ring with outrage. "Put that bag down and get the hell out of my house."

"It's not your house, babe. It's a vampire's lair." Jackson came closer, his words soft as though talking to an actual "babe" with a tantrum. "A young and dangerous vampire. You're nothing but the plaything of the moment."

He snatched at her arm. She ducked out of reach and retreat into the kitchen.

"This is my *home*." It was true. Her refuge in the middle of nowhere had become her haven from the world. She felt safe here and always had. Because of Dominique, she realized, despite what he was—or maybe because of it. On some level she had always known, always felt safe here. "If a vampire can't chase me off on day one, you're sure as hell not going to drag me out now."

"Don't be stupid. When he gets bored with your attitude, he'll kill you."

"Dominique is my friend."

Jackson dropped the bag and rounded the counter. "Bullshit. That's what he wants you to believe."

Cassidy backed up to the sink. "He can't compel me without my permission," she argued, borderline panicked now that he might actually drag her from the cottage, kicking and screaming.

"You've had no training to resist compulsion. He's messing with you."

"No. He's not. Believe me. I've seen him—"

"You can't trust him," roared the red-faced, steel-eyed, six-foot-plus male mountain before her.

She knew he was capable of a temper, but he'd never directed it toward her. When he started forward with grim purpose, her stomach dropped into her ankles. Her hand groped frantically in the sink behind her, snatching up the first thing she found, which turned out to be an impressive-looking bread knife.

Jackson stopped in his tracks.

"I trust him, Jackson. I trust Dominique because he put his life—his *immortal* life—on the line for me. *You,* on the other hand, couldn't even be bothered to open your freaking mouth on my behalf when your father and uncle shredded my dignity at a dinner table."

He raised both hands in a gesture of calm that stood in stark contrast to the vein-popping fury distorting his face. "Listen, babe, you're confused right now. You don't want to do anything that can't be undone."

Confused? Cassidy's nerves were raw, but she recognized a gaslight attempt when she saw one. She gripped the knife harder as her shaky insides settled into quiet certainty. "Get out."

"Babe..."

"And stop calling me that. Do I *look* like something that needs to be coddled?"

"No. You look like someone who's out of her mind."

"I don't think I've ever seen things more clearly."

Jackson made a sudden lunge for her, but those lessons about maintaining total awareness of her environment paid off when she anticipated the move and turned in time to put the knife tip directly to his throat. He froze instantly.

"I'm done letting anybody tell me how I'm feeling and what to do, be they human or not. This is my home, and this is where I stay. Now, *get out.*"

He held her irate stare, assessing, then took several slow steps back, fists clenching by his sides. "If that's how you want it. We'll talk about this some other time. If you live that long."

She didn't lower the knife until Jackson was halfway out the door. Then she side-stepped to her bag sitting on the kitchen table. "Wait. You forgot something." Unzipping the side pocket, she pulled out the Striker family engagement ring and tossed it across the room for him to catch out of the air. "Eddie doesn't want to marry you either."

As usual, Dominique listened for her heartbeat when he returned to consciousness. Tonight he found it just down the hall. He inhaled, seeking her scent—and found that much closer.

With a powerful shock, he sat up. The instinctual panic quickly gave way to anger. "Cassidy!"

"Sleeping beauty awakes." She made no effort to raise her voice from the living room. "Bad dream?"

He didn't bother with clothes. He was out the door and in her face a second later. She almost spilled her laptop to the floor in surprise, but to her credit—and his relief—there was no hint of fear. "Why am I still here?"

"Where else would you be?"

"You were in my room today."

"Oh." A pink blush infused her freckles. "You knew I was there?"

"You touched me. I. Can. Smell. You."

"Yeah, okay. No use denying it then. I checked on you." She shrugged and shut the laptop. "Your door was unlocked."

Frustration continued to gnaw at him, but the anger subsided in the face of her wide, innocent eyes glistening with unshed tears. Watching her disintegrate last night had torn him apart. He had intended to betray her trust for one reason and one reason only—he didn't expect to have to live with that memory for long. He had intended to maintain control while at his human worst, only to end up losing control over his inhuman worst. Or had he? How had the beast slipped its chain and not killed her? How was it that in that moment, he had never felt stronger and more vulnerable at the same time?

No better than Aurelius, she had called him. No fear in her tear-streaked face. Only hurt. Disgust. Contempt. It should have been enough. He prayed it was enough. Yet here he still was, and he still remembered. As did she.

Pointless. All of it pointless. Like his existence.

The last of his ire drained away. He surrendered to the sofa beside her. "Why?"

"I was curious," she whispered.

"What did you find?"

"You were sleeping."

"I was defenseless," he growled. "Why did you not take me out into the sun?"

Her mouth dropped open. Was it possible the thought had never even crossed her mind? He wished he could will himself to die right there on the spot.

"Why would I do that? That would have killed you, wouldn't it?"

He couldn't look at her anymore. Leaning on his thighs, he slumped into himself. "As would a sword through my neck. As I told you."

Silence stretched as she comprehend his meaning, what he wanted of her—what he had *always* wanted of her. The heat of her hand brushed against his bare back, then vanished as she changed her mind about touching him.

"No," she said, her voice semi-steady. "If you seriously want to off yourself, you're going to have to do it without my help."

"After all you have seen? All I have told you? What else can I do to persuade you that a thing such as I does not deserve to exist?"

"The only way I would ever want to hurt you is if I believed you wanted to hurt me."

"Just knowing about me is dangerous. That knowledge alone separates you from the rest of humanity. Every thought, every decision you make from here on out will be determined by what you now know."

"It'll take some getting used to, I'll give you that. But how is this different from other life-changing events?"

"I could kill you. By accident or on a whim. Just like that." He snapped his fingers to illustrate. "Whether you stay here or leave, as long as I exist—and crave you—your life is in danger."

She was quiet for a while, watching him, mouth pressed flat with a stubbornness that defied all reason. Then she shook her head. "I know you won't hurt me, and...you need me."

"*Merde,*" he murmured, dark suspicion tingling between his shoulder blades. "What would make you think that?"

"Serge told me when I tried to help him, before he told me to run. No, wait..." A small frown appeared, then vanished as her brows rose. "Oh. Wow. He didn't just *tell* me, did he? He used that weird voice."

"He compelled you," Dominique clarified, a whole new kind of aggravation bubbling through his innards. He had abandoned Serge in the Keys to buy himself some precious hours of privacy, and still that idiot's meddling interfered.

Cassidy chuckled. "Good thing he did. Otherwise, I might have had a different reaction this morning." Sobering, she continued, "Which was what, by the way? Your sordid attempt to get me to hate you?"

"It would be better for you if you did," he said tightly.

"I'm sorry. I can't do that. I've seen your heart too often, my friend. I know you too well."

"Then grant my request as a friend. Drag me into the sun. End this nightmare for me." Soon he'd be begging on his knees.

She shook her head. "Never, *mon ami.*"

With a furious growl, Dominique sprang to his feet and moved so fast it took her several seconds to spot him by the door.

"Be sure to thank that filthy old blood-drinker for saving you from me twice now," he sneered. "And for leaving that bruise on your neck."

34

WRETCHED HEARTS

The front door slammed in Dominique's wake, rattling the windows. Cassidy stared at it, dumbfounded by the sheer storm of misery. She'd seen it this morning in her bed. She'd sensed it today while studying his lifeless body. She heard it in his voice now.

And yet, after everything she believed she understood, everything she had done, trying to help him, she still hadn't understood the true depth of his despair. For a long moment, she felt overwhelmed and powerless in the face of it.

Then her jaw clapped shut. No. She would not let him push her aside. This required a serious intervention, and clearly there was no one better than her to deliver it.

"Dominique, wait!"

She hurried for the door and burst onto the porch—where she came to an abrupt halt as something scrambled away and tumbled off the stairs.

Cassidy leaned over the rail. There was just enough light from the front windows to make out a figure. "Serge? What are you doing here?"

He sat up, bug-eyed, and glanced toward the dune. Then he got to his grimy bare feet and looked up at her. "Sweet one. Where you are, I am."

"Really? Just how long have you been stalking me?" she asked, unable to muster more than mild irritation. Twice, Dominique claimed, this ragged apparition had saved her life. His innocent, hapless manner made him difficult to take seriously. Likely, this was a fatal mistake made by many of his victims.

A mistake she had made.

Cassidy retreated, her hand going to the place on her neck where the bruise had been. Dominique's parting words registered only now. Serge had put it there. He had attacked her. The fog surrounding that night unraveled. Memories tumbled out. She and Jackson had walked the beach to talk, reconnect. Serge materialized out of nowhere. He had a beard then and a crazy light in his eyes. "Wait here and see nothing," he ordered Jackson, who did as told. Serge grabbed her, forced her head back, and...

Her backside bumped up against the door. She stared at this dubious, fidgety version of the nightmare that had crushed her neck with his jaws to drink her blood. The terror had lasted only a moment before she fell into a strange euphoria and wondered why Jackson looked so angry.

"You remember," Serge said with hushed awe. "I never meet them again, you see. They never remember."

"Why?" she said, bewildered. "Why would you do this to me? Why me? Jackson was there. He must have gallons more blood than I do."

The vampire sidled up the steps. Sand trickled out of his clothes. Dry seaweed hung in his hair. "But he is not made of light. Not like you. You...you are like the sun at midnight. I have never seen anything like you. I had to know you. I had to see all the shadows you cast through time. I may not have been as gentle as I could have," he concluded, looking contrite as a guilty puppy.

"Shadows?" Was this vampire-speak or lunacy?

He nodded and giggled, warming to the conversation. "I see, you see. I see the future in the shadows people cast in time."

"Uh-huh. So you think you've seen my future, is that it?"

Serge gave her an affronted look. "I have had your blood, sweet one. I don't *think* anything. I *know* your future."

Lunacy, she decided. But as long as he believed she needed to be protected for this future, she wouldn't dream of arguing. "How nice. Is it something good?"

To her mild alarm, he didn't answer right away. Head tilting to the side, he stared at her—or rather, *through* her—before drifting closer still. "I have had Dominique's blood, too," he said, his voice lowering to a whisper, almost drowned by the rustling breeze. "It is his future that is written in your blood."

Her skin crawled violently. She hugged herself.

"You feel it, the connection," Serge murmured.

He was so close; his mossy forest scent enveloped her, swirling in the briny ocean air. She wanted to get away from him. And she hung on his every word. Just words—she recognized the sound of a compulsion by now, and this wasn't it—but they resonated with something deep within her.

He shook his head. "So rare, that harmony. Almost...unimaginable." His tone grew fervent. "The blood-child has a destiny, and you are the key."

Cassidy shivered. On a ragged inhale, she forced herself to step back to reality. Such as it was these days. "He seems to think that his destiny involves me dragging him into the sun."

Serge hunched his shoulders. "I know."

"You do? And you leave it to a human to try and talk him out of that? He said you were his friend."

"He did, yes," he agreed, brightening. "But that is not his destiny. You will not betray him. Even when he begs you to."

"Destiny," she cried, throwing up her hands in frustration. "I don't give a rat's ass about his destiny. He's in *pain*, you flaming idiot. So much so, he wants to die. *That* is what I care about right now. Or did you put that in my head, too?"

Serge scurried back to the edge of the steps. "No. That is your destiny."

With that, he vanished.

Cassidy looked around and listened. Palm fronds clattered in the breeze. Surf rolled. Crickets.

She huffed out a breath and retrieved her flip-flops and flashlight. Walking back out into the moonless night was like walking into nothingness. Only the bobbing circle of her light existed. She followed it down the narrow path across the dune, past the towering shadow of a soughing pine. Along the way, startled land crabs reared up, waving their pincers.

From the beach, the cottage and its glowing windows were no longer visible, but she could make out the horizon where the tiny beacons of passing ships stood out from the fainter lights of the stars. Her beam swept around. Empty beach and churning waves.

"I know you're out here, Dominique." Was he watching her even now? Serge probably was. "Talk to me, Dominique," she called. "Dominique?"

Nothing.

Cassidy shut off the flashlight and settled cross-legged in the sand, waiting for her eyes to adjust. Oddly, it worried her more that one of those ornery crabs could sneak up on her than the fact that vampires could as well. She felt invisible sitting there. After a while, she felt light, too, insubstantial, dissolving into the darkness. *Like vampires,* she thought, a powerful sense of quiet despair invading her. Voices—French voices—drifted in this void, begging for help.

Aidez-moi, mon amour. Je vous prie.

Cassidy blinked, not sure if she'd heard the words or only imagined them. "Dominique?"

"*Oui.*"

He sat beside her—right beside her, the way he often did in her dreams—a bright silhouette, glistening with wetness. To her amazement, she found his sudden appearance more expected than alarming. What she didn't expect—and greatly appreciated—was that he wore his sweatpants now. He must have retrieved them from the cottage before joining her. Also, two bottles of Perrier, one of which he handed to her.

She cracked open her bottle. "You went swimming? In complete darkness?"

"I no longer swim. I can only sit on the bottom."

"For how long?"

"As long as I need to. I do not need air," he added and drank. Water he apparently did need.

She wondered why he might "need to" sit on the ocean floor, then she remembered those mysterious mangled sharks that washed up on this beach sometimes. Somehow she knew there would be another one come morning. Apex predators, Jim had called them. Clearly not quite apex enough.

She took several refreshing swallows of the sparkling water and solidified her resolve. Now or never then. "Aren't people easier to catch than sharks?"

She sensed his eyes on her. "Maybe I am lazy tonight," he told her, the French accent growing clipped. "And in no mood to travel or dispose of bodies."

"Hmm. I don't understand why you'd bother with that."

"Don't you?" he whispered.

The tension in his voice alone could have drawn blood, and she sent a silent thanks to the undead nutjob who had compelled her to have no fear in Dominique's presence.

"Think about it. There's a resort five miles down the street from here, offering a wide variety of international...dishes to choose from." She indicated the direction with her bottle. "Go drink your fill and leave the bodies where they drop."

An uncanny stillness settled over him. Was it shock? Or lurid fantasies? No matter. Keeping her tone reasonable, she gunned the engine and braced for impact.

"No, really. Isn't that how the vampires always buy it? By pissing off a bunch of humans who then track them down during the day? Don't be so damn careful. Leave a trail of bodies to your doorstep. You'll be amazed how quickly they'll find you.

They'll assume you're dead and carry you away. On the way into the coroner's van—poof!—there you go. No, wait, stop. Would you survive that inside a body bag? Oh, that would suck, waking up in a morgue. Okay. I see where that might not work. Scratch that." She erased it with her free hand. "But otherwise, doesn't that sound simple? I can't believe you haven't thought of that, brilliant as you are."

A small choked noise escaped him. "You. Are. Mad."

"How so? Isn't that what you want? Someone to do you in? Because obviously you can't do it on your own. I mean, what could be simpler than sitting out here at sunrise? Do you know how many suicidal humans would envy you that option? What the hell is stopping you?"

No reaction.

She leaned close and lowered her voice. "Unless, of course...you don't really want to die."

The little green bottle shattered in his hand. Glass shards thudded into the sand.

Cassidy straightened. "Right. Truth can be a bitch." Would he disappear now? From her side—and her life? She held her breath, waiting.

He turned his beautiful, empty face toward the sea. "It is not simple at all," he began softly. "We cannot harm ourselves. The beast's will to survive is stronger than any logic, any sense of decency or honor we might still cling to. In the end, it always wins."

"So...you have no choice?"

"None."

"And...you had no choice about...the deaths you caused in the beginning?" While sitting with his inert body today, she had speculated about this at length. Strong as he was, he could not stay awake during the day. Something as benign as sunlight was deadly to him. Was his reaction to fear equally unavoidable?

She sensed him tense, as though meaning to argue. Then his shoulders dropped, and he hung his head in an unmistakable gesture of surrender that squeezed her heart.

His voice was low and thick with human emotion. "When I was first transformed...the beast claimed me for many nights. I didn't realize that my father was...my first until much later, when the madman who made me told me what I had done. He declared that nothing mortal would ever matter to me again." Dominique shook his head. "It was a lie. My family still mattered. Jeovana still mattered. When she came to the island soon after, I escaped to see her. I was convinced that in her arms I would wake up from this horror. Instead—" He hesitated before finishing quickly. "Instead, I discovered that no human lover can survive me."

"Oh my God," Cassidy whispered, unable to suppress a shudder.

"*Oui. Mon Dieu.*" He scoffed with a meaningful tilt of his head. How many times had she, under the influence of wine, high spirits, or outright delusion—almost tempted him across lines of no return she didn't even know existed? Too many. Yes, they'd definitely be keeping things platonic.

"That morning, I waited for the sun to take me, only to learn that the thing I had become would not allow it. I woke up the next night buried deep in the sand with no clear memory of how I got there. Obviously, if I was to end myself, I would need help. Stupidly, I asked my sister, Anastasie. When I told her what I was—what I had done..." He closed his eyes and fell silent.

"She was terrified," Cassidy murmured.

"*Oui.* That night, I learned how very much the beast loves terror."

"I'm so sorry."

"Sorry? You are *sorry*?" Dominique spat under his breath. He leaned towards her, crowding her. "Keep your pity. I have enough of it for myself. What I want—what I *need*—is your outrage. I lust for your contempt more than I do for your blood. Do you understand?"

Cassidy didn't move until he retreated with a disgusted snort.

"I understand you had no choice."

This brought a low, decidedly inhuman growl, which she ignored.

"You had no idea what was happening to you. You were out of control, a victim of forces you couldn't comprehend. That's tragic beyond words, but it doesn't deserve the death penalty."

He considered this. "You sound very sure of yourself."

"Maybe as an outsider, I see things more clearly than you?" She imagined that a human in somewhat similar circumstances would get locked up and medicated, but he wouldn't be sent to death row regardless of how badly he might want to go there. No one would lock up Dominique. His penance was to live with what he'd done—what he was still doing. That he agonized about it at all meant that he was no true monster. His human soul was alive and fighting to be heard.

In the end, wasn't that what mattered most?

"Perhaps," he allowed. The corner of his mouth twitched.

Cassidy smiled, satisfied, and emptied her Perrier. At least she got him thinking in a new direction. No telling where that would lead him—or them? For now, sitting in companionable silence, watching the ocean stir beneath a blanket of stars filled her with a peace and gratitude she hadn't known in years.

Finally, she gave him a gentle nudge. "C'mon, friend. I'm starving."

35

MEMORIES OF THE SUN

Always, she surprised him. Always, she touched him in ways he never imagined. She knew him. She knew him better than he knew himself, and Dominique no longer cared how. He wallowed in the enchantment of Cassidy.

When he rose and helped her to her feet, she wrapped her arms around him. He let her, too hungry for her touch, but bracing for the sting of that infernal silver ring against his back. It didn't come. The ring was gone. Her cheek warmed his shoulder, and he closed his eyes to savor the heat of her body pressed so close. His fingers found their way into her hair, caressing the soft waves.

"I'm mastering the sneaky," she said, laughter in her voice.

His arms tightened around her, drawing her into him like a golden breath of life—and redemption. *"Touché, ma belle."*

Much as he knew he should, he could not refuse her compassion. The best to be hoped for was that he would not repay her by taking more than she could give. He needed her more than he would have believed possible. He existed tonight because of her. More than that, he *wanted* to exist because of her. She was the sole voice of reason in his senseless world.

She *was* his world.

And she would never be his.

There was no future for her with him, nothing that wasn't filled with peril and impossible desires. But for this night, she was with him, and he basked in the gift of her acceptance.

Serge loitered in the shrubs, cackling, but stayed clear of them as Dominique guided Cassidy by the hand through the darkness. For the sake of his hypersensitive eyes, she kept the flashlight off.

Back at the cottage, he threw himself into making dinner with all the enthusiasm of the newly saved. She quizzed him about the preparations, and he showed her how to dice, mix, and measure. He used the last of the ill-gotten fish for the entrée with a special improvised lemon pepper cream sauce. Her interest and unfettered appreciation of his efforts suffused him with pleasure.

"You could open a restaurant," she suggested, gesturing with her fork. "Open only for dinner. It's perfect."

Dominique couldn't help himself. He tossed back his head and laughed as he hadn't laughed since before he lost the sun. He laughed until he cried, slumped over the kitchen counter in a blissful heap. Though perplexed and hesitant, she laughed with him.

"Let me in on the joke now?" she said, wiping her face when he quieted at last.

"Ah, *chérie*. How should my guests pay for their meals? Shall I ask them to donate a pint of blood on the way out? Or perhaps meet the chef in the pantry for a swift embrace?"

Cassidy fell victim to another paroxysm of hilarity.

Mon Dieu! *She laughs at my perversity*, he thought, losing the last of his heart to her.

She calmed enough to sip at her glass, then broke down anew and ended up snorting wine out her nose. Dominique watched, fascinated by her hapless attempts to regain her dignity.

"That's so not right," she declared.

"It would be the only appealing aspect about such a venture."

"And here I thought you enjoyed cooking."

"Food no longer holds any interest for me, so I don't enjoy working with it. My pleasure lies in your enjoyment of what I make. Anyone else—" He shrugged. "I truly don't care."

Cassidy pushed a piece of fish through the creamy sauce. "Well, if this is what you can do when you don't like what you do, I'm sorry I never got to try your cooking before." She looked up. "Dominique, if it's really so unpleasant, please don't do it anymore. I don't think I can enjoy it knowing that."

He tilted his head and smiled. "You missed the part where I told you that *you* are my pleasure." Color bloomed in her cheeks. *And my salvation,* he added silently, leaning across the counter. "Cassidy, *ma belle amie.* When you first came here, not much about me was human. You made me remember who I was. You make me want to be that man again. Sometimes when I'm with you...I forget. For such a gift, I will gladly work a kitchen." And he would never tire of watching her freckles glow against that furious blush.

"I don't know what's worse," she murmured. "Dominique the flirt, or Dominique the sincere vampire?"

He beamed at her and used his most seductive French accent. "We are both equally devastating, *non*?"

They laughed for most of the rest of her meal about this and countless other nonsensical matters. Not until they both tackled kitchen cleanup together did he see an opening to ask one of his more burning questions.

"What happened to the ring?"

Her voice went flat. "It's over. Enough said."

Nowhere near enough. But the determined set of her shoulders made it clear the discussion would end there—or maybe not.

"He knows about you," she said, hanging up the towels.

"I know. We had a brief alliance in Key West." At her surprised look, he added, "Your welfare was a mutual interest."

Cassidy nodded. "Okay, well, he's completely recovered from his encounter with Arie. He put two and two together all over the place." She sighed. "But he doesn't understand a thing."

"Perhaps you are not giving him enough credit." Dominique cringed at his own words. Little credit as he gave Jackson—though recovering so swiftly from a compulsion of that magnitude was impressive all by itself—the human man harbored deep feelings for Cassidy and would have to be her future. No one else would understand what she had experienced—or have any hope of persuading her back into a human existence. "He knew what he was going up against when he tried to rescue you from the Roman. He risked his life as surely as I risked mine."

Cassidy propped a hand on her hip, gesturing with the other. "And now he's convinced that you're not to be trusted, all this evidence to the contrary."

Dominique swallowed his amusement. No, she definitely wasn't giving Jackson enough credit. He hadn't had a chance to give the man or his mysterious knowledge much thought, but now it occurred to him just what an aberration Jackson Striker was. Humans who were aware of vampires without also being enslaved to one were unheard of—at least as far as he knew. Serge, who didn't seem bothered by Jackson, might know differently. Then again, most nights, Serge flirted with madness.

Dominique dropped onto the sofa and booted his laptop, his curiosity piqued. "How much do you think he knows about us?"

"They," she corrected, plopping down beside him. "The Striker family. He said they've known about vampires since the sixteenth century."

"Promising," he murmured and launched some of his more nefarious apps.

"Promising? Promising for what?"

Dominique typed for a minute, searching, issuing commands.

Cassidy scooted closer, hanging by his shoulder, her intoxicating proximity all but evaporating his reason. The heat of her body radiating into his bare arm made him wish he had opted for a long-sleeved shirt instead of the T-shirt he grabbed earlier.

"Is that...? Striker Capital? You're hacking their network?"

"Every networked device they own." The attack geared up now, originating from co-opted systems around the globe, bouncing across continents and satellites, converging on all things Striker anywhere, public, private, or secret. He put the laptop aside. This would take a while.

Cassidy looked between the scrolling screen and him. "Why?"

"Information, *chère*, about my condition. I have spent months searching for any scrap of knowledge about what happened to me and why. Where it began. What it means. Anything to give me a reason to go on. Or even hope for a cure."

Her eyes rounded. "A cure? You think there might be a cure, and you wanted me to kill you? What is wrong with you?"

"You still need to ask?" He smiled, rueful. "You were an opportunity I could not refuse. Or thought I could not. In any case, I have found nothing credible about my kind, much less a cure."

"Did your sire tell you anything at all?"

"He showed me more than he ever told me," Dominique scoffed. Memories rose like muck from the bottom of a sulfurous river, things of which he had never spoken before. "He showed me how to transform others, because he made them over and over. He chose them because they somehow caught his attention, the way I believe I did when I killed Anastasie's assailant with my bare hands. He fed from them every night until they were near death with his poison burning in their veins. Then he forced me to give them my blood to turn them into what we are."

He paused, recalling the iron grip on his body and the nails slashing into his wrist. "The blood forges a bond between a sire and a youngling, a connection that allows the two to communicate telepathically. I believe he didn't give us his blood in order to remain hidden from us, hide his knowledge from us."

"So there was another one when—"

"A woman, yes. She blocked me from her mind and never spoke to me. I never even learned her name." Chills crawled over Dominique's shoulders, recalling those ghoulish nights not all that long ago.

"What happened to her?"

"I killed her, and every one of the spawn he forced me to make." Cassidy stared at him. He lifted a shoulder. "He maintains a perpetual army of two by manipulating the new youngling into trying to kill the one whose blood has made them. One always dies. It wasn't long before I became as silent as she had been. I didn't want to know them, because I would have to kill them. Or they would kill me."

"But...but that makes no sense. Why?"

"Ah yes. Why." Dominique rubbed both hands over his face and shoved his fingers through his hair. "I asked him that every night. Whatever his reasons, he had no interest in explaining himself to me. I was merely his current champion fighting cock, bound to him not by blood but by an unspoken promise that one night...one night, all would be revealed." He spread his arms in a dramatic gesture before him.

"He never did, did he?"

"No." Dominique leaned on his thighs, his mind speeding back to those months spent traveling from island to island on a yacht with a human crew compelled to within an inch of automatons. Nights of empty monotony and growing desperation. "I tried to push him. The night I pushed too hard...he left me exposed to the dawn. He carried me to safety, but not before I passed out, convinced I was about to burn."

A quiver ran through Cassidy, drawing his awareness back to her luscious warmth.

"I was his. He would not end me, he would not answer my questions, and when I attempted to escape, he tracked me down. I considered letting the next youngling win, but it was impossible. The beast refused. Or I could not condemn another to take my place. I don't know which."

"Do you think...could he have compelled you?"

"*Of course*. He could have commanded anything of me or anyone," he said, thoughtful. His voice dropped to a whisper, almost believing he was summoning the creature by naming it, almost smelling its fire-ravaged-forest scent in the air. "I believe...Kambyses was ancient long before Aurelius walked the sun."

Cassidy paled, the implied degree of supernatural power not lost on her. "How did you get away?"

"Orchestrated deception. But now I wonder if even that was part of the game he played with me—or maybe still plays." The idea grew in his gut like a flame catching kindling; Kambyses would hunt him until the end of time. Aurelius had all but confirmed this. Word had gotten out about Dominique among the ancients. Aurelius had even known his sire's pet name for him—Nico.

Dominique closed his eyes until the unease ebbed, drowned out by Cassidy's quiet, understanding presence. Her heartbeat whispered in his own blood, lending him the strength of her convictions. Somehow, his existence was less horrific in her company, almost bearable even.

"After I escaped, I returned to St. Barth and staged my death so my mother and sister could go on with their lives. Which is why you found my obituary there," he added with a small nod in tribute to her sleuthing skills. She said nothing, continuing to give him the gift of her undivided attention.

"After that, I traveled, looking for others like me. The few I found all wanted to kill me sooner than answer questions, so I came here." He waved at the surrounding house. "My mother inherited this cottage from an aunt. While we were children, my parents would bring us here almost every year to spend time as a family, away from the restaurant. And of course, to visit my father's favorite place, Disney World." Dominique grew pensive. "This is the closest thing to home I will ever have again. Here I have peace."

"Until the human moved in, and you decided to check out. What if I had done what you wanted today? And maybe tonight, you'll discover that cure on the Striker's systems?" She gestured at the laptop on the glass tabletop.

The intrusion had tripped alarms, and large sections of the network dropped offline in defense. That there was something to find was no longer in doubt. It would take more than one night to uncover, though.

Even Cassidy understood all the red X's. "Or you could just try asking them."

"I could," he murmured, but his attention took a sharp turn back to the quickening pulse in her neck. Perhaps a ride on the bike was in order before it got too much later. "I will try harder to find the answers I need. Somehow."

"You better," she said with such indignation his mood lifted despite himself.

"Or what? Would you miss me if I could sit in the sun instead and be done with it all?"

"Hell, no. I just don't want to sweep your ashes off the porch." She gave his arm a light push. "Idiot. What do you think?"

"That you might miss me—a little."

"A little," she agreed with a lopsided smile that flooded his chest with even more warmth than her casual touch did.

Before he knew what he was doing, he reached around her shoulder and pulled her against his side fast enough to make her squeak with surprise. To cover his own sudden awkwardness, he gently wedged her neck in the crook of his elbow in a move he had performed a dozen times during their practice session. She knew the counter-move needed to free herself. She didn't.

Instead, she relaxed, and the soft heat of her body settled against him like a banked coal. *Que Dieu l'aide*, he could even feel her heart beat against his ribs. What was he doing? Somehow he kept his voice steady as he said, "One sneak attack deserves another, *non*?"

She laid her head against his shoulder. "I won't fight; I'm not in the mood."

He loosened his hold. "Is that what you will tell an attacker when he takes you unaware?"

"Oh, Dominique," she said with a mildly exasperated sigh and a wave of one hand. "Just...do it already. It's not like I could stop you."

"Do...what?"

She turned her face up to him, and he brushed the hair out of her eyes to meet her speculative gaze. "I see how you look at me. I can guess what it means."

"Do you?" he asked carefully.

"You're hungry, aren't you?"

He leaned his head back on the sofa cushions and stared at the whirling ceiling fan. "I'm not hungry, *ma petite*. Not like that." Again, she surprised him.

Again, she wasn't done.

She shifted around under his arm to sit, facing him, with her legs tucked beneath her. "But you want to...bite me. Right?"

Dazed by the sheer thrill of the idea alone, he closed his eyes. "I'd have to be blind not to see it."

"I'm sorry, Cassidy."

"Don't be. I...I want you to."

His eyes snapped open. "Why?"

"Because I want to pay for dinner?" she offered with a one-shouldered shrug.

"Try again. This is no trivial thing you suggest."

"You did it before."

"By accident. Serge stopped me from..."

"He's still here, isn't he?"

He stretched his hearing, sifting through the noises surrounding the house. Wind, waves, insects, a troupe of raccoons, but no hint of her guardian angel's presence. There hadn't been for some time. "You would put your life into that madman's hands?"

"No, Dominique. I'm putting my life in your hands, and not for trivial reasons, either." She hesitated. Color flared back in her cheeks as her gaze dropped. Her heart thumped in his ears. Then she nodded to herself, tucked her hair behind her ears and licked at her lips as she met his gaze again. "I...I need to feel that connection again. That moment when...when you were part of me. Also...can you see what's in my mind when you...?" She raised a questioning brow.

He only managed an abbreviated nod.

"In that case, maybe you'd like to see this place during the daytime again? And the beach? And the bridges in the Keys—"

Dominique scrubbed a hand over his face to restart his thoughts, which had crashed and burned against the inside of his skull. He had scarcely begun feeding like this—sipping really—while flooding his oblivious prey with fantasies instead of terror. What she suggested staggered him. Her total awareness of him, and her shared memories. Memories of the day...of sunlight!

A helpless little sound strangled in his throat. The sharp tips of his canines emerged in eager anticipation.

Serge! he bellowed. By giving the old one his blood, he had permitted him into his mind for a while, allowing him to track his thoughts, emotions, and location. The reverse was not true, however. He had no idea where the little fiend lurked. Dominique would have to take it on faith that he continued to hover—because they were well past the point of no return.

"I know you can do this," she said. Her hot, unexpected touch on his arm drove his fingers into the upholstery beneath him.

The entire room glowed with brilliant colors and razor-sharp contrasts. In the midst of it all, Cassidy's golden aura swirled with the pulsing river of her life.

"I'm not so sure." Raw lust rolled in his voice.

"I am. You would have been out that door by now if you thought you might hurt me."

He shifted toward her. His nostrils flared, taking in her scent, his monstrous black eyes locked with her unblinking ocean blue stare. "Do you have *any* idea what you are tempting me with?"

"I do now," she whispered, breathless. She held up a finger between them. "There is one thing. I...I want to see it this time." With that, she turned over her arm, exposing her wrist.

Had she taken off her clothes with an inviting sway of her hips, she could not have inflamed him more. Every vein in his body ached for her blood, and his wits fluttered like frightened birds. Dominique closed his eyes. Control. He had to maintain control. Otherwise, the beast would ride him into the abyss. She was certain that he could. He was sure only of not wanting to let her down.

Forcing himself to concentrate on how and where to bite, he traced the vein that ran the brightest from her inside elbow down to the delicate bones of her wrist where the line lay exposed, a thin, blue worm. She shivered when he sniffed at it.

"Cassie *amour*. You smell like the sun," he said, entranced, before closing his mouth—and teeth—over the pulse. Blood washed his tongue, warm copper spiced with pepper and wine. For three beats of her heart, he drifted in darkness, savoring the taste of her and nothing more.

Then a flood of sunlight swept him away.

36

No Fit Company

Sometime after midnight, Dominique stood over a body drained of blood. "*Merde.*"

So much for merely sipping his prey without Serge hovering over his shoulder. After drinking from Cassidy the night before and stopping on his own before the euphoria knocked him senseless, he was certain he could manage this.

But Cassidy had welcomed him into her arms and mind. This clueless young thug was far more apprehensive about the embrace of a stranger. The beast pounced. The rest was inevitable. Dominique's body still thrummed with the ecstasy.

He wiped the back of his hand across his mouth. It shook a little. What a fool he was.

Retrieving the phone from his pocket, he dialed a number he had seen only once before when he casually perused Cassidy's phone. When his call hit voice mail, he dialed again, and then again.

"Who the fuck is this?" a man's sleep-roughened voice demanded.

"*Bonsoir,*" he said and waited. After several seconds of dead air, he ventured, "You missed me, *non?*"

"What the fuck do you want?" Jackson Striker sounded wide awake now.

Dominique hesitated. The words he really wanted—needed—to say refused to emerge. Instead, he said, "I need to see you."

"You're joking."

He let the silence speak for itself.

"Why?"

"I will explain when we meet. Where will you be in two hours?"

"You think I'm going to agree to meet with you in the middle of the night? How stupid do you think I am?"

"I think maybe you are curious?"

This gave the human pause. "What guarantee do I have that I'm going to walk away in one piece and with a full blood supply?"

Dominique stared at the corpse by his feet. "I truly only wish to speak with you."

Long pause. "Fine. In *four* hours I'll be at the municipal airport, getting on a plane to Buenos Aires. I can spare a few minutes then. Don't be late." Jackson didn't wait for a confirmation before disconnecting.

Four hours later, and an hour and a half before sunrise, Dominique cruised through downtown Orchard Beach, along roads that stretched like empty raceways under the glow of yellow sodium lights. A strange mixture of reluctance and purpose welled deep inside him, fueled by the joy he'd known in Cassidy's arms the night before.

For hours they had lain together in a swoon after he sipped her vein, his starving soul twining with her generous spirit, their surrender to each other complete. Their minds locked like pieces of a puzzle, conjuring a shared dream of sunlight and memories, both ecstatic and abysmal. Together they laughed and they wept, understanding all and hiding nothing. They were more than one. They were whole.

"All is as it must be," Serge had said later when Dominique joined the would-be oracle on the front porch after he deposited a gently snoring Cassidy in her bed.

For once, Dominique didn't argue. Nothing had ever felt so right. As had Serge's proclamation soon thereafter when he declined an offer to ride: "Tonight, your destiny begins."

Stupidly, he believed this was the fool's dramatic way of saying he deemed Dominique ready to hunt on his own without making bodies.

It means nothing, he chided himself now, but couldn't quite shake the sense of something momentous hanging over him. The night oozed portent.

At the airport entrance, the large, sleepy-looking guard handed him a parking pass and pointed out the hanger with the SICI logo emblazoned on the side. Jackson's sleek white Audi stood nearby, alone in the glare of a floodlight. Dominique pulled the bike up next to it. He looked around while shedding his helmet and gloves.

The hangars and office buildings were lit, and a line of blue lights marked the single runway, but there was no activity anywhere. The main doors to the SICI hangar stood partially open. Silhouetted against the bright interior, a figure paused at the edge of night, hands tucked into the pockets of his Dockers, white polo shirt crisp. Dominique detected only one heartbeat, a slightly accelerated thumping against a backdrop of subtle machine noises. Jackson was alone.

Whether to put the human at ease or delay the inevitable, he couldn't say, but he took his time pulling off the jacket. Also, the fresh blood scent of tonight's hunt still clung to the leather, presenting a distraction he could do without. As he draped the jacked over the seat by the helmet, damp night air caressed his bare arms and ruffled his hair.

"Do I even want to know why there's a machete strapped to your ride?" Jackson called.

"I don't know. Do you?"

Jackson didn't. As he retreated into the hangar, he said, "I need to get this damn door unjammed before the crew gets here. You can do your talking while I do that."

Dominique followed, his reluctance deepening, but seeing no way around having this conversation.

Inside, a Gulfstream jet sat with its door gaping and interior lights on, only in want of a pilot and an open hangar. Jackson walked toward the far wall and a control panel.

"I need to know your true sentiments for Cassidy," Dominique said.

Jackson shot him a dubious scowl over one shoulder. "Well, let's see. I saved her from certain rape. She saved me from committing suicide. In the two years we lived together, she became the only woman for me. I proposed and brought her home, and not even two months later she dumps me for someone who can't stay awake during the day and maintains a questionable diet. At knife-point, I might add. So how do I feel? I don't know. You tell me, Nicky."

"She does have a knack for attracting troubled souls," Dominique murmured. In her mind he'd seen all this and more, witnessed Jackson's varied personas and actions, experienced all her emotions every step of the way. Remembering the bliss of lying in her arms almost made him spin on a heel and rush back to her, to touch her again, merge with her for the rest of this night, and every night thereafter for as long as his poison contaminated her blood.

"I'm not fit company for her," he said instead.

Jackson turned away from the control panel, his hand hovering over it. Standing with his fingers pushed into the pockets of his leather pants, Dominique held his stare and studiously ignored the pulse ticking in the human's muscular neck. If only he could trust himself to drink without killing, this would be so much easier.

"Did you have a point?" Jackson said.

"I think you need to make more of an effort to be the man she deserves. Show her you are the only man for her."

Jackson's face colored. "And how do you suggest I do that? At gunpoint maybe? Is that considered a good foundation for a relationship in France?"

Dominique raised a brow. "No."

"If you really feel that way, how about you stop drinking her blood and compelling her? That would be enormously helpful right there. Better yet, why don't you just go the fuck away?"

"If it were so simple, I would compel her tonight to forget I even exist."

"It *is* that simple."

"She knows too much. She has seen more than she can ever forget, even if she allowed me to compel her." Dominique came closer, his voice lowering. "And you are the only one she can speak to about any of it. There can be no one else to share her life now." He paused, riveted by the thunder of the human's racing heart as he leaned closer still, drawn like a moth to flame. "There is no need for secrets between you," he whispered. "And that is a good foundation for any relationship anywhere. Even in America, *non*?"

Teeth grinding, Jackson eyed him down his nose. "Get. Away. From me."

An artery pulsed within striking distance, and Dominique's canines ached to pierce it. He took two careful steps back. He remembered to stop breathing, too. Amazing and fortunate that the outrage pulsing through Jackson had not morphed into terror. It was close, though. The man teetered on a razor's edge.

"You've made your point." He wiped at the sweat pouring off his forehead. "I'll talk to Cassidy again. But...you're going to stay out of her life. Is that clear?"

Dominique closed his eyes. Despair cleaved through him, but he nodded. She would have a chance to live a full and happy life in the sun...without him. "*Merci.*"

"You're the damn weirdest vampire I've ever met."

"Oh? You have met many?"

"None like you."

Dominique shrugged and relaxed now that he had accomplished his purpose here, and Jackson's anxiety subsided. "Perhaps this is because I did not have the benefit of a proper blood-drinker education."

"And why's that, if I may ask?"

"My sire had no interest in providing it."

"Huh. That sucks," Jackson said and turned back to the screen. He touched several controls, succeeding only in creating another blinking red light. "Fuck."

"I wonder if maybe you might have some more information for me?" Dominique ventured, daring to hope. "About my kind?"

"I might...damn. I don't suppose you know anything about tech?"

He allowed himself the smallest of smiles. "I might."

"Have at it. Fuck knows it can't get any more hosed than it is." Jackson massaged the back of his neck, and Dominique's eye caught on the two partially amputated fingers. "Everything's been acting up since yesterday."

"Has it?" Dominique recognized the damage caused by his hacking efforts. He could fix it with three simple commands. Not that he was about to. The hangar doors, however, were innocuous enough.

He touched the screen. It went blank.

A rumble rolled through the cavernous space, and they both turned to look. At the far end, the massive doors slid shut.

"Nice, Nicky," Jackson drawled. "Now you've got me curious. Does everything you touch die?"

Dominique tried to reconcile the snide words with the strange excitement gleaming in the cold, bright eyes.

A new sound filled the air, a mechanical humming that issued from the ceiling's corners. Basketball-sized spheres rotated there. An instant later, they ignited blinding beams of light that swerved through the enormous space.

"Well, now you've done it," Jackson said.

Dominique shaded his eyes against the stinging glare with one hand. "What is this?"

"My uncle's idea of a security system. Can't say I've ever seen it kick in. But of course,"—he paused to watch the beams converge on Dominique—"I've never seen a bloodsucker in here either."

Dominique gasped. The exposed skin on his face and arms crawled with heat. Red-hot needles pierced his eyes, rendering him blind as he staggered backwards, throwing his arms across his face.

The beams followed.

He scrambled faster, crashed into a wall. Blisters popped on his forearms and the back of his neck. Blood ran down his sides and spine. "Do something!"

"Working on it," Jackson called from the vicinity of the control panel. He didn't sound all that concerned. "Did I mention our systems have been a mess?"

Dominique tasted blood as the beast seized his body with every panic-fueled survival instinct it possessed. With a tremendous burst of speed, he streaked away, only to crash into another wall. The impact shattered his shoulder with a sharp crack. The beams found him, and again he bolted. Again a wall stopped him. The thick aluminum sheeting dented under the explosive force of impact. This time, it was his back that took the brunt of the collision.

Somewhere, a door slammed. He raced around the perimeter to locate it. There were three—all of them steel and electronically locked—and no sign of Jackson.

Finally, he hurtled toward the only possible cover, the jet. Inside, the lights shafted through the large windows, luminous fingers seeking their prey. Dominique shot between them, past lavish leather seats and into the darkened sanctuary of the galley.

He slumped over the sink, gasping. His limbs spasmed with pain and exertion. Sinister wisps of smoke drifted off his skin.

In his heart, human terror warred with the beast's rage. Every cell in his body screamed TRAP!

"Please tell me you're not dripping blood all over the rug," Jackson's tiny voice said from the overhead speakers. "You can't imagine how expensive those things are to clean."

Through the red haze of his vision, it took Dominique a few seconds to spot the small camera mounted near the front of the cabin. "Please tell me you are actually trying to turn off your 'security system.'"

"Oh, don't worry. I'll get it turned off." Pause. "As soon as the sun's up."

"*Va te faire foutre*," he growled.

"I did say you needed to go the fuck away, didn't I?"

Dominique straightened and assessed his surroundings—his very expensive, very mobile cage. With the beast all but off its leash, he darted down the length of the cabin and snarled directly into the camera. "You foul, useless *coward*. I agreed to your terms."

"What can I say? I guess I don't trust you all that much."

He stood just beyond the reach of two of the light beams, but could feel them lying in wait for him. They were bright enough to reflect off the shiny walnut walls and heat the exposed skin on his hands and face.

No way out.

Tonight you meet your destiny, blood-child.

The wrath in his chest became still and cold. He was at the mercy of yet another madman. They were becoming a perpetual plague in his miserable existence. He considered reaching out to Serge on their new blood bond, but dismissed that idea instantly; the old pirate wouldn't stand a chance against these high-tech systems. Not that he was likely to even show up, given how he considered Dominique's dealings with Jackson "destined." No, there were no allies to be had here; he was on his own.

His body tightened as the beast surfaced fully.

"You do not trust any of us, do you, Jackson?" he said, staring directly into the camera lens.

The calm tone, together with the transformation of his face, made Jackson hesitate. When he spoke, animosity poured from the speakers like acid. "The first vampire I ever met tore my twin brother to pieces right in front of me. Do I trust you? Seriously? What do you think, you blood-sucking motherfucker?"

"What I think is that you underestimate me," Dominique said and bared his fully extended fangs in a lethal grin.

Then he released the beast.

The next morning, Cassidy found the door to Dominique's sanctuary wide open and his bed empty. Her disappointment in morphed into unease when she checked for messages on her phone over coffee and found none. He was spending the day elsewhere without explanation.

He'd been in good spirits last night before embarking on a "quick outing," the precise nature of which he tried—and failed—to conceal from her. The telepathic bond forged by his feeding from her was too strong to hide anything when they were near each other. He would siphon a pint or two from a body he intended to let walk away. Even Serge gave his blessing. What could have possibly gone wrong?

Eddie, who sprawled on the kitchen counter like the lord of all he surveyed, gave her a narrow-eyed look.

"Right," she muttered. "Everything."

Resolving to put the issue aside until sundown, she geared up for another shift in the trenches at the *Orchard Beach Gazette*. The previous day, Monday, matters there had reached a whole new level of unpleasant. It was the day after the weekend that had flipped her world on its axis, and she had rushed in late to hostile glares from Jim and sympathetic glances from the others. There were no secrets in an office this small, and by noon everyone knew she had overreached her rookie position by horning in on veteran Jim's turf. But they also knew how close she had been to the scene of the latest murder, and after she mentioned it had been Jackson who discovered the young man's body, expectations for her report rose exponentially.

While Jim fumed, she made calls to the Monroe County Sherriff's office in Key West, as well as the medical examiner in Marathon and—because she had true first-hand knowledge—asked the sort of leading questions that resulted in fresh and useful quotes. She didn't bother calling Jackson, freely placing words of shock, horror, and chilling details in the mouth of "the man who was first on the scene." He owed her that much, she reasoned.

"Kiddo, this is great stuff. Way to go, running with that exclusive source," Larry rumbled when she let him read an early draft. Then he chuckled and more quietly added. "That should knock Jim down a peg or two."

Jim lost no time trying to knock *her* down, though. "Lucky break," he sneered as he sailed past her cubicle. "Don't plan on building a career on that."

She buried her frustrations under a bland smile. She would have much preferred to write the truth, an exposé about marauding vampires. But that *really* wouldn't have helped her career—or her continued existence if it had attracted the attention of the subject-matter.

To Cassidy's relief, today was nowhere near so tense. She appeared early, brewed a pot of coffee that could dissolve spoons, and lost herself in a tall stack of obits and copy edits. She maintained a quiet, friendly, ever-helpful attitude, the perfect employee who had learned her place in the food chain. It was easy now that it didn't matter anymore. Beyond the paycheck, nothing here in the so-called real world mattered. Not anymore.

She even worked late and then dawdled in the grocery store until after dark, because that was easier than sitting at home waiting for the sun to set. When she hauled her bags through the front door and announced her presence, only Eddie mewed a greeting. The rest of the house lay silent. No hint of Dominique brushed her mind.

With a heavy sigh, she piled her groceries on the counter and walked down the hallway in search of his presence, if nothing else. The small, cluttered room looked dingy in the yellow light of a rickety table lamp, the action hero patterned sheets crumpled on the twin bed. A few black shirts and pants hung in a closet otherwise stuffed with boxes, but there were no bike leathers or boots—and no vampire.

Cassidy brushed her fingers over the smooth scabbards hanging on the wall. Disappointment crowded around her heart. The electric thrill of his bite, the mind-blowing communion it forged between them, had rocked them both. Time had ceased to exist as they lay in each other's arms, stunned as their mental edges blurred, one into the other. Sharing their minds, their memories, their souls...those were the greatest intimacies either of them had ever experienced, bar none. What it all meant, she dared not consider. For now, she wanted only to live in this moment with him. The future, whatever it held, would get here soon enough.

Had Dominique thought about it, though? She'd felt hints of his trepidation before they became high on each other and the world disappeared. But once he was away from her? With a clearer head? What was he thinking?

With her eyes closed in concentration, she reached out for him. No answer. He wasn't nearby. A visit to the shed confirmed this; it stood open and empty. There was, however, a vampire.

She gasped when her flashlight caught the bedraggled, curly-haired figure standing not ten feet away. "Serge?"

He stared at her, and Cassidy struggled with a growing sense of disquiet. She switched off the flashlight—no point annoying an unstable vampire by shining it into his eyes—and tried for a casual air. "Have you seen Dominique?"

"Your destinies unfold," he said in hushed, reverent tones.

Cassidy cringed. *Not this again.* "Dominique," she repeated, speaking slowly. "Do you know where he is?"

The silhouette drooped as he appeared to turn away from her.

She took an impatient step toward him. "You had his blood. Doesn't that mean you're plugged into his head? Even at a distance? Where is he? Is he alright?"

Serge looked up, only the glint of his eyes visible in the starlight as he whispered, "The future, sweet one, is now."

37

Judge, Jury, and Executioner

In the operations office, Jackson checked the monitors again before sunset, confirming that all systems reported armed and ready. The equipment towers held a fortune in state-of-the-art technology, running military-grade software. The whole controlled an impressive array of defenses masquerading as standard airport structures. Any vampire foolish enough to step onto the airport grounds would trip one of the fine-tuned sensors and activate the same type of high-speed light cannons that had so effectively cornered Nicky in the hangar.

Although how effectively was a matter of opinion.

Garrett Striker had stepped off his Gulfstream earlier in the afternoon with three more kills to his name and in high spirits—until his brother, Warren, informed him he would take Garrett's plane to a business meeting in Brussels.

"What happened to yours?"

"Ask your nephew."

"Forty million dollars," Garrett muttered now for what had to be the twentieth time.

Jackson winced, but held his tongue. His uncle would eventually stop griping about the damage done to the plane. It was a small price to pay for what they were about to capture.

Dumping his equipment duffel on the desk, Garrett jerked open the zipper, retrieved his Glock, and confirmed a bullet was in the chamber. Then he slid the weapon into the shoulder holster he wore over a standard white SICI polo shirt. While never part of any military, he had trained with several paramilitary security groups, maintained lethal combat instincts, and kept himself in peak physical condition. Garrett Striker was a hunter, born and bred.

Another gun appeared from the bag, though that was too generous a term for the thing. An amalgamation of batteries, bulbs, concentrators, indicator, and triggering mechanism, it looked more like a clumsy attempt at a sci-fi fantasy weapon. It had some heft, however, and good balance, and Garrett continued to make regular enhancements. Compared to this version of the light gun, the one that had failed to subdue the vampire that took Justin's life was a sparkler next to a Hollywood spotlight. When he pulled the trigger, a crisp, round brilliance appeared on the desk.

Jackson checked the charge on his own light gun. "Ready."

The containment room beyond the security door was really another hangar, a thirty-by-forty foot steel box. The full-spectrum lamps mounted on the thirty-foot ceiling came up to blast the space with an intensity equivalent to high noon at the equator. No vampire could tolerate such exposure for any length of time, which was great motivation to stay under cover in the crate. Not that breaking out of the fifteen-foot titanium cube taking up the center of the room was in any way realistic, even for a supernatural being.

Garrett stood in front of the silver-coated bars that made up one side of the enclosure. With hands on his hips, he eyed the pale, still body stretched out along the far wall. "You trapped a rogue youngling in a forty million dollar plane. What in God's name were you thinking?"

"He figured out we were in his house and came after us. Or me rather, since you weren't here. I triggered the cannons once he was inside. And don't you dare tell me about the plane again," Jackson flared, seeing his uncle's white-lipped expression. "It was a tool. How was I supposed to know he'd trash it?"

A prime understatement there. The only way his father's plane could have sustained more damage would have been to fall out of the sky and explode on impact.

Garrett waved an authoritative finger at him. "Those cannons were never intended to trap anything, only keep things *out*. Now you're telling me you allowed yourself to become a target as well?"

"I saw an opportunity, and I took it. Don't tell me you wouldn't have done the same." Close enough. Never mind the result—or even the astronomical price tag—if Garrett ever found out how close he'd gotten to the vampire long before springing the trap, none of this would matter. In his uncle's eyes, Jackson would be deemed too stupid to live.

Garrett shook his head. "Dumb, Jack. Very dumb. There are proper ways to do these things. You could have gotten us all killed."

Jackson squeezed his mouth shut and checked his watch. Another minute, two tops. "I had the lab run his blood this afternoon. Don't suppose you're interested in the result?"

"Oh, why not?" Garrett said, spreading his arms wide. "Let's see what other fiascos you've brought down on our heads."

Jackson smiled tightly, savoring the anticipation, and forced himself to sound casual. "According to the preliminaries, it looks like his genetic deviation will come in at around one percent." Pausing for effect, he added, "Maybe less."

Garrett's eyes narrowed. "That can't be right. You messed up the draw."

It was the serum that carried a sire's fragile DNA payload. Once there was enough of it established in a host, the immune system succumbed, and a small dose of vampire blood triggered the transformation into an entirely different species. With each successive generation, the genetic signatures evolved, adapting to different hosts, but the Striker labs had analyzed enough of them over the years to isolate most of the common DNA. The lower the genetic deviation, the closer it was to the root of the family tree—the original vampire.

"Really? A fucked up blood draw would cause results like that? Give me at least some credit, will you? It's correct. Our baby vamp here offed another one last week, who was about two thousand years older. He didn't do that without a sire at least that old, possibly even first generation."

Garrett stared at his nephew in annoyed bewilderment. "And how, in God's name, would you know what he did last week?"

"You sent me to Key West to find things. I found things."

Quiet laughter floated from the crate. "Ah, Jackson, *cher*, what a trickster you are." The soft words were hard to make out through the hiss of the white noise generators mounted on top of the crate. They neutralized the vocal frequencies the vampire might use to compel them, leaving only an impression of his voice, like the whispers of a ghost.

"I'm in no mood for your games tonight," Jackson said.

"But you play them so well." In the back of the crate, the captive was sitting up. "Is there anyone at all that you do not deceive?"

"Oh good," Garrett said. "We've got ourselves a talker."

Fuck. That's all he needed. The bloodsucker spilling his guts to Garrett about Jackson's screw-ups. He should have killed him today while he had the chance. Fuck the sire.

The vampire rose to his feet and approached the front bars, without an ounce of inhibition about his nudity. Jackson had waited until an hour after sunrise before venturing into the debris-filled plane to retrieve the unconscious vampire from the lavatory. Before he dragged him into the crate, he had drawn the blood sample for the lab and pulled off every shred of clothing. From here on out, nothing would protect this creature's pale hide or non-existent modesty.

The knowing smile dropped a chill into Jackson's gut. The vampire was done playing at being human. "I changed my mind. You do not deserve her. But then...she is no longer yours, is she?"

"You leave Cassidy out of this," Jackson said between grinding teeth.

"Ah, but why? Of all the reasons I am here, she is the only one that truly matters, *non?*"

The bastard came even closer, took hold of the silvered bars with both hands and almost pressed his face to them as well. His fingers sizzled on the silver. The reflected shimmer from the full-spectrum lamps turned the front of him the color of poached salmon. A tangled shock of hair protected his eyes from the worst of the light, but Jackson could see that they were slits of glittering darkness. The vampire's mouth opened, fangs extended. "You are wasting your time. Cassidy is mine. For as long as I live."

"I can fix that in a hurry." Jackson's grip tightened on the light gun.

"Mmm," the vampire taunted and stepped back. A layer of his skin remained stuck to the bars where it curled and blackened. "Did I mention she is delicious? And so very willing. In *every* way."

Jackson's whole body swayed forward, then straightened again. He knew better than to give in to the impulse to rush at the crate. "Son of a—"

Garrett shot him a sharp look. "He's got your number, kid, doesn't he?"

And he knew how to use it, too. The vampire's suggestive words shot a spike of rage up his spine. Even now, standing there, arms loose by his sides, the creature flaunted his blatant sexuality, his grace, his sleek power. Jackson reminded himself that Cassidy couldn't have been seduced into sex with this demon for the simple reason that she still lived. The vampire was playing emotional mind games with all of them, nothing more. As long as he didn't start talking about their impromptu alliance in Key West in front of Garrett, Jackson could deal.

Jackson let out a long breath and schooled his expression into neutrality.

Apparently satisfied with that display of self-control, Garrett turned back to the crate. "Since you've already met my nephew, allow me to introduce myself. I'm Garrett Striker, hunter, judge, jury, and executioner. And your ass is mine."

"Is it truly?" The soft French accent sounded bemused.

"As you've discovered, you have no way out of here. We've done this far too long. We know what we're doing." To emphasize this point, Garrett aimed the light gun at the floor inside the crate and triggered the beam before sliding it across the vampire's bare feet. They erupted into bloody blisters. With a sharp hiss, the vampire scurried back.

"Let me tell you what's going to happen," Garrett continued. "The only way you're leaving here is as a pile of ash in a garbage bag. But you do have a choice about how you get there. If you're a good little bloodsucker and cooperate, we'll be quick about it. If not—" He shrugged, hefting the weapon. "Well, we've got time." When there was no response, he added. "So how do you feel about inviting your sire to join us?"

The vampire drew back his upper lip in a fanged, contemptuous sneer. "You are mad."

Garrett raised the light gun. The vampire's trunk lit up bright as day for less than a second before the target twisted away at such speed he seemed to vanish. A long growl drew their attention to a far corner of the crate. His torso was raw scarlet, but already healing.

"Want to see the wide angle setting? Bet even you can't move that fast." Garrett twisted the lens several notches and pulled the trigger. This time, the beam lit up the entire enclosure. There was nowhere for the vampire to go, though he tried, and tried hard. There was a blur of motion, punctuated by violent bangs, sledgehammer strikes against the titanium walls. When the hammer crashed against the bars, the entire box vibrated like a struck gong.

Stunned, Jackson watched as the vampire desperately tried to squeeze through a narrow gap, reaching straight for the light that broiled him. His skin reacted to the silver coating. Strips of it shriveled and peeled off, sticking to the bars in black crusts. His shoulder and several ribs collapsed with loud cracks and squeezed through. Still, Garrett fired. The guttural roar of rage shifted and became an earsplitting howl, a rising wave of sound—the primal essence of inconceivable pain.

When the scream finally stopped, the vampire slid to the ground and fell back, unconscious, his body a broken, bloodied shell enveloped in a haze of smoke.

Garrett studied his handiwork with a critical eye. "Give me some earplugs, and I can do this all night."

"Isn't this a bit extreme?" Jackson said.

"They usually run away from the light."

"That's not what I meant."

"I know what you meant." Garrett cut a penetrating look at him. "You're not getting squeamish, are you, kid?"

He wasn't sure what he felt, but squeamish wasn't it. "What good is he to us like this?"

"Plenty. Watch."

Jackson did. The flattened shoulder and ribcage expand-ed, returning to their previous shape, balloons filling with air. Bones popped and snapped back into place, and a thin new layer of skin slithered across the raw flesh, stemming the ooz-ing blood. The energy the vampire spent to heal himself was tremendous. That he would run out of healing powers long before the gun ran out of battery power was obvious.

"Ready to call daddy yet?" Garrett said. "No one else is ever going to find you here. Or hear you. These walls are as sound proof as it gets. Your blood bond is your only hope."

The vampire lying on the floor chuckled. "*Petit imbécile.* I have no blood bond with my sire. Consider that a gift."

Garrett sighed and shook his head as he checked the battery levels on his weapon. "If that's how you want to play this, fine. We're going to be here for a long, *long* time."

He aimed and pulled the trigger.

38

FOUNDATION BUSINESS

Every inch of Cassidy's body prickled with alarm the moment she set foot inside Dominique's deserted sanctuary late on Thursday afternoon. She had narrowed the plausible reasons for his absence to one—her safety. Something was threatening her, and he was shielding her by drawing attention away from her. Nothing else made any sense. It was this or he was dead, and that she refused to contemplate.

But now she wondered if there was another possibility.

The wall beside the door...was empty. Only holes remained where the hangers had been. They were gone, along with the samurai swords. As were all the electronics.

The realization washed over her like a rogue wave: Dominique's most valued possessions had disappeared—during the day.

Cassidy dropped to the edge of the bed, frozen with fear. Someone had been here today, in her house. Were they still here? She herself had only just returned home from another exhausting day at the *Gazette*. Suddenly, the familiar walls felt sinister. Her heart thudded hard as she looked around, wide-eyed and unseeing, listening, not daring to draw a full breath.

The air conditioner kicked in. The vents whistled. When the door swayed on its hinges, her skin crawled.

A shaggy black face peered around the corner.

Cassidy sucked a relieved lungful of air. "Eddie!"

The enormous cat padded in, a question mark in his tail, relaxed in a way he would never be if there were strangers in the house, or if he had been recently disturbed by same. She gave him a vigorous scratch behind the ears. "Am I ever glad to see you."

Eddie head-butted her hand, then stopped to look down the hallway. The tip of his bushy tail twitched, undecided, as something silent and invisible captured his full attention. It was still daylight, though, which ruled out several possibilities, both good and bad.

"More lizards, buddy?"

He flinched and flattened his ears. Cassidy straightened. Was that a car door?

Eddie circled in place and disappeared under Dominique's bed.

She made it only halfway down the hall before someone knocked a jaunty rhythm on the front door. When she opened it, she wondered if she wasn't dreaming again.

Garrett Striker stood on her porch, sharply dressed in a blue blazer, polo shirt, and jeans. He pulled off his sunglasses before looking her up and down, taking in her slightly wrinkled blouse and skirt.

"Miss Chandler. I'm so sorry to disturb you."

Her eyes widened. A polite Garrett Striker? That couldn't be good.

"I believe we've gotten off to a bad start, you and I. What do you say we go for a ride and get to know each other better?"

"Excuse me?" She couldn't have heard right. This man had gone out of his way to make her feel inadequate every other time they met. Now he was—what?—*propositioning* her?

"You are the girl who has turned my otherwise intelligent and capable nephew into a bungling idiot who can't stay out of situations that could get him killed."

"What?"

"Since he got home from school, all his troubles seem to begin and end with you, and I intend to find out if we can limit the damage to a forty million dollar airplane or if maybe we'll all be dead by this time next week."

Cassidy stared at him, slack-jawed, before giving herself a mental shake. "I'm sorry, but Jackson and I are no longer together. I thought he told you. Whatever you think is going on with him has nothing to do with me." She slashed a flattened hand through the space between them, underscoring her statement. Not that she wasn't concerned about Jackson if he really were in trouble. But she wasn't about to take his uncle's word for it.

"On the contrary. It has everything to do with you, my dear. Or should I say...*chérie*?"

Apprehension swarmed up her back on a million tiny feet. "I don't know what you mean."

"Come now, Miss Chandler. We all know the sort of company you keep these days." He flashed a positively wolfish grin. "I think we have a lot to talk about."

Cassidy still had no idea what he mean. Nor did she want to. "You need to leave," she said with as much force as she could muster and made to slam the door in his face.

He caught it with one hand high on the door. "I'm sorry. I should have mentioned that this is not a request."

It only took a second. One glance out of the corner of her eye, at the now wide-open front of his jacket, and Cassidy's world stopped. Garrett Striker had come packing heat. He didn't lower his hand, letting the jacket fall back into place, until he saw her notice the holstered gun.

All thoughts of using some of Dominique's fancy moves against Garrett drained away. There was little chance of her tackling a man of his size and training to begin with, but if she wasn't prepared to take that weapon from him and—more importantly—*use* it, her chances hovered well south of zero.

Simmering panic or not, she'd need a lot more motivation before she'd go there.

"You really know how to impress a girl," she said faintly.

"I thought you'd come around." He stepped aside and gestured toward the huge black SUV hulking in the yard. "Shall we? We're wasting daylight."

Dazed and moving with robotic stiffness, Cassidy retrieved her bag and followed Garrett Striker to his car. Serge's odd words from the night before rang in her ears. Something monumental was afoot.

When Garrett closed the passenger door, sealing her into the Cadillac's rich leather interior, every cell in Cassidy's body wanted to tear it open and run. Except that if he caught her, he might truss her up like a parcel. And if he didn't catch her, he'd probably shoot her.

She stayed put.

Garrett dropped the charm act and remained silent as he eased down the narrow lane. The sound of blood rushing in her ears overpowered the soft, classical music playing on the satellite radio.

Think, Chandler, she admonished herself. If an opportunity came along, it wouldn't do to miss taking advantage because panic paralyzed her. Besides, she didn't have all the facts, and Garrett had so far done nothing beyond being creepy. Maybe he really did only want to talk.

The late afternoon sun blazed in a cloudless sky, and Cassidy retrieved the sunglasses from her bag, pushing them onto her nose. Then she finger-combed her hair and worked it into a braid. The action relaxed her, sharpened her focus. It would also keep her hair out of the way during whatever was to come.

When they stopped at a red light, she again considered making a run for it, but ruled it out when she realized how closely Garrett watched her. He'd have her wrist in a vise grip as soon as she reached for her seat belt release. Judging by the look on his face, he was already three steps ahead of her.

Cassidy rallied her nerves and pulled her mouth into a gullible smile. "Gelato."

"Excuse me?"

"If you want to take me somewhere so we can talk about whatever it is you want to talk about, well, I love gelato. I hear there's a new place downtown that serves it. I've been dying to try it. Just couldn't afford to."

No reaction. At all.

"Light's green," she pointed out. "Gelato to the right?"

They went straight.

"Why don't you tell me how much you know about our family," he prompted.

She bobbed her shoulders. "Movers and shakers in global financial markets and more money than God. Oh, and issues with their women having careers beyond charity events and procreating. I think that about sums it up?"

The fingertips of Garrett's left hand rubbed together in thought. "What about the Striker Foundation?"

"I...I guess Jackson might have mentioned it," she hedged, not sure how much to reveal of the little she recalled. "It has something to do with...um...vampires."

"God damn stupid kid," Garrett muttered, knuckles going white on the steering wheel.

"It's not like I don't know about them."

"Exactly, Miss Chandler. That's the problem right there."

"I don't understand."

"Unfortunately for all of us, at some point you will."

"Meaning what?"

"Did Jack also tell you how we lost his brother?"

This abrupt change of topic gave her pause. "Grizzly bear?"

"Interesting. As much of a fuss as he makes about you, I would have sworn he told you the truth."

"Not a bear?" Her skin crawled. That was all Jackson had ever told her to explain his scars and Justin's death during an "Alaska hiking trip with Uncle Garrett." He never gave details, and—seeing the remembered horror still reflected in his eyes—she never asked.

He shook his head. "Vampire."

She blinked, stunned. Just like that, everything clicked into place—Jackson's reaction to Dominique, his fervent warnings and determination to get her away from the cottage, even following her to Key West. "That...explains a few things."

"It explains Jackson. Not much else."

Cassidy said nothing more, mentally reeling. Several minutes passed before she realized they were traveling on an obscure access road and approaching a back entrance to the local airport. He triggered the unmanned gate to open via remote control and drove right up to a sizable, bright white hangar. On its side, SICI's swooping green and gold logo glowed in the evening light.

"Are we going somewhere?"

"On the contrary. We've arrived."

He ushered her inside the hangar where a single jet gleamed in a pool of utility lights. Her steps faltered when she noticed a seat protruding from the shattered cockpit window. Wires coiled from the interior walls and ceiling. She stopped. No, not just the cockpit window. *Every* window was veined with cracks, splintered, or gone completely. A jumble of bulky things lurked in the shadows within.

"Forty million dollars," Garrett said behind her with a heavy sigh.

"What happened?"

"Jack turned stupid into an art form. Probably because he can't stop thinking with his dick where you're concerned."

She glanced at him, wary. "Jackson did this? Why?" She looked back at the gutted plane. "How?" The damage looked way beyond anything a single man could do. A single vampire, however... Out of nowhere, all the hairs on her arms stood at attention.

"Don't worry, Miss Chandler. All I need from you is a moment of your time and we'll call it even, shall we? Over here, please."

Garrett directed her toward a back corner. He stayed behind her until he had to key the code for a door. "After you."

The space inside felt cramped by a desk and two tall racks full of humming computer equipment, complete with a sea of flickering indicator lights and rivers of cable pouring out of the ceiling. "Security systems," Garrett explained. "My specialty."

"A lot of good it did your plane."

"The least of my concerns. This way." He propelled her through another door, which boomed shut behind them with the weighty finality of steel, sealing them into an echoing gloom. The only light here came from several desk lamps scattered on a row of workstations along one wall, leaving the rest of the space shrouded in obscurity. A large square structure of some sort loomed in the center some twenty feet away, drawing her eyes. A deep, chilling silence seemed to emanate from it.

"What the hell is this place?"

"The Foundation," Garrett said. He smiled then, in a slow, smug way that made the back of her neck tingle with the uncomfortable awareness that she was alone with him.

Sobering, he pointed to a plastic chair beside a desk. "Sit."

The moment she did, he grabbed her right arm and snapped on a pair of handcuffs he swiped from a desk drawer. Before she could even think about reacting, he had shackled her to the desk.

She yanked at the restraint, her throat suddenly too tight, breath too thin. "What the—"

"A precaution. In case you don't like needles."

"In case I don't *what*?"

From a drawer, Garrett produced a pair of latex gloves and various steri-sealed supplies.

"Oh my God. You're even crazier than I thought."

"I prefer 'dedicated.'" He shed his blazer and tossed it over another chair. The gun, he left in the shoulder holster, a not-so-subtle warning. "I won't need much," he promised as he pulled up another chair. He pulled over the desk light to illuminate her arm before snapping on the gloves and going to work.

"Do you even know what the hell you're doing, Mr. Director of Security?"

He applied the rubber tourniquet with a hard yank. His face betrayed no emotion as he uncapped a needle that looked thick enough to relieve her of a gallon of blood inside of five minutes.

"No, no, *no!*" The last word came out in a squeak as he jammed the needle into her arm without ceremony, missed the vein, and tried again. And again. Cassidy squirmed and sucked air through her nose, keeping her mouth clamped shut. She was not about to give him the satisfaction of crying out.

"If there were an easier way to do this, I would," Garrett said as he snapped a vial in place. When it started filling with her blood, he released the tourniquet. "I'm a little out of practice, so bear with me."

"Is that actually an apology, you sick bastard?" she burst out.

"If I'm wrong, I'll apologize later." He searched her face. "But I doubt it."

"Wrong about what? What the hell do you think I am?"

"We'll know in a couple of minutes." He wiggled the needle in her arm, fishing for a better angle. "The last time I doubted my instincts, eight people died. If that happens again, this family is finished. So I hope you can appreciate my caution."

"No, I have no freaking idea what you're talking about," she panted. That damn needle felt like it was going straight through her elbow joint.

When the vial was full, Garrett stuck a cotton ball on the injury and told her to bandage herself up with the supplies he pushed toward her. He moved two desks away, popped the cap off the vial, and transferred a measure of blood into a large test tube. Then he added drops of solutions from various little bottles.

"It's a simple analysis we perform on everyone who becomes involved with the Foundation." He set the tube into a rack, pushed a button on his watch, and sat back, studying her. "We'd hate to have another Rafael on our hands."

She flexed her arm to test the Band-Aid she had just applied. A sizable bruise already bloomed in the crease. "Who?"

"Someone who, like you, spent more time with vampires than he should. But we didn't know that about him before we hired him to be a driver for the family." His smile was so tight it approached a sneer. "He was at the wheel when my brother's first wife and their four children died. He drove them into oncoming traffic. By the time the fires were out, eight people were charred beyond recognition, Rafael included. Only after we examined his personal effects did we understand he'd done it on purpose."

A chill descended over her. She knew about the accident that had killed Warren's first family, but no one had ever hinted at this horrifying twist.

"Why would he do that?"

"A difference of opinion regarding his vampire mistress."

"I see," she said, mystified. "And what does all that have to do with me? I have no intention of killing anyone, I promise you."

"Not yet." His watch beeped, and he picked up another bottle, unscrewing the top. "This test will tell me how likely you are to go postal on us should we have the same difference of opinion. The higher the concentration of a vampire serum in a human's blood, the more effective, not to mention persistent, that vampire's compulsions become. Sometimes for long after the serum has dissipated."

Cassidy curled a clammy hand around the table leg she was shackled to as she watched Garrett lift the bottle and count several more drops into the tube. Again, she felt the sharp pinch of Dominique's teeth in her wrist, remembered the euphoric effect of his poison—serum—in her blood, the blood Garrett now swirled under one of the desk lamps. The blood that changed color, first turning purple and then blue. A beautiful electric-blue that reminded her of the sky above the meadow where her soul had first touched Dominique's.

She didn't realize she was smiling until she caught Garrett watching her and sobered.

"Doesn't look like I'll be apologizing, Miss Chandler."

39

THE ONLY THING

Cassidy was loaded—to the "proverbial gills" as Garrett explained before suggesting that her best course of action would be to put a gun to her head and pull the trigger. Assuming she could still make her own decisions. The loathing in his voice was palpable, and, for the first time, made her think that her chances of walking away from this place unscathed were less than good.

Garrett busied himself typing into a workstation, ignoring her requests for explanations and demands for release, even the threat of legal consequences. Cassidy worked her wrist in the cuff, but her hand would not slide free. The desk, she discovered, was bolted to the floor. "Son of a bitch." Her captor didn't glance up.

Breathe, Chandler. Think. She looked around more carefully for clues, tools, or opportunities. As she did, a monitor on his far side kept tugging at her attention. Something about it was familiar, a blue flame dragon on the screen. The login box it held filled and emptied, filled and emptied, over and over again, trying and failing to gain access. It was a very long password...

This was Dominique's laptop. There was only one reason it would be here—the last thing she wanted to believe.

"Jackson, you freaking son of a bitch," she said with a great deal more feeling.

The corner of Garrett's mouth tilted up. "Adding it all up, I see."

A cascade of noises like small gunshots echoed through the murky cavern. Soft light filtered in and grew, along with a building hum and a peculiar rushing hiss.

"What's happening?" she asked, bewildered.

He didn't look at her. "Sunset."

Though clearly not in here. More than two dozen feet up, the ceiling was packed wall to wall with the biggest lamps she had ever seen.

The structure in the center of the room melted from the shadows, becoming a dull gray cube the size of two garbage trucks. A ladder leaned against one side. Garrett got up and went to stand in front of the cube, grim-faced, hands on hips. A minute dragged by, and the lights reached maximum brilliance, their hum growing into a drone.

A sudden, explosive bang made her leap up, only to be painfully checked by the handcuff cutting into her wrist.

"There's our—" Garrett said before a deafening, agonized scream drowned him out. A tremendous wave of pain and rage surged through her, driving tears into her eyes.

Dominique!

The sound and the wave subsided. Silence. He had caught the scent of her blood in the air, but shut her out again the instant he sensed she was alive. Like smoke in the wind, he disappeared from her awareness.

Garrett was beside her now. "It's titanium. He can't get out."

She could hardly find her voice. "What have you done?"

He took a key ring from a drawer and unlocked her handcuffs. As they fell away, he stepped back and pulled the gun out of its holster, but kept the muzzle pointed at the floor.

"Here's what's going to happen. You're going to get up, walk to the front and say hello. After that, you're going to prove me right and try to kill me."

The idea was as appealing as it was insane. "With my bare hands?"

"You won't care."

She glanced at the gun. "And...you'll kill me. In self-defense?"

"Probably."

Cassidy got up, locking her knees, not quite trusting them to hold her. She couldn't even imagine what would cause her to attack a man with a firearm. Aware of little but the weapon behind her, she forced her feet to move, and rounded the corner to the front of the box—the cage—and peered past the narrow vertical bars. Then she stood and stared, trying to make sense of what she saw. The almost unrecognizable thing huddled in the far shadows—the animated corpse draped in raw skin.

She wanted to weep. She wanted to rage. Shell-shocked, she did neither. "Why? Why would you do this to him?"

"He's not human."

"But he was," she cried, facing the man with the gun. "And he's still a living being. He feels pain. He's *suffering!*"

"By his own choice. All he has to do to make this stop is call his sire through their blood bond. Instead, he wants to tell us stories, first about how he has no blood bonds, then how he killed his sire. Which, in their world, is impossible."

You're telling them what? she thought at Dominique and sensed him recoil. If they believed him, they would have no reason to keep him alive.

"I think he hasn't screamed loud enough yet," Garrett said. "He will eventually. They all do. Then we can put them both down and put this behind us."

All her blood drained to her feet. "Put them...down?"

"It's what the Foundation does. And we're damn good at it, if I say so myself."

Dominique's mind brushed against hers, a whisper of an impression. He wouldn't fight them, not even if he could. At long last, he had found a way to die.

The breath rushed out of her. *Over my dead body.* Very deliberately, she turned and took a single step toward the cage.

"You should know, Miss Chandler. The only blood he's had lately is his own."

Dominique's warning was a great deal less vague. His panic battered at her, willing her to stay back.

She took another step. So much for this powerful vampire's control over her. "If I'm going to die here, Mr. Striker, I'll take his fangs over your bullets any night."

"Then, by all means. Be my guest."

Dominique withdrew a little farther. Silent terror and hunger exploded out of him with enough force to make her sway on her feet. *Do not ask this of me.*

She kept moving forward. *Help me prove this wacko wrong, Dominique. I know you can.*

I have no control!

Which is what he expects—a bloodthirsty monster that'll tear me apart. But you're better than that, and you know it. You know it in your heart. Just like I do.

Not tonight! The vampire sprang up and paced in the back of the cage, frantic, searching for a way out that wasn't there.

Right. Guess that explains why you're over there. While I'm...here. She wrapped one hand around a cool titanium bar.

Dominique turned into a blur, crashing back and forth between the two sides like a hyper accelerated projectile before landing in a corner where he rolled up into a tight ball. *Merde!*

"He doesn't look all that happy to see you," Garrett remarked, a frown in his voice.

"He doesn't want to hurt me, but he...can't—" A flaky black substance crackled between her fingers. She pulled her hand away from the bar and watched it drift into the direct glare of the overhead lights. With a tiny puff of smoke, the flake disintegrated into fine gray powder. The stuff littered the floor—both in front of and inside the cage.

Cassidy stared at the powder. Ash. She glanced back at the bars. Blood and skin…or what was left after the silver coating finished with it. The air reeked of charred flesh.

White-hot rage exploded in her chest. She glared over her shoulder.

Garrett raised the gun.

Suddenly Dominique was there, hands sizzling on the bars, his voice a hoarse whisper. "No."

"I want to kill him. For what he's done to you, I want to kill him." Tears blurred her vision.

"You must not. You cannot."

Cassidy turned to search his gaunt face and the deep, glazed black pools of his eyes shimmering behind the matted shock of hair. Smoke curled around his clenched fingers. The stink of burning flesh scratched her sinuses.

She extended her right hand into the prison and reached for his face.

He jerked back with a sharp hiss. "No." When he let go of the bars, fragments of blackened skin remained stuck to them.

It was her first good look at him, and the sight made both her insides turn over. Dominique's skin wasn't just raw. Large patches of it were completely gone. Only the thinnest film covered the withering muscle and bone of his left arm and side. He dropped to his haunches and put his forehead down on his knees, unwilling to see her reaction to his condition.

Cassidy's legs buckled. She slid down the bars. Her hand settled in the ash inside the cage, palm up. "Eat. You need to eat."

For interminable seconds, he didn't move. Then, slowly, Dominique brushed his fingers against hers. Physically, his touch was the caress of a corpse. Mentally, it was an electric current igniting her soul. *Ma belle amie. Feeding now only prolongs the inevitable. I cannot last long like this, and I yearn for this misery that is my life to end. I only hoped that you would never know what happened to me.*

Cassidy gripped his fingers, pulled his presence deeper into her mind by its virtual scruff. *But I do know. And I won't let you do this. I'm not letting you give up. You, my friend, are not going anywhere.*

I no longer have a choice. He stirred a little, his attention captured by the leaking Band-Aid in her elbow and the bruise growing around it.

How did this happen, Dominique?

Still watching her injury, he showed her in a stream of agonizing memories: his decision to let her go so she could live free of his darkness, and his relief at Jackson's willingness to give her that life…the betrayal, the trap of light, Jackson's bottled rage…Garrett's sick pleasure at Dominique's suffering…

In her chest, her heart twisted, then ripped right down the middle. She trembled. *I brought them into your life…*

For this reason. My "destiny," as Serge would say, non?

Serge is an idiot!

He speaks the truth. This is a fitting end for me, and you are the key to make it happen. Now you must allow Jackson to keep you safe from things such as me. He is angry and frightened, but he is not evil.

But his uncle is. She gave him her own memories of how she got here, what Garrett had done to her and why, and what he surely meant to do to her still. The well of despair within Dominique expanded into a gaping chasm.

You see why I can't do that, don't you? If you die, your blood is on their hands as well as mine. They could never trust me, and they'd be right. With her free hand, she yanked off the small bandage and squeezed the puncture until it oozed. *I don't know how, but I'm going to get you out of there, and you'll need your strength. Eat.*

She felt him struggle, but when the shiny bead of blood turned into a rivulet, he leaned toward it. As he did, she caught sight of his back—and smothered a cry. Bare ribs and knobby spine protruded from a spongy red and black pulp of tissue, as if he'd been sitting in front of a blowtorch.

Dominique licked at her arm and shivered. The tiny wound closed with a prickle. His grip tightened around her hand, but he did not bite her. *Do you see why even all you could give me would not be enough to recover my strength? The only thing you can do is make that monster finish me quickly. Then live your life in peace...for me.*

Jackson entered the containment room and felt a punch to the gut. There before the crate, on her knees, clinging to the bars...

"No, Cassidy, get back!"

"Finally. I was wondering when you might show up," Garrett said. He stood off to the side, holstering the Glock. "You're missing quite the show."

"What the fuck have you done, you insane fucking bastard?" Jackson railed.

"How about saving your incompetent ass? Did you really think she wouldn't figure it out? If not today, next week, next month or even next year? You can *not* leave a compromised individual at large. You *know* that."

"She's not Rafael," Jackson snapped and pulled the small, full-spectrum flashlight from his pocket. There was no time to get a light gun from the chargers in the outer office.

"Do not go near her. She'll push you into his reach."

"At which point, feel free to shoot me." Jackson pointed the light and switched it on as he marched straight at the front of the crate.

"She's full of serum, Jack." Garrett sounded as beside himself as Jackson had ever heard him and looked like he would have tackled his nephew physically if he wasn't already within the vampire's reach. "She's his creature."

"Not for long." Jackson came up behind Cassidy's hunched back, keeping the brilliant beam trained on her and the part of the crate immediately in front of her.

Her tear-streaked face blinked up at him. "Oh. Is that what you used at the beach?"

He hesitated. "Yes, that's how I saved your life on the beach. With this light." He held out his free hand, coaxing. "Come on, Cassidy. Come with me. Let me save you again."

"I don't need saving," she whispered. "Turn that off."

Jackson glanced around the crate, most of it obscured now in empty shadows. Where was he? He resisted the temptation to swing around the beam, leaving Cassidy exposed. She had an arm reaching through the bars.... And then he saw it. The vampire was curled up right in front of her—in her shadow. "Son of a bitch!"

"Turn it off, Jackson. *Please*, turn it off," she begged, pulling herself to her feet. "I'll come with you if you do."

"Over my dead body." He angled around to get a clear line of sight. She moved with him, the emaciated vampire ghosting in her shade with remarkable agility. Jackson came closer.

"Jack, no," Garrett yelled. "For the love of God, leave her be. She's in no danger from him. He needs her alive. Don't you see that?"

The only thing Jackson saw was Cassidy near a demon who could tear her limb from limb, even through the bars. Keeping the light trained on her face, he reached out quickly, grabbed the braid hanging across her shoulder, and pulled hard. With a shriek, she twisted around.

The vampire's skin-and-bone arm shot out. The impact was like a nail driving through his hand, and Jackson was sure the next—and last—thing he would feel was that jaw closing on his wrist. Instead, Cassidy, off-balance, crashed into him and sent them both tumbling to the floor. The flashlight shattered as it hit the ground. He wrapped his arms around her and pulled her close. "I've got you. You're going to be okay."

"You imbecile," Garrett barked.

"You idiot," Cassidy said, squirming to get out of his embrace.

Jackson cursed as he released her and searched her arms for bite marks. He found only an impressive bruise. No delicate feeding this time, obviously. It was a miracle she still lived. Come dawn, he would put that bloodsucker down, and to hell with the sire and Garrett, too. Then he'd not let her out of his sight until every molecule of serum had dissipated from her system.

Garrett grabbed Jackson's wrist and pulled it up hard in front of Jackson's face. Two ugly gashes ran across the back of his hand, oozing blood where the vampire's nails had raked him. Now that he noticed them, they started burning like a mother. Jackson inhaled through clenched teeth. Garrett dropped his arm, disgusted. No need to say it. Half an inch closer to the crate and Jackson would have suffered his twin brother's fate.

During the commotion, Garrett had retrieved the light guns from the office, for he had them both now, raising them up, aiming into the crate. When he pulled the triggers, the interior lit up bright as high noon in the Sahara.

The vampire turned his scorched back to the blast and curled up small. His piercing, inhuman screams were the stuff of nightmares.

A hard grip closed on Jackson's arm. He looked down to see Cassidy shake violently. Her mouth gaped in a silent scream of her own. Then her eyes rolled up, and she slumped forward into his arms, unconscious.

The back of her shirt was soaked—in blood.

40

Under the Influence

Spiders. Spiders crawled on her shoulders. With scratchy, hairy legs.

Cassidy came to with a start.

"Easy. You're safe."

That it was Jackson telling her this made her feel anything but. That she lay naked face-down in a bed—Jackson's bed at the Striker mansion—further bore this out. His hand on her arm chilled her.

"Just a minute. I'm almost done."

She shivered. He dabbed along her spine. The tingling moved with it.

"What are you doing? What's happening?"

"I'm healing your wounds. I doubt you'll be shocked if I tell you I'm using vampire blood on you."

She pushed herself up. "*Whose?*"

He pressed her back down. "I have no idea. We keep some in storage for testing."

She waited for him to finish, taking the reprieve to figure out what had happened to her. That infernal light had lit up Dominique's back. The fiery agony, too powerful to contain, had flooded through their link. But more than the feeling had reached her. Apparently, her skin had burned along with his.

"Garrett wouldn't let me take you to the ER. So I improvised," Jackson explained. "All done."

Cassidy sat up and pulled the red satin sheet up around her. "*Your uncle* wouldn't let you. Of course."

His eyes slid away from hers as he screwed the top onto a small black vial.

"Since you always do everything he says, it's all his fault, then, is it? He's the reason you trapped Dominique? So Garrett can cook him alive?" Her gorge rose, remembering the bones, the charred flesh. The burning stink still clung to her hair.

He gave her a hard, assessing look. "You realize he's not human, right?"

"Garrett's the one who isn't human. But Dominique *was* human recently. And he wants to be again."

"Right," Jackson scoffed. "Next you'll tell me he's got you believing in Santa Claus."

"He hasn't sugar-coated anything for me. I've seen the worst of what he is *and* the best. You've seen it, too. He wanted to leave and asked you to take care of me, for God's sake. As if I'd let you."

"Games, Cass. They play games with people and manipulate them into whatever situation suits them. They can't be reasoned with, bargained with, or trusted. Ever. And there is no help for them but to put them down like the rabid wolves they are."

She narrowed her eyes. "You realize that's not what Garrett is doing, right?"

His lips flattened and paled before he said, "We've been dealing with them for centuries, since the first of us became a vampire's pawn. My ancestor thought he was 'befriending' the creature and ended up dead when his 'friend' got tired of him. His sons read their father's journals, realized what had happened, and went after it. Once they knew what to look for, they found hordes of these scheming, lying, murdering demons, and we've been ridding humanity of them ever since. That's our purpose, Cass, our only purpose. How it's accomplished—" He shook his head. "Doesn't matter."

"Wow," she whispered. How had she almost married this man? How could she not have seen this ruthless, self-righteous alien living inside him?

Jackson's phone chirped. He answered it. "Yes, she's conscious." He studied her. "Go ahead." Pause. "No, nothing. Okay."

He slipped the phone back in his pocket and turned away. "Good news. You're far enough away here to not be affected."

"Affected," she repeated, confused. Then she realized what he must mean and wanted to vomit all over the expensive sheets. Dominique would burn, but his suffering would not reach her. Her throat clenched against the smoke she suddenly imagined choking the air. She closed her eyes and concentrated on filling her shrinking lungs. This was not the time to lose it.

"We've never seen that before," Jackson continued while rummaging in a small bag on the vanity. "His serum is something else if he can mirror his own reactions to you like that. Can't wait to meet the sire."

"No, you won't," she murmured on a slow, stabilizing exhale.

"And what do you know about it?" he wondered, sounding casual.

She opened her eyes and stared at the back of his head. No answer here would deter these human monsters from dragging out their torture of a young vampire who never asked for any of this and only wanted it all to end. "Nothing you clearly haven't figured out already."

Where the hell were her clothes? Why had he stripped her down to her panties? She had to get out of here.

"I doubt it, but it's not like I can trust anything coming out of your mouth right now, anyway." He came to sit on the edge of the bed. "Just like I can't trust you to stay put in here for a while?"

"Not even if I have to leap naked through a second-story window, no," she promised, unable to keep the vehemence from dripping from her tongue.

"Yeah, that's what I thought." Suddenly, he gripped her forearm and yanked her close.

Cassidy yelped when he struck her shoulder. A stinging burn followed. "What are you doing?"

"Just making sure you don't do anything stupid, babe. It's for your own good."

The room wobbled and spun around her, and her whole body collapsed into uncooperative jelly.

Jackson pulled the sheet up under her chin. "Don't worry. You're safe here."

Burn in hell, she tried to scream or say or even whisper, but her eyes closed and she thought no more.

———————

"What if you're wrong?"

"I'm never wrong."

From the SUV's backseat, Cassidy watched Garrett give Jackson a withering look. Even nursing a sedative hangover as she was, she recognized the warning. A muscle jumped in Jackson's jaw, but he said nothing more to his uncle. He looked over his shoulder. "How're you doing back there, Cass? More coffee?"

"Go to hell."

Kept unconscious all night, Cassidy had awakened to find herself tied hand and foot. The rage she flew into caused Jackson to dose her again for, he claimed, her own safety. The second time she woke, she was too light-headed with hunger and thirst to put up a struggle. She wolfed down the sandwich, fries, and soda waiting for her.

Now she nursed the last of something semi warm, sickeningly sweet, and overly caffeinated. The handcuffs on her wrists forced her to hold the paper cup in two hands like a child. She toyed with the idea of using her shackles to strangle Garrett, the driver, but realized she wouldn't do anyone any good injured or dead in a wreck. Staying alert was imperative.

If only her toes weren't still half-asleep. She wiggled them in her sandals like stiff little sausages. The rest of her was doing somewhat better, though a shower would have been nice. She wore one of Samantha's long sun dresses—pilfered from the house laundry, judging from the delicately sweaty scent of it—which only added to her sense of disorientation.

A nauseous knot of anxiety congealed in her gut as they arrived at the SICI hangar near sundown. Jackson took the cuffs off before they let her step out of the car and ushered her inside. In the office, Garrett pulled two light guns off their charging bases and headed for the door to the chamber of horrors. Apparently, he had big plans for the evening. She should have strangled him while she had the chance.

Scanning the room for anything that might gain her an advantage, something familiar caught her eye. Dominique's dragon scabbards leaned in a far corner, looking a little like lost time travelers among the humming towers of technology.

Cassidy shot Jackson an ugly look. "Like you couldn't buy your own? You had to steal his?"

He glanced at the swords, his mouth compressing into a white line. Without comment, he took her elbow and propelled her after Garrett through the next door. The first whiff of smoke made her go light-headed, and a swarm of fuzzy black dots threatened to blot out her vision. *Don't you dare faint,* she admonished herself.

Garrett pulled up a plastic chair in front of the cage. "Sit, Miss Chandler. You might as well be comfortable."

Cassidy dropped onto the seat with more relief than she cared to admit.

In the shadowed rafters above, switches tripped, and the sun lamps buzzed and hummed like a swarm of hornets as they warmed up. Her skin prickled with foreboding.

"Here we go," Garrett said beside her as he checked the light guns.

The vampire's reaction was much less violent tonight: no sound, no movement. As Dominique regained consciousness, despair engulfed Cassidy. He no longer thought in words, only raw emotion, and she realized it was more the beast than Dominique in that cage now. She moaned softly. *I'm here. Don't leave me now.*

Slowly, he turned toward her. Nothing human looked out of that skull face. But in her mind, she could still feel his heart.

"Good evening," Garrett said. "Tonight, we have a special treat for you." He gestured at Cassidy. "Someone to share your...experiences with."

Dominique propped himself up. Apprehension shuddered in the connection between them.

"If you're going to be the martyr and let me kill you rather than summon your sire, she is going to die with you."

Beside her, Jackson cursed under his breath.

"She is nothing to me," rasped the beast on a faltering growl that barely rose above the hiss of the white noise generators.

"Let's put that to the test, shall we?" Garrett raised the light gun and lit up the cage.

The moment the light found Dominique, Cassidy's world dissolved in fire. Searing heat surged over her and through her. It blinded her and cooked her, made her convulse and scream...scream until her throat bled.

Minutes later—or maybe just seconds—it finally stopped. The worst of the agony retreated like an outgoing tide as she gasped and shuddered. A hand grabbed her shoulder, keeping her from sliding out of the chair. Her skin stung with burns, and her face felt too small for her head.

As her vision cleared, the room seemed to swim in a cold gray haze. In the cage in front of her, Dominique's unblinking stare was fixed on Garrett.

Their tormentor dropped into a crouch a solid ten feet away. "I know you can sit here all night with me. A lot longer if I find it in my heart to throw you a rabbit or two now and then. Weeks, at the very least. Months maybe. Or even years?" He swung the light gun over at her and activated it. It was just light now, no heat, but she flinched and turned away. "How long do you think she'll last? I'm guessing if she makes it longer than an hour, it'll be a miracle."

Swept up in a surge of rage, Cassidy bolted out of her chair. Dominique was in no position to help them. It was all up to her now. She took a step and turned, gearing up to kick that glorified flashlight out of Garrett's hand and break his wrist while she was at it. But then those fuzzy black dots swarmed in and the floor moved beneath her feet. A second later she fell back hard onto the plastic chair, Jackson's hand hard on her shoulder.

"You will not let her die," Dominique said. If compulsion rode his words, it was as weak and flattened by the hissing white noise as his voice.

Garrett bared his teeth in a wolfish grin of unfettered malice. "You've got that backwards, my blood-sucking friend. As contaminated as you've left her, what I will *not* do is let her live."

Cassidy's every muscle tensed as she tried—and failed—not to react. Somehow this wasn't a total surprise, not given all she had seen so far, but hearing it out loud made it very clear: He was going to kill her. Or...was this some twisted game played to coerce Dominique into cooperating? She glanced at Jackson who stared into the cage, vague-faced, hands on hips. She looked back at his uncle and the handgun he kept holstered within easy reach. No, what Jackson believed didn't matter. He wasn't the one prepped for a shootout. If Garrett wanted to, he could kill all three of them.

Dominique reached a similar conclusion. His fury dissipated in an icy blast of shock.

Garrett rose to his feet and moved a dial on his vampire weapon. Its subtle whine pitched higher. "So I'm giving you a choice. I can arrange for something quick and painless for her later, or...she can die here with you. Like this."

Cassidy watched him raise the gun as if in a slow motion nightmare...watched the overhead lights glint off the bulbous barrel...his finger close on the trigger. She drew half a breath, bracing, then the light engulfed Dominique again. He tried to shield her from the worst of it, but he was no match for the roaring agony. It hit her like the breath from a blast furnace.

This time was worse. This time, she could actually feel her skin sizzle and split and pull away from her flesh. This time seemed to go on for hours. She wanted to scream, but beyond an initial shriek, she could make no sound with the lungs that seemed to burn in her chest.

Eventually, the heat stopped building, then receded, though even her bones—or Dominique's—felt like they glowed. Blood trickled down her arms, dripped from her chin. She could taste it in the back of her throat, copper mixed with salty tears.

"*Arrête...*" said a wet, labored voice she barely recognized.

She opened her swollen eyes to see that Dominique had collapsed into a smoke-shrouded heap, a corpse in waiting, no sign of the beast. *Cassie...*

I'm here, she called, even her thoughts shaking.

"I'm all ears," Garrett drawled.

"I will..." Dominique convulsed in a violent cough that ended in a clump of something wet and dark smacking onto the floor. "I will summon him," he rasped. There was not an ounce of challenge left in his body or his mind. "I will summon my sire."

"Now, was that so hard?" Garrett said, spreading his arms wide.

"It will"—another gasp—"take a while. He's far..."

"That's alright. He can have all night to get his ass here. And if he doesn't make it, well, we'll just have to do this again tomorrow, won't we?"

Dominique, what are you doing? Cassidy thought at him, bewildered.

There was no response.

41

SAMANTHA

"What do you think you're doing now?"

"What does it look like?" Jackson reached into the mini-fridge tucked beneath the desk in the facility office and retrieved a black vial. "Fixing the damage you caused."

Arms crossed over his barrel chest, Garrett lounged in the swivel chair beside the cot they had set up for Cassidy. "Don't even think about it."

"For fuck's sake. Look at her."

"I am. She's exactly how I need her."

Cassidy sat on the cot and didn't react. She fingered the damp, red-stained towel Garrett had tossed at her almost an hour ago "to keep the blood off the floor." It was the only kindness he would grant her, and Jackson's temper and nerves had finally reached a point where he couldn't sit still any longer.

In contrast, Garrett had gained the ice-cold calm of a hunter lying in wait. "Our friend in there knows everything she's feeling. The more uncomfortable she is, the more motivated he'll remain."

"So you're going to leave her like that all night?"

"And tomorrow and the next night, too, if that's what it takes."

"You piece of shit."

"Speaking of, now is not the time to lose yours, kid."

Jackson put the vial back in the fridge. Her injuries weren't all that serious. A sunburn, really, with a couple of burst blisters thrown in. Not painful enough anyway, to dim the hateful glower she fixed on him.

"Coward," she mouthed.

"How about water? Do you think that might be okay?" he mocked.

"Fine. You can fetch me one too, while you're at it."

Water bottles lived in the hangar's utility fridge. Jackson wished he could have slammed the office door behind him, but being on a resistor, it refused to cooperate with his mood. He often wondered what his uncle was capable of in the name of Foundation business, but he hadn't put killing humans high on the list of possibilities. Now he wasn't so sure. He couldn't come right out and ask Garrett in front of Cassidy. The vampire had to believe that Garrett would kill her. Which meant Cassidy had to believe it.

"Fuck," he said, slamming the fridge door with a satisfying *whomp*. They'd have one hell of a "discussion" once she was safely out of earshot.

Jackson's phone rang. Samantha, he saw when he pulled it off its belt holster. His thumb hovered, ready to send the call to voice mail. She'd call back. And text. Call the police to report a missing person. His sister never called for trivial reasons. "Shit." He answered the call.

"Jack. Oh my God, I'm so glad I reached you."

"Sam? What's wrong?"

"I'm in the hospital." Her voice sounded even younger and more helpless than it usually did.

"What? What happened?"

"I was a-at-attacked."

"Attacked? What do you mean attacked? How? What happened?" He struggled to project calm for her benefit.

"When I left…left the studio, they…they… oh, Jack, it was ho-horrible. So fast. I don't know…I don't…" She dissolved into sobs.

He dropped the waters onto a workbench and headed for the hangar door. "Easy, Sam, easy. I'm on my way. Do you hear me? I'm on my way. I'll be there in ten minutes."

She gulped air now, hiccupping. "Y-es. Thank y-ou."

Cursing, he broke into a run. What horrendous timing. He called Garrett while laying rubber across the parking lot.

"Are you insane? You can't be out there tonight!"

"Watch me." Jackson disconnected the call. As he squealed through the gate, he shot the surveillance camera his middle finger. Garrett could go fuck himself in there. Cassidy was stable and would be okay for a while. There was at least one person he cared about he could help tonight.

He parked behind the hospital and jogged for the ER entrance when she called.

"Jackson. Over here, baby bro."

"What?" He peered into the gloom beyond the walkway lights, unsure he had heard her voice. There she was, two rows over, waving, her golden hair in disarray, but unmistakable.

"Sam?" he said, changing direction. "What the fuck?"

Samantha stood by her Prius, keys in hand, giving him a tear-stained smile. She wore her favorite white yoga cover up as though having just finished teaching her classes. "Oh Jack, I'm so sorry about all that drama earlier. Please forgive me."

"You said you were attacked!"

"Oh, I was," she confirmed brightly. "But I realized I didn't mind."

Jackson stared at her, reeling. His body tensed, already acting on what he still refused to comprehend. His hand went for his pocket and the flashlight. It never got there. Something had a hold of it—and of him. He never felt the bite, but knew it was happening when his thoughts swam in erratic patterns like a school of fish moving as one to make space for a predator moving among them. *Oh, hell no!*

Drawing on years of training, he focused, concentrating on a singular thing—outrage. It cleared his head long enough for him to try writhing free, impossible though that would be.

"Don't hurt him," Samantha pleaded, leaning over him, a hand hovering by her mouth. How had he ended up lying on the ground between the cars? *Fuck.*

"Get your filthy mouth off me," he croaked.

A deep, thrumming growl filled his hears. The invisible horror in his head grew. His vision disappeared. Jackson gasped.

When he came to, he lay sprawled across the backseat of Samantha's car. The door by his feet was open, and his sister peered in with wide, worried eyes.

"Are you alright?"

He clutched at his neck. Nothing. Not even an ache. He'd been nailed by something powerful in total control of its instincts. Somehow that idea didn't jibe with the hand-wringing, owlish little man standing beside Samantha. He looked bedraggled, clothes torn, curly hair unkempt—and familiar.

"You," Jackson said. "I was wondering what rock you'd disappeared under."

"Hmmm," said the vampire, narrowing his eyes. "Stubborn, this...thickheaded."

Samantha heaved a dramatic sigh. "Yes. That sums up my baby brother. Is that going to be a problem?"

"His light is bright," the bizarre apparition said with some reluctance, as if that might make up for a dumpster full of shortcomings he clearly perceived in Jackson. He patted her arm. "We must go, golden one."

"Of course." Samantha got behind the wheel. The vampire shoved Jackson's feet off the back seat and dropped into it.

Jackson scrambled to the far side of the car. "What the fuck, Sam. What have you done?"

"Helping a new friend, of course. His name is Serge. He's three hundred years old. Can you believe it?" She looked over her shoulder at him, her gentle face aglow like he hadn't seen it since the Christmas morning she found a pony tethered by the tree. "Magical," she intoned. "Just magical."

"Nightmare," Jackson corrected. Samantha had to be compelled out of her gourd and would be of no help in getting them out of this disaster. He had to take control, and fast.

They were still in the hospital parking lot. He could open the door and... No, he had to stay here. He had to—*God damn it, no!*—help Serge. And Dominique. He closed his eyes and tried again. His fingers closed around the door release, but he didn't pull it. Couldn't pull it. Sweat broke out across his forehead and upper lip in clammy beads. He swallowed the sour taste of panic and slanted a look at the vampire.

Serge watched him with a pleasant, half-friendly smile on his broad face. Apparently satisfied that Jackson wouldn't bolt, he reached over his shoulder, pulled down the seatbelt and clicked it into place. "It's the law. Buckle up," he told Jackson and erupted into a gale of giggles.

Jackson wiped his forehead with one hand. *Get it together. Concentrate.* What the fuck had happened here? How did he get tripped up again? And now his uncle would get dragged into this mess, too. Of course, they were in this mess because of Garrett, so maybe that was as it should be.

Uncle Garrett, he thought, a spark of hope flickering to life. Uncle Garrett was at the operations office in the hangar. Every sensor and surveillance camera for a mile around fed back to there. He'd know the second Serge breached a border, even inside a car. Yes, Garrett would see them coming, curse his nephew's name and then meet the threat in classic Garrett Striker style—with all guns blazing. With a little luck, Jackson and Samantha might even avoid becoming collateral damage.

Oh, fuck, Samantha... He couldn't wrap his head around his sister bumbling around in all this, compelled and no longer blissfully clueless.

They were almost at the airport.

"What's your part in this? You're not Nicky's sire," Jackson asked the vampire in the backseat with him. God help him. These conversations were becoming unacceptably common.

Serge cocked his head and grinned in a way that verged on unhinged. "How do you know?"

"His blood says his sire is a great deal older than you."

"Yes," Serge said slowly, stretching the word into a hiss. He watched Jackson like a hawk eyed a juicy mouse. "You should be glad I come instead, foolish boy."

Maybe so. An ancient might have finished him before he even knew it was there. Like that thing in Key West, the creature Dominique had bested...

"Okay, here we go," Samantha announced. "Blanket time."

"What time?"

"You're sitting on them, dummy," she admonished. "Hurry up. I'm almost at the gate."

Serge yanked several Mexican yoga blankets out from under Jackson's butt, sending him slamming against the door. In a blurring whirl, the vampire made a blanket burrito of himself. Jackson blinked at the innocuous pile now bunched beside him. "Son of a bitch."

The blanket giggled. No sensor or camera would detect a supernatural presence in this car now. The fiend would know this, of course. He would have learned it from Jackson's mind. Which explained why Samantha's blankets lay at the ready rather than in the trunk, their usual home. "Fuck."

"Good evening, sir," said the guard at the gate, ducking low to see him in the back seat. Samantha had announced his presence as her ticket to enter. *Stop this car. I'm being kidnapped,* he wanted to shout. Instead, the alien that had body-snatched him waved a pleasant acknowledgement. They rolled up to the SICI hangar a minute later with no hint of a light cannon coming online anywhere.

The blanket sighed, blissful.

Samantha got out, walked around the car, and opened his door. "C'mon, Jack. Let's go get this hideous system turned off."

"Yeah, right. You're out of your mind if you think I'm going to do that," he said, but lead the way into the hangar.

She stopped when she saw the ruined plane. "Someone was pissed. Dominique?"

"Forty million dollars' worth of pissed. Garrett won't let me forget it."

"Serves you right," she sniffed. "How could you? From all I've heard, Dominique is a sweetheart."

Jackson almost tripped. "You should reconsider your sources, sis."

By the time they reached the office door, he felt Serge's hold on him loosen somewhat. The distance between them was growing too great for the demon to maintain firm control. He stared at the panel. Pin, thumb print, disengage lock.

"Well?" Samantha prompted, baby blues wide.

He opened the door.

The office was empty. A high-pitched scream echoed faintly from the containment room.

"Is that Cassidy?"

Jackson knew it had to be. He shouldn't have left. He *really* shouldn't have left.

"The system, Jack. Hurry." Samantha pushed him toward the server racks, propelled by the same compulsion he felt, but which she was far less able to withstand.

He had to stop this, get control, get Cassidy out of here. His fingers flew over the keyboard. Indicators started going red as components dropped offline in groups. A minute later, all the humming in the room ceased. He looked at the blank screens, horrified. It would take half an hour for all of this to boot back up and calibrate. In the meantime, the humans here were defenseless as babes. "We're so fucked."

"Serge is on his way," his sweet, innocent sister said and opened the door to the hangar.

Jackson touched the twin St. Christopher medals, but dared not think as his hunter instincts took over, formulated a plan, and executed it on autopilot. With his mind carefully empty, he moved up behind his sister, the *katana* in hand, raised and ready.

The vampire's alien presence closed in around him again. When it could get no closer, he stepped into the open door and brought down the blade.

42

Not This Night

Garrett's fist connected with Cassidy's jaw, snapping back her head and making it ring like a struck gong. She flailed on the chair, her vision blurring. He clamped a hand around her arm, keeping her in the seat. Her stomach spasmed and filled her mouth with thin, sour vomit, but her mind shrieked with rage. Or, more accurately, the reflected rage of Dominique's beast.

"Ready to tell me what's going on yet?" Garrett said.

Dominique paced behind the bars, a growling, half-burnt apparition straight out of hell. Several minutes ago, he burst into a rampage that drew Garrett back to the cage with Cassidy in tow and cursing Jackson for being a brainless boy who was going to get them all killed.

"Fine. I can do this all night." Garrett drew back his fist again. Cassidy screamed.

"He comes!" Dominique rasped. "He comes for you."

The fist lowered. "Excellent. Now, tell me something I don't know."

Dominique stepped closer to the bars. His solid black eyes glistened, unblinking. The fangs in his open mouth had never looked sharper. He was all nightmare incarnate.

"He will cast you into darkness," he hissed. "He will hunt you and make you his. You will beg to die."

"Spare me the fantasies." Garrett raised his fist again, and Cassidy cringed. "Where is he?"

A soft boom echoed through the towering space, followed by...silence. Gone was the hiss of the white noise generators and the buzzing hum of the lights—and the lights themselves. As they faded quickly, night fell like a death shroud. The beast's malevolent whisper slithered clear and cold, like a snake made of ice. "He will cast you into darkness."

Cassidy shuddered. No, it couldn't be. He couldn't really have called his sire, could he?

Garrett cursed under his breath. A generator kicked in somewhere. The desk lamps switched back on, and a set of florescent emergency lights flickered to life, casting everything into the equivalent of pale moonlight. He marched for the nearest workstation, hustling her, staggering, along with him. By the time Cassidy realized his intention, Garrett already reached for the light gun sitting beside the keyboard.

Adrenaline kicked her in the gut and merged with what was left of the caffeine. In a whirl of ferocious, instinctive motion, she spun around and slammed her elbow into Garrett's kidneys. Air whooshed out of him, and his hold on her loosened. Tearing free, she darted for his wrist, grabbed and twisted it, and shoved it up his back until he doubled over and dropped to his knees. On the way down, his head smacked the corner of the desk. He collapsed in a heap, limp and still.

Heart hammering, hands shaking, she reached for the light gun. It took three tries before her numb fingers had a tight enough grip on the thing to smash it against the desk's edge. Shards of glass and plastic clattered over Garrett's still body.

"Run, Cassidy." The words drifted through the fogbank clogging her head. "Run."

She took one step back, eyes locked on Garrett's slack face. Blood trickled from a cut slanting across his forehead. Her ribs closed in on her lungs, squeezing all the air out of her body. She bent over, wheezing.

She had acted without thinking. Might have killed a man.

She didn't want to be here. She had to be here.

No way out. Trapped.

The dim expanse of the room oscillated around her.

Breathe, she admonished herself. *Keep it together, Chandler.* Easier thought than done. Her throat only grew tighter.

"Cassie *amour*. You must run."

She looked up sideways at the cage. Dominique lay at the front, watching her through the bars. No sign of the beast, only an impossibly broken human shell. He turned his face away.

Cassidy clenched her hands on her thighs and fought for air.

"Breathe," he whispered. The single word brought back the last time panic had run her over. *Slowly. Deeply. In with the nose. Out with the mouth.* Her hand clutching at his, at Dominique...at safety.

A massive breath shuddered into her and dissipated the haze as she exhaled it again. Another one and the panic subsided like an outgoing tide. Certain knowledge took its place—Dominique was her haven. Nothing else mattered.

"I'm not leaving you here."

"You must. Save yourself."

"I can't." She closed her eyes for a moment to let the truth settle deep into her bones. "I can't lose you, too," she whispered. "Not yet. Not like this."

To this, Dominique had no reply, no doubt sensing the truth in her mind. It was the same sentiment that had driven him to surrender himself to his fate. He more than cared for her—he loved her. The feeling was mutual. Which meant the night would come when he—like everyone else she ever loved—would be lost to her. But it wouldn't be *this* night. And it wouldn't be because of her.

Or because she was too afraid to act.

She straightened and looked around. Door. There had to be a door to the cage. The ladder. Of course. The entry had to be on top. That way, whatever was inside wouldn't have any leverage to push against it. But it would still be locked. How? She'd seen keys in a drawer here last night. As good a guess as any.

Retrieving the sizable key ring, Cassidy hiked up her dress and scrambled up the ladder. "Please tell me you didn't really call your sire."

"*Sotte!* What are you doing, foolish woman?"

"What do you think? Hang tight. This won't take long," she said, more to convince herself than the irate vampire in the cage beneath her. Four padlocks secured a titanium crossbar as thick as her arm, an overkill clearly designed to make it as time-consuming as possible for anyone to do exactly what it was she intended to do. She dropped to her knees beside the hatch and got started. The keys rattled in her fingers as she selected the first candidate in the dim emergency lighting and fumbled it into each of the locks in succession.

They will stop at nothing to keep you from releasing me. Please. I am not worth your life.

"And now that they know they can yank your chain with me, they won't stop looking for me either. We're in this together, whether you like it or not."

The first of over ten identical keys didn't work on any of the locks, neither did the second. The third finally clicked open a lock. She whooped her relief and flung the thing aside, clear off the roof. "One down."

Dominique was silent until she undid and dispose of another lock. *What do you think I will do when you release me?*

"Run like hell, of course. What else would you do?"

I have never been this hungry, chérie.

"Okay, then..."

Or this angry. A wave of that rage simmered over her again, making the back of her neck cramp. *I will have blood for what they did to us.*

She faltered with the fifth key. "No. You won't kill them."

Because I did not kill you? You are my heart, Cassie. I can no more hurt you than I can let them live.

Cassidy swallowed a dry knot of renewed anxiety. *You do that, you're going to live up to their worst expectations of you.*

She jammed the key home and twisted. Click. The third lock followed the others off the roof. *Why do you think I can let them go?* Dominique wondered, drifting in genuine confusion.

Because I believe in you. The real you. Like you believe in me. The next key jammed in the last lock, and she struggled to pull it back out. *Even when I don't.*

Something dragged against the floor down below. A miserable groan followed. Garrett.

She jerked so hard on the stuck key, when it came out, the key ring flew out of her hand. It smacked against the metal roof. Cassidy leapt after it, landing with a thud.

The reviving motions became more energetic. *Shit!*

Somewhere outside, someone, a woman, screamed. Though muffled, the sound made her freeze in shock. Who? Why?

Steps clanged up the ladder rungs.

Cassidy, stop.

The last key slid home, twisted. The lock snapped open and dropped away.

"Stop right there."

She looked up to see Garrett Striker coming over the edge like a SWAT team commando moving in on a terrorist leader. His gun—the one that fired real bullets—was pointed straight at her.

Dominique's most resonant voice, no longer obscured by the white noise generators, throbbed in the air, every syllable dripping with compulsion. *"You will leave her alone!"*

Doubt flitted across Garrett's face, confusion clouding his determination. His hand shook, but the gun didn't move away.

Instead, he pulled the trigger.

43

Acts of Desperation

Jackson's first kill exceeded his wildest fantasies: at night with the target running free *and* while under a compulsion. Against all the odds, yet clean, swift and decisive, a thing of sheer, triumphant beauty. He reeled with the euphoria of it—or would have, if not for his sister, splattered in blood, on her hands and knees beside the vampire's headless body, screaming, incoherent, a woman gone insane.

In the containment room, a gunshot rang out, followed by an unearthly shriek. Dropping the bloody sword and leaving Samantha to have her nervous breakdown in private, Jackson bolted for the door. Inside, in the flickering emergency fluorescents, Garrett was running toward him and gestured for retreat. His face was bright red with anger, and blood flowed from a gash across his forehead. "Get out! Run!"

"Where is she? What have you done?" Jackson shouted as he raced for the crate. Deafening roars reverberated off the towering walls, vibrating with rage, promising annihilation.

Garrett grabbed his elbow and pulled him toward the door. "That bitch unlocked the hatch, and I can't secure it. He could be free any second. We have *got* to get the lights back on in here."

"Where is she?" Jacksons snarled, shaking off his uncle. There was so much adrenaline pumping into his bloodstream, he could fight an army of bloodsuckers right now. Fuck, he'd already killed one—with ease!

The hatch jolted violently, again and again. Something was shaking loose. Up there on the roof lay a small, still hump. Cassidy. A red haze obscured his vision.

"Son of a bitch!" Jackson's fist slammed into his uncle's jaw. The older man staggered backward.

He didn't stick around to see if Garrett recovered. He bolted for the crate. If he was quick enough, he might secure the hatch before all hell really broke loose—and then get Cassidy out of there before it was too late for her. If it wasn't already.

Another gunshot. The bullet pinged off the floor by Jackson's feet. He kept running.

"Get back here. Leave her to him. That's where she wants to be."

"Over my dead body," Jackson shot back, gambling that if his uncle took him by his word and hit something vital, it would be by accident. It wouldn't matter. Nothing mattered anymore. He had put down his first vampire. He drew the line at killing humans, a line Garrett clearly had no problem crossing. If Cassidy didn't make it, the Foundation be damned, Garrett Striker was going down.

Two more times the gun went off. The reports exploded off the metal walls. He stumbled up the ladder, the metal bars vibrating in his hands from the vampire's efforts to free himself.

Cassidy lay face-down, one hand on the crossbar she hadn't pushed aside quite far enough. A slick pool of red spread around her head and disappeared in a neat line along the edge of the hatch.

"Oh God, please no." He dropped to her side, turned her over and wanted to throw up. Blood. Blood everywhere. In her hair, on her face. Her neck, shoulder, chest. Impossible to tell where it came from. Only that there was too much.

Beside him, the hatch continued to rattle powerfully. No doubt the vampire was gaining strength from Cassidy's blood dripping into the crate. The crossbar securing the hatch was within seconds of knocking free. He lunged and slammed it back into place.

The captive's long, agonized scream shivered through Jackson. Somewhere deep in his core, the sound harmonized with his own emotions. He looked at Cassidy's face, ashen beneath the smeared blood. The stench of ash filled his nostrils—and his memories. White ash, ancient ash, glittering in the morning sun. Foolish young vampire risking his existence for a human girl, battling a foe he had no hope of defeating, while Jackson...remained useless.

The moment he decided, before he could change his mind, he took what might well be his ultimate gamble. He pulled the crossbar all the way back.

Silence.

Jackson hauled up the hatch as though watching someone else do it, someone else inviting certain death. He let it drop and stepped back. Way back.

An apparition flowed out of the opening, a Halloween horror rising from a grave. Dominique had protected his face, torso, and belly from the worst, but the rest of him looked like the victim of a fiery plane crash. In vampire terms, he was the embodiment of hunger.

Jackson didn't move—hoping against hope not to draw attention.

When Dominique hesitated at the sight of Cassidy covered in all that blood, Jackson thought his gamble was about to get them both killed after all. Those eyes were turning pitch-black with hunger. The fangs were out. This was the end.

The monster's attention belonged to Cassidy alone. His burnt claws shook as they moved over her—searching for injuries. Jackson released the breath he didn't realize he'd been holding. But new fury gripped him when he saw where all that blood was coming from. Garrett had shot her in the head. It was a long, narrow wound, not a direct hit, but blood welled from it furiously.

When Cassidy stirred, Dominique brought his wrist to his mouth and drove his fangs into it, tearing savagely. He couldn't have more than a few drops of blood left, yet what he had he gave, rubbing it into the hideous damage with gentle, circular motions. He murmured in soothing French, probably listing all the ways he planned to exact revenge.

Cassidy groaned, then came to with a sharp inhalation. She struggled to sit up and clutched her head in both hands. "Damn that man."

"Cass?" Jackson said, unable to keep quiet any longer. "Are you alright?"

She looked up and blinked as though startled to see him there, crouching on the edge of the roof. "I've been better."

"Me, too," he said, thrilled to hear her speak coherently. He grew apprehensive again, however, when he noticed the vampire staring at him without even a hint of an expression.

Cassidy noticed, too. She put a hand on Dominique's arm. "Don't. Plea—"

Jackson found himself grabbed by the shirt collar and free-falling into the nothingness of those monstrous eyes. "You live because of what you have done for her tonight," the vampire said. The gut-churning, charred blood stench of his breath wafted over Jackson's face. Jackson's own blood drained to his ankles. "You owe her your life. Never forget that."

Jackson's mouth refused to work, so he gave a single, stiff nod. An instant later, he collapsed to his hands and knees, feeling ill and unsure if he was still alive—or if he would stay that way until Garrett got the lights back on.

"Dominique...no!" Cassidy shouted. She clambered down the ladder and followed him on unsteady legs.

Dominique banged on the door with tremendous blows. It was blocked, but not locked—which, of course, it wouldn't be since the entire system was down.

"Fuck."

By the time Jackson made it off the crate, the door stood open, and the vampire was gone.

44

VAMPIRE GAMES

Gunfire erupted as Cassidy burst through the office door. She threw herself to the ground, into the splintered remains of the desk. Pain spiked through her shoulder, and her head pounded as if that damn bullet had made it into her skull and ricocheted around inside.

Screams followed the gun shots—human and supernatural, male and female. Biting back a scream of her own, she peered over the toppled mini-fridge. The air was thick with acrid electrical smoke and coppery spilled blood.

Dominique stood in the door to the hangar. Blood trickled down his emaciated arm from a fresh injury in his shoulder, a pain she had felt through their link a moment ago. By his feet, a pair of legs angled into the room, keeping the door propped open. They wore stained, slightly ripped trousers and...no shoes.

"Oh God."

Garrett was visible out in the hangar near the wrecked plane, gun in one hand, Dominique's *katana* in the other. It was coated with blood.

Oh God.

Savage outrage pulsed from Dominique's mind, and the need to dismember Garrett Striker slowly bit by bit seized her. She flexed her hands against the fridge, eager to rip his skin, shatter his bones, watch the blood flow, and hear his screams. But Dominique didn't act on any of these impulses. Instead, he stood, staring at the upper portion of the corpse, which was hidden from Cassidy's view.

"You want a piece of me, do you?" Garrett taunted as he backed away. "Well, what are you waiting for?"

There was a small desperate whimpering sound. Cassidy froze. Serge?

Dominique disappeared.

Garrett stopped moving, gaping through the now empty doorway into the office—at Cassidy.

No, not her, or at least not only her. She glanced back to see Jackson standing behind her, as unexpectedly alive as she was, given a hungry vampire in a rage and on the loose. A vein stood out on his forehead over the glare he leveled at his uncle.

A series of small explosions blasted through the hangar. Streams of glass shards, metal strips, and plastic casing rained from the ceiling and ricocheted across the concrete floor. Dominique had scaled the walls and was systematically destroying the light cannons he had shown her in his memories, taking no chances of them activating again.

"You're on your own, kid," Garrett shouted over the din before turning on a heel and running for the nearest exit.

"When the fuck am I not?" Jackson snapped under his breath and turned to the equipment rack, where a few of the trashed machines still whined and sparked, indicator lights flickering in pitiful fits.

Navigating a wave of dizziness, Cassidy got up and staggered for the door—and stopped. There lay Serge, spreadeagled in a pool of blood. And kneeling by his side...

"Sam?"

Samantha lifted her tear-stained face. Blood spatters caked her tangled hair and smeared across the giant Ohm emblazoned on her white shirt. "Cassidy, look what he did to Serge." She lowered her gaze to the face that stared back in slack-jawed astonishment.

"He shouldn't be—" Cassidy broke off when she realized just how much blood there was on Serge's shirt, on the floor, and splattered across the wall. The injury must be massive. Like a severed limb, or... Samantha's small, crimson-coated hands didn't just cradle Serge's head, they were holding it in place against his neck.

Cassidy put the back of her hand to her mouth to ward off the nausea punching her stomach. "What are you doing?"

"I'm trying to fix him. He thought this might work. Just before..." She leveled a glare of pure contempt at her brother.

"Oh God."

"Fuck." Jackson slammed both fists onto the keyboard before sending it flying off its shelf with a violent sweep of his hand. Apparently, the anti-vampire systems wouldn't be operational again anytime soon.

More gunshots. Cassidy turned to see a tall storage cabinet topple over right in front of a far door near Garrett. Dominique was moving so fast he was all but invisible, but she could feel him all around. His wrath filled the vast space like a hurricane.

Garrett sprinted across the hangar, scanning all around, smoothly pointing the gun this way, then that, covering every angle in rapid succession. He fired when another cabinet crashed sideways in a far corner, spilling tools and canisters. Pausing by the nose of the ruined plane, he took aim and fired again, but the cabinet, propelled by a blur of motion, was already screeching the entire length of the hangar. As it slammed into place across the last door, the gun clicked empty in Garrett's hands. Tossing it aside, he brought up the sword in front of him.

Dominique circled closer, most of his movements too fast to follow, creating an illusion of growling, ravenous specters moving in for a kill.

Garrett swung the sword in wild arcs, hitting nothing, and screamed red-faced defiance. "Is that all you've got, you blood-sucking punk?"

"Fucking vampire games," Jackson spat. "Filthy demons."

A stone lodged in Cassidy's chest. *Please, Dominique. Don't do this. Prove them wrong. Just go.*

"C'mon Serge," Samantha implored. "Wake up. We need you." Cassidy couldn't bear to look. Her heart was breaking for the surprising little vampire and the woman he had obviously compelled, but these things would have to wait.

Serge groaned.

Cassidy and Jackson turned their heads as one. The formerly headless body moved. His hands and feet twitched with the uncoordinated efforts of a newborn, and his eyes rolled like those of a crazed animal.

Samantha squealed. "Yes, that's it! You've got it!"

Jackson hissed between clenched teeth. "I don't believe this."

Someone was running. Garrett. He sprinted back to the office, keeping his eyes on the rafters and sword at the ready. He made as if to dive through the door, then lunged for Cassidy instead.

She didn't even have time to think about moving out of his reach. He had her by the arm and swung her around. Vertigo turned her body to rubber. That bloody blade waved in front of her, daring anyone to come to her rescue. Jackson shouted something incoherent. Samantha just screamed.

The sword aiming for her throat disappeared. Garrett jerked behind her, and the hands grabbing her tore away. She staggered, arms waving for balance.

Garrett slammed to the concrete nearby, pinned beneath an infuriated vampire.

Dominique roared into his face, fangs gleaming, letting the prey see his burnt and battered body compact and morph into the pure skeletal horror of a vampire at his very worst. By the time he struck at Garrett's jugular, Dominique was gone. Only a terrifying manifestation of absolute rage remained.

Cassidy sensed him dive into the void with willful abandon, shedding his humanity like a snake shed its skin. "No..."

"Get it off me! Get it off me!" High-pitched terror cut through Garrett's voice, sending a shiver of alien pleasure through her.

Jackson appeared beside her, now clutching the *katana*. By the time she realized what he intended to do, he already swung it up and back, preparing to bring it down on Dominique. She flung herself on the beast's iron scaffold body with bone-jarring force.

"Cass, no!" he stood over her, the blade held high, ready to sever a neck—which right now would be hers along with Dominique's, possibly Garrett's as well.

She clamped her arms and legs around the feeding vampire and buried her face in his ragged, blood-matted hair. The burnt ice stench made her belly roll. Pleas flew from her lips. "Please, please, *please* don't do this..."

He gulped hard and fast. Rapture surged with every beat of Garrett's heart.

Prey.

Terrified prey.

The beast trembled with ecstasy.

Garrett choked out a hoarse, wordless sound soaked in mortal fear. He thrashed like a landed fish, striking at anything he could reach. His fist pounded her head where the bullet had grazed her, making her cry out. Dominique reached out with lightning speed, captured Garrett's wrists, and confined them without missing a beat.

Jackson was screaming, but his words only registered as background noise to the roaring euphoria and her whispered pleas. "You do this, you justify everything they have done. You'll be no better than them. Don't do this, Dominique, I beg you."

But he kept drinking. Deep swallow after deep swallow, the blood's strength pounded through him harder and harder. The prey ceased struggling, its mind now under the vampire's complete control.

Death was coming for Garrett Striker.

Cassidy tightened her hold on Dominique's body and his mind, reached for him, her rock, her everything. He was slipping away into the insatiable hunger and cold fury, turning his back on her...leaving her world. Her life. *Dominique...you are breaking my heart...*

Her head snapped back. Pain seared across her scalp and down her neck. Jackson had her by her braid again. "Damn it, Cass, don't make me hurt you."

But he *was* hurting her and badly. She wobbled to her feet. It was that or risk having her neck broken. Once upright, she kicked out at him. There was no grace or intention to the maneuver; it was wild and frantic, and had only the element of surprise going for it, which proved quite enough.

The top of her foot landed a solid thump in Jackson's groin. He doubled over, the air leaving him in a spasmodic *whoosh*. He let go of her hair in favor of curling around his genitals. She grabbed the wrist of his sword arm and wrenched. Jackson dropped like a rock, the *katana* clattering to the ground. She picked it up, then stood over him, breathing hard, head spinning.

"Bravo, *mon trésor*."

She looked up. Dominique sat beside Garrett, watching her with soft, human eyes. Though still haggard and smeared with gore, his face looked a little fuller. The skin on his burned left arm was a shade less see-through. He wiped at the blood on his chin with a wrist.

The man lying beside him stirred, and Cassidy felt a sense of grudging relief to see the bastard still among the living. Garrett opened his eyes to the vampire peering down at him.

"Garrett Striker," Dominique said with a slow, hard smile. "Your ass is mine."

Serge, too, roused. He sat up—drenched in blood and looking wan, but fully restored—and giggled. The sound was full of madness and joy—and anticipation.

45

THE QUESTION OF WHY

Cloaked in the darkness of a moonless night, Dominique slowly rode his bike up to the cottage. Only starlight edged its roof. An expectant hush hovered in the drowsing palms crowding around it. The yellow VW Beetle—now sporting Florida plates—slumbered in the carport.

A strange sense of anxious anticipation filled him as he locked the motorcycle in its shed. After a week of steady feeding, he almost felt normal again. His instincts and reflexes were still a little dull, or he might have noticed the giant new flat-screen TV flickering in the living room instead of pausing to wonder about the new set of steps to the porch.

Nor did he register the blood-drinker presence until he stepped through the door.

A familiar wet forest scent permeated the air-conditioned interior. Of Serge himself, only the top of his head and wide, staring eyes were visible over the sofa's back. Though the volume was next to nothing, the low, ominous bass strains thrumming from the speakers were unmistakable.

Dominique picked up the remote and paused the shark attack in mid-chomp.

Serge popped upright, quivering. "Blood-child?"

"*Bonsoir, mon ami.*"

He darted from behind the sofa to look Dominique over more closely. "You appear much better than last I saw you."

Which had been the night they escaped the Striker Foundation's "facilities" together. After a night of communal hunting, they parted ways. Serge returned to Cassidy's side as her guardian while Dominique concentrated on healing himself.

"As do you," he said, eyeing Serge's neck. The red line where the sword had severed his head was gone. He still marveled at the old fool's unaccountable good fortune. The moment the sword had struck Serge, all he thought about was keeping his head on his shoulders. Samantha, from whom he had fed to deepen his control of her, had picked up on the fantastical urge to reassemble him, and had done exactly that.

"I have seen this trick tried," Serge explained once they had fed for a while and hunger no longer ruled their every thought.

"But have you ever seen it work?"

Serge beamed. "I have now."

"Did I not tell you to stay out of my house?" Dominique said now without rancor. Except for Cassidy, there was no one he would rather see.

"The sweet one invited me," Serge announced, puffing out his chest. "She and the golden one have introduced me to the wonders of this age." He glanced at the TV with a delicate shiver. "And the horrors."

Dominique turned away to hide his amusement. A stack of DVD cases teetered on top of the new player plugged into the new TV. He shuffled through them. Action, adventure, horror, and—he raised a brow—romantic themes predominated.

"You should go, blood-child. She waits for you. As does your future." Serge gave him one of those penetrating looks that seemed to reach beyond the ordinary world. Then he snatched the remote, dove back behind the sofa, and let the watery slaughter continue.

Dominique retreated to the bathroom. He stripped off the jeans, T-shirt, jacket, and boots he had compelled off one of his feeds, and stepped beneath the steaming spray of the shower. His skin was intact again, his flesh restored, but the once raw nerves stung where the hot water pelted him. He soaped and scrubbed vigorously, washing away what remained of the filth.

If only he could do the same with his memories of the time spent as Garrett Striker's captive, when he prayed for death. His prayers had gone unanswered. He lived, free again, and the more time passed, the more he needed to know why—in terms more concrete than having a "destiny."

The bed in his sanctuary was made up with a new set of navy-blue sheets that somewhat complimented the outdated décor. The old linens with the cartoon figures had vanished like his childhood innocence. Several fresh shirts and a pair of gym pants—all black—sat neatly folded on the foot of the bed. His phone was on the dresser along with his laptop, and on the wall, in their rightful place, hung the samurai swords. Perplexed, he caressed the gleaming dragons on the scabbards. From Garrett's mind, he knew Jackson considered these blades his trophies. Why and how they were back here, he couldn't imagine.

The mystery of the swords didn't matter, though, not compared to the question of why Cassidy had risked her life charging to his rescue like an enraged lioness. In his pain-ravaged state, he had caught fragments of her reasoning, but nothing coherent. Nothing that convinced him she wasn't acting on—or reflecting—his own most desperate desires.

Dressed but damp and warmed to the core by fresh blood and hot water, Dominique moved up the stairs. The blood-drinker squirming on the sofa ignored him.

In the upstairs hall, the cat was on patrol. It gave him an agitated glance before deciding that the gecko clinging on the wall held more interest. "Good hunting, little brother," he murmured and slipped into Cassidy's bedroom.

She lay poured into the bed, her heart quiet and steady. He inhaled her somnolent scent and reached for her mind. Nothing. He squatted beside her and touched the point over her forehead where her life force coalesced. The disturbance rippled around her until she woke, blinking up at him.

"*Salut*, Cassidy."

"Hi," she said and sat up, rubbing the sleep out of her eyes. She had cut her hair, and not just a little. It now framed her head in a copper-shot cloud of waves that hardly brushed her shoulders. She turned on the lamp on her nightstand and studied him in its soft light.

"You have taken in another stray," he said when she remained quiet.

"Oh, is he down there watching *Jaws* again?"

"Again?"

"It's a ritual. I suspect he's really rooting for the shark." She gestured. "Take off your shirt."

Puzzled, he complied, then sat where she patted the mattress, his bare back to her. "Your hair...I like it."

"Hmm. I got tired of people pulling it." Her hands whispered over his sensitive new skin. "Scars," she murmured. "Your back is nothing but scars."

"For now. It still heals."

She caressed his left arm and shoulder. "Your tattoo is gone. You've lost your sun."

Impressions of her mind reached him through her touch, but at a great distance, and only because he looked for them. Vague rays of joy jumbled among shadows of dismay and anger.

"No, *mon amour*," he whispered. "I cannot lose what is in my heart."

She paused her survey. Then her arms came around him, and her face nestled against his neck. Dominique closed his hand over her forearm, caressing her wrist with his thumb. It was a tremendous effort not to pull her around and embrace her the way he truly needed to. Not just her body, but all of her...and always.

"You can't stay here during the day," she said. "The Strikers want you more than ever."

"I know. But I...we...will be nearby." He would spend his days cocooned in the dune with Serge, his home no longer safe now that the hunters would stalk him here. He had no illusions about Jackson's motives and dared not assume that his truce with the hunter had been anything but temporary and for Cassidy's sake alone.

"I even got a huge promotion and a raise at work to encourage me to stick around." Pause. "Jackson actually said so when he gave me back your swords."

He leaned his head against hers, closed his eyes, and faintly registered the rest of Jackson's sentiments, which she could not get herself to utter; the hunter would have his trophy again—when the prey was dead. "He knows I will not leave you." When she said nothing, he continued, "So, Garrett Striker lives?"

She nodded. "He needed three units of blood and gave the ER docs hell for wanting to put him through all kinds of tests to figure out how he lost it in the first place. He was on a plane at sunrise the next day, heading out to who-knows-where."

Dominique allowed himself a small, smug satisfaction. The threat he had planted in his tormentor's mind was taken seriously. "He runs from me until my serum has left him."

"Looks that way. He told me if he were ever bitten and was at risk of being manipulated by a vampire, he'd put a gun to his head and pull the trigger. Guess he changed his mind." She sighed. "I know how hard that was for you, letting him live. Hell, I wanted to kill the bastard myself. But you proved them wrong. That's all that matters."

Dominique trailed his fingers over her arms, still draped across his shoulders. "I don't know. Did I?"

"Oh, I think Garrett really will kill himself if you get even close to turning him." Cassidy lay on her side and looked up at him. "You won't do that, will you?" He became distracted by her teeth worrying her plump lower lip, and how the hem of the sleep shirt slid up her thigh. His body cried out with the need to kiss her, touch her, hold her, show her all that lived in his heart.

"Force him to exist as what he hates most? Poetic justice, *non?*"

"Yes. Poetic justice. But...that man as a vampire? In your world forever? That sounds like more of a torture for you than him."

"Garrett Striker is a man in old pain," he said, recalling the memories he had torn from the man's mind. Memories of soul-destroying losses suffered at blood-drinker hands. Cold brutality was all he had left. Dominique could almost understand it.

Cassidy gave him a dubious look. He shrugged. "Truly, I have not given him much thought. I have been too busy healing and appreciating my continued existence. Such as that is."

"You're really glad to be alive, then?"

"Beyond measure."

"Then you won't attempt suicide by vampire-slayer again?"

"That was unexpected."

"You sure as hell jumped on it when you had the chance."

"A fair result of my incompetence, *non?*"

"No. A result of knowing me. They would have never known about you if not for me."

He brushed his thumb over where the bullet had grazed her skull, aching to know her thoughts. The scar was thin and concealed by her hair, but it was there and always would be. The mind that lay beneath it bristled with stubborn determination. He dropped his hand.

"Is that why you risked your life to free me, then? So you would not have my blood on your hands?"

She shook her head. Her heart thumped faster. "They gave us no choice. Either we both lived or—"

"*Non.* The choice was yours alone. And you know how hungry I was. What I can do."

Her eyes flashed with challenge. "You risked your eternal life for me when I didn't even realize I needed help. How can you even question what I did?"

"Because by saving my life, you are risking the lives of everyone who crosses my path, perhaps for a very long time to come. How do all those lives outweigh mine?"

She propped herself up on one arm. "What's gotten into you now?"

"You know it's the truth."

Her cheeks colored as she looked away.

"Cassie. Why?"

"Was I wrong to believe in you?" She cut him a sideways glare. "Fine. I'll play. Why don't you tell me, Dominique, how many have I killed already by setting you free? How many lives did it take for you to recover this far? How many more before you're fully healed? How many victims of mysterious, violent assaults are going to make the headlines soon?"

The vehemence stunned him. Apparently, he had pushed her over a line into uncomfortable emotional territory, but rather than succumb or flee, the lioness went on the attack. Here she would not go without a fight. She would sooner tear out his throat.

"None," he murmured.

"I see. Hid the bodies that well, did you?"

Unable to help himself, he smiled.

Wary disappointment shuttered her face. "So the Strikers were right about you after all."

"No, no, *chérie*," he sputtered, heart squeezing flat in his chest. "No one died. Not the night you set me free, and not since."

"You expect me to believe that?"

"*Oui*, yes. I do. Serge was there in the beginning. He would have stopped me taking lives, but he didn't need to. I could have devoured dozens, but I only pierced the veins of hundreds. Every time, I became stronger. Every time, I gained more control. Every time, I remembered your cry in my soul. I will not—cannot—betray your faith in me." Emotion threatened to choke him. "Don't you understand what you have done for me?

You seduced the monster I am. You and only you are the reason I have not killed anyone, not even when I was nothing but hunger and rage."

Her eyes glistened. He felt his own sting.

"This week I have drunk more blood than ever before, but I have made no bodies, and no one remembers me. No one even came close to sustaining the kind of damage I did to that *fils de salope,* Garrett Striker. No one has died, Cassidy, because you believed in me. Because you reached me when nothing else could."

"But why can't I reach you now, Dominique?" she said on a half-stifled sob. "Why are you shutting me out when you tell me all this? What are you hiding from me?"

He took her face in both hands. Only echoes of her confusion reached him. "The connection is too weak now. Too little of my...serum remains in you. Too little of your blood in me."

She took a hold of his wrists. "Then fix that. Now."

"Nothing would please me more."

"What's stopping you?" Pain in her eyes. Pain in her touch. Pain of his doing.

It was all he could do not to take her into his arms and do as she asked. "Please, I need to understand. Why did you free me?"

"I told you why. Why won't you believe me?"

"If you freed me out of guilt or even self-preservation, I have no place in your life. I must leave you in peace. Not infect you again and again and keep you by my side."

Tears spilled from her eyes. "You mean leave. You want to...oh God, you want to leave." She twisted away. The anguish in her voice slid through him like a blade.

"No," he said quickly, shaking his head. "No, Cassie. No. I want to drown in you every night of my existence." He continued in a hoarse whisper. "But if I do this—if we become one again—you cannot get free of me. And I won't let you bind your precious mortal life to all the horrors of mine for something as trivial as guilt." Or because she considered him a stray cat in need of rescuing. Or even friendship. None of that would do. If he could resist taking lives at his worst now, he could—and would—resist taking advantage of her.

"Guilt? You think I'd want this because of guilt?" She wiped at her face with a quick, angry motion and rounded on him. "Everyone I've ever loved has broken my heart in one way or another. They've left or lied or died. Only you have come back to me, Dominique. You've even let me into your literal *soul*, and been nothing but honest with me—the way you are right now, whether I like it or not." She heaved a hitching breath. "That's why I freed you. Because I can't imagine my world without you. You are my home, Dominique. I can't lose you. You mean too much to me."

He placed a hand on hers where it lay in the rumpled sheets and squeezed. "And you to me," he said softly, shaken by the words he had dared not hope for. "Wherever you go, Cassie, I will be by your side, and I will share with you my heart and soul. For as long as you will have me."

A watery smile. "That could be a while."

Only the rest of her mortal life. A pang of guilt surfaced. "You understand I can never give you all that you deserve?"

"You give me all that I need."

"I can never give you the day."

"We'll have the nights."

"Or children."

"Seems to me we already adopted one. He's three...hundred."

Despite himself, Dominique relaxed. "I suspect he has adopted us."

Cassidy threaded her fingers with his. "Make love to me."

He stifled the impulse to retreat, wary. "You know we cannot."

"Yes, I know. And that's not what I meant." With a gentle tug, she pulled him into her arms, and Dominique shook with the effort not to crush the life out of her in return. What she meant was abundantly clear when she tilted her head aside to present her neck.

A soft sigh of surrender escaped him as he closed his eyes and let his mouth find its way to the pulse beneath her skin. Just a kiss that made her shiver delicately. Then another, deeper, and he thought he might faint with the pleasure of her sweet blood. Moments later, her soul blossomed in his awareness and embraced him.

In his dark heart, the scattered pieces of his being tumbled together, making a new whole.

He was home. They both were.

46

THE SUN AND HER HEART

Cassidy thought she knew what to expect when her blood flowed into him...and he flowed into her. She was wrong. Darkness swallowed her. Thunder engulfed her.

Stunned, she drifted in a mighty rumble that seemed to come from everywhere and struck her flesh like velvet hammers. Cool eddies swirled over her skin. She was under water. Blurry light filtered down from above, and she kicked toward it until she broke the surface with a splutter, finding herself in a large, natural pool. The source of the reverberation lay at the far end, where a massive waterfall crashed down from a staggering height—easily a hundred feet or more—in a perpetual explosion of sound. The air vibrated with the concussive force, and mist churned around the impact zone, glittering like diamond dust in shafting sunlight.

As she struggled to regain her bearings, the thunder ebbed, and the edges of the pool melted out of the fog, revealing a shoreline of impenetrable jungle. Huge leaves and thick vines rustled in the breeze generated by the fall. Wet earth and rock and fecund vegetation rode the wind...along with the cool bite of snow.

Do you like it?

Someone surfaced between her and the waterfall, and it took her a moment to recognize Dominique. The normally wild black hair lay sleek against his skull, and the long planes of his face were no longer the color of moonlight, but glowed with the deep tan of someone who spent long days in the sun. An uncertain smile lit his warm, gold-flecked eyes.

I'm...speechless, she thought, answering both his questions. There was nothing not to like about this place—or this version of him. The vampire she knew was gone; the man he had been was back, at least for the moment.

His smile widened, flashing strong white human teeth and deepening the dimple in his stubble-smudged cheek. Then he ducked under. As he swam past in the clear depths, she saw the wavering outline of his long, graceful limbs against the pool's dark bottom. Long, graceful, *nude* limbs, she noted, arching a brow. Her own sleep shirt still floated around her, getting in the way and feeling increasingly like an intrusion. She submerged to slip out of it, and after only a moment's hesitation, pulled off her underwear as well. As the clothes left her hands, they melted away, disappearing from this world. With a deep sigh, she closed her eyes, tipped back her head, and relished the currents eddying around her body, making her feel deliciously exposed and safely cocooned at the same time.

When she opened her eyes again, she stared straight up the waterfall and into a cloudless, cornflower-blue sky where an enormous helix turned slowly and radiated light like the sun. She had seen it before when they shared their minds, but not like this. Not this strong, this vibrant. Dominique wasn't aware of its presence, leaving her to puzzle about it on her own. Now, however, she thought she knew what it was. The helix was Dominique's true self, his soul. The water, the endless falling river rushing toward her, pooling around her, supporting her...it flowed from the spiral's brilliant core.

And it was no simple river.

It was emotion, flowing from his soul into hers, on and on and on without end—eternal...like him.

For a while she could only stare, breathless, overwhelmed by the power of the water, of what it represented. Then, out of nowhere, she saw herself in a sea of light, wind-tossed hair framing her smiling, freckle-dusted face like a lion's mane. Her eyes glowed with an almost unearthly blue fire.

Startled and amazed, she turned to find Dominique watching from near the edge of the pool, his heart in his face, waiting to see how his declaration would be received. More than showing her how he felt, he also offered his memories of how, in the days they had spent apart, thoughts of her had given him the strength to sustain himself without doing harm. The anticipation of this moment, of reuniting with her, had filled his every waking thought. But what she would do with this knowledge—and how far they would venture into this reality—was now up to her.

Silly vampire, Cassidy thought, swallowing her tears as she glided toward him. Thoughts of him had sustained her as well these past few days, especially the certain knowledge that he would be back, that somehow the connection they had forged while racing on the edge between life and death was real, profound, and unshakable. She had faith in him, in them, together.

He was kneeling in the shallows, on a bottom made of small, shifting pebbles. Awed wonder infused him as she approached; she was there, aware of him, part of him, a miracle he was still trying to wrap his head around. Also, the water was clear enough to conceal little of her curves, which seemed to her rather more voluptuous than she recalled.

"My heart is yours, Cassie, *mon amour.* Always." It was a whispered prayer in the waterfall's rumble, but the words resonated clearly in her mind.

She touched his face, thumb stroking a prominent cheekbone. "And my heart is yours, Dominique, my love. Always."

They leaned their foreheads together, and a soul-deep sigh lifted their shoulders in tandem. Sanctuary, at last.

A moment later, her gaze dropped past the surface ripples and down his front. She blinked, unsure, then smiled. The water may be refreshingly cool, but his body didn't seem to mind that, not entirely. This body, at least, here in this place where nothing was real except their thoughts and feelings. The look he gave her when she sat back bordered on bashful.

"Is this..." She cleared her throat, cheeks heating.

The widening smile confirmed what she already knew; the interest burbling in him was anything but platonic. "This is what I was before." On a more suggestive note, he added, "And how I would have reacted to you."

Cassidy tried to imagine how she would have reacted to him, this perfect male specimen with a dancer's powerful body and runway model's beguiling face. Even as a human he had been something out of a fantasy, something otherworldly, traveling in orbits she might glimpse but never enter. "You would have intimidated the hell out of me."

His dark brows furrowed with regret as he murmured something in French. *That would have been a tragedy.*

"Mmm," she said and watched his mood shift into a new, more distracted gear. With a light grasp, he took her hands and spread wide her arms to regard her body in a way that made every inch of her bare skin tingle. "What...um...what would have happened if we had met...before?"

The dimple in his cheek deepened with alarming mischief as he leaned closer and purred at her ear in tones more seductive than anything she had ever heard before from him or anyone else. It didn't matter that he spoke in French; every word—every intention—formed in gasp-inducing detail in their joined minds. More than that, he hinted at his words with his hands, roaming delicate trails across her body. Cassidy shivered and sighed and grabbed at his shoulders, and by the time he stroked her hips and reached around to clutch her buttocks, far more than her cheeks burned.

"Promises, promises," she said, voice raspy with need, and pressed her face against his damp hair to drink in his scent. Snow and ice and starlight—with a sharp, new edge of something primal, something her body understood. Her knees spread of their own volition. He caressed down the outside of one thigh before drifting up the inside.

"You're such a...tease." The last word escaped on a soft gasp as his fingers reached their destination and proceeded to do exactly that. Before she could draw another breath, he had her by the back of the neck and brought his mouth to hers in a leisurely exploration of a kiss that mirrored what he was doing beneath the water. *Oh God. Looks and talent, too.* Her whole body threatened to melt like the butter in his skillets.

Better than my cooking, non?

Cassidy was barely coherent. *Mmm, I'm not convinced. Try...harder.*

He groaned. *You are a demanding critic.*

Desperate for the kiss—and everything—to deepen, she reached for his face. Still, he held back, denied her, teased her, drew out the moment until she thought she might lose her mind. When he finally met her demands, stars exploded in the back of her eyes as she shuddered against him and moaned into his mouth.

He held her in his arms and trailed kisses along her neck and collarbone while she recovered her senses. Only water swirled between her thighs now, and that was nowhere near enough to appease this maddening hunger he had kindled. "I need...more." *I need you.* Oh God, how she needed...

"*Je sais, chèrie,*" he said. *I know. I have always known.* Something in his husky voice, in his unfocused thoughts, the way his fingers splayed against her back. She sensed more than saw the spiral pulse in the sky. It was like a wave of energy sweeping through the glade, rushing in the trees. *You have always wanted me.*

"Yes." No sense denying it. He had smelled the interest coming off her from moment one. But this was more than that, she realized suddenly. What she was feeling, that ache in all her most sensitive places, wasn't just hers alone. "And you have always wanted me...in every way."

"*Oui,*" he admitted softly. His thumbs ran down her spine as he breathed the desire wafting off her skin. Unlike her, his control over his lust was absolute, even while he thoroughly enjoyed hers, feeding on it as he had fed on her blood. This was as far as he would go, even here in their own sunlit reality where he was human and she was supposedly calling the shots. So much for that.

Wait. If she was in control here, why did she accept this?

Sensing her shifting attitude, his hands stilled. Hers slid from his shoulders, across the tight muscles of his chest, and...hesitated. No, there was only so much temptation he would allow himself, even here. He still didn't trust his own reactions.

Cassidy pressed her lips together and ignored the subtle command to cease. Her seeking fingers slipped over his rock-hard belly. *You're such a...cocky bastard.*

When she seized hold of said not-quite-ready-for-action cock, his warning growl quickly morphed into a helpless little groan that made her smile. Matters firmed up nicely at a brisk clip. His head fell back, eyes closed, sensuous mouth curving with bemused surrender. *And you love that about me,* he thought, entranced.

She kissed his exposed throat, "Oh, *oui.* I do." Then, as her hands worked their magic, she closed her teeth on the satiny skin over his jugular.

Another violent pulse swept in, whipping up waves across the pool's surface. Rolling her eyes upward, she could see the helix contract and spin faster. She felt it twist inside both of them, tearing at his control and driving her on—the way his hands gripping her buttocks drove her on to straddle him and...

They jolted in surprise. What little still separated their minds unraveled along with the distance between their virtual bodies, and there were no words for the male and female sensations echoing between them.

This time, when the helix pulsed, she could feel it throb in their bones.

His warm human eyes vanished. Icy black shadows took their place as his face blanked and paled. The waterfall roared, and the gusting winds wailed like a swarm of hungry phantoms. *Know me...*

"I do," she said again, more softly. It was more than Dominique with her now, though thankfully his alter ego remained confined to the inkwells of his eyes—his aroused and curious alter ego. The part of him that, ultimately, wanted only one thing. She cupped his cheek and gave it to him. "Yes, I know all of you, Dominique. And with all of my heart, I accept...and love...and need...all of you."

For a long moment, he didn't seem to have heard. Then, his unblinking obsidian gaze never leaving hers, he moved closer, crowding her until she lay back. As she did, the water receded and their bodies dried. Soft, moss-covered ground rose to meet her. Tremors shook him, but he pushed on, nestling into her.

Only then did the shadows drain from his eyes, and a shaky smile surfaced on both their faces. Mon Dieu...*my brave lioness. You are glorious!*

It was the last coherent thought either of them had. What remained of their boundaries evaporated once they began to move together.

They were one.

They were everything.

47

WHAT IS AND WILL BE

Later, much later, they lay spent and dazed, a single mind in two bodies. Had they died? Did it matter? They thought not. Not with such love in their hearts.

Eventually, the pearlescent mist thickened into a fog, erasing the jungle and muting the waters. Then the fog dissipated, and the light dimmed. The waterfall's rumble faded to the murmur of the sea beyond the dune. Its wind became the lazy breeze from the overhead fan. The scent of snow mingled with the musty tropical decay of the cottage and...sex.

Dominique tensed. Cassidy's eyes snapped open.

Together they lay spilled across the bed in a tangle of limbs. One of his hands twined with hers, the other was stuck under her butt. He had his bare hips wedged between her bare thighs, his pants nowhere to be seen. Ditto for her sleep shirt—and her panties.

Her breath caught. *This was real?*

He lifted his head from her chest with a violent start. Mon Dieu, *what have I done?*

The astonished look on his face made her giggle and playfully run her toes up the back of his leg. *Oh, I would think that's obvious.*

Her attempt at distraction fell flat.

I lost myself. I lost control. I almost...I could have...

"No. No, Dominique, you didn't," she said quickly and took hold of his face, capturing his wide, human, borderline panicked eyes with hers. "You didn't."

Another moment of indecision hunched his shoulders, his expression one of fierce, vulnerable beauty. "*Mon Dieu*." He glanced down at their erotically snuggled bodies.

She gave him her most seductive smile. "That was some fantasy, love."

"*Mon Dieu*," he said again and collapsed half on top of her, boneless with dawning relief. She stroked his wild, thick hair, trying to soothe his jangling nerves while his mind raced, looking for answers, riffling through clues. It came to an abrupt halt at a memory of the night they met, when she had refused his compulsions without realizing what she was doing.

I was desperate, she thought, remembering the sweaty, furious mess she had been, and the obnoxious, barely dressed apparition he presented.

Dominique nuzzled into her neck and inhaled deeply. *No, you were aware of me, Cassie. That is how you refused me then, and why you survive me now. In this bond, we are one. Even the beast understands this.*

A bond that seemed to grow stronger every time they renewed it. His thoughts swerved. Curious, she followed. While feeding from Garrett, he had gleaned a treasure trove of information over which he had agonized ever since. Vampires were not just humans with sun allergies and a specialized diet; they were a whole different species, transformed by a virus that altered their DNA. There was no "cure" for such a thing, no going back. This was his life.

And the only thing that made it tolerable was this woman in his arms, the only living thing who knew him completely—and loved him anyway.

His fingers found and laced with hers again to squeeze in mute gratitude. Outside, the first whispers of dawn crested the horizon, but he ignored them. Worry still gnawed at him.

Every time he pierced her skin, he infected her anew with this blood-drinker virus, which very likely was what made this miraculous link possible.

Cassidy gripped his hand tightly in encouragement. She knew the risks. She accepted them.

Yet, the uneasy shiver up her back was mutual. They were dancing at the edge of a firestorm, and the price, eventually, might well be the one thing neither of them wanted to give up. Her humanity tethered him to the man he wanted to be, and Cassidy had experienced enough of blood-drinker life in his memories to know that crossing that line would change more than her body. Maybe these were just echoes of Dominique's sentiments, but they were too much a part of each other for that to matter. Her humanity was a cornerstone of their relationship.

So she would venture into an immortal world as a fragile mortal. Countless dangers awaited her at his side. Dangers he might not see in time to protect her.

His lightning-fast thoughts raced off into darker territory. To derail them, she stroked his scarred back, down toward those firm buttocks. When he didn't respond, she said, "I'm okay with us taking this one night at a time. We'll figure it out. Together."

He looked up again to see the calm conviction in her eyes. His own stung, and not just because the windows grew brighter.

"Who knew vampires were such worry warts?" she said and cradled his bristly cheek. He leaned into the touch and smiled, his body suddenly too small to contain all that he felt. "*Je t'aime,* Cassie."

"I know. I love you too."

He kissed her wrist. "What we are doing...if we are not very careful...this might transform you, regardless. Only more slowly."

"Show me a relationship worth having that isn't transformative."

The corner of his mouth twisted in wry appreciation of this double-edged truth.

With a small frown, she considered his new knowledge of blood-drinker science—such as that was, given the source. "I think what's really happening here is that you're 'enslaving' me."

That familiar mischievous glint lit his eyes. "Perhaps." Feather-light, he trailed a fingertip down her nose, causing it to flare.

She bit her lower lip, sensing where he was going with this. The finger traced along her jaw and down her neck, leaving electrical tingles in its wake. "I am enslaving you to my touch."

Her breath hitched as said touch settled expertly on her quaking breast. With blunt teeth, he nipped at her chin, then he was at her ear, dripping words like warm honey. "You, *mon amour*, will never again judge my cooking to be superior to lovemaking. This, I promise you."

Cassidy couldn't resist. "I don't know. I may need to see more evidence."

"Such a demanding critic," he purred, and accepted the challenge. The sun rumbled in his awareness, but he took his time with a deep, moan-inducing kiss.

They didn't bother with imaginary worlds this time, enjoying each other, loving each other, in the reality of the little cottage by the sea. The sky had grown noticeably lighter by the time they finally collapsed again, side-by-side, sated into a stupor deep enough to blunt, for the moment, his creeping anxiety about the looming dawn. A minute, maybe two, was all they had left.

Their hands reached for each other amidst the tangled sheets. In the gentle stroke of his thumb against her skin, Cassidy heard again the thunder of the waterfall—along with an absolute truth: Whatever perils their future held, Dominique would not desert her. She could count on him to be there—as her champion, her partner, her lover, her friend. More than anything else tonight, it was this that finally undid her. Sensing her shifting mood, his thumb stilled.

"But you did enslave me, Dominique," she said in a strangled whisper.

He turned to her, expression soft as he followed her thoughts. She spoke them aloud anyway, giving them substance. "The night you told me that love has no secrets"—even as he longed to share every one of his with her—"that night you enslaved my heart."

"*Non, mon amour*," he said, gathering her back into his arms. "That night, we enslaved each other."

Thank You For Reading

If you enjoyed this book and have a moment, please consider leaving a brief review wherever you purchased this book or on Goodreads to help others discover this series. Thank you!

If you would like a free eBook, sign up for my mailing list and also be the first to find out about new releases and special offers.

Mailing list signup: https://skryder.com/mailinglist

Acknowledgements

My heartfelt thanks go to my family, who puts up with all the time I spend buried in my notepad or laptop, or just staring off into space, talking to myself. You will never know how much your love and patience means to me.

More thanks go to:

Aleksina Teto, second-edition editor, for her stupendous attention to detail, not to mention French language expertise. I'm still breathless.

Máirín Fisher-Fleming, first-readier, for her sharp eye and in-depth knowledge of English, French, and motorcycles. I couldn't have finished this tale without your unflagging encouragement and friendship.

Simone Christian for her sage advice on Aikido, firearms, and dragons.

Kara Wills for her eye-opening critiques and enthusiastic support.

Karen Ann Dell for her expert input regarding the survivability of gunshot wounds.

And last, but certainly not least, many thanks to all the wonderful writers I have met over the years who have generously given of their time and expertise via conferences and workshops as well as individually. You are too numerous to list, but I am forever in your debt.

About the Author

S.K. Ryder writes paranormal and science fiction fantasy featuring fish-out-of-water characters forced to deal with reality gone wrong. Her stories reflect her deep love of nature and are filled with adventure, suspense, humor, and romance. Though she currently calls South Florida home, she has lived in Germany and Canada and has traveled widely, usually in the hot pursuit of wild and scenic spaces. When not writing or working as a freelance programmer, she enjoys plotting her next scuba diving or river rafting trip, beach combing, or just getting lost in a book. Should push comes to shove, she can also bake a halfway decent cake and stand on her head, though not (usually) at the same time.

Find her online at https://skryder.com

BOOKS BY S.K. RYDER

DARK DESTINIES SERIES

Dark Awakening (Prequel)
Dark Heart of the Sun (Book 1)
Dark Lord of the Night (Book 2)
Dark Reign of Forever (Book 3)

For a complete list, visit:
https://books2read.com/SK-Ryder